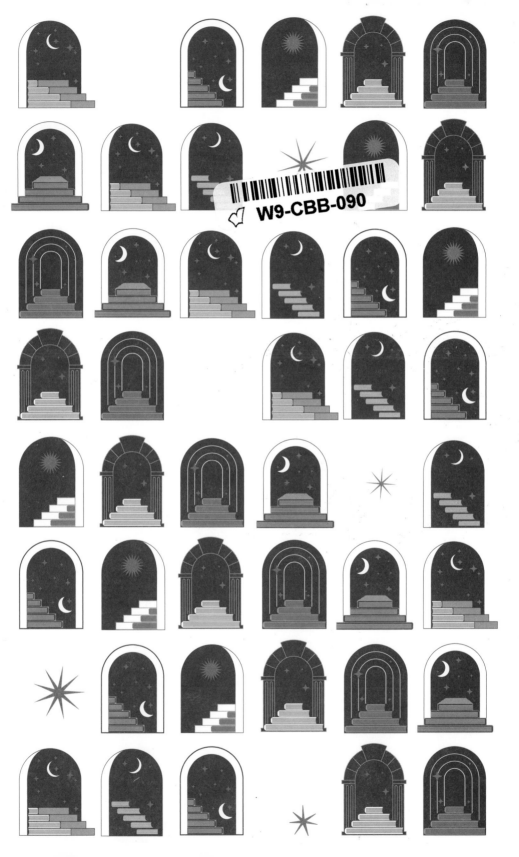

W9-CBB-090

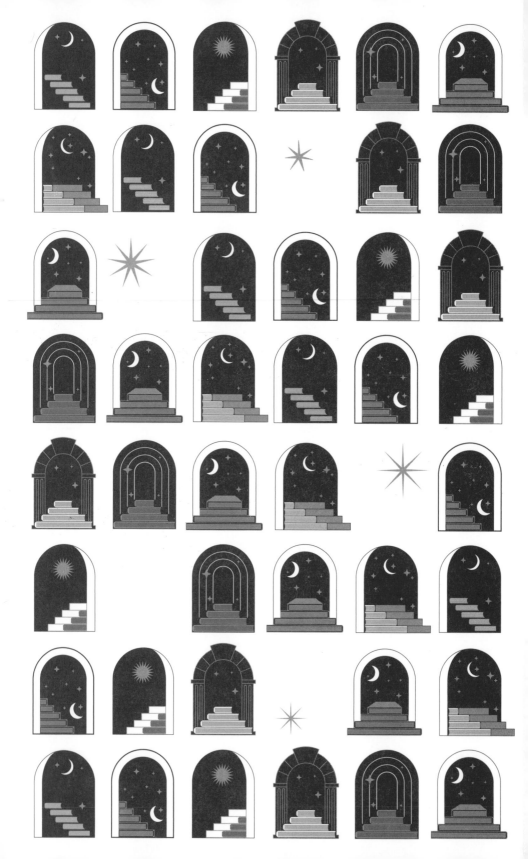

THE BOOK
OF DOORS

THE BOOK

A NOVEL

OF DOORS

GARETH BROWN

WM
WILLIAM MORROW
An Imprint of HarperCollinsPublishers

HarperCollins books may be purchased for educational, business, or sales promotional use. For information, please email the Special Markets Department at SPsales@harpercollins.com.

FIRST EDITION

Designed by Nancy Singer

Interior art © Unusual Corporation/Will Staehle

Library of Congress Cataloging-in-Publication Data has been applied for.

ISBN 978-0-06-332398-8 (hardcover)
ISBN 978-0-06-335900-0 (international edition)

23 24 25 26 27 LBC 5 4 3 2 1

Dedicated to my wife, May, for all the memories
made and the adventures still to come
(NMINOO! VWDDR!)

THE BOOK
OF DOORS

DOORWAYS

The Quiet Death of Mr. Webber

In Kellner Books on the Upper East Side of New York City, a few minutes before his death, John Webber was reading *The Count of Monte Cristo*. He was sitting at his usual table in the middle of the store with his overcoat folded neatly over the back of his chair and the novel on the table in front of him. He stopped for a moment to take a sip of his coffee, closing the book, and marking his place with a soft leather bookmark.

"How are you doing, Mr. Webber?" Cassie asked, as she made her way through the store with a stack of books under her arm. It was late in the day and Mr. Webber was the only customer.

"Oh, old and tired and falling apart," he replied, as he always did when Cassie asked how he was. "But otherwise I can't complain."

Mr. Webber was a regular face in the bookstore and one of the customers Cassie always made an effort to speak to. He was a gentleman, softly spoken and always neatly dressed in what appeared to be expensive clothes. His age showed in the wrinkled skin of his hands and neck, but not in the smooth skin of his face or his full head of white hair. He was lonely, Cassie knew, but he carried it lightly, never imposing his loneliness on others.

"Reading *The Count of Monte Cristo*," he confided, nodding at the book. The bookmark stuck out at Cassie like the tongue of a snake. "I've read it before, but as I get older, I find comfort in rereading favorites. It's like spending time with old friends." He coughed a self-deprecating laugh, signaling to Cassie that he knew he was being silly. "Have you read it?"

"I have," Cassie said, hitching the pile of books up under her arm. "I read it when I was ten, I think." She recalled long rainy days one autumn weekend when *The Count of Monte Cristo*, like so many other books, had taken her away.

"I don't remember being ten," Mr. Webber murmured with a smile. "I think I was born middle-aged and wearing a suit. What did you think of it when you read it?"

"It's a classic, of course," Cassie said. "But the bit in the middle, that whole section in Rome, that was too long. I always wanted to get to the revenge stuff at the end."

Mr. Webber nodded. "He certainly makes you wait for the payoff."

"Mmm," Cassie agreed.

The moment expanded, the silence filled by the soft jazz music playing through the speakers on the wall.

"Have you ever been to Rome?" Mr. Webber asked, rubbing his hands together as if they were cold. Cassie knew that he had been a pianist and a composer before he had retired, and he had the sort of long, delicate fingers that would dance easily across a keyboard.

"Yeah, I've been to Rome," Cassie said. "I don't remember much about it." She had spent a week in Rome years earlier when she had traveled around Europe and she remembered it well, but she wanted to let Mr. Webber speak. He was a man full of stories of a life well lived, a man with more tales than people to tell them to.

"I loved Rome," he said, relaxing back into his chair. "Of all the places I traveled, and I traveled a lot, Rome was one of my favorites. You could walk around and just imagine what it was like five hundred years ago."

"Mmm," Cassie murmured again, watching as Mr. Webber's attention drifted off into his memories. He seemed happy there.

"You know, I stayed in a small hotel near the Trevi Fountain," he said, suddenly seized by a memory. "And they would bring me coffee in bed every morning, whether I wanted it or not. Seven A.M. sharp. A quick knock and then the old woman who ran the place would march in, bang it down on the nightstand, and march out again. On my first morning I was standing naked in the middle of the room just contemplating getting dressed, and then she burst in, coffee in hand. She gave me one look, up and down, thoroughly unimpressed by what she saw, and walked back out again." He laughed at his memory. "She saw me in my . . . entirety."

"Oh my god," Cassie said, laughing with him.

He studied her as she laughed, drawing a conclusion. "I've told you that before, haven't I?"

"No," she lied. "I don't think so."

"You indulge me too much, Cassie. I've turned into one of those old people who bore youngsters with their stories."

"A good story is just as good the second time around," she said.

He shook his head, as if annoyed at himself.

"Do you still travel, Mr. Webber?" Cassie asked, pulling him away from his annoyance.

"Oh, I never go anywhere now," he said. "Too old and too weak. I doubt I'd survive a long flight." He clasped his hands over his stomach and stared at the table, lost in that thought.

"That's a bit morbid," Cassie said.

"Realistic," he said, smiling. He looked at her seriously then. "It's important to be realistic. Life is like a train that just keeps getting faster and faster and the sooner you realize that the better. I am hurtling toward the final stop, I know that. But I've lived my life and I've got no complaints. But young people like you, Cassie, you must get out and see the world while you can. There is so much to see beyond these four walls. Don't let the world pass you by."

"I've seen plenty, Mr. Webber, don't worry about that," Cassie said, uncomfortable with the conversation turning toward her. She nodded at the books under her arm. "Let me take these through the back before my arm falls off."

She headed past the coffee counter—now closed for the day—and through to the windowless cave of boxes and staff lockers in the back room. She dropped the books on the cluttered desk for Mrs. K to deal with the following day when she opened up.

"Cassie, I wasn't trying to tell you how to live your life," Mr. Webber said, when she reappeared, his expression serious. "I hope I didn't insult you."

"Insult me?" Cassie asked, genuinely puzzled. "Don't be silly. I didn't give it a second thought."

"Well, what I mean to say, really, is please don't let Mrs. Kellner know that I was suggesting you might abandon her and her bookstore."

"She would ban you for life," Cassie said, grinning. "But don't worry. I won't say anything. And I'm not going anywhere anytime soon."

As she tidied mugs and plates from the tables, Cassie looked around the store. It was everything a bookstore should be, with shelves and tables laden with books, soft music always playing in the background, and lights dangling on cables from the high ceiling, creating spots of brightness and cozy gloom. There were comfy chairs in corners and in between the shelves, and mismatched artwork on the walls. The paint hadn't been redone in ten years, and the shelves had probably been first bought in the 1960s, but it felt appropriately shabby rather than rundown. It was a comfortable place, the sort of store that felt familiar the first time you stepped through the door.

She nodded down at Mr. Webber's coffee cup. "Do you want a last refill before I close up?"

"I've had more than enough," he said, shaking his head. "I'll be up and down like an elevator all night to pee."

Cassie pulled a face, half amused, half disgusted.

"I offer you a window into the life of an old person," Mr. Webber said, unapologetic. "It's a constant pleasure. Now, give me a few minutes to gather my strength and then I'll be out of your way."

"Take as long as you want," she said. "It's nice to have the company at the end of the day."

"Yes," Mr. Webber agreed, gazing down at the table, his hand resting on the cover of his book. "Yes, it is." He looked up and smiled at her a little shyly. She patted him once on the shoulder as she passed. At the front of the store the large window spilled soft light out into the night, a fireplace in the dark room of the city, and as Cassie perched on her stool, she saw that it was starting to snow, flakes spiraling like dust motes through the haze of light.

"Lovely," she murmured in delight.

She watched the snow for a while as it grew heavier, the buildings across the street a crossword puzzle of lit and unlit windows. Passersby pulled their hoods up and ducked their heads against the onslaught, and diners in the small sushi bar directly opposite Kellner Books peered out at the weather with chopsticks in hand and concern on their faces.

"The best place to enjoy a stormy night is in a warm room with a book in your lap," Cassie said to herself. She smiled sadly because someone she missed had once said those words to her.

She glanced at the clock on the wall and saw that it was time to lock up. At his table Mr. Webber was sitting with his head tilted awkwardly to the side, like a man who thought he'd heard someone calling his name. Cassie frowned and a finger of unease tickled something deep in her gut.

"Mr. Webber?" she asked, rising from her stool.

She hurried across the store, the easy-listening background jazz jangling against her sudden unease. When she put a hand on Mr. Webber's shoulder he didn't respond. His expression was fixed, his eyes open and lifeless, his lips slightly apart.

"Mr. Webber?" she tried again, even though she knew it was pointless.

Cassie knew what death looked like. The first time that she had seen death, many years previously, it had stolen from her the man who had raised her and the only family she had ever known. Now death had come again, and this time it had taken a nice man whom she hardly knew while she had been distracted by the snow.

"Oh, Mr. Webber," she said, as sadness swelled within her.

THE EMTS CAME FIRST, BUSTLING noisily into the store and shaking snow from their clothes and hair. They were energetic, like there was a chance of saving Mr. Webber, but as soon as they saw him all of their urgency drained away.

"He's gone," one of them told her, and the three of them stood around in an awkward silence like strangers at a party. Mr. Webber watched nothing in the middle distance with glassy eyes.

Then the police came, a young man and an older man, both of them asking her questions as the EMTs lifted Mr. Webber from his chair and strapped him onto a stretcher.

"He comes in the evening, two or three times a week," she explained to them. "Just before the coffee counter closes for the day. He gets a drink and then sits there and reads his book until I close up the store."

The young police officer looked bored, standing with his hands on his hips and watching the EMTs as they worked. "Probably lonely," he said.

"He likes books," Cassie said, and the cop looked at her. "Sometimes we talk about books we've read, books he's reading. He likes the classics." She realized that she was prattling even as the words continued to tumble from her lips. She folded her arms to stop herself. Something about the police made her self-conscious, excruciatingly aware of everything she was saying and doing.

"Right," the cop said, watching her with professional indifference.

"I guess he liked talking to you, ma'am," the older cop said, and Cassie thought he was trying to be nice. He was thumbing through the contents of Mr. Webber's wallet, seeking an address or next of kin. It seemed oddly obscene to Cassie, like rummaging through someone's underwear drawer.

"Nothing like a pretty lady to give an old man something to look forward to," the younger cop said, a mischievous smile tugging the corner of his mouth. The older cop shook his head in disapproval without looking up from Mr. Webber's wallet.

"It wasn't that," Cassie snapped, her words sharp with irritation. "He was just a nice man. Don't make it something it wasn't."

The young cop nodded an approximation of an apology but made no attempt to hide the loaded glance he then threw at his colleague. He walked to the door to hold it open for the EMTs.

"Here we go," the older cop said, pulling out Mr. Webber's driver's license. "Apartment four, 300 East Ninety-Fourth Street. Nice neighborhood." He returned the driver's license to the wallet and folded the wallet shut. "We'll let you know if we need any more information," he said to Cassie. "But call us if you think of anything." He handed her an NYPD business card with a phone number on it.

"Like what?" Cassie asked.

The cop shrugged loosely. "Just anything we need to know."

Cassie nodded as if this were a good answer even though it wasn't. "What about his family?"

"We'll deal with that," the older cop said.

"If he has any," the younger cop added, waiting by the door. He wanted to go, Cassie saw; this was boring for him, and she hated him for it. Mr. Webber deserved better. Everyone deserved better.

"You gonna be all right, miss?" the older cop asked her. Everything about the man seemed tired, but he was still doing his job, and doing it better than his younger partner.

"Yeah," Cassie said, frowning in annoyance. "Of course."

He watched her for a moment.

"Hey, sometimes people just die," he said, trying his best to say something consoling. "That's just the way of it."

Cassie nodded. She knew. Sometimes people just died.

CASSIE STOOD AT THE FRONT of the shop and watched them go, the ambulance first and then the cop car. Her own reflection was a ghost in the window—the tall, awkward girl dressed in thrift shop clothes: an old woolen crewneck sweater, and blue jeans that were almost worn through at the knees.

"Goodbye, Mr. Webber," she said, absently pulling the sleeves of her sweater up to her elbows.

She told herself not to be sad—Mr. Webber had been old, and he had died peacefully and swiftly, it seemed, in a place that gave him joy—but her sadness was stubborn, a constant bass note rumbling in the background of her thoughts.

She picked up the phone and called Mrs. Kellner at home.

"Dead?" Mrs. Kellner said, when Cassie told her what had happened. The word was a bullet from a gun, a short, sharp bang.

Cassie waited, and she heard a long, tired sigh.

"Poor Mr. Webber," Mrs. Kellner said, and Cassie could hear her shaking her head. "But there are worse ways to go. Certainly Mr. Webber would think so. How are you, Cassie?"

The question surprised Cassie, as it always did when someone inquired about how she was doing.

"Oh, I'm fine," she lied, brushing it off. "Just shocked, I guess."

"Mmm, well. It comes to us all, and Mr. Webber was a good age. It's sad, but no reason to be depressed, you hear?"

"Yes, ma'am," Cassie said, enjoying Mrs. Kellner's robustly given kind advice.

"You lock up now and get on home. It's a blizzard out there and I don't want you getting hypothermia. That's an instruction not a request."

Cassie said good night to Mrs. Kellner and got to work tidying up, wondering how well the Kellners had known Mr. Webber. They seemed to know most people who came into the store regularly. Not that Mr. Kellner knew much of anything anymore, dementia having stolen his memories from him a few years ago. Cassie's mind wandered, trying to remember when Mr. Kellner had last been in the store. It had been years, she was sure. Now Mrs. Kellner barely spoke about her husband at all.

When Cassie swept the floor around the coffee tables, around Mr. Webber's seat, she saw his copy of *The Count of Monte Cristo* still lying on the table by the half-empty coffee cup. The sight of the book hit her like a punch in the gut, as if Mr. Webber had been taken away without his most prized possession. Then she saw another book next to it, a smaller book with a brown leather cover, faded and cracked like weathered paint on a door. Cassie hadn't noticed the book earlier, not when Mr. Webber had arrived, not during all the activity with the EMTs and the cops. Had she just overlooked it?

She cradled the broom against her shoulder and picked up the book. It felt oddly light, as if it was more insubstantial than it should have been. The leather spine creaked pleasantly as she opened it. The pages were thick and coarse, and covered in what looked like scribbled text in dark ink, but in a language and script that Cassie didn't recognize. As Cassie flicked through the book, she saw that there were sketched images and doodles as well, some dotted around the text, others taking up whole pages. It looked like a journal of some kind, a place where someone had collected their thoughts over many years, but chaotically so. The text didn't run in a single direction; it was up and down and cutting through and curling around images.

On the very first page of the book Cassie saw a few lines, written in the same handwriting as the text on every other page, but in English:

This is the Book of Doors.

Hold it in your hand, and any door is every door.

Below those lines there was another message, written in a different script. Cassie gasped when she saw that it was a message to her:

Cassie,

This book is for you, a gift in thanks for your kindness.
May you enjoy the places it takes you to and the friends you find there.

John Webber

Cassie frowned, surprised and touched by the gift. She flicked through the pages again, stopping about a third of the way into the book where a single page had been given over to a sketch of a doorway. The doorway was penned in simple black ink, the door wide open, but through the opening Cassie saw what appeared to be a room in darkness, with a window on the far wall. Beyond that window was bright sunlight and a rich blue sky, the many colors of spring flowers in bloom among vibrantly green grass. Everything was sketched in black except the view from the window; that was drawn in full, glorious color.

Cassie closed the book, stroking the cracked leather.

Had she been so kind to Mr. Webber? Had he meant to give her the book that evening? Maybe he had taken it out of his pocket while she had been distracted by the snow, just before he had died?

She debated what to do for a moment, wondering whether she should call the cops and tell them about the book, both books. She could just see the younger cop rolling his eyes . . . *"Some crazy person's notebook he wanted to give to you . . . ?"*

"Stupid," she muttered to herself.

Mr. Webber had wanted her to have it. She would take it as a memento of the nice man who had often kept her company at the end of the day. And she would take his copy of *The Count of Monte Cristo* as well; she would see that it got to a good home.

When she left the store a short while later, wrapped up in her old gray greatcoat and burgundy scarf and bobble hat, the sharp edges of the wind cut into her, but she didn't notice, so distracted was she by the contents of the odd notebook. After only a few steps she stopped under a streetlight and pulled the notebook from her pocket, entirely unaware of the figure watching her in the shadows of a doorway across the street.

She flicked through the pages again: more text, lines seemingly drawn at random as if the pages could be taken out of the book and placed together in a different order to reveal some grand, secret design. In the very center of the notebook she saw that a hundred or more doorways had been drawn in neat rows right across the two pages, each of them slightly different in shape or size or feature, as varied as the doorways on any street. It was odd but beautiful, enigmatic and inviting, and Cassie wanted to pore over the pages and dream about whoever it was that had spent so many hours scribbling in the book. It felt like a treasure to her, this book, a mystery to occupy her mind.

She wiped snowflakes from the pages and slipped the book back into her pocket, then started on her way through the snow-silenced streets, heading for the subway three blocks away, her mind alive with images and strange words scribbled in black ink.

The figure in the doorway did not follow.

The Favorite Game

When Cassie reached home, she took Mr. Webber's copy of *The Count of Monte Cristo* and found a space for it among the paperbacks on the bookcase at the end of her bed.

The bookcase was a map of her life: the books she had devoured as a child; books she had bought or picked up on her travels through Europe; the books she had read and treasured since living in New York. Her own battered copy of *The Count of Monte Cristo* was there, an old paperback that had originally belonged to her grandfather. Cassie remembered reading it in her grandpa's studio back in Myrtle Creek, wedged into a beanbag in the corner as he had worked, the smell of wood and oil in the air as heavy rain beat the ground outside. She pulled the book off the shelf and flicked the pages, catching the ghost of a scent that made her heart crumple at the memories and emotions it conjured, the contentment and comfort of those days in her childhood.

She slid the book back into its place and pulled off her old sweater to dump it in the laundry pile. She caught her reflection in the mirror on the back of the door and regarded herself dispassionately. She was always slightly disappointed whenever she saw herself in reflections or photographs. To her own eyes she was too tall and too thin. She thought her hips were too narrow and her chest too flat, and her eyes were big and wide like a startled deer's. She never wore makeup, because she had never really learned how to do it, and her blond hair was always flying off in different directions no matter how much she brushed it.

"You home, then?" Izzy called from the living area.

"Yeah," Cassie said. She opened the bedroom door, pushing her reflection out of sight, and wandered through to find Izzy cross-legged on the couch, dressed for bed in an oversized T-shirt and pajama bottoms.

"How was the work thing?" Cassie asked. "Must have been good since you're at home and in your pajamas."

Izzy rolled her eyes wearily. "We went to a few places. Couple of guys tried to pick us up in the last bar we were in. This big guy tried to use his charm on me. He was horrible. All muscles and monobrow. He suggested that we go down to Times Square together and watch the lights."

"Wow," Cassie said.

"Right?" Izzy agreed. "Who the hell wants to go to Times Square? The only people interested in Times Square are tourists and terrorists."

Cassie smiled, enjoying the sound of her friend's voice and the distraction from her lingering sadness. The journey home on an empty subway train and through snow-smothered streets had felt long and lonely.

"I said that to him," Izzy continued, as Cassie joined her on the couch. "'Nobody cares about Times Square except tourists and terrorists.' He acted all offended, like I'd said something awful." She pulled a face, affecting a lower voice. "*That's so distasteful, you know terrorists kill people.*"

"That's pretty special," Cassie said, grinning.

"It kinda spoiled the mood, so we called it a night. Lucky too." She nodded at the window, the snow still falling.

Izzy worked in the jewelry department in Bloomingdale's and every couple of weeks she would go out drinking with her colleagues after work. Her world was full of expensive products and rich people and wide-eyed tourists. It was a world Cassie neither understood nor cared about, but Izzy loved her job. At one time she had wanted to be an actress. She had moved to New York from Florida as a teenager with dreams of singing and acting on Broadway. When they had first met Izzy had been working at Kellner Books while auditioning and performing in tiny theaters. After a few years of getting steadily nowhere she had given up on her dream.

"Can you think of anything worse?" she had said to Cassie, one evening when they had gone for drinks at the rooftop bar of the Library Hotel. "Being thirty-something and watching all these beautiful young women come into the same auditions as you, looking at you exactly how I look at all the older women now? The world has an endless supply of beautiful women, Cassie. There's always a newer, younger one coming along. I am not a good enough actress that my looks don't matter."

Cassie and Izzy had worked together at Kellner Books for over a year, and they had fallen into being friends almost immediately. They were very different people, with different interests, but somehow they had always gotten on well. It was a natural, easy friendship, the type that comes out of nowhere and changes your life. When Cassie had started looking for an apartment to rent, Izzy had suggested that they try to find a place together to save on costs. They had shared a third-floor two-bedroom walk-up in Lower Manhattan ever since. Their building was on the edge of Little Italy, above a cheesecake shop and a dry cleaner's. It was cold in the winter and hot in the summer, and because of the landlord's subdivides none of the rooms were the right shape or size, and none of the furniture really fit where it should. But it worked for them, and they had continued living together even after Izzy had left the bookstore to work at Bloomingdale's. Izzy tended to work during the day while Cassie preferred to work the late shift and weekends. As a result they often didn't see each other for days at a time, but that stopped them from getting in each other's way and prevented the living arrangement from spoiling the friendship. Every three or four days their paths would cross, and Izzy would give a rapid rundown on all the events in her life while Cassie listened. And then, when Izzy's stream of consciousness ran dry, she would look at Cassie with a maternal expression and ask, "And how are you, Cassie? What's going on in your world?"

Izzy looked at her now with that expression on her face, her hair tied up in a mess of curls behind her head. She was a beautiful woman, with high cheekbones and large brown eyes. She was the sort of woman department stores loved to have behind their counters, the sort of woman who might have been a film star if she had been able to act. Cassie felt plain in comparison, but Izzy had never done anything to make her feel that way. That fact said everything about the sort of person Izzy was.

"What's going on in my world?" Cassie preempted.

"What's going on in your world?"

"Nothing," Cassie said. "Not much."

"Come on," Izzy said, unfolding her legs and jumping up to wander over to the kitchen counter. "Let me get you a classy mug of wine and you can tell me your nothing and not much."

Izzy switched on the lamp by the door, splashing soft light across the walls.

"Mr. Webber died today," Cassie said. She looked down, realizing she was still holding the book he had given her. She had meant to leave it on the bookshelf in her bedroom.

"Oh my god, that's horrible," Izzy said. "Who's Mr. Webber?"

"Just this old guy," Cassie said. "He comes into the store every now and then. Gets a coffee and reads."

"God, it is so cold, what is with this weather?" Izzy muttered, closing the door to the hall as she padded back to the sofa and passed Cassie a mug. They didn't drink wine from glasses, not in the apartment.

"I think he was just lonely. And he liked the bookstore."

"So what happened?" Izzy asked, pouring the wine. "Did he trip and fall or something? My uncle Michael died like that. He fell, broke his hip, and couldn't get up. Died on his living room floor." She shuddered.

"No, nothing like that," Cassie said. She took the mug of wine even though she wasn't interested in drinking it. "He just died. Just sitting there. Like it was his time."

Izzy nodded but seemed disappointed.

"That's what the cops said anyway," Cassie reflected. "'Sometimes people just die.'"

Izzy settled more comfortably into the sofa, crossing her legs beneath her. Cassie took a sip of wine, and they were companionably quiet together for a few moments.

"Look at the snow," Izzy murmured, gazing out the window. The buildings on the opposite side of the street were almost hidden by the storm. The wind seemed to have died but the flakes were bigger and softer now, tumbling slowly but steadily from the sky.

"It's so pretty," Cassie said.

"What's that?" Izzy pointed at the notebook in Cassie's lap, and Cassie passed it to her, explaining about the gift.

"Leather," Izzy observed. She opened the book and flicked through the pages idly. "Wow. This looks like a crazy person vomited some word soup. Wonder if it's worth anything?"

"Probably not," Cassie said. It annoyed her that Izzy's first thought was about monetary value. That wasn't the point. "Anyway, it was a gift."

"I think Mr. Webber was sweet on you, Cassie," Izzy said, smiling mischievously, as she handed the book back.

"Stop it," Cassie protested. "It wasn't like that. He was a nice man. And he did a nice thing."

Izzy sipped her wine, her eyes slightly glazed. "Okay. Let's not wallow. Come on. Let's think of happier things."

"Like what?" Cassie asked, placing her mug on the table. "I can't drink this. I'll fall asleep."

"Lightweight," Izzy murmured. "Tell me about . . . tell me about your favorite day."

"What?" Cassie smiled, although she remembered the Favorite Game. They had played it often in the store when things were quiet and there was nothing to do. One of them would ask the other to talk about their favorite something . . . favorite meal, favorite holiday, favorite bad date. It passed the time.

"Tell me about your favorite day," Izzy repeated. "What was your best day ever?"

Cassie thought about the question, gazing out the window to the snowy world, cradling Mr. Webber's book in her lap.

"I tell you what *wasn't* my favorite day," Izzy said, interrupting Cassie's thoughts. "That day on the Greyhound."

"Oh god." Cassie groaned and smiled, remembering the trip she and Izzy had taken to Florida several years earlier to visit Izzy's cousin. The two of them had spent almost twenty-four hours together on a Greyhound bus to Miami, alternating between terror and hilarity at the events they endured. "Remember that man who smelled like he went to the toilet on the bus without leaving his seat?"

"Oh, don't remind me," Izzy said, covering her mouth as if she wanted to be sick.

Cassie turned her mind to better days. She remembered when she was much younger, days in the house she grew up in, just her and her grandfather, or just her and a book, but she wouldn't talk about those. Those memories were too precious. She thought instead about the traveling she had done before she had moved to New York, after her grandfather had died. She had taken a trip to Europe by herself, partly to grieve and partly to work out what she wanted to do with her life. She had backpacked from city to city, mostly by herself but occasionally making friends: a handsome German boy in Paris, a young Japanese couple in London. There had been a couple of middle-aged Dutch lesbians she had met in Rome whom she traveled with for a few weeks because they seemed to think she was innocent and in need of protection. Cassie had promised to keep in touch with these people but never had. They were walk-on parts in her life. Although they were lost to her now, those people and those warm, sunny days across Europe were among her happiest memories.

"I remember when I was in Venice," Cassie said.

"Ooh, Venice," Izzy said. "Nice." Izzy had never been out of the country, but she had often spoken about going back to Italy, to where her family originally had come from, talking about it in the way people speak of dreams that they know will never really happen.

"I was staying in this hostel," Cassie said. "And I had the room to myself. Just nobody else there, not at first. It was run by this middle-aged couple with young kids. They were so nice. I can't remember their names now . . ." She thought for a moment, searching her memories but coming up empty. "But they treated me like a daughter."

Izzy rolled her head to the side, resting it on the back of the sofa as she listened.

"The street I was on," Cassie continued. "It was a narrow, cobbled street with all these yellow and orange buildings with big wooden doors and small windows with shutters. I'd probably never find it again if I ever went back there. Well, there was a bakery across the street, and I'd sleep with the windows open because it was so warm."

"Mmm, warm is nice," Izzy said, sounding sleepy.

"And in the morning, I'd wake up to the smell of baking bread and pastries." Cassie sighed at the memory. "Just the best smell in the world. And you'd hear the locals talking and laughing as they met each other. The coffee shop at the end of the street would put out tables and chairs, the waitstaff clattering and banging even though it was early, and all the locals would stop by for a cappuccino on their way to work or whatever."

"I want to go to Italy," Izzy said.

"Every day I'd jump out of bed and run down the stairs," Cassie continued. "The property had this big old wooden door. You'd open it and the bakery was right across from you, usually with a queue of people waiting to buy whatever they needed."

"I love bread," Izzy murmured. "Can't eat it. Goes straight to my hips. But I love it."

Cassie ignored her, caught in the net of her own memory for a few moments.

"I'm going to put this away," she said, nodding at the book in her hand. "And I'm going to make a coffee or something, otherwise I'll be asleep before you."

"I'm not sleepy," Izzy said, with her obviously sleepy voice. "It's a lie."

Cassie smiled and pushed herself off the couch.

She was remembering Venice again, thinking about the coffees she'd had at the café on the corner, the crusty bread she'd eaten for breakfast, and as she reached for the door to the hallway she felt a shudder, a moment of oddness where the world seemed to tense and release within her.

And then she opened the door and found herself gazing out onto that small, cobbled street in Venice she remembered from her holiday, quiet and dark and glistening with rain.

Venice

Cassie's brain did a backflip and asked her what her eyes were playing at. Then her mouth fell open in disbelief.

There was a world where her apartment hallway should have been. There was cool air and moisture and the slightly damp, fresh smell of a different place. There was darkness, but it was closer to light than the snow-filled darkness of New York City.

In front of her, in the bakery she had visited during those days in Venice, a light came on, punching a hole into the drizzly gloom. She watched as a man moved about inside, a blurred figure beyond the rain-streaked window, and she realized that this wasn't a picture she was looking at—this was moving, this was real!

"Oh my god," she said, astonished.

"Are you coming or going, babe?" Izzy asked, in a world that still made sense. "Close the door; there's a howling wind going right up where it shouldn't go."

"Izzy," Cassie said, in a voice that sounded very far away. "Come here."

In Venice, in the bakery that shouldn't have been there, the man beyond the glass was taking off a dark coat, walking through a doorway at the back of the store to hang it up somewhere.

"Come here, Izzy," Cassie said again, her voice strangled and tight.

"What is it?" Izzy asked. "Oh shit, have we got rats again?"

Cassie didn't reply. She forced her eyes shut, counted to three, and then opened them again. The street was still there. The rain, the cobbles, the man in the bakery. Cassie saw now that the sky above was not full dark, the day was coming, and a detached voice at the back of her mind said: *Of course, Italy is six hours ahead of New York. It's morning.*

Then Izzy was standing beside her. Cassie turned her head to watch as Izzy's eyes widened, as she processed the same impossibility that Cassie was still struggling with.

"Am I having a stroke?" Izzy said, her voice a monotone. "Cassie, am I fucking high?"

"It's impossible," Cassie said slowly, not answering Izzy's question. "It's amazing."

"What the fuck is this?" Izzy asked, the question a gasp of incomprehension.

"It's Venice," Cassie exclaimed. "It's the place I was just telling you about."

"Why is it in my apartment?" Izzy asked, skirting around the edge of hysteria. "I need to pee! Where's the bathroom?"

Cassie let go of the door handle and reached forward with her hand. Izzy grabbed her.

"What are you doing?"

"What?" Cassie asked in reply.

Izzy released her and they both watched as Cassie stretched forward through the threshold of the doorway. She felt the tickle of a breeze, the tiny kiss of raindrops. She wiggled her fingers and then turned her hand over, palm up. She giggled in disbelief and delight and pulled her hand back into the room. Both she and Izzy inspected it closely.

"Rain," Cassie said, peering at the droplets on her skin. "I felt the breeze," she said, smiling, looking back through the door again.

It was unbelievable. Another place, a city in another country across an ocean, was just beyond the doorway. Cassie's mind chewed on that slowly, like someone savoring a favorite meal.

"What are you saying?" Izzy asked.

"I'm saying my hand was in Venice," Cassie said. "My body was in New York, but my hand was in Venice."

Izzy was struck dumb.

"How can this be?" Cassie asked herself in a whisper.

They gazed through the doorway in silence. It was impossible to look away. Across the street there was a second person in the bakery now, indistinct shapes through the rain-streaked window, like scribbles in charcoal.

"What do we do?" Izzy asked, and Cassie thought it was the first time she had ever heard Izzy sound uncertain. She was always so confident, and so obvious about her confidence.

"I want to go," Cassie murmured.

"Go? Go where?"

"Go to Venice," Cassie said, gesturing ahead of them. How could she not want to go? It was another place, far away, a place she loved, and it was *right there*, right in front of them.

"We can't go to Venice!" Izzy gasped. "I am in pajamas and socks. And you . . . I don't know what you're wearing but you don't have any shoes on either."

"I need to know it's real," Cassie said, barely hearing Izzy's protestations. It looked real. And it felt real. "Stick your hand in, Izzy."

Izzy regarded the world beyond the doorway warily.

"Please," Cassie begged. "I want to make sure it's not just me, I'm not hallucinating this."

Izzy crossed herself—something Cassie had only ever seen her do once before, when a pedestrian had been struck by a car on the street many years earlier—and then stretched her hand out. Her fingers breached the threshold and Izzy narrowed her eyes, like she was expecting pain. Then her hand was out into the street that shouldn't have been there, and Cassie put a hand over her mouth anxiously. She wanted it to be true, this miracle, this impossibility. She wanted to believe things like this could happen.

Izzy laughed in disbelief. "It's cold," she said. "I can feel the air."

"Yeah," Cassie said happily, delighted that Izzy felt it too, that it was real. "And the rain?"

"Yeah, and the rain." She waggled her fingers just like Cassie had done, and then pulled her hand back into the apartment to inspect it, shaking her head.

Cassie wanted to step through the door. She wanted to go to Venice. She wasn't scared by what she saw; there was nothing to fear here, only something to wonder at and delight in.

"Don't," Izzy said, as if reading Cassie's mind. "What if you can't get back? What if you get stuck in Venice in the rain in your socks and you can't get back?"

Cassie hesitated, Izzy's caution an anchor to her joy, holding her back.

"I'll take a photo!" Izzy said. She reached into her pajama pocket and pulled out her phone to take a shot of the doorway and the street beyond. Then she stepped back and took a few more shots, showing Cassie in front of the doorway. "Smile!" Izzy said.

Cassie smiled distractedly. She wanted to step through the door. That was all she wanted.

"Hold on, I'll take a video," Izzy said. "Wave your hands or something. Go."

Cassie lifted her free hand to point to the doorway.

"Looks like Venice," she said. "Where our hallway should be." Then a slightly manic laugh escaped from her. "It's crazy!"

"Put your hand in again," Izzy instructed.

Cassie leaned into the doorway, pushing her hand through, and then taking a step and poking her head out after it.

"Cassie!" Izzy exclaimed.

Cassie felt Izzy grab her and pull her back.

"It's really real," Cassie said. "I can't believe it."

"That's enough, it's freaking me out now."

Before Cassie could respond Izzy grabbed the door and pushed it shut. It juddered in the frame and the women stared at it silently. Then Izzy turned her head and met Cassie's eyes, asking a question. Cassie nodded and Izzy opened the door once more to reveal their hallway, the awkward narrow space with the door to the bathroom and their bedrooms and their coats and shoes by the entrance to the apartment. Cassie's breath exploded out of her, relief and disappointment washing over her in successive waves.

Izzy immediately looked at her phone. Cassie crowded close, their heads touching, and they peered together at the photos Izzy had taken, the video footage of Cassie standing by the doorway and then leaning in—or leaning out?—before a yelp from Izzy and the footage was cut off.

"How is it possible?" Izzy wondered.

Cassie stood at the doorway and put her hands on her hips, only realizing as she did so that she was still holding Mr. Webber's book, that she had been gripping it all through the miraculous discovery of Venice in their hallway. She lifted the book, thumb running over its brown leather cover. She was aware that the book felt warm in her hand now, and heavier than it had been when she had first picked it up in the bookstore.

"It's the book," she said, saying it as she examined the item again. It didn't just feel heavier, it felt more *solid*, as if there was more substance now between the covers.

"Huh?" Izzy grunted.

"It's the book," Cassie repeated. After a moment she sat down, picked up the mug of wine she hadn't drunk, and downed it in one gulp.

"What do you mean it's the book?" Izzy demanded.

"The Book of Doors," Cassie said, flicking to the front of the book and reading what was written there, above where Mr. Webber had left his own note. "'. . . any door is every door.' I was thinking about that street, that doorway in the place I stayed," Cassie said. "I was holding the book and thinking about it and then I felt . . ." She shuddered.

"Felt what?" Izzy asked.

"Felt strange. And then I opened the door and Venice was there. The Venice I was just thinking about." Cassie felt wonder dawn within her like the best and most beautiful sunrise ever. *Could it be . . . ?*

Izzy stared at her, absorbing this. Then she said, "Are you out of your mind? You think a book did that?"

Cassie shrugged, with an expression inviting other explanations.

"I know you love books, Cass, but magic books that can transport you across the world?"

"The Book of Doors," Cassie said, savoring the sound of it. She flicked through the book, her finger stopping on a random page. It was the page she had seen earlier, the sketch of the doorway with the dark room and the window looking out on flowers and sunshine. This time, however, there was no window. This time, through the sketched doorway, she saw a street and cobbles, the window of a bakery. It was the street she had just gazed upon, and Cassie's mouth fell open in disbelief. She flicked through the pages again, trying to find the image she had seen earlier, but it wasn't there.

"The book has changed," she murmured to herself, excited by this revelation, excited by yet another impossibility. It felt almost as if the book was alive somehow or talking to her. "Look," she said to Izzy, holding the book out and feeling herself getting hysterical. "Look at this image! This was a different picture before! Now it looks like that street!"

Izzy took the book and peered at it.

"It's that street, isn't it?" Cassie asked, needing Izzy to confirm what she was seeing.

"It might be," she said cautiously, as if she didn't want to admit something that was clearly impossible.

"Oh, come on," Cassie said, taking the book back and looking at it again. "It's definitely that street. But it was something different earlier. It's changed."

Cassie's mind spun for a moment, her whole body trembling. "Is it magic?"

"A magic book," Izzy said, raising a skeptical eyebrow.

"Why not?" Cassie asked. "You saw what just happened."

"If you're so sure it was the book, do it again." Izzy closed the door to the hallway and pointed at it. "Go on, make something else appear."

Cassie thought about it, realizing that she wanted to do just as Izzy demanded.

She *wanted* to open the door to another place again.

She *wanted* to use the strange, wonderful book.

It was tantalizing her, offering something astonishing in a world of so little astonishment.

"Better get our coats," Cassie said. "And you better go pee first."

Magical Midnight Tour of Manhattan

Where do you wanna go?" Cassie asked, standing in front of the door, her stomach somersaulting. Izzy had been to the toilet and had changed out of her pajamas and they had both put on coats and shoes. Cassie was holding the Book of Doors in her hand.

Izzy shrugged. "Not Italy," she said. "Somewhere we can walk home from if we get stuck."

"Right," Cassie said. She thought about the bookstore, because it was her favorite place, a comfortable place, but then Izzy suggested something better.

"I know," she said. "The roof terrace at the Library Hotel. Remember?"

Cassie did remember. The Library Hotel had been their favorite place to go for drinks after work, in the days before Izzy had left Kellner's. They still went occasionally, but not as often as when they had worked together. It was a place Izzy loved because they could sit outside, surrounded by the towering buildings of Midtown Manhattan, drinking expensive cocktails and watching rich young people socializing. Cassie had loved the view, the opportunity to gaze out at all the windows of Manhattan.

"Yes," Cassie said. "Good idea."

"You pick a place too!" Izzy suggested. "We go to my choice and then your choice!"

Cassie smiled, liking the idea. "What, like a magical midnight tour of Manhattan?"

"I love it!" Izzy exclaimed, her eyes shining.

"Okay," Cassie said, facing the door to the hallway again. "The bar at the Library Hotel."

She took a moment, thinking about the bar at the hotel, the door to its roof terrace, gripping the Book of Doors in her hand. She nodded decisively, reached forward and pulled the door open, and saw only their hallway.

"Shit."

"What happened?" Izzy asked. "What went wrong?"

"Like I know!"

"Well, what did you do last time? Just do that again. But not Venice." Cassie met Izzy's gaze.

"It should be easier," Izzy said. "It's a few miles away! Venice is across an ocean!"

"You wanna do it?" Cassie suggested, offering her the Book of Doors.

"Uh-uh," Izzy said, stepping backward.

Cassie sighed and turned her attention back to the door. She closed it again and tried to calm her breathing—why was her heart racing so much? She tried to remember what she had done the last time.

She had been thinking of Venice. Of the street, the bakery. The door. She had been remembering—no, not just remembering, she had been *visualizing* that door in Venice. And then she had felt funny . . .

She closed her eyes and thought of the door to the roof terrace of the hotel, a glass door cold to the touch, grimy on the outside. She visualized reaching for it as she reached for the door handle.

Then she felt it again, that fizzing, funny pressure all through her, and a detached part of her mind exclaimed: *You're doing it!*

"Look!" Izzy gasped.

Cassie opened her eyes and looked down. The book felt heavy in her hand again, but now she saw that something else was happening. There was a glow, or an aura, around the book, like some sort of intangible shadow but gloriously colorful like a rainbow. Cassie moved her hand back and forth and the rainbow aura followed the book's movement, swimming lazily in the air.

"It's glowing!" Izzy said.

Cassie turned her eyes to the door. She reached for the handle and pulled.

And the door wouldn't budge.

"Huh?" she grunted in surprise.

"What is it?" Izzy asked. "What now?"

"The door won't move."

Cassie looked down at the book. It was still glowing with that strange multicolored aura. It still felt heavy and solid in her hand. Something was happening.

She looked at the door again and yanked two or three times.

"It's like it doesn't open," she muttered.

After a moment, Izzy said, "The door at the bar opens outward, doesn't it?"

Cassie immediately realized she was right. The door—the normal door to the hall—would pull open toward them, just like the door in Venice. But if she was standing in the bar of the Library Hotel and stepping out onto the roof terrace, the door pushed away from them.

Cassie pushed. Their door had somehow changed, and it now moved in a way that was normally impossible. "No way," Cassie murmured in amazement. The door swung back, cold air rushing in to meet them like an excited dog.

She looked down and saw the aura around the book dissipating, blown away by the breeze, and the book grew lighter in her hand once again.

She met Izzy's gaze.

"Come on!" Izzy said, and the two of them tumbled out onto the roof terrace of the Library Hotel, giggling like children.

The night was alive with snow, the sky beyond the terrace swirling and white, the lights of the city blurred and indistinct. The tall buildings were giants silently watching, shrouded by the storm.

Izzy led Cassie to a bench at the far end of the roof and opened an umbrella on the table to shield them from the snow. There was a man out on the terrace with them, sitting at the other end of the roof and drinking by himself, but otherwise they were alone in the snow. "Wonder if we can order a drink," Izzy said, peering through the window to the bar inside. There was a pianist, sitting on the other side of the glass from them, and the sound of his music drifted out into the night and swirled in the sky with the snow.

"This is unbelievable," Cassie said, shaking her head in wonder. How could they have traveled across the city? She looked down at the book in her hand, the simple brown notebook, and realized that she loved it. It had come into her life and it was weaving miracles.

"It's freezing but I don't care!" Izzy said, throwing her laugh out into the storm. "We are at the Library Hotel!"

"I know!" Cassie exclaimed. "Come on!"

She pulled Izzy out from beneath the shelter of the umbrella and into the snow, leaning on the balustrade at the edge of the terrace to stare down into the canyon of Madison Avenue. It was an arctic world down there, the snow piling up quickly, all the streetlights and headlights blurred by the storm. A few adventurous people were trudging through the drifts, heads bowed and hoods up. Behind Cassie and Izzy, in the bar, the pianist finished a slow number and started something faster, some sort of jazzy arrangement of a big band classic that Cassie vaguely recognized.

"Take my hand," Izzy said, grinning.

"What?" Cassie asked, looking at her friend as she squinted against the snow.

"Dance with me, Cassie!" Izzy said.

"You're drunk!"

"Yes!"

Izzy pulled Cassie close and for a minute they danced to music from the bar, just them and the snow and the piano notes pirouetting in the cold night sky.

"This is crazy," Cassie said, as they collapsed into the seats under the umbrella, wiping snow from their faces.

"I still think I'm dreaming," Izzy said. "Did we just dance in the sky?"

"Some crazy person grabbed me and made me fox-trot," Cassie agreed.

Izzy smiled and watched the snow, shaking her head. Behind them the pianist finished the piece and moved back to something slower, something more suitable for late night in a New York bar.

"What could you do with this ability?" Izzy asked a few moments later. "If you can go anywhere whenever you want?"

Cassie thought about it.

"Never need to catch the subway to work?" Izzy suggested. "Just walk from the bedroom to the bookstore."

Cassie smiled at the thought of that. "I quite like the journey to work, sometimes. Not when it's cold, though."

"Cold is the worst," Izzy agreed. She looked over her shoulder into the bar. "I really feel like getting a drink."

Cassie's mind was playing with possibilities. "Never have to use a public restroom again."

"Oh my god, yes!" Izzy exclaimed. "How good would that be? No more hovering to pee."

"I can just use the bathroom at home," Cassie said. "Anytime I want."

"But what if you do that and I'm in there?" Izzy asked. "What if you walk in on me peeing?"

"Please, you use the bathroom with the door open anyway. I've seen it all before."

"You know, it's lucky you ended up with that book," Izzy said, shuffling close to Cassie on the bench for warmth. "I mean, rather than someone else, someone less good. Think about what you could do with it if you were not a nice person."

Cassie was quiet, not wanting to turn her mind to such thoughts. She wanted to play with the possibilities and enjoy the excitement, not wallow in worries.

"Imagine a sicko who can get in and out of any woman's bedroom," Izzy said. "Anywhere in the world."

"Yeah," Cassie said.

"You could go to another country and commit crimes and come back here and nobody would know who you were. Even if people thought it was you, you would have the perfect alibi of being in a different country."

Cassie nodded silently.

"Or a thief," Izzy continued. "In and out of any safe. Don't need to break in. Don't even need to step into the bank. You could open the safe door and reach in. Or any jewelry shop. Nothing would be safe."

"Okay," Cassie said, scowling. "Can we not list all the horrible things someone could do? This is amazing, Izzy. It's like . . . the best thing ever. A magic book that can take me anywhere I want to go! Don't spoil it!"

Izzy held up her hands in apology.

They sat for a moment in silence, but Cassie grew impatient to use the book again. She wanted to see where else they could go.

"Shall we go somewhere else?"

"Okay," Izzy said. "Somewhere warmer."

They made their way back to the door to the bar and Cassie saw that the man drinking by himself was still there. He glanced at them, dark eyes flicking to Cassie and then to Izzy, and then away to the surrounding buildings. Then Cassie used the book again, just as she had in the apartment, and it felt heavy and there was a burst of rainbow colors around her hand, and it all seemed even easier than the last time. And then they were through the door to the bar but arriving instead somewhere else.

They traveled to the New York Public Library, the reading room where Cassie spent many happy hours, now dark and quiet, the storm beating against the tall windows. They tiptoed around the darkness like giggling ghosts, Cassie terrified that there would be some alarm or a security guard who would discover them. And then they used a door at the side of the reading room to travel to the Strand Bookstore, just south of Union Square, one of Cassie's other favorite haunts in the city. With each successive doorway Cassie was sure tedious reality would return and steal this fairy tale away from her, but each time she was proved wrong. The world was suddenly wondrous and full of possibility.

"I'm hungry," Izzy said, as they stood in the Strand.

"Ben's?" Cassie suggested, referring to the twenty-four-hour deli a few blocks from their apartment. It was the place where they had waited for over two hours to meet the rental agent on the day they had first moved into the apartment, and the place where they now went for take-out and sandwiches.

"Ben's," Izzy agreed.

Cassie opened a door at the back of the bookstore and they stepped into Ben's Deli a mile across the city. They sat at the back of the deli and Izzy ate pancakes and bacon with a Coke, while Cassie sipped a coffee and tried to contain her excitement.

"Look at me," Izzy complained miserably. "I am disgusting. It's midnight and I am doing this to my body."

"There's nothing wrong with your body and you know it."

"There might be if I keep eating like this. Have you seen my aunts? They're all huge. That is my genes, Cass."

"Why are you eating, then?"

Izzy shrugged. "My mouth is bored, and I've been drinking." She clattered her fork onto the plate and pushed it away. "What are you gonna do about the book?"

"What do you mean?" Cassie asked.

Izzy frowned at her. "Well, you can't just keep it, and keep using it like this, can you?"

Cassie didn't understand. "Why not?" she asked. "It was given to me. It belongs to me."

"You don't know anything about it, Cass," Izzy said. "It might be dangerous."

Cassie sighed, hating the warning, hating that she understood it. She thought for a few moments as Izzy sipped the last of her Coke.

"I could try to find out more," Cassie conceded. "About the book, about Mr. Webber."

"How are you gonna do that?" Izzy asked. "He's dead, remember?"

"I'll ask Mrs. Kellner. She might know more about him. He was a regular customer."

Izzy nodded. "Until you know more, you probably shouldn't play with it. You don't know what it might be doing."

"We've been playing with it all night," Cassie said.

"Yeah," Izzy said, her expression serious. "Still. I wouldn't."

"Shall we go home?" Cassie asked, avoiding the subject. "I'm tired."

WHEN THEY GOT BACK TO the apartment, walking through snow-covered streets arm in arm, they lay in Cassie's bed together, both of them unable to sleep but trying to keep warm. They spoke about the

Book of Doors, the crazy, fabulous magic and what it could mean. Cassie realized she was happy, lying with her best friend in the darkened room, talking about amazing things; the night was cold, but her heart was warm.

At some point Izzy got up to go to her own bed and Cassie was alone. She removed the Book of Doors from beneath her pillow and held it in her hands, rubbing the cover with her thumb. She flicked through the pages again, amazed by the dense text and the finely drawn images. She tried to identify the languages, but many of them didn't even seem to use symbols she recognized. She flicked to the front of the book, to Mr. Webber's message, and felt her mouth drop open again when she saw that his words were gone. The front page now contained only the few lines saying what the book was. There wasn't any sign of Mr. Webber's message, no trace of ink, no indentation.

Cassie couldn't believe it. It was another piece of magic, but she found that the disappearance of Mr. Webber's words pained her a little. She dwelled on that for a moment but then her mind turned back to what the book could do, to the gift that had been given to her. That *Mr. Webber* had given her.

"It *is* real," she insisted, in a whisper.

But she had to prove it to herself one more time. Despite Izzy's reservations she knew she wanted to use it again. Who could turn down magic? Who would refuse?

She climbed out of bed and tiptoed to her bedroom door.

She thought of the holiday she had taken in Europe years before—the best months of her life—and she knew that the book could let her have that sort of happiness again.

She closed her eyes and tried to remember another doorway from her travels. She remembered the hostel where she had stayed in London. She remembered that door, the dark wood, the pair of tall narrow windows, the way the door had screeched whenever it was opened. She felt the book grow heavier in her hand and when she opened her eyes, she saw that same halo again, as if the book existed in a cloud of rainbow air.

"It's beautiful," she murmured, the light reflecting on her face.

She reached out for her bedroom door, holding the Book of Doors in her other hand, and when she opened it, it screeched like her bedroom door never did and Cassie felt a smile of delight on her face, even as the rainbow halo dissipated.

She peeked around the edge of the door and saw that street in London she remembered so well, a gray morning and rain and cars parked along the sidewalk. She was watching this foreign city across an ocean from the comfort of her own bedroom.

"Wow." She giggled. Cassie couldn't remember the last time anything had made her feel so elated, but she felt it now.

She closed the door, shaking her head as she did so, not because she regretted what she was doing, but because she couldn't believe what she had just done.

She returned to her bed, holding the book between both hands and gazing at it like it was the face of a lover.

She could do magic.

She could return to any door she had ever been through, anywhere on the planet.

Drummond Fox in the Snow

Drummond Fox was in the snow, with ghosts.

He stood at the edge of Washington Square Park, thinking of a day a decade earlier when his world had changed.

He didn't know why he had come—it was stupid really, dangerous even—but he had felt the need to come back to this place to remember the friends he had lost.

Drummond lowered his face against the weather and walked north toward the fountain, his mind a chaotic jumble of memories and emotions from that day so long ago. Laughter and hugs and long walks. And then screams and light, blood and darkness. A few moments of madness in Manhattan that had marked the dawning of a more dangerous time. The start of his life as a wanderer. The creation of the Shadow House. All of these things had come from that moment ten years earlier.

He reached the Washington Square Arch and stepped into its shelter. He was cold, his old coat offering little protection from the weather, but he didn't want to leave just yet. He stood motionless for a while, letting the wind chill him, watching the park. After a few moments he realized that he wasn't alone.

A shape formed beyond the fountain, and Drummond felt his heart kick into a faster rhythm. The figure grew larger, nearer, and Drummond watched as a man emerged from the snow and stepped into the space beneath the arch next to him.

"Mr. Fox," Dr. Hugo Barbary said. The man smiled, but to Drummond it looked like the satisfied expression of a predator upon cornering its prey. "What luck to meet you here, of all places? I don't know whether to be surprised or disappointed in you that you would actually come back."

They were standing only a few feet apart, close enough that Barbary could reach out and touch Drummond if he wanted. Drummond tried not to show his fear.

"Hugo," he said, his tone neutral. He pointedly turned his gaze back to the storm, refusing to be intimidated, but slipped his hands into his pockets to be ready.

Barbary was a large, round man with a big bald head and dark eyes behind the thick frames of his spectacles. He was dressed in a three-piece suit beneath a long overcoat, the waistcoat stretching taut over his stomach, and he wore a large fedora, sheltering his face from the snow. He was carrying an old-fashioned leather bag by his side, like a doctor on a home visit.

"People have been looking for you, these past ten years," Barbary said. "A lot of time and effort has been spent trying to locate you."

Drummond said nothing.

"What luck that I am the first to see you again." Barbary was South African, and although his accent had softened over many years of moving around the world, it was still there in his odd, clipped vowels.

"It sickens my soul," Drummond said, and Barbary tilted his head as if interested, "that a man like you is still alive when much better people died here for no good reason."

"Ouch," Barbary said, grinning. "I won't take that personally. But what happened ten years ago was nothing to do with me. I wasn't even here. If I recall, I was out in Thailand chasing down some bloody book that turned out not to exist. Have you ever been to Thailand? Bloody hot. Hated the place. Everything they eat is full of lemongrass. It all tastes like medicine and soap."

"What do you want?" Drummond asked, tired of the man, tired of his fake bonhomie.

Barbary hummed thoughtfully, like a man studying a menu. "I want your books. I am just trying to decide whether or not I have to kill you first."

Drummond nodded to himself. "It's always about the books, isn't it?"

Barbary shrugged. "What else would it be about?"

Drummond said nothing, watching the storm. It was a curtain between the two men and the world. In that moment, surrounded by the snow, the safety of other people and brighter places felt very far away.

"What do you have, Librarian?" Barbary asked, taking a step closer to Drummond, his eyes finally revealing the hunger of his soul. "What have you been carrying to keep you safe all these years?"

"I am not the Librarian anymore," Drummond replied. "There is no library. It's gone."

It caused him pain to even acknowledge this truth, but he showed none of it on his face.

"That's what I heard," Barbary said, scratching his cheek idly. "Gone but not forgotten, eh? Many people are looking for the Fox Library."

"Many?" Drummond asked skeptically. "I didn't think there were many left. I thought *she* had seen to that."

"Oh, it's not so bad," Barbary said. He removed his hat and ran a hand over his bald head. "I'm still here. There are others. Fewer than there were, that's true. She's picking people off one by one and taking their books. But it's Darwinian, isn't it? Survival of the fittest. I'm sure she'll find me sooner or later, but I am okay with that. We'll see how good she really is."

"She'll get to you," Drummond said. "No one is safe. I know. I've met her."

Barbary eyed Drummond for a moment as if considering this sobering assessment.

"Some people are safe," he countered. "Those with the right sorts of books. The most powerful books."

"Is that you, Hugo?" Drummond asked. "Are you carrying a powerful book these days?"

"Foolish of you to come to New York," Barbary said, ignoring Drummond's question. "You must have known it was a risk."

"I had a craving for a hot dog," Drummond murmured.

Barbary laughed once, the noise echoing around the arch above them.

"I'm tired," Drummond said. "Can we get to the bit where you try to kill me, or where you leave me alone, please? Either is fine, but, you know, sooner rather than later."

"Why don't you just give me your books?" Barbary suggested. "Save me some trouble. I'll let you live. I won't even tell anyone I saw you."

"How many books do you have now, Hugo?" Drummond asked. He was carrying three books himself, two in one pocket, and one in the other. He had gripped them as soon as he had slipped his hands into his pockets moments earlier, reassuring himself that they were there. The Book of Shadows was alone in his right pocket, open and bent back upon its spine. Drummond had grown used to carrying the book this way over the years. It was always ready for him to tear a corner from a page, to disappear into the shadows. In his mind he heard the words of the Book of Shadows like they were a good luck charm: *The pages are of shadows. Hold a page and be of shadow too.*

"It's not the number of books that matters, is it?" Barbary replied. "It's what one does with them."

"Book of Pain?" Drummond asked. "That was always your favorite, wasn't it?"

"You wouldn't want me to use the Book of Pain, Drummond," Barbary said. It was almost sympathetic, like he was concerned for Drummond's health. "I'm very good with it. I enjoy it."

The two men held each other's gaze, Drummond giving no ground despite the fear that was tensing all his muscles. Then Barbary smiled. "There he is," he said. "There is the Librarian. Backbone of iron. Just like when he ran away and left his friends to die."

It was Drummond's turn to look away then, to gaze off into the swirling snow.

"I wonder what favors the woman would grant me if I told her where you were?"

Drummond met Barbary's gaze again, assessing the threat.

"Nah," Barbary drawled. "I think I'll just kill you and keep your books for myself."

He jerked forward suddenly, an arm shooting out like a piston, but by the time it reached where it was going Drummond had moved.

"You have to catch me first," Drummond said, one step away. In his pocket he tore a corner from a page in the Book of Shadows and clenched it in his hand. Almost immediately he felt that fragment of paper grow heavy in his palm, and as the weight increased he vanished into the snow, becoming shadow himself, intangible and invisible.

Hugo squinted into the storm, his mouth a tight line of annoyance. "I know you're here," he said loudly. "You've shown your face now. I'll find you, Librarian. Be sure of that."

Drummond said nothing, refusing to move even as Barbary waited, even as the cold gnawed at his bones. The larger man lost his patience first, muttering under his breath after a few minutes and turning away. The storm swallowed his huge shape almost immediately.

Drummond waited for a while longer, just to make sure that Hugo really had gone, then he headed north out of the park, keeping himself hidden in the shadows until he was on the street again. Once he was there, he opened his palm to reveal the scrap of dark paper with its rainbow aura. The wind lifted the paper as it grew lighter, as the rainbow aura died, and the scrap fluttered away on the breeze. Drummond emerged from the shadows, substantial once more.

He struggled through the weather along Fifth Avenue toward Midtown, leaving footprints in the snow behind him.

THAT NIGHT DRUMMOND STAYED AT the Library Hotel in Midtown, knowing it was a risk to stay somewhere so on the nose but not caring. He had been to Washington Square Park to remember, and now he just wanted to drink and sleep and forget.

He paid for a room, ignored the haunted eyes of the gaunt, dark-haired man in the mirror in the bathroom as he washed his face, and then took himself to the rooftop bar. He ordered whisky and looked for a seat, but the room was full of the sort of people who made him feel out of place—rich, or pretending to be, overly confident and carelessly callous about their wealth—so he took himself out to the roof terrace. He sat in a corner, under an umbrella, and nursed his drink. There was open sky high above him and towering walls of windows all around, the buildings of Midtown forming an enclosure of concrete. The snow was still heavy, big soft flakes turning the world white and hazy.

Drummond sipped his whisky and lifted the glass in a silent toast to the friends he had lost a little over a decade ago. To Lily and the food she would cook for him whenever she visited from Hong Kong. To Yasmin and her patience with his lack of historical knowledge and the stupid questions he bothered her with. And to Wagner and his regular phone calls from Europe just to check in on how Drummond was doing, making sure he spoke to another human being at least once a week. Drummond missed his friends still, and he had carried their memories with him as ghosts, constant companions on all of his wanderings over the years.

He was growing old and growing tired and he didn't know how much longer he could keep wandering, but he didn't know how to stop, and he had nowhere to be. For ten years he had been on the move, using the books in his possession to protect him—the Book of Shadows to pass unseen; the Book of Memories to make people forget about him when he needed them to; and the Book of Luck to bring him good fortune. The books had helped him during that time, and he had existed untroubled other than by his own thoughts. He didn't mind the loneliness, he had been solitary for most of his life, but the constant need to move had become tiring. More than anything, he missed his home.

But now Hugo Barbary had seen him, and Drummond wondered how that could have been possible when he carried the Book of Luck with him. It seemed like the very opposite of good luck. But Drummond knew luck wasn't a straight path—he had learned over the years that it was a curving road with detours and hidden exits. Maybe the luck of having been seen by Barbary wasn't obvious to him yet.

Drummond sipped his whisky, realizing that his mind was enjoyably unfocused. He returned to the bar for another drink and then came back to his spot on the roof terrace.

He thought about Barbary then, one of the worst men he had ever known, a monster dressed up like a gentleman. He wondered if perhaps he should have let Hugo take him. It would have been poetic, in a way, dying ten years after the massacre, in the same spot. It might actually have been a relief, a release from the burdens of his life and the fear of the woman.

The sudden sound of laughter punctured the white noise of the storm, pulling his attention from his thoughts. Two women stumbled through the doorway from the bar onto the terrace, both of them squinting and lifting their hands against the snow. The women looked toward him and then turned away to find another seat at the far end of the roof, away from Drummond.

Drummond looked elsewhere, but his heart was suddenly racing, as if a nightmare had just woken him in the middle of the night.

He had seen something, a burst of fireworks light up the darkness.

He told himself it was impossible. On this night, of all nights, and in this place.

But he had the Book of Luck in his possession, and such things happened to lucky people.

He waited, knowing he had to be sure before he did anything. He was aware of the women dancing drunkenly in the snow, and then returning to their seat and chatting to each other for a few minutes. And then they got up again and headed back toward the door to the bar.

He watched, studying them, memorizing them. A tall blond woman, a shorter dark-haired woman. He met their eyes, one after the other, and then turned away again as if not interested in them.

When they stepped through the door to the bar, he saw telltale rainbow light reflected on their faces for a brief moment, colors he knew so well. And when he craned his neck to look, Drummond didn't see the women appear on the other side of the glass.

"Fuck," he muttered, knowing then that the women had the Book of Doors, as impossible as that seemed.

"Book of Doors," Drummond muttered. A book that his family and other book hunters had been seeking for over a century. A book many people doubted even existed. Just his luck to stumble upon it.

He had to find the two women.

They were in immense danger, the like of which they couldn't possibly comprehend.

The Illusion in the Desert

In a luxurious house between the ocean and the desert, Hjaelmer Lund stood at the window and stared out at the darkness. There was nothing to see now that night had fallen, but the previous morning, when they had first arrived, the floor-to-ceiling windows had provided a breathtaking view out over the Pacific Ocean. Now all Lund could see was his own reflection in the glass.

The house was a grand, modern single-story complex, with big rooms and wide corridors, lots of sandstone and marble and the minimalist feel of an expensive hotel. It sat on a bluff to the north of Antofagasta, down a private road off Route 1, in between the Pacific Ocean and the Atacama Desert. The house had been built so that it faced away from the city, with a view that would make you think you were alone in the world.

"Sit down, Lund," Azaki muttered behind him, from the sofa in the center of the room. "Nobody wants to come into a room and see you standing there."

Lund was a giant by any measure, six feet eight inches tall, so large that he was impossible to miss and intimidating without intending to be. He understood the point Azaki was making and moved away from the window to sit on the couch.

"Here they come," Azaki said, smoothing down his tie. "Let me do the talking."

Lund raised an eyebrow, as if saying: *When do I not?*

The doors to the hallway opened and Miss Pacheo appeared in her wheelchair, Elena behind and pushing the chair into the room. The old woman, frail and wrinkled but with eyes full of life, lit up at the sight of Azaki. Miss Pacheo was a long-term multiple sclerosis sufferer, and she spoke next to no English. Elena, as well as being her assistant, was her translator. Once Elena had parked the old woman she took a position on the end of the couch and started to translate as Miss Pacheo spoke.

"Mr. Ko, Mr. Jones," she said, using the fake names Azaki had given. "Miss Pacheo is keen to hear how your search has gone."

Azaki bowed politely, affecting the Japanese academic that he was pretending to be. Azaki was Japanese by ancestry, but he had been born in California. He was a neat, short man, always well presented, with jet-black hair and a handsome, symmetrical face. "Please tell Miss Pacheo that we are incredibly grateful for her hospitality, and for access to her family's private library."

Elena translated as Azaki spoke. Lund glanced at Miss Pacheo and saw her grow attentive as the message was relayed.

"Please tell Miss Pacheo," Azaki continued, "that we are very sorry to say that we found no books of particular academic interest or historical significance."

They had spent two days meticulously searching the Pacheo library for special books, but they had found nothing. Lund glanced toward the old woman again and saw her face fall with disappointment.

"I am very sorry for the trouble we have caused," Azaki said. "I know Miss Pacheo was keen that her family's library might be of some interest."

Azaki had found out about the Pacheo library a month or two earlier, during a week in Santiago when he'd gone drinking with a local academic. He had researched the family history, learning about a library that had originated with books brought over from Spain a century or more earlier, but which had been added to over the years by the Pacheo family as they had grown wealthy from their shipping business. He had sent a letter, claiming that he and Lund were academics touring South America in search of historically significant books. It had been enough to get them through the door, and after that Azaki's charm had won over the old woman sufficiently that she had granted them access to the library.

"She's dying," Azaki had explained to Lund, on the drive out to the house on the first day, even though Lund hadn't asked. "She has no children and she's never been married. She wants a legacy. So that's what I am offering her the possibility of."

Now Miss Pacheo accepted the news with a slow nod of the head. After a moment of silence she spoke a few more words to Elena.

"Miss Pacheo thanks you for your time," Elena said. "She is disappointed. But she appreciates the effort you have gone to."

Azaki nodded. Lund could tell he wanted to leave now. There were no special books here. Only sadness and a life ending.

"Thank you," Azaki said, nodding again.

The room was silent then, Miss Pacheo's eyes fixed on the floor, Azaki standing politely with his hands clasped in front of him like a servant awaiting an instruction. Elena was watching Miss Pacheo and Lund was watching her.

"Oh, Miss Pacheo," Elena said, standing up suddenly.

The old woman was crying, a quiet, dignified sort of weeping, individual tears rolling down the lines of her face.

"Again, I am very sorry," Azaki tried.

Elena smiled politely, but Lund could see that in that moment Azaki was an irritant for her.

Miss Pacheo smiled through her tears and said a few words that needed no translation.

"No need to apologize," Azaki said, dropping his eyes slightly.

As Elena tended to the old woman Azaki pointedly looked away, turning his eyes around the living area. They had been in the room for only a few minutes on the previous day, before they had been led to the library in the east wing of the house. Lund saw Azaki frown at a series of large photographs on the back wall, black-and-white images of a building that Lund didn't recognize. It looked almost like a building from some fantasy film, with towers and arched windows.

"That's the Sagrada Familia," Azaki said, pointing. "In Barcelona."

Elena glanced up. "That's right," she said.

Azaki walked over to the wall and studied the photographs. "So many pictures of the same building," he said.

Elena handed a tissue to Miss Pacheo, and the old woman dabbed weakly at her cheeks as she watched Azaki.

Elena smiled a sad smile. "Miss Pacheo always wanted to travel to Spain one day," she said. "Back to where her family came from. Her father always told her about the Sagrada Familia and she wanted very much to see it. Sadly, her illness and her age mean it is now not possible."

Azaki studied the photographs in silence for a moment or two. "I have seen it," he said finally. "I have been to Barcelona, I have seen the Sagrada Familia."

Elena smiled politely, all but saying: *That's very nice for you; now will you please leave?*

Azaki looked at Miss Pacheo in her wheelchair for a moment. Lund could see him wrestling with a decision, his kindness arguing with his fears.

"Elena, I feel bad for having disappointed Miss Pacheo. I know she is very ill. If it would make amends for her disappointment, I would like to offer her a gift."

Elena's eyebrows lifted in surprise.

"I would like to give Miss Pacheo the chance to visit the Sagrada Familia."

THEY LEFT THE HOUSE AS a group, Miss Pacheo at the front pushed by Elena, Azaki and Lund behind, following a path of flagstones away from the property and toward the barren, sandy landscape along the coast. The Pacific Ocean was roaring in the darkness off to their left, the air heavy with salt and spray.

"This will do," Azaki said.

A vast plain of orange-brown sand extended away from them into the darkness, and the only light came from the spotlights around Miss Pacheo's house a short distance behind them. Azaki bowed his head for a moment, one hand slipping into his pocket to hold the Book of

Illusion. He closed his eyes, and Lund knew that he would be imagining whatever he wanted to conjure, painting with his mind. He knew that if Azaki were to have withdrawn the book from his pocket, a dance of lights would have lit the night, the Book of Illusion surrounded by a haze of soft colors as Azaki worked. Miss Pacheo and Elena watched Azaki questioningly, but Lund turned his eyes to the barren plain, the sound of the ocean in his ears.

After a moment there was movement, a swirl of dust and sand in the darkness. And then the movement became more distinct, and the swirl became solid, and that solidity spread. Nothing became something and a vast building with spindle-like towers stretching high above them emerged suddenly from the darkness. The effect was of the huge building speeding toward them and then stopping suddenly with a shudder just beyond touching distance.

Miss Pacheo squeaked and threw her hands up to her face. Elena jerked backward, away from the illusion of the huge building. Azaki kept his eyes closed, and as he did so the surface of the cathedral became more detailed, as if a sculptor were chiseling away unwanted material from a masterpiece.

"The Sagrada Familia," he said.

Elena gaped, her mouth wide, and she took a few steps to the side, to see that this building had three dimensions, that it was not just a picture.

Azaki was sweating slightly, Lund saw, as if this illusion was a strain for him.

"Perhaps some light?" Azaki suggested.

A moment later ribbons of color filled the air above the Sagrada Familia, like the northern lights but in many different hues, waving and blending together. It was colors like those that Lund had seen coming from the book, whenever Azaki used it.

Elena said something in a language that Lund didn't understand, and then looked at the old woman. Miss Pacheo was pushing herself up, her eyes bright and shining, the lights in the sky painting colors on her face. She reached for Elena, flapping her hand urgently, and Elena hurried to her and supported her weak frame.

Together the two women stumbled into the doorway of the church.

Azaki kept his hand in his pocket as the women explored the illusion he was sustaining.

Lund stood with him, watching and waiting.

A SHORT WHILE LATER, IN the car back to Antofagasta, Azaki was staring off into the darkness through the passenger-side window.

"Was that stupid?" he asked, even though he knew Lund wouldn't answer. "I am just so tired of misleading people. Giving them hopes and dreams. It wouldn't be so bad if we found something; then at least it's worth it."

Lund didn't think Azaki had been stupid, but he didn't say anything to that effect. He just kept driving. That was his job. To drive, to protect, to wait and see what was happening and then do what he was asked. This was his life with Azaki: traveling the world, staying in nice hotels, and waiting to see what Azaki wanted to do. It had been like this for almost nine months now, ever since Lund had rescued Azaki from a group of drunken men in a bar in San Francisco. Lund had been working as a bouncer and occasional barman, just the latest in a string of jobs he had taken over the last fifteen years, as he had moved in a long slow arc across the southern United States. He had been a laborer, a pool digger, a gardener, a bouncer frequently, a bodyguard once, and a barman more times than he could remember. It was simple, unchallenging work, jobs that were easy for someone of his size, build, and demeanor. For all of his adult life, ever since he had left the small town in northeastern Canada where he had grown up, he had stayed in one place for only as long as it took him to grow bored and restless, and then he would move on. He never wanted for much other than food and a bed and he was happy with his straightforward existence.

And then, in a bar in San Francisco, a drunken Azaki had won a game of poker, cleaning out three men who hadn't planned on being out of pocket, particularly not to some "short, drunken Jap." Lund had watched the exchange as it had warmed from friendly banter to unhappiness to outright violence, and then he had stepped in just before Azaki was about to be beaten into the ground. Lund had stood up to the men and they hadn't liked it, so he had beaten them into the ground instead.

When he'd finished with the men Azaki had asked him if he'd wanted a job.

"I've just lost my bodyguard," he said. Then he barked a laugh. "Perfect time to get into a fight in a bar, I know. I'll pay you well. You just need to travel with me and be my bodyguard."

Lund had gone with the man, partly because he'd been bored with San Francisco, but mostly because when he had been watching the game of cards, he had seen Azaki look at his cards and then change them to a better hand, hearts changing to spades, spot cards to face cards. It had amazed Lund, and he had become interested in this man.

They had traveled together for almost two months, up the West Coast from San Francisco and then across to Chicago and south again, following the Mississippi. Azaki was easy company. He didn't demand much and spoke only occasionally. After a while he had started to tell Lund about his life. He was a third-generation Japanese American and he was a disappointment to his family.

"They wanted me to be straight, married, and a doctor or an engineer. Such a cliché, right? Turns out they got a gay, single artist. I wanted to do something creative like my great-grandfather."

Azaki's great-grandfather had been a famous card magician in the mid-twentieth century. Azaki had researched all about him in his youth, and had studied magic himself, as well as art and music, while ostensibly studying medicine at college. It was during his research for rare books on magic that he had found the Book of Illusion. Lund knew this because Azaki had finally revealed the truth about the book during a night of protracted drinking in Memphis. Azaki revealed more when he was drunk.

"This is it," he had said to Lund, showing him the small black book. It was covered in fine gold patterns, like the backs of expensive playing cards. "This is everything I am," he had said sleepily. "It is a magic book, my friend Hjaelmer Lund. And there are lots of magic books out there. I know. I've seen them. I've had friends who had them, just like me."

Azaki had seemed sad for a moment, and then his face had brightened. He had handed the book to Lund and told him to look at it. Lund had flicked through the pages and seen that they were filled with line-drawn scribbles, sketches of people and places and items.

"Drawings," Lund had said.

And Azaki had nodded. "It's the illusions the book creates. When I make something appear, I can find a drawing of it in the book. Let me show you what it can do!" he had said. "All I need to do is hold the book and imagine what I want to see. I can make you see whatever I want."

As Lund had watched, Azaki had gripped the book. And then there had been lights, a haze of bright colors dancing and swirling around the edges of the book. Lund had felt his mouth drop open, the first moment in his life in which he had felt genuine amazement.

"Look," Azaki had said, nodding at Lund's empty plate, now loaded with food again.

Lund had reached out to touch the food. It felt real. It looked real.

"I can smell it," he had said.

"It's all illusion," Azaki had said, and Lund had seen that he was smiling proudly.

Then Azaki had visibly relaxed, placing the book on the table, and the haze of lights had disappeared as if someone had flicked a switch, and Lund's plate had been empty once again.

"And look at this," Azaki had said, opening the book. He flicked through pages until he found what he was looking for. Then he turned the book around and showed it to Lund—a rough, scribbled drawing of the plate of food he had just seen and touched and smelled.

"Fucking unbelievable, right?" Azaki had said.

Lund had simply nodded, because it was exactly that: fucking unbelievable.

He didn't know why Azaki had told him his secret, but he assumed Azaki had decided that Lund was simple in some way. It wasn't unusual. People saw Lund's size, and if they spent any time with him, they noticed how he didn't say much and therefore assumed he was stupid. Lund was happy to be underestimated, and as much as he liked Azaki and his easy company, he had no plans to disabuse the man of the notion that he was a bit slow.

WHEN THEY MADE IT BACK to the hotel on the edge of the port in Antofagasta, Azaki said that he was going for a drink in the bar, alone. Lund got the message and went straight to the top-floor suite. He took a beer from the minibar and stood at the window for a while. Lund could see the port, and he liked the view. He liked to see the activity, the people at work.

Lund sipped his beer and thought about Azaki. Beneath it all he was a soft man, a kind man. Lund didn't see that as a failing; it was a big part of what had kept him traveling with him for so long.

Azaki returned to the suite earlier than Lund had expected, a little over an hour later. He took a beer from the minibar and joined Lund on the couches.

"I think we'll go back to the US," Azaki said. "I feel like we should go to New York."

Azaki had a faraway look in his eye. He got that way sometimes when he was sad, or drinking, or sad and drinking.

"Okay," Lund said. He didn't mind. He had been to New York only once before when he'd been much younger. He would enjoy a return trip.

After a few beers, and while they were both slumped on the couches in different corners of the room, Lund said, "Do the thing."

Azaki sighed theatrically, but Lund knew he liked to show off his skills.

"Okay," Azaki said. He pulled out the Book of Illusion and held it in his hand, closing his eyes briefly. The book glowed in many colors, and then similar colors lit up the room as a whole, a waterfall of rainbow sparks showering down upon them from the ceiling. Lund relaxed back into the sofa and enjoyed the illusion, feeling himself easing down into sleep.

"Enjoy it," Azaki said. "Tomorrow a new adventure starts."

Lund lifted his bottle to reciprocate and turned his eyes back to the lights.

He didn't imagine they'd find anything the next day; they hadn't found anything in the nine months he had been traveling with Azaki, but he was happy to go along for the ride, happy to learn all about the hidden world of magic books.

Mr. Webber's Apartment and Izzy's Investigations

The next morning, after a night of little sleep and lots of excitement, Cassie went in search of answers, and she took the Book of Doors with her.

Her first stop was Mr. Webber's building on East Ninety-Fourth Street, a four-story redbrick building with a black fire escape zigzagging down the front that was covered in a fat layer of snow. The door to the building was locked—she tried it, but it rattled securely. Cassie thought for a moment, and then reached for the Book of Doors in her pocket, imagining opening the door and stepping straight into the hallway beyond, but when she pulled the handle, the door remained stubbornly shut.

"What?" she asked the day, the word a swirl of breath coughed into the air.

She glanced around, making sure she was still alone on the street, and removed the book from her pocket. She tried again, checking to make sure the Book of Doors was surrounded by its haze of rainbow light as she pulled the handle, but the door to Mr. Webber's building still didn't budge.

"Why doesn't it work?"

She stood motionless for a moment, thinking about the puzzle. The journeys she had made the previous evening had all started from doors that were unlocked—the door in her apartment, the door on the hotel roof terrace. The only difference that she could think of was that the door to Mr. Webber's building was locked—she couldn't walk through it *without* using the Book of Doors, so why should she be able to walk through it using the book?

"Can't unlock locked doors," she said to herself. The Book of Doors could transform one doorway into another, but only if the first door was already unlocked.

"Huh," she murmured, as the conclusion settled and solidified. It felt right. She could get through a locked door only by traveling from an unlocked one. She needed to test the hypothesis.

Cassie walked back out onto Second Avenue, swinging her gaze across to the far side of the street and back, whistling happily to herself. She found a Citibank, the building it occupied covered in scaffolding that provided a canopy over the doorway. The Citibank itself was just a square room with five ATMs and no staff.

"Perfect," Cassie murmured.

She reached for the door, the other hand in her pocket and holding the Book of Doors. She remembered the door she had just tried to Mr. Webber's building, the feel of the handle in her hand. She remembered the cold metal, the sound as it had rattled in the lock. She remembered— she *felt*—all of this as she was aware of the book changing in her pocket, growing more solid. She glanced down and peered into her pocket, see- ing sparking lights like fireworks in a cave, and she smiled to herself as she pulled the Citibank door open and stepped not into the bank, but into the hallway of Mr. Webber's building, a block south and around the corner. The world was suddenly quiet, the smell of warmth and wood in Cassie's nose.

"Cool," she murmured, as the door banged behind her, sealing off Second Avenue. Relief washed over her, and she realized she had been worried by the locked door on the street, worried that the magic wouldn't work anymore.

She pulled the Book of Doors from her pocket and flicked through the pages to that drawing of a doorway. Where once there had been a dark room, and then a street in Venice, the image now showed the hallway Cassie was standing in. She found herself staring at that draw-ing, and then lifting her eyes to compare it to her surroundings.

"Unbelievable," she murmured, smiling.

She scampered up the stairs to the top floor. The door to Mr. Webber's apartment, the only door on the top floor of the building, was locked. She knocked smartly, and the sound bounced around the walls and off the tiled floor like a rubber ball. She waited, but there was nobody home.

Cassie thought about how to get into Mr. Webber's apartment. Now that she had seen the door, now that she had *experienced* the door she wanted to open, she just needed an unlocked door to get through it.

She realized what she had to do. She took another good look at the door, reaching out and gripping the handle, just as she had with the street door. And then she headed back down the stairs and onto the street, around the corner and back to the Citibank, slightly irritated by having to retrace her steps, but delighting in what felt like mischief and magic, in her secret adventures.

A few minutes later she opened the door to the Citibank for a second time and stepped into a darkened hallway behind Mr. Webber's locked door. Unable to stop herself, she looked at the drawing in the book again, and she saw that it had changed once more, showing the gloomy interior of Mr. Webber's apartment.

"It's magic," she said, shaking her head slowly. It was as thrilling as the first time she had used the book the previous day; more so, even, because now she was testing what it could do, she was exploring the impossible. She was developing a relationship with the book.

She walked along the corridor and into an open-plan living area with two large windows facing the street. Beams of gray, watery morning light stretched across the space. The walls were lined with bookshelves, all of them full and neatly arranged. A wingback armchair sat by a window with a footstool in front of it, and a two-seater sofa sat in the middle of the room facing a small, square television on a wooden unit. The kitchen area was to her right. The whole place smelled of wood and leather and books and coffee.

Cassie ran her eyes around the bookshelves. She saw Dickens and

Dumas, Hardy and Hemingway, plays and literary theory and music scores. There were modern books as well, fantasy and science fiction and horror, paperbacks in bright colors filling one set of shelves. But there was nothing like the Book of Doors, no other magical notebooks.

She found a second short corridor on the other side of the living room, three doors along its length. She ignored the bathroom and looked into the gloomy room on the right of the corridor. There was a single bed pushed against the wall and an old cupboard in the corner. A small window looked out onto a courtyard behind the building. Inside the wardrobe Cassie found clothes, but the clothes of a younger woman rather than an older man. She wondered if Mr. Webber had had a girlfriend at one time. Or a relative maybe. There were books here, arranged in a neat line along the window ledge. Paperbacks, classics and contemporary books, an eclectic mix. Cassie nodded as she ran her finger across the spines, appreciating the taste of whoever had brought the collection together.

The main bedroom at the end of the hall was a much bigger room, with a double bed against the far wall, a single window similar in size to the two in the living area, and a built-in cupboard on the left that was full of clothes, and shoes neatly arranged on the floor. These were Mr. Webber's clothes. She recognized scarves and jackets, the faint smell of whatever toiletries he had used. Sadness fell upon her again at the loss of this man she barely knew, but she pushed it away.

She closed the cupboard door and walked over to the window, watching a delivery truck wobble down the snowy street as she wondered what she was doing. There was nothing significant in the apartment.

Why had she come?

What had she hoped to achieve, really? Or had it just been an excuse to play with the Book of Doors?

She walked back into the living area, the comfortable space full of books and daylight. It was a quietly joyful place, Cassie decided, a place where Mr. Webber would surely have been content.

"Why did you give me the book, Mr. Webber?" she asked to the room. "And where did you get it? What is the secret behind it?"

She waited, but there was nobody there to answer her.

"HOW ARE YOU, DEAR?" MRS. Kellner asked when Cassie arrived at work. She had walked through the cold lunchtime air from Mr. Webber's building, slipping and sliding occasionally on the frozen snow where the sidewalks hadn't been cleared, and her face felt windburned and dry.

"Fine," Cassie said.

Mrs. Kellner nodded approvingly. "That's good, dear."

Mrs. Kellner called everyone "dear," regardless of whether they were old or young. She was a woman of indeterminate age herself, and to Cassie's eye she hadn't aged in the six years since Cassie had first met her. She was short, solid, and always well presented, the sort of woman who would stare down a crisis like it was barely the worst thing that had happened to her in the previous half hour.

Cassie had been a customer of the bookstore before she had been an employee. In her first few months in the city, after returning from Europe and while she was still sleeping in hostels, Cassie had toured the bookstores of New York. Kellner Books had been her favorite—it was easy to get to, away from the tourists and busy people of Midtown, and big enough to have a good selection of books without being so big that it was impersonal and soulless. She had ended up visiting most days of the week, becoming known to the staff, and even rearranging books when she found them in the wrong place on the shelves. After months of this Mrs. Kellner had taken Cassie aside and had offered her a job.

"You're here often enough; you might as well get paid."

The truth was, as Cassie had found out weeks later from Izzy, Mr. Kellner had been diagnosed with Alzheimer's and he was already showing the signs of a rapid deterioration.

"He's not going to be able to do anything in the store soon," Izzy had told her, as they'd tidied up together at the end of one day. "And Mrs. Kellner is going to be doing less because she'll be looking after him. So she needs more help. And you have an honest face."

"All the best liars do," Cassie had joked.

Sure enough, Mr. Kellner had slowly faded as a presence in the shop. He was a man as tall and slight as his wife was short and solid, with disheveled hair and a kindly way about him, but Cassie had only just started to get to know him at the point he had stopped coming to the store. In the last few years Mrs. Kellner had barely mentioned her husband and Cassie had never felt comfortable asking how he was doing.

"Go get a coffee," Mrs. Kellner instructed her now. "You look tired." It was her usual sort of kindness, offered as a mild scolding.

Cassie put her stuff in the back—her coat, and her bag with the Book of Doors within it—and then stopped by the coffee counter. The shop wasn't busy, just a few students with their laptops at the coffee tables, a couple of regular customers browsing, so Cassie chatted with Dionne for a few minutes while her coffee cooled, describing what had happened the previous evening as dispassionately as she could.

"Poor Mr. Webber," Dionne said, shaking her head and clucking her tongue.

"You served him yesterday, right?" Cassie asked. "Before you finished up?"

"That's right," Dionne said, leaning on the counter.

"Did you notice . . . ?" Cassie hesitated but wasn't sure why.

"Did I notice what?"

"Did you notice if he was carrying a brown book? Like a little notebook?"

Dionne laughed. "Honey, at the end of my shift you're lucky I notice if I'm serving a man or a woman or a goddamn alien. I take the order and give them their coffee. I don't notice what books they're holding."

"Right," Cassie said.

"You okay, honey?"

"Just tired," Cassie said, lifting the coffee. "Need this."

Cassie wandered back toward the counter at the front of the store and settled on her stool.

"Mrs. Kellner?" she asked, trying to sound casual.

"Yes, dear?"

"Did you know Mr. Webber?"

"What do you mean did I know him? I knew him. He came to my store and bought books. Is that what you mean?"

Conversations with Mrs. Kellner were often like this. She had to tell you that you were stupid before she answered your question. There was no malice in it; it was just how she spoke.

"No, I mean did you know anything about him?"

"I know he was old and not eating enough. A man that age and that thin, like he would snap if he fell over. It wasn't right."

"Has he always been coming here?" Cassie asked.

"That's awful English, my dear, 'always been coming here.'"

Cassie gave the older woman a look, a look she wouldn't have dared to give her even a few years earlier. Mrs. Kellner sighed and gazed off into the shop.

"Mr. Webber was a good customer," she said, and Cassie knew that this was high praise. "He's been coming to this store for as long as I can recall. I remember him when he wasn't so thin. When he was working. He was a handsome man, tall and strong." The old woman smiled to herself. "He was always alone," she said, looking back to her computer. "I don't remember him ever coming in here with someone else. I wondered if he was gay, actually, but you don't talk about things like that with customers, do you? But he was a good customer. We're running out of those." She was quiet for a moment, lost in her thoughts, and then added, "There was that woman that one time . . . he went home with a girl once, much too young for him. I think she was homeless or something. Maybe he was trying to help."

Cassie waited for more.

"Or maybe that was someone else," Mrs. Kellner said, shaking her head. "I've been doing this so long I get mixed up."

Mrs. Kellner went back to work. Cassie tried to work but found her thoughts constantly turning to the Book of Doors, to its many pages of mystery. She wanted to sit with it and pore over the details.

IZZY TURNED UP AT THE bookstore in the late afternoon, clattering through the door and kicking snow across the floor. Her hair was dampened down by the cold air and her cheeks were almost comically red.

"My dear Izzy," Mrs. Kellner said, embracing Izzy by the counter as Cassie looked on. "You look like a doll, look at these pink cheeks."

"I look like I'm frozen is what I look like!" Izzy muttered.

Mrs. Kellner held Izzy at arm's length, running her eyes over her like she was a grandchild she hadn't seen for years. "When are you going to stop selling those expensive baubles, mmm? Come back here and sell things that make the world a better place."

"Sorry, Mrs. K, but the expensive bauble people pay better. If you want to match what they pay me, I'll be right back here."

"Ah, money. Young people only care about money. There's more to life than money, dear." Mrs. Kellner picked up a stack of books and drifted away toward the back room.

"That's easy to say when you live in a multimillion-dollar apartment on the Upper East Side!" Izzy muttered to Cassie, leaning across the counter.

"She just misses you," Cassie said. "What are you doing here? I thought you were working today?"

"Just finished," she said. "Do you know what time it is? Never mind. I need to talk to you."

"What about?"

"About the . . ." She looked around and then lowered her voice. "Teleporty book."

Cassie almost smiled. "Not here," she said. A woman approached the counter, pushing a toddler in a stroller. The toddler was holding a large picture book out in front of her like it was a steering wheel. "Give me ten minutes and then I'll take an early break. We can walk and talk."

THEY WALKED ARM IN ARM, holding each other close for warmth and stability on the icy sidewalk. Cassie's bag was slung over her shoulder, the Book of Doors within. The street was busy with people and noise and traffic fumes, everyone wrapped up warm, their breath curling in the air. The sun appeared to have been swallowed by heavy gray clouds that threatened further snow. They walked in silence for a few moments, and Cassie found herself thinking about the many other times she and Izzy had walked arm in arm like this—to and from work in those early days of their friendship; to dinners with friends; to nights out when Izzy had been looking for dates and Cassie had been desperate to get home to whatever book she was devouring. It was their shared history together, and to Cassie it seemed almost as if they had always known each other, as if they were sisters.

"What did you want to talk about?" she asked.

Izzy nodded, staring ahead of them along the urban canyon. "I couldn't sleep last night," she said. "I mean, I probably did, when I went back to my room. Couple of hours maybe."

"Yeah."

"But it was like that sleep when you've got to get up early for something. You keep waking up and . . ." Izzy shook her head. "I kept watching the video we took, you know, of . . . ?"

"Yeah," Cassie said again. They waited at a crosswalk for the lights to change, and then crossed the street with the crowd, two groups of pedestrians coming together like opposing armies in a battle, before separating again and moving off in different directions.

"When I got to work, I couldn't stop thinking about it, so I was googling all day."

"Busy day in Bloomingdale's, then," Cassie observed. "What were you googling?"

Izzy rolled her eyes. "The weather in Minnesota! What do you think, Cassie? Your teleporty book. I was googling that."

Cassie bit her lip, uncomfortable with the idea that Izzy had done anything about the book without first discussing it with her. "What did you find out?"

"Nothing," Izzy said. "I was interneting like some PhD student for hours. I was looking at every website and every message board. Every vlog and blog and god knows what else. And I found nothing. No references to teleporting books or the Book of Doors or anything. Nothing."

"Huh," Cassie said, surprised by her own disappointment. "Why are you here, then, if you found nothing?"

Izzy gave her a disbelieving sidelong glance. "Don't you get it?" she asked. "The internet knows nothing about your book."

"Yeah, you said that."

"Cassie," Izzy said, speaking to her like she was stupid. "Google knows everything. *Everything.* I bet I could find your shoe size and Mrs. K's tax returns. And this book, it's not a normal thing, is it? It's the sort of thing that people *would* know about. So how come there's nothing there?"

Cassie thought about the question. Something heavy settled in her stomach, a sensation she didn't like. She refused it, ignored it.

"Oh, come on, Iz," she said. "You're worried because you found nothing. If you *had* found something, you would have been worried too."

"It's like someone is watching, deleting all references to things like this," Izzy continued, her voice low and hurried. "I don't like it."

"You're overthinking!" Cassie said, forcing a laugh she didn't feel.

"And you're under-thinking!" Izzy snapped, and Cassie looked at her in surprise, seeing for the first time how serious Izzy was. "I know you walk around in this daydream all the time like nothing matters and nothing can hurt you, but this is giving me the creeps! You need to go to the police, get them to investigate that Mr. Webber . . ."

Cassie pulled a guilty face that Izzy interpreted straightaway.

"Cassie," she said, sounding disappointed.

"I might have visited his apartment this morning," she said.

"Cassie, someone might have seen you! And how did you get in . . . oh . . ." Izzy cut herself off, and Cassie nodded confirmation. "I am not sure you should be using it like that. Not until you know more about it. It could be dangerous."

"I didn't find anything," Cassie said, narrowing her eyes as she turned her face to the wind. "It was just the apartment of an old man. I didn't rummage through his drawers or anything, but it just felt like there was nothing there."

Izzy was shaking her head, looking at her feet as they walked, obviously unhappy.

"Come on, I'd better get back," Cassie said.

They reached the end of a block and started to head back. As they turned something caught Cassie's eye, a figure, a familiar face. Across the street a man was watching them—a dark-haired man with a gaunt face, dressed in a dark suit, and Cassie realized she had seen him before. He was the man from the previous night, the man sitting on the terrace at the Library Hotel. She held his gaze as she walked, craning her head to keep him in view.

"What is it?" Izzy asked.

"Nothing," Cassie lied, smiling at her. "Nothing."

She glanced back and the man was no longer visible through the traffic.

"We've taken longer than I thought," Cassie said, suddenly uneasy. "I'm going to use the book to get back."

Izzy's face crumpled in unhappiness. "Cassie . . ."

"Please, Izzy, just trust me."

Something in her tone halted Izzy's protestations. They turned down the next street and found a large deli. Moments later they stepped back into Kellner Books, away from Second Avenue, and away from the man who had been watching them.

Book People

In New Orleans, in her townhouse in the French Quarter, Lottie Moore, the woman better known as the Bookseller, received a message she had long expected, providing information about the Book of Doors.

She read the email carefully, feeling her pulse quicken, and then she read it again to make sure she had the details secure in her mind. She got up from her desk and walked out to the balcony. She leaned on the metal railing under the shade of the cypress tree that stood in front of her house and stared down the length of Orleans Street, toward the spire of St. Louis Cathedral in the distance. It was a warm day for the time of year, but not too humid. The breeze pleased her, and she let it wash over her as she contemplated things for a while. Then she pulled out her phone to call the book hunter Azaki. She'd had a long time to think about who to ask for help, and Azaki had been the one she had settled on.

"Madame Bookseller," Azaki said, when he answered.

"Thank you for taking my call," Lottie said. She knew that Azaki was not a fan of hers. The only time they had previously had contact had been several years earlier, when Azaki had sold her a book. He had done it out of necessity, to survive, rather than because he was happy for a special book to be sold on the open market.

"What can I help you with?"

"Where are you?"

Azaki didn't answer immediately. "Let's say South America."

"I understand your caution, but this conversation is strictly confidential."

"South America," Azaki said again. He was a cautious man. Lottie didn't blame him.

"I am going to be honest, Mr. Azaki," she said. "I need someone trustworthy, someone careful."

"For what?"

"I have intelligence about a special book that has emerged in New York."

"I'm listening," Azaki said, his voice briefly obscured by the sound of traffic and street noise.

"I am not at liberty to reveal how I know what I am about to tell you, but I believe the Book of Doors has surfaced."

"The Book of Doors," Azaki said. "Are you sure?"

"I am."

Azaki was quiet for a moment. "Interesting."

"I need someone trustworthy to retrieve it."

"To bring it to you, to sell?" Azaki asked.

"Of course," Lottie said. "Imagine the profits. Even after my cut, you would have enough to run and hide for the rest of your life. That's what you want, isn't it?"

Azaki didn't answer. He was scared and in need. That was what she was bargaining on.

"If that book falls into the wrong hands . . ."

She knew what he meant. *Who* he meant. But she didn't say anything.

"Tell me what you know," he said finally.

Lottie told him the details. "I am asking for your help, so I will pay for your flight to New York, if you tell me what airport you want to leave from."

"No need," Azaki said. "I can afford a couple of tickets."

"A couple?"

"Me and my bodyguard," he explained. "I've got a new guy. Big guy. Very good with his hands. Does anybody else know about this?"

"Probably," Lottie said. "But if they don't yet, they soon will. It will be a feeding frenzy."

"Yes," Azaki agreed.

"I want you to do one other thing for me," Lottie said. "Something a bit more unusual. And this is why I am coming to you. One of the women with the book, her name is Isabella Cattaneo."

"What of her?"

"If she is alone when you find her, I want you to bring her to me."

"What?"

"I want you to bring her to me."

"Why?"

"I need to protect her."

"Protect her from what?"

"That is not your business. Will you do it? Recover the book and bring the woman to me?"

Azaki thought about it for a moment, and all Lottie heard was wind and traffic.

"Let me get to New York," he said finally. "I'll be in touch once I'm there."

He hung up.

Lottie put her phone away and leaned on the railing again. She wasn't worried about the Book of Doors; she knew that would come to her one way or another, and she would make her final sale and get out of the business once and for all. Azaki was really just insurance on that point. What she really needed Azaki for was to bring her the woman. That was the main thing. Because she had made a promise and she always kept her promises.

DRUMMOND FOX, ONCE THE LIBRARIAN but now a wanderer, woke up that morning with the women he had seen the previous evening in his mind. He felt an urgency to find them, to save them from whatever fate might befall them. He showered and dressed and then took his three books from the bedside table—the Book of Luck, with its golden cover and golden pages; the Book of Shadows; and the Book of Memories. He lingered on the Book of Memories again, opening the cover and looking at the neatly penned text on the first page, just as he had a thousand times before over the years.

This is the Book of Memories.

Share it, to share a memory,
Give it, to give a memory,
And take it, to take a memory.

Drummond had often thought about taking his own memories, for-getting all about the special books and the woman and the Fox Library and just starting a new life. It had been tempting, but he had always resisted. He resisted again now, because he had a purpose. He had to find the women with the Book of Doors.

He slipped the Book of Memories into his pocket alongside the other two books. They formed a slight bulge against his hip, but he was comfortable with that, it was how he knew they were always there—they were so light and insubstantial normally, it was easy to forget he had them. He stepped out into the cold morning, the wind burning his cheeks, and walked the snow-covered city without direction, down the long avenues in the shadows between the tall buildings, along streets wide and narrow. He bought a hot dog from a street vendor, washing it down with a Coke, and then he walked some more, trusting to his luck.

It was lunchtime when he saw them. He was standing at a crossing in the Upper East Side, waiting for the lights to change, and he spotted the two women on the opposite corner. The blond one saw him, glancing across the street and meeting his eyes with a serious expression. They held each other's gaze for a few moments but by the time he had crossed the street, slipping on the snowy sidewalk and stumbling and falling, the women were already at the end of the block. When he reached that corner only moments later there was no sign of them. The only place they could have gone was a deli, the first door along the street. Drummond entered the store, but it was empty other than the old woman behind the counter.

He returned to the street and stood there, breathing heavily, looking around to make sure he hadn't missed anything. There was nothing but doorways to apartment buildings, nowhere for the women to have gone unless they lived on that particular street.

But Drummond didn't think that was the case. He thought there was a different explanation, and he was even more sure than he had been the previous evening.

It was the Book of Doors, as unbelievable as that seemed.

DR. HUGO BARBARY KEPT ONE block away from Drummond Fox all through the man's morning wander. Hugo had been a hunter before he had become a book hunter, and it had been easy for him the night before to follow the man's tracks in the snow, all the way from Washington Square to the Library Hotel. Barbary had booked his own room in the same place, and a sizeable bribe to the concierge had made sure he was notified whenever Drummond left the building. Barbary had followed him all morning, wondering what the man was up to.

Barbary knew that Drummond Fox would have books. Nobody survived for ten years without being found, without some sort of help. Especially given the kind of people that were looking for Drummond.

Barbary had only two books himself, more than enough to fill his life with the sorts of pleasures and riches he enjoyed. And they were powerful books too, certainly powerful enough that he had been left alone so far. But someday, sooner or later, people would come for him, he knew: the bastard Okoro from Nigeria, or someone like him. Or the woman herself. It was an arms race to see who could collect the most books and the most power. Hugo was confident in his own abilities, and knew he inspired fear in others. But he also knew that it would be wise to have more books in his possession if he could. Books the like of which the Librarian had used to evade detection for ten years. Such books might be very useful indeed.

Barbary watched from across the street as Drummond Fox stood on the corner, a slightly puzzled look on his face, as if he had just lost something important.

Then the man walked again, heading south from the Upper East Side back toward Midtown.

Hugo didn't mind. He liked walking, it kept him healthy.

AT ABOUT THE SAME TIME in London, where it was early evening rather than the middle of the day, Marion Grace was waiting for her sister at a busy Italian restaurant in Covent Garden. Marion hadn't seen her sister for over five years—she rarely met anyone, anymore—but her sister had emailed asking for an urgent meeting. So Marion had left her apartment in the Docklands and made her way to Covent Garden. She had felt nervous and uncomfortable during the journey and had only really relaxed a little when she had reached the restaurant and had been given a table in the back corner.

"When the booking was made," the waiter explained, "a quiet table was requested. I hope this will do?"

Marion smiled her thanks, grateful that her sister had been considerate enough to think of her fears. She had settled in to wait. The waiter had brought bread in a basket and then a drink, and then Marion had been distracted by her phone for a minute, wondering if there was a message from her sister, and when she looked up again the woman was there, watching her from across the table with her very dark eyes and her beautiful face.

Marion gasped. The woman stared at her without expression.

Marion turned her face toward the restaurant as if looking for help, but nobody else would know who the woman was. None of them would have seen anything other than an attractive woman in a flowery dress.

"You," Marion said, her voice trembling.

The woman met her gaze, saying nothing.

Marion swallowed and her throat felt very small.

"I was meeting my sister," Marion said.

The woman held her gaze, then slowly shook her head.

"You," Marion said. "My sister, is she . . ."

"Your sister is gone," the woman said simply. Her voice was quiet, her words almost whispered. Marion looked away in dismay.

She thought about running, but how could she run? She was an old woman who had spent five years in hiding. And who knew what books the woman had?

"What do you want?" Marion asked, her voice shaking now. "What do you want from me?"

The woman caught the attention of a passing waiter. He bent at the waist to listen, and she said something close to his ear, and then the man bobbed and hurried away.

"I don't know anything," Marion said. "Please. I've been living like a hermit for five years. I haven't spoken to anyone."

The woman was inspecting the basket of bread as Marion spoke. She picked up a white roll and sniffed it.

"What did you do to my sister?" Marion asked, although she didn't want to know.

The woman met Marion's gaze and slowly tore the bread roll in two down the middle. Then the corners of her mouth twisted up in a smile.

"I don't have my book," Marion said then, and the woman's eyes again flicked up to her, as she put a piece of the bread in her mouth. The waiter reappeared with a glass of champagne and placed it down. The woman chewed the bread, watching Marion silently.

"I don't have it," Marion insisted. "I didn't want it. I didn't want you to come looking for it."

The woman sipped her champagne and pulled a face of disappointment, inspecting the drink through the glass and smacking her lips, as if it didn't taste like she had expected.

"You wouldn't have wanted it even if I did have it," Marion said. "What would you do with the Book of Joy?" Marion's mouth turned down, her hatred finally overcoming her fear. "Joy is the last thing that you care about."

The woman ate some more of her bread.

Marion watched her, waiting.

Waiting for something.

Waiting for the terror.

"I sent it to Drummond," she said finally. "I sent it away over ten years ago to keep it safe, all right? That's what you've done to this world. You made me hide the Book of Joy because that was better than you getting it."

Marion was surprised by tears in her eyes. She didn't know if these were tears of fear, tears for her sister, or tears for the world that this woman had created.

"That is what you did," she said, wiping her eyes with her hand. "Don't you have any shame?"

"Where is the Fox Library?" the woman asked, the sound of her voice so low that Marion had to lean in to hear what she was saying.

"I don't know where the Fox Library is," Marion said, suddenly panicked. "Why would I know? I wouldn't want to know! Nobody wants to know because it just means you'll come for them, doesn't it?"

The woman was looking at the bread roll, but her eyebrows lifted as if asking: *Really, that's what people are saying?*

"Only Drummond Fox knows," Marion said. "If you want to find the Fox Library you need to find him. I don't know why you are asking me!"

The woman said nothing. She was such a beautiful woman, Marion thought, such darkness wrapped up in such a lovely package.

"You'll never find Drummond Fox," Marion said, feeling her fear slip off her shoulders like a discarded coat. She was going to die, she knew, and it was incredible how freeing that thought was. She smiled to herself, and the woman dropped the uneaten part of her bread onto the table. "You haven't found him in all these years and you're not going to find him now, are you?"

The woman looked at her with her blank, beautiful expression.

"Oh, this is the best news I've had for years," Marion said, clasping her hands together in a moment of delight. "Oh yes! If you don't have him, you'll never find the Fox Library, will you?"

Marion actually laughed, and with the release of tension it felt as if the air around her relaxed slightly too.

She looked at the woman and saw how empty she was, how lacking in any sort of human substance. She was like a portrait of a woman, Marion thought, beautiful but without life.

Then the woman reached across and laid a hand on Marion's arm, her mouth a sudden, vicious sneer. A moment later Marion felt immediate, immense pain, as if a huge hand had grabbed her heart and was squeezing it.

She gasped and thumped forward onto the table, cutlery and glasses rattling. She died in moments, her eyes seeing her own contorted reflection in the metal water jug, the face of an old woman screaming.

THE WOMAN WALKED SOUTH FROM Covent Garden to the embankment along the Thames, caressing her quiet fury and hating the bustling, active world around her.

She was furious that all of her work had been for nothing. The Book of Joy was out of reach. She had tolerated a transatlantic flight, and now had to tolerate another to return home.

She walked up onto Westminster Bridge, the Palace of Westminster lit up and shining like gold in the evening gloom. The bridge was teeming with busy people, with the comings and goings of humanity. People were chatting as they walked, smiling, or pushing past each other. The woman moved through it all without expression, like a shark gliding through schools of fish.

She wanted to cause pain, she wanted to bring suffering. That was always true, but it was particularly true on this day, given her disappointment. It was not enough to have killed the old woman in the restaurant. That had been an instant, unsatisfying necessity. The woman felt the need to calm herself with some more substantial suffering, to make the world sing out in agony for her to hear.

The day grew darker as night approached, as the woman crossed the bridge, and the people she moved through looked around in the gloom, as if somehow aware of what moved among them, as if suddenly uneasy but unable to place the reason why.

The woman saw a young mother walking toward her and hand in hand with a girl, perhaps eight or nine years old. The girl was bouncing as she walked, and she was dressed in a cream coat and white stockings. She wore earmuffs over her head and her cheeks were reddened by the chill breeze swirling off the Thames. The girl was smiling as her eyes took in the sight of the House of Parliament, of the clock tower piercing the sky. She was bright and healthy and alive, and the mother seemed so happy, so pleased with herself, so smug about what she had brought into the world. The woman hated it all.

The woman let herself move toward the pair as they neared, and as she did so she removed the Book of Despair from her bag and clasped it against her chest, like a woman on her way to church clutching her Bible. She felt the power of the book, the despair, bubbling in the air around her. Darkness leaked from the edges of the book as she brought it to life, but nobody looked her way.

The child passed by, and the woman reached down to let her fingers brush the girl's soft, pink cheek. Despair poured out of her like water from a jug, gushing into the child through that brief moment of contact. The woman was thrilled by it, by the agony that coursed through her and into the vibrant, youthful body.

Immediately there was an anguished wail, and as the woman kept walking, she glanced over her shoulder to see the mother squatting down with concern, holding her child in both hands as worry creased her brow.

The child cried as emptiness filled her up, and the woman thought the girl's eyes looked darker now, as dark as the night sky behind the Palace of Westminster.

The child's face was scrunched up and red, tears rolling down her cheeks as she shrieked at the sudden horror she felt, as she sang the woman's song. She turned her head to look at the woman, as if she knew the source of her agony. The girl watched the woman through her tears even as her mother hugged and fretted over her, as other passersby on the bridge threw glances at the pair and moved around them.

And the woman looked back and smiled at the girl: *Yes, child,* that smile said. *It was me. My gift to you.*

The child would never smile again, the woman knew. She would never know happiness or joy. She might not even live to adulthood, so destroyed by the misery and despair that the woman had passed to her.

And that satisfied the woman. She too had been an innocent, happy girl at some point, before the change had come to her. Why should any girl be happy and smiling, when she could instead be singing her pain into the world for the woman to hear?

The woman carried on her way, the shrieks of the despairing child flying up to the sky behind her, a delightful, dreadful song.

A Night of Travel

Evening, and Cassie was alone in the bookstore. She was sitting at the counter with the Book of Doors in her lap, slowly turning the pages and running her eyes over the scribbles and images. Most of it was meaningless to her, but her eyes lingered on the pictures and the doodles. Doorways, open and shut, and corridors. There were faces too, men and women, children and adults, and Cassie wondered who these people were. Had they owned the book before her? Would Cassie's face one day join them on the pages? What had happened to them?

For the first time Cassie asked herself if Izzy could be right about there being a risk with using the book. But in response Cassie's mind turned to the previous evening and her last conversation with Mr. Webber. He had been telling her to get out and see the world, telling her stories of his travels.

Surely that had been because he had been planning to gift her the Book of Doors?

Surely it was a message?

Cassie put the book aside and started cleaning up before closing the store. As she cleared mugs and plates from the coffee tables she remembered a dinner with her grandfather, many years before, the two of them at the table eating stew, when her grandfather had admitted to her his dreams of traveling.

"I get so excited just driving one town over," he had told her, spooning stew onto her plate. "That road, going all the way to anywhere, and I could just keep going. Imagine getting on a plane to a whole other country. Being up there in the sky with the whole world passing below you."

Her grandfather never got to travel. His life had been work and bills and responsibilities and raising Cassie, and she was sure it was always something that he had planned to do in that middle-distance place called "someday," but "someday" had never come for him.

For that reason, but mostly because she wanted to, Cassie knew she wouldn't stop using the book. She wasn't going to turn her back on magic and impossibility.

That night Cassie locked up the store and then used the door to the back room to transport herself to Europe, to places she had visited years earlier. She traveled first to Venice again, the street she had seen from her apartment the previous evening. She stepped through the doorway and out onto the cobblestones. It was a cold, dry night and Cassie turned for a moment, marveling at the sight of the street, her eyes glistening. She squatted down and placed a hand on the ground at her feet, reassuring herself it was real. The door she had just come through was still ajar and she saw the interior of Kellner Books there, an impossible sight that made her heart race with excitement.

"It's real," she said. "It's all real."

She closed the door, watching New York all the while through the narrowing gap like someone trying to catch the fridge light going out. Then she stood on the spot and just breathed in the Venice air. It was the hours before dawn and the streets were dark and quiet. Cassie felt tears welling in her eyes, tears of joy, tears of amazement.

She turned to her right and walked for a few moments, her footsteps echoing around her. She came to the end of the street, where it met a narrow stretch of canal that doglegged around a few awkward corners and then under a pedestrian bridge before disappearing through a crack between two tall buildings. The water of the canal was perfectly still, like black glass. On the other side of the canal there was a small square—a campo, Cassie remembered—with an old stone well in the center. In the daytime the restaurants around that square would set up tables and chairs, and in the middle of the day the sun would be directly overhead, and the world would be warm and bright. Cassie had spent many happy hours in that square, drinking cheap wine and reading. Now the square was empty, the surrounding buildings as noiseless as mourners gathered around a grave.

Cassie turned away from the canal and retraced her steps, wiping the tears of happiness from her eyes. She passed the bakery, knowing that soon enough the bakers would be there kneading dough and firing up the ovens, and the small café on the corner and then turned left into a passageway between two buildings.

It was like walking through a geological fault, the sky a zigzag crack high above. Cassie had loved just wandering, the first time she had been to Venice, exploring these secret passageways, and the surprises they led to—unexpected canals halting her progress and forcing her to turn around; or a tiny square surrounded by towering buildings in crumbling red brick, windows shuttered against the midday sunlight and old Italian women in heavy dark clothes talking loudly and gesturing at each other in doorways. This was the city in the daytime as Cassie remembered it, but as she walked now it was a different place. The narrow passageways were almost creepy, claustrophobic, and she started to torment herself with thoughts of strange people appearing at the end of the passage and blocking her exit.

She shook off her overactive imagination as she emerged into a long, wide square. The buildings around the edges of the space were mostly quiet, but there were a couple of lights on, late-night life behind shutters. The buildings were beautiful to Cassie's eye, shabby with their lumpy bricks and cracked yellow and orange plasterwork, but so evocative of a different time and place, of history and stories and all the people who had lived and continued to live in this amazing city.

Cassie drifted through the passageways and piazzas, heading south and east until she came to the Grand Canal and the Rialto Bridge. The tourist shops on the bridge were all closed and silent, but there were a few other people here despite the hour, drunken young tourists lingering at the edge of the bridge and giggling and whispering; a man with a camera on a tripod over his shoulder, seeking the best spot for the sunrise; and a couple of young Asian men sitting glumly on large suitcases as though they were too early or too late for something. Cassie found a spot by herself between the backs of the tourist shops and the edge of the bridge and gazed out on the broad canal. It was cold here, away from the protection of the buildings, a chill wind moving with the canal waters and brushing against her. But Cassie didn't care; she stood for a few moments and just absorbed the sight of Venice at night. The water of the Grand Canal was moving silently, gently, and she heard the faint knocking of the nearby boats bumping against each other in their tethered sleep. The sky was clear, dotted with stars, and a gibbous moon splashed ripples of milk into the black water.

She wanted to stay there forever, by herself, enjoying the beautiful, sleeping city. But she started to shiver with the cold, and then the rumbling noise as the two Asian men trundled their suitcases away pulled her out of her reverie. She continued through the streets, following the tired chatter of the men ahead of her until she found herself standing on one corner of St. Mark's Square, the red-orange campanile directly in front of her like a square pencil standing on end. She saw the two Asian men far ahead, across the other side of the square, wheeling their suitcases onward.

Cassie headed left to walk along the front of St. Mark's Basilica where it squatted at the eastern end of the square, with its cluster of garlic-bulb domes and crucifix points piercing the sky, the ornate gold in the mosaics above the doorways glinting in the moonlight. She reached the edge of the Grand Canal again, just beyond the basilica, and saw a fleet of gondolas tied up in rows, awaiting the morning and the tourists and the activity. Cassie turned, stretching her hands out by her sides and laughing as she threw her head back to gaze up at the stars spinning above her.

"I'm in Venice!" she called out, not caring that the sound of her voice clattered in the night, galloping off around the square like a horse. "I'm in Venice," she said again, more quietly.

She wiped her eyes, feeling tears there once again, and walked back across the square. She remembered how busy it got in the daytime, the hordes of tourists disgorged by cruise boats, the waiters and pigeons flapping about. She was glad to be there by herself, in the silence, but already she was impatient to be somewhere different, to taste a different treat.

She entered a passageway on the far side of the piazza and walked for a few minutes until she found what she was looking for: a small hotel on a crooked little square, the light on above the doorway to the lobby. She pulled out the Book of Doors and held it in one hand, letting its soft rainbow light wash over her face as she remembered another doorway, in another ancient city, and then she opened the door to the hotel to reveal a side street in Prague.

She stepped out onto the cobbles—lumpier, rounder cobbles here than in Venice—and turned back to the doorway to the youth hostel she had stayed in years before.

The streets of Venice now lived inside that youth hostel, it seemed, and Cassie giggled at the thought as she pulled the door shut.

She walked to Prague's Old Town Square, where elegant old buildings faced each other across an expanse of cobbles, an audience around a dance floor that Cassie skipped across as joy filled her heart. A flock of pigeons, startled by her skipping dance, scattered into the sky with a tattoo of panicked wingbeats.

She walked through the Old Town, along streets just as narrow and crooked as those in Venice. But where the buildings were lower and less crammed together, she could see more of the sky here, and the walls were never as close to her as they had been there. Cassie wandered past darkened cafés and chocolate shops she had visited years ago and emerged onto the Charles Bridge over the wide Vltava River. Just like in Venice, it was colder by the water. The breeze off the river was strong, making Cassie shiver in her coat again, but she ignored it, leaning on the bridge wall between the old lamplights and the cast-iron statues. Prague Castle was slumbering long and low at the top of the hillside, lit up with floodlights in the darkness, and another bridge spanned the river in front of her. Beyond that the hillside rose up where the river curved out of sight. The sky was cloudier here than it had been in Venice, the stars shrouded.

Cassie turned her eyes back the way she had come, toward the Gothic tower at the end of the bridge. It still looked like a face to Cassie, the archway and the windows forming the image of an outraged man, the tall roof resembling a hat upon his head. Cassie smiled at the thought and stamped her feet to warm them.

The sun would rise over the tower, she knew. She had come here for the dawn when she'd been in the city years before, getting up early with a group of three other American tourists. Cassie smiled to herself, remembering that morning, how they had wandered sleepily through the quiet streets, wrapped up in scarves and coats against the cold, their breath white mist in the air. They had gathered together in the middle of the bridge, chatting and waiting until the sun splashed bright light across the world. It had been a fabulous sight, an image burned into Cassie's memories.

They had waited until the sun was fully up in the bright blue sky before going for coffee and pastries and chat. It had been an easy, casual friendship with those other tourists, requiring nothing of her, and Cassie knew she had been happy then, happy and free like she never had been before or since.

"Until now," she said to herself, lifting her eyes from the cobbles and staring south along the river. With the Book of Doors she was free. She was able to go wherever she wanted whenever she wanted, like she had her own fairy tale magic carpet. Nobody else had a life like this.

Cassie kept walking, over to the far side of the river and off the Charles Bridge onto the cobbled street that climbed the hill up to Prague Castle. The buildings here were painted in pastel colors, pinks and whites, and they were ornately decorated like wedding cakes. Farther up the hill the street widened and became lined with cars, and then opened out onto a grand square, the towers of a cathedral on the far side. A bus hummed past, a couple of tired faces gazing out at Cassie, and then a few other cars, and Cassie saw more people crossing the square, wrapped against the cold and heading down the hill toward the Old Town. The city was starting to come to life.

She checked her watch. In New York it was just after eleven in the evening, but in Prague it was after five in the morning. She had been walking for over two hours. She felt a rumble somewhere in her stomach and realized that she was hungry. She smiled, remembering the breakfast she had most loved during her time in Europe. But that was somewhere else, in a different city, in a different country.

She found another hotel on another side street and holding the Book of Doors and splashing colorful light into the dark morning, she opened the door and stepped out of the budget hotel she had stayed in during her weeks in Paris, near Gare du Nord.

The world was suddenly wetter and colder and busier. A mist or drizzle hung in the air like a thin curtain, making everything appear blurry and indistinct. It was still dark, but a few cafés and hotels were open, neon signs buzzing brightly in the gray drizzle. Buses with illuminated interiors, and cars with glowing dashboards and ghostly faces behind the wheel, trundled past. Cassie walked north, retracing steps she had taken years before, and headed for a café directly across the road from the front entrance of the Gare du Nord train station. She had loved going there to eat hot croissants and drink black coffee, and to watch all the Parisians come and go, particularly during rush hour.

When she reached the café, she sat at one of the outside tables, beneath the canopy. She ordered a coffee and a croissant from the jolly old waiter—a man who whistled to himself whenever he walked, it seemed—and then she relaxed in her chair, enjoying the ache in her legs and the chill air on her cheeks. The streets grew busier and noisier as she drank her coffee and ate her croissant, and other people joined her at the tables along the front of the café, filling the air with cigarette smoke and conversation and the yapping of a small dog on a woman's lap.

Cassie loved it. She loved seeing another, ordinary part of the world going about its business, the sounds, the smells. She realized, as she picked the last crumbs of croissant off her plate, that she loved the *stories* she was seeing—the many different lives being played out in front of her. Each day, in every place she went, she was bumping up against other lives, a million other people at the center of their own stories, and Cassie loved to touch them all.

As she lingered over her coffee, she removed the Book of Doors from her pocket and flicked through the pages again, her eyes resting on sketches she hadn't noticed before, fragments of unreadable text. Every time she opened the book it seemed she found a page she hadn't seen yet. Or maybe, she thought, the book was constantly changing, always something different, just like the places she visited.

When she was done, she paid for her breakfast with a credit card and stepped out from under the awning back into the refreshing morning drizzle. Daylight was closer, she saw, as she retraced her steps back to the hotel, a gloomy, wintry sort of daylight that wouldn't fully chase the shadows away. She was bustled and bumped as she pushed against the flow of pedestrians, but she was happier and more contented than she had been for many years. She reached the door of the hotel, the Book of Doors in her pocket, and opened the door to her bedroom in New York across an ocean and several time zones. Behind on the street in Paris a young couple glanced toward her, perhaps catching a glimpse of the rainbow light from Cassie's pocket, perhaps seeing something through the doorway that didn't make sense, but Cassie closed the door before they could react, before they could be certain about what they had seen. Minutes later she fell into bed exhausted and elated, the Book of Doors held against her chest like a child's soft toy as she slept.

When she dragged her tired body into work the next afternoon, Mrs. Kellner took one look at her and asked, "Are you coming down with the flu? You look half dead."

Cassie smiled sleepily. "I'm fine," she said. "I was up late with a book, that's all."

Possibilities and Reservations

When Cassie got home from work the evening after her night in Venice and Prague and Paris, she was ready to travel some more, to return once again to the places she had visited eight years earlier. She shrugged out of her coat and wandered into the kitchen, planning to make a sandwich to fuel her for her travels. As she reached for the fridge her eyes landed on a postcard stuck to the door, the sort of thing that had been there so long it had become invisible. The postcard had been sent by Izzy's parents several years earlier, from a trip they had taken to Egypt, and it showed an image of a church at the end of a courtyard, an open doorway in the foreground. Cassie studied the image for a few moments, her hand resting on the fridge handle, her mind quiet.

Then there was a realization of possibilities that set off fireworks in her stomach. Her mind asked, *Could you . . . ?*

Cassie had never been to Egypt. She had never stepped through the doorway in the image on the postcard. But she wondered if she could. She wondered why she had assumed the Book of Doors could only take her to doors she had previously been through, or through doors she could touch in real life.

"'Any door is every door,'" she murmured to herself.

She forgot all about her sandwich and peeled the postcard off the fridge door. She padded through to her bedroom and closed the door behind her. The Book of Doors was still in her pocket. She pulled it out and held it in one hand, the postcard in the other, her eyes on that image and the doorway in a faraway place.

"Come on," she murmured to herself, closing her eyes and trying to visualize, trying to *feel* the doorway in Cairo.

A short while later, after several failed attempts, Cassie opened a door onto darkness and warm air, a courtyard with palm trees. To her left, at the end of the courtyard, the twin towers of the Hanging Church of Cairo held identical crucifixes up to the sky. In the distance she could hear the noise of a city, different from New York's. As she stepped out under the Cairo sky, she looked behind her, through the old wooden doorway, and saw her small bedroom, the soft light of her lamp, her bed with the blind pulled down over the window.

"Oh wow," she said, on a sigh of amazement.

The Book of Doors was so much better even than it had seemed the previous evening. The whole world was available to her, every city and every street; anywhere a doorway was to be found was a place she could travel to in moments.

She was still holding the postcard in one hand. She looked down at it and then back up at her surroundings and giggled in disbelief.

It was overwhelming, and her heart fluttered with excitement as she tried to come to terms with this truth, as she struggled with why Mr. Webber had given her this gift. What had she done to deserve this miracle?

She shook the questions away, refusing to be melancholy.

"You are in Cairo!" she scolded herself.

She was on a continent she had never even set foot on before. She gazed up at the church with its silent, simple beauty, just enjoying the experience of a new place.

That night she spent hours finding pictures of doorways from around the world in places she had never been and traveling to them, experimenting with what was possible. She visited cities in the US that were new to her, opened doors to an observation deck high above Tokyo, a library in Beijing, and a hotel in Rio de Janeiro where she crossed the lobby and then stepped through another doorway back into her bedroom.

She was testing the Book of Doors, seeing what it was capable of, what the limits of this miracle were. She found no limits.

She could go *anywhere*.

IZZY WAS WAITING WHEN CASSIE arrived home after work, late the following evening, and they spoke for the first time since meeting at the bookstore a couple of days previously.

"How are you doing?" Izzy asked, gazing at Cassie from the couch.

"All good," Cassie said lightly, slipping off her coat and tossing it onto the end of the sofa. She put her bag on the kitchen counter to pull out the sandwich and fruit she had bought on the way home. She had planned to have a quick meal before traveling.

"You look tired," Izzy said, standing up from the couch. "Like you need sleep."

Cassie nodded. She took a bite from an apple and dumped her bag down at the end of the sofa along with her coat. "Must be all the fruit I'm eating."

Izzy smiled politely.

"What's wrong?" Cassie asked, sounding more challenging than she meant to.

Izzy sighed and looked away for a moment.

"You can tell me," Cassie said, more gently. "It's okay."

"Come and sit down."

They sat, facing each other from opposite ends of the couch. Izzy took a few moments, as if trying to pick the words she wanted to use.

"You're still using the book, aren't you?" Izzy said.

Cassie didn't reply, neither confirming nor denying the accusation.

"It's not safe," Izzy said.

"You can't say that," Cassie argued.

"You don't know what it is or where it came from or what it's doing!" Izzy said, her words tumbling out. "All you're seeing is the adventure it's letting you have. But you don't know the cost!"

"What cost?"

"There's always a cost to things like this!"

"There are no things like this!" Cassie shouted, suddenly frustrated. "Nothing, Izzy. We're talking about magic!"

"It scares me," Izzy admitted, her voice quiet. "And it scares me that you are not scared by it."

Cassie took a moment to think about Izzy's words, trying to look at them from all angles to see if she was being unreasonable. She didn't like Izzy being unhappy, but she couldn't contemplate the idea of giving up the Book of Doors. It was everything that her life had never been—it was a plaything of impossibilities, of excitement and mystery and wonder. She didn't understand why Izzy couldn't see that.

She took another bite of her apple, thinking about how to make Izzy see, how to make her understand. "Can I show you something?" she asked.

Izzy's eyes narrowed, as if sensing a trap. "Does it require me to go through a door to somewhere else?"

Cassie put her half-eaten apple on the coffee table, wiped her hand on her jeans, and then held it out toward Izzy. "Just come with me? Just once?" she said. "Please."

Izzy held her gaze for a moment, then relented.

"Okay. But I'm not holding your sticky apple hand."

CASSIE LED IZZY THROUGH A door and into a large circular room with floor-to-ceiling windows all around. There were people milling about and the sound of light conversation, but the space wasn't busy.

"Where are we?" Izzy asked, taking in the faces of the other people in the room.

"Come," Cassie said, urging her on with a flick of her hand.

They walked toward the window wall and the view opened up in front of them, an endless expanse of buildings and streets in all directions beneath a hazy blue sky. In the distance, on the horizon, a giant shape loomed, perfectly symmetrical and triangular, topped with a cap of white.

"Whoa!" Izzy exclaimed, as she took in the view.

"Tokyo," Cassie said, her eyes fixed on the streets spread out below them. "This is the observation deck of the Tokyo Metropolitan Government Building, to be exact. And that . . ." She pointed to the shape on the horizon, tapping the glass with her forefinger. "That is Mount Fuji. Have you ever seen a more mountain-looking mountain?"

Izzy smiled. "I thought New York was the best city in the world . . . This is . . ." She shook her head slowly. "This is like New York times ten."

"Yeah," Cassie agreed.

Izzy enjoyed the view in silence for a few moments. "But you could buy a ticket and fly here, Cassie," she said, looking at her. "Tokyo is here with or without the book."

"It's not really about Tokyo," Cassie said, letting her gaze linger on Mount Fuji.

"I don't get it," Izzy complained. "What's it about, then?"

They waited, silent once more, as an old Japanese couple walked slowly past them. Then Cassie answered.

"You know my grandpa died?"

"Of course," Izzy said. "Lung cancer."

Cassie nodded. "But nothing else, right? That's all I say. 'Lung cancer.' And then people nod and make out they understand, and we move on. I never say any more than that because it's too hard, and I'm scared that if I let it out, I'll never stop letting it out and it's all I'll be, just this never-ending grief and . . ."

She pulled her eyes away from the view and saw the look of concern on Izzy's face. The words dried up in her mouth. Izzy placed a hand on her arm.

"My grandfather raised me," Cassie explained. "After my mother left me with him because she was an addict. Then she died of an overdose. And then he lost his wife, my grandmother, when I was an infant."

"Jesus."

"No, it was fine. I never knew my mother, or my grandmother. I had a happy childhood. My gramps was the best dad I could have had. The best parent. It was just me and him. He gave me my love of books. He'd read to me when I was little, and then I'd read by myself. He was a carpenter, and he had this workshop next to our house. There was a big beanbag in the corner, and I'd sit there after school or on weekends when he was working, and I'd just read. We didn't have much money, but we were fine."

Izzy nodded, frowning a little as if not understanding the point of the stream of memories.

"He got cancer when I was eighteen," Cassie said. "It came out of nowhere, just one of those things. By the time he had symptoms it was too late. I was with him through those months when he died, Izzy. Someone with cancer, they don't die in one moment. It's a long slow death over weeks and months where everything that person is gets stripped away from them. It's . . . dehumanizing."

"Couldn't they do anything?" Izzy asked.

Cassie smiled sadly. "We didn't have good insurance. He'd put all of his money into the house. And by the time he was really ill he didn't want to take any money out of the house to pay for medicine. He said it was for me. He said he knew he was dying, and nothing would change it. I asked one of the doctors once if he could have been saved if we'd had the right insurance. She said she didn't think so, but I don't know if I believe her."

Cassie felt her eyes watering as she let the bad memories in, the thoughts she usually kept locked away. She turned from the view and walked along the window, watching the room, the other tourists wide-eyed and excited, the staff going about their business. Izzy walked beside her.

"He was in so much pain at the end," Cassie said. "Days of agony in his bedroom. In the dark, sweating, coughing blood."

Cassie shuddered, trying to throw off bad memories like a dog shaking off water.

"You know he never got to do anything with his life?" she said, looking at Izzy. "He raised his daughter and then his wife died. And then his daughter died. And then he had to raise me. And all the while he just kept working, giving me a happy childhood. He always wanted to travel, but I don't think he ever even left the state, not in the time I was with him. And what does he get for it? A horrible, painful death before the age of sixty." Cassie shook her head. "It's not right."

"No," Izzy agreed.

"This world is awful and mean and I hate it . . . but books have always been a place I can go. When I was young and when my grandpa was dying. I prefer books to the real world."

"I get it," Izzy said. "Life sucks."

"And now I have this," Cassie said, lifting the Book of Doors from her pocket, holding it in front of her. "I don't know why it was given to me, but it was. And Mr. Webber was a nice man. A man who loved books. So I refuse to believe it is anything bad. I have to believe it was given to me so I can live the life my grandpa never got to live. I can do it for him."

Izzy contemplated that. "I get it," she said again.

They stood at the window, looking toward the sun.

"Can we go home, please?" Izzy asked.

"Yeah," Cassie said. "I mean, we can come back whenever we want, with the book."

"Yeah," Izzy said, her voice a little flat.

"I'm hungry, shall we go to Ben's?"

"Sure," Izzy said.

They used the door to the women's toilet at the edge of the observation deck and stepped into Ben's Deli, back in New York. They walked through the store, nodding at the familiar faces behind the counter, and took seats at a table in the back. It was after midnight and the deli was mostly empty, only one other person there, but Cassie was in her seat before she realized it was the man she had seen before, on the hotel roof terrace, and then on the street a few days earlier. She gasped, even as the man raised his eyes and saw her, as realization flashed across his own face. He stood up quickly, as if he had something important to say, and walked over to their table.

"You've been following me," Cassie said, and she was aware of Izzy's head jerking up to look at her, and then at the man.

"No," the man said. "I haven't been following you, and I didn't know you were going to be here. It's just luck. But I'm glad you're here. My name is Drummond Fox, and you are in incredible danger."

A Stranger at Ben's Deli

orry, who are you?" Izzy asked, and Cassie could see her friend was immediately on the defensive, immediately protective of her.

The man pulled out a chair and moved it around to sit at the end of their table.

"Oh, feel free, take a seat," Izzy said.

"Please indulge me," the man said.

Before Izzy could answer one of the deli staff arrived, a young guy who flicked his chin at them to invite an order.

"Coffee, please," Cassie said. "And give me a chocolate chip cookie as well."

Izzy glanced at Cassie, as if perhaps surprised that she wasn't put off by the man sitting at their table. "Coke," she said. "And a grilled cheese sandwich. With pickles."

The guy wandered away.

"You've got until the food comes to tell us who you are and why you've been following me," Cassie said.

"I told you, I haven't been following you."

He looked tired, Cassie thought. His eyes were dark circles set in a gaunt face. He was dressed in the same black suit and white shirt that she had seen him wearing previously, the clothes of a banker or a lawyer, but there was something rumpled and disheveled about him, like he had been fired from his job and hadn't bothered changing his clothes since. He was older than them, perhaps in his forties, with short brown hair that was going gray at the edges. His body was as thin as his face, but there was a sense of physicality about him, like he was a man who spent more time walking than he did sitting in a car or behind a desk. As Cassie studied him, she decided he wasn't an obviously handsome man—his face was all angles and corners—but there was something about those dark eyes that was interesting, something that made her want to keep looking at them.

"I don't think you realize the danger you're in," he said, sounding almost apologetic. Cassie and Izzy exchanged a glance.

"Danger?" Cassie asked, moving back slightly.

"Not from me," the man said, raising a hand to mollify her. "There are other people."

"Why would we be in danger?" Izzy demanded.

The man sighed; he seemed so tired. "Because of the book," he said.

The server returned and placed Izzy's and Cassie's drinks on the table.

"I don't suppose you have any whisky, do you?" Drummond asked. The server shook his head.

"Didn't think so," Drummond murmured to himself.

"What book?" Cassie asked, as the server retreated to the counter.

Drummond nodded, a gesture of approval. "You're right to be cautious," he said. "But I know you have a book, a very special book that lets you do unusual things."

Cassie held his gaze for as long as she could, but then she glanced at Izzy, and the man read that as an affirmation, responding with a nod of his own. Then he threw a nervous glance at the street door.

"What are you?" Izzy asked. "Irish or something?"

The man smiled at that, and it made his face handsome, as if all of his good looks were tucked away until he was happy. "No, I'm not Irish," he said. "Look, I am sorry about this, but you have to be serious now." He glanced back and forth between them. "I can help you, I can protect you, but you have to trust me."

"What kind of name is Drum and Fox?" Izzy asked.

Cassie could see that Izzy was stalling, trying to avoid committing to anything. Cassie watched the man as he digested the question. She was not scared of him, she realized, this man in his crumpled clothes, with his dark eyes; this man who was handsome when he smiled. She was uncertain of him, but not scared.

"Drummond," the man said. "Not 'Drum and.' It's Drummond. I'm not Irish, I'm Scottish. It's a Scottish name."

"Drummond," Izzy said, trying the name out in her mouth.

"Since we are doing introductions . . . ?"

Cassie and Izzy exchanged a glance again, conferring in silence about whether to answer.

"I'm Cassie," Cassie said.

"Very pleased to meet you, Cassie," Drummond said, nodding his head slightly.

"I'm Isabella, Izzy for short," Izzy said, but grudgingly, giving her name only because Cassie had.

"Izzy," Drummond said. "It's a pleasure. Now. I've seen the book you have. I saw you holding it on the roof terrace at the Library Hotel when you were dressed like you shouldn't have been there. I saw you using it, I saw the colored light. And then I saw you on the street a couple of days ago and you disappeared into thin air. I think I know what you have."

"Okay," Cassie said cautiously.

"How do you know about all of this?" Izzy asked.

"I have some experience with these sorts of books." He snatched another glance to the street, his eyes flicking back and forth quickly as if searching for something.

"Books?" Cassie asked, catching the plural, her heart skipping a few beats.

"Yes, books," Drummond said, looking at her. He smiled again, genuine warmth in his eyes. "You didn't think yours was the only one, did you?"

"I didn't think about it," Cassie said, and Izzy shook her head.

"There are books," he said. "And there are people who want the books, and they will do whatever they can to get hold of them."

"I told you," Izzy muttered to Cassie. "I told you it wasn't safe."

"This place is lovely . . ." Drummond said, gesturing at the seats around them. "But we have to go somewhere else to talk. Somewhere people won't find you. Just for a while until I can tell you what you need to know. It's not safe here."

They stared at him silently, neither of them moving. Cassie met his dark eyes and saw a plea there, but she couldn't bring herself to respond.

"You don't trust me," he concluded.

"You think?" Izzy said.

"We've just met you," Cassie elaborated.

Drummond seemed to think about things for a moment. "I understand," he said. "Like I said, it is good that you are cautious. But I need you to trust me, for your own sake. As an act of faith let me show you, I have a book too." He withdrew a small book, about the size of a notebook, about the size of the Book of Doors, but the cover and the edges of its pages were golden, like it was layered with gold leaf. "This is my book," Drummond said, holding the volume carefully. "This is the Book of Luck. If I have it on me, I will always be lucky. It is why I found you, because it was lucky for both of us."

Cassie and Izzy both gazed at the book. It was a beautiful thing, more so even than the Book of Doors. Cassie wanted to ask questions. She wanted to take the Book of Luck and open it to see what was written inside, what images were drawn there. She wanted to know what it could do and where it had come from, whether it too would produce a halo of fabulous colors in the air. And she wanted to know more about this mysterious man, with his Scottish accent and dark eyes. But before she could do or say anything the door to the street opened at the far end of the deli and all three of them looked in that direction as a man entered. He was a tall, bald man with round glasses and a leather bag in his hand. He was dressed in a three-piece suit beneath a long raincoat.

"Shit," Drummond muttered, returning the Book of Luck to his pocket.

"I'll take that," the bald man said, his voice booming from his chest as he sauntered toward them.

Drummond stood up slowly, pushing his chair back and taking a few steps toward the newcomer. "You've been following me, Hugo."

"Of course," the man said. He placed his bag on the floor at his feet and slipped one hand into the pocket of his overcoat. "I told you I would. And now I want your books."

"Who's that?" Izzy asked, and the man flicked his eyes to her.

"Dr. Hugo Barbary," the man said, nodding his head slightly. "Delighted to make your acquaintance. Who are your friends, Drummond?"

"Nobody," Drummond said. "I was lost and asking for directions. Not from around these parts, am I?"

The man smiled, enjoying the answer. "Give me the book that you just put back in your pocket, and any others you have, and I won't kill them."

Cassie felt her stomach drop, and Izzy gasped and looked at her in shock.

The server appeared behind Barbary with Izzy's food in his hand. "Hey, excuse me, bro," he said, trying to pass him.

"Fuck off," Barbary said, without turning his head.

"Hey," the server barked in protest. Before he could finish the thought Barbary snapped his arm up, like he had just touched something unexpectedly hot, and the man was thrown backward through the air as if he had been hit by a truck, clattering to the floor and sending Izzy's food skittering into the corner. As the server landed, Barbary withdrew the hand that was in his pocket, and Cassie saw that he was holding a book. As he moved his hand a trail of purples and reds followed it through the air.

"Look!" Izzy said. "He's doing that thing!"

There was a reaction behind the counter to the commotion, the other staff hurrying to their colleague's aid, but before they got far Dr. Barbary jerked his free hand again, his face a grimace of annoyance, and both men shot upward and crashed into the ceiling. They dropped back to the floor, ceiling tiles and dust following them. Dr. Barbary walked back to the front of the deli, rainbow colors trailing after the book in his hand like a ribbon in the air, and casually locked the door. He turned the Open sign to Closed and both Cassie and Izzy jumped up from their seats. There were people on the street, walking past in either direction, but nobody was paying attention to what was going on inside Ben's Deli.

"If your book is what I think it is," Drummond said, turning his head to speak to Cassie over his shoulder, "now is the time to use it. Please. Your life is in danger."

His eyes begged her to act. She hesitated, her heart pounding in her chest, her eyes flicking to the bald man as he walked back toward them. He swung his hand sideways through the air and one of the tables flew up and smashed against the wall, the rainbow colors by his other hand pulsing angrily.

"Give me your fucking books!" he shouted, his face a knot of fury, his voice making Cassie flinch.

He swiped his hand again and all of the remaining tables and chairs slid suddenly and crashed against the right-hand wall, like furniture on a ship in rough seas.

"There's nowhere to go," Barbary said. He flicked his wrist and the server who had been carrying Izzy's food jerked three feet into the air and then slammed down onto the floor again with a groan. Barbary casually kicked his head, not even looking down as his foot connected with a wet crunch.

"Jesus!" Izzy yelped.

"Time to go," Drummond said. "Please!"

"Where are you going to go, Drummond?" Barbary asked.

Cassie reached for Izzy with one trembling hand. "Come on," she urged. They clasped hands and darted toward the toilet at the back of the deli.

"Just give me the books and I'll let you go," Barbary said. "Probably."

"Did he kill them?" Izzy gasped in horror. "Did he kill that kid?"

Cassie didn't answer. She slipped her free hand into her pocket and gripped the Book of Doors. She concentrated on a destination, a place far away, and she felt the familiar sensation in her arms and the pit of her stomach, the way the Book of Doors seemed to change in her hand, and then she opened the toilet door and saw a nighttime street, and she felt cold air on her face.

"Come on," she said again, pulling Izzy through the doorway.

Drummond ran to join them, his lean body moving with surprising speed, his feet pounding the tiled floor and a grimace on his face.

"Close it!" Izzy ordered, as they watched Drummond racing toward them, the bald man farther back in the deli.

"Wait!" Drummond pleaded.

Cassie hesitated, unsure what to do, but Drummond seemed terrified, his eyes wide and white. She couldn't leave him.

"Close it before he reaches us, Cassie!" Izzy said again.

Drummond jumped through the doorway and collapsed onto the pavement in front of them. Cassie slammed the door shut just as an expression of surprise crossed the face of the bald man in the deli, as he realized perhaps that they were not fleeing to hide in the toilet.

Drummond stood up slowly and brushed himself down. Then he exhaled heavily, relief flooding out of him, his arms trembling slightly. He looked down at them, frowning at his own body.

"I thought you'd leave me there," he admitted to Cassie. "Thank you."

"Okay," Cassie said, after a moment.

"Do you believe me now that you're in danger?" Drummond asked.

"Yes," Cassie admitted. Suddenly her whole body was trembling, shock coursing through her, and she felt like she wanted to collapse at the knees or be sick or do both at the same time. "Yes, we're in danger."

The Woman

The woman arrived back in Atlanta on an overnight flight from London, eight hours stuck in a tube with too many people. She escaped the plane and hurried through the airport, every interaction grating on her nerves, and climbed into the car she had parked a few days earlier before her trip.

It was a short drive home, two hours north through Georgia from Atlanta, heading into the Blue Ridge Mountains. She didn't mind driving; she enjoyed it, in fact, to the extent that she enjoyed anything, because it was something she could do without having to deal with anyone else. That was what she preferred. On those rare occasions when she had no choice but to be around other people—international travel, for example—the woman could affect a superficially normal demeanor to manage any human contact that she couldn't avoid. But it was exhausting to her, tolerable only when absolutely necessary.

The trip to London had been disappointing, and it annoyed her that she'd had to endure all the pain of the journey there and back for little benefit. The only upside had been that one more book hunter was now dead. And she now knew that the woman—Marion—had at one point possessed the Book of Joy. And now it was in the Fox Library. Another special book locked away out of reach.

The woman didn't know what she would have done had she been

able to obtain the Book of Joy. She would have added it to her collection, undoubtedly, because she desired *all* the books. But she wouldn't have had much use for joy. Unless the book could have been used to *remove* joy as much as to give it. That might have been interesting.

She considered the possibilities as she drove.

Her home was deep in the woods, in the north of the state on the edge of the Arkaquah Valley. The house was a large timber cabin that had been built in the late 1990s. It had three bedrooms upstairs and a big kitchen and a lounge and a utility room downstairs, and a wraparound porch where her parents used to sit on nice evenings. Both the woman's mother and father were now dead, buried elsewhere in the woods on the twenty acres of land attached to the property. She didn't grieve for them. She barely thought of them.

Most of the house was now neglected, rundown and falling apart, and from the outside it almost looked derelict. The driveway from the turn off the main road was overgrown and not maintained, but the woman didn't mind that, because it meant the house was almost a hidden, secret place.

She pulled into the drive, killed the engine, and then climbed out into the thick, damp air of late morning. She climbed the stairs to the cabin, unlocked the door, and headed inside. The woman kept one room for herself, the smallest bedroom, which had always been hers. It was set into the roof with slanting walls and skylight windows, and it was spartan and clean to the point that a casual observer might describe it as empty. When she had been a child, the bedroom had held many more things, the bits and pieces of a girl's life. But the woman was not that girl anymore. That girl was lost, and most of her belongings had been jettisoned many years before.

She opened the windows to let in the susurration of the trees. At night the area around the cabin was pitch black, and as a girl, that darkness had terrified her. She had refused to leave the house after dusk, especially not alone, hating the vast, inhuman emptiness of the countryside. She had always wanted to live somewhere brighter and more alive, somewhere with more people and laughter. Now, things couldn't be more different. The woman liked being alone and she savored the darkness and solitude of night in the woods. She hated the scratching irritation of other people, the noise and the activity, the smell.

The woman stripped out of the clothes she had worn on the flight. She enjoyed clothes and how they looked on her body. She enjoyed dressing herself and trying on different outfits, almost as if her body were a toy to play with, as if it wasn't her own. In some ways, she knew, this was the truth. The body belonged to Rachel Belrose, and the woman wasn't her anymore, not really.

She showered, washing off the smell of other people, and pulled on a simple nightgown. She removed four books from her purse—the Book of Speed, the Book of Mists, the Book of Destruction, and the Book of Despair. They were her favorite books, the books she used most often, at least in part because they were easy to use. They required nothing of her other than to have them in her possession. Other books required her to do specific things, or to give them to people she wanted to use them on. The woman preferred to be free of such restrictions, and she usually found her favorite books were all that she needed.

She padded back downstairs and then descended into the basement. Here were the guts of the building, the boiler and the pipes, old timber and tools. On one wall her father's gun case hung, the weapons and ammunition still inside. Her father had always liked to hunt, but he hadn't enjoyed it so much in those last few days of his life when the woman had hunted him with his own handgun. The woman had enjoyed using the gun on him, and on the others in the subsequent years. It had been a fun toy, until she'd had the books.

The basement was dug out of the earth, with a poured concrete floor. It was lit by a bare bulb hanging from a wire. The woman pulled the cord to switch it on and the bulb swung gently, the light sloshing back and forth across the floor. In one corner of the room an old mattress was pushed against the wall. The woman had used that mattress before, when she had kept people down here, experimenting on them. In recent years she had experimented with different ways to use the Book of Despair. That book always intrigued her—she relished the idea of using despair as a weapon; that spoke to her on some level. She thought back to using the book on the young child in London and her insides buzzed.

It had satisfied her immensely. She had gifted that girl such pain, such enduring misery.

In the opposite corner of the basement, cemented into the floor, was an old iron safe. It had been her mother's when she had been alive. The woman's mother had been a vet and had kept certain drugs in the safe. The woman had never understood why, and no longer cared. The drugs had long since been discarded and the safe now held only the woman's own belongings: the books she had gathered over the years of hunting.

She opened the safe and placed three of her books alongside their three siblings, six books of the seven she owned in total. She held on to the Book of Despair because she'd had a thought on the flight back from London, an idea of something she could try with the book. She meant to work on that in the coming days.

The woman closed the safe and returned to her room, where she slept for many hours, the Book of Despair in the bed next to her. She slept a dreamless sleep of the dead.

ON THE DAY AFTER HER return from London the woman started researching other books to hunt. It was what she did. She existed, and she searched for books. She had an insatiable hunger for the books, a hole inside her that could only be filled by acquiring more of them. Sometimes, when she had to, she ate and she slept, but eating in particular was a chore to her.

The woman started her research by trawling the various secret message boards known to book hunters and collectors. The books were becoming rarer, she knew, and that made the hunt more enjoyable for her. The fewer books there were out in the world, the more she possessed.

Sometimes, on rare occasions when she actually reflected on what she was doing and who she was, she wondered what she would do once she had all of the books. The drive, the insistent need to find and collect books, was everything she was. But once she had them all, what would she do with them?

She didn't like to think about these sorts of questions, because it was at such moments when she felt at her most vulnerable, when she felt the girl whom she had once been watching her from deep inside. That girl despaired at the woman. That girl screamed and shouted at all that had been done. Like a prisoner in a windowless room the girl banged and thumped and pushed at the walls, and only in those quiet moments when the woman asked questions of herself could she hear the girl.

Better not to think, she knew. Better to focus on the task.

There were more books out there, more owners to track down and destroy.

And there was the Fox Library.

She had seen the Librarian once, many years ago. But she had been younger then, distracted by her enjoyment of killing and using the books, and the Librarian had gone, disappearing into the air before she could take him. It had been a good night, rewarding her efforts with three books, but she still felt disappointment whenever she thought about how he had escaped her. Such a missed opportunity. Everywhere she had been, every book hunter she had met and interrogated and tortured since that night, she had asked the same question: *Where is Drummond Fox? Where is the Fox Library?*

He would be the prize, she knew. He would be the key to the Fox Library, wherever it was.

"Drummond Fox."

She spoke rarely, almost never. Speaking was a function of engaging with other humans, and she had no interest in that. But she spoke the man's name now, as a promise to herself.

"Drummond. Fox."

THAT EVENING, AFTER COMPLETING HER research, and doing some work with the Book of Despair, she retrieved the Book of Destruction from the safe in the basement and walked out into the woods in the darkness, navigating by memory and by moonlight. She found the place where she had buried her father after killing him. She had been sixteen, only a few years after the moment she thought of as her change, when she had shifted from being Rachel Belrose to what she now was. Her mother had lived for seven months after her father had died, only because the woman had experimented with how long a person could survive. She had been impressed by what her mother had endured. The loss of fingers and toes, limbs, her eyes. The woman had loved inflicting pain on her mother, even more so than upon her father. She loved the sensation of the suffering of others. It made her feel alive. It was when she had tortured her mother that the woman had come to appreciate that this was her purpose in life: to bring pain into the world, to make other living things suffer.

Her mother's last words, before the woman had taken her tongue and lips, had been: "What did we do to make you like this?" It was a question of exhaustion and defeat, a question that hadn't really sought an answer and the woman hadn't given one. Her parents had done nothing to make her the way she was. Except maybe to take her on holiday to New York, to take their girl to where she just happened to be in the wrong place at the wrong time, to be *changed*.

The woman—or perhaps some residual remnant of the girl, in those early years—had buried her mother next to her father, as if thinking they could keep each other company in the afterlife.

The other seventeen bodies scattered around the woods were not so blessed with company. They were alone in their miserable eternity. But the woman remembered them. She remembered how each of them had suffered, the sound of their pain. She thought about them often. Them and the other people she would make suffer in the future, the pain she would inflict.

Out in the darkness by the graves of her parents, the woman stood in silence and felt the air brush her skin. She heard the rustling of the leaves. At a different time in the year the woods would be alive with the buzz of insects, but it was winter, and life was hiding and hibernating. It felt to the woman as if she were alone, but she knew there was still life out there. Not everything was asleep.

The woman closed her eyes and gripped the Book of Destruction, stretching her feelings out into the world in a wide circle. Her mind was like creeping fingers, finding the insects and vermin, the birds in the trees with their feathers puffed up to keep them warm. She held all of these things in her mind, and in her hands the Book of Destruction glowed in the darkness, illuminating her face from below.

Then the woman sneered, a sudden burst of fury, of need, and the Book of Destruction pulsed once, an angry eruption of light with the woman at its center, stretching out wider and wider like ripples in a pond, and everything alive that it touched died suddenly. The insects in the undergrowth, the spiders spinning their webs. They all stopped, destroyed instantly by the woman and the book.

There were no screams, there was no yell of agony, but the woman *felt* all the pain, the sudden absence of life, the moment of terror in each and every living thing as it knew it would be no more.

As the light dissipated through the darkness, as the Book of Destruction fell silent, the woman hummed to herself happily, like a dinner guest full after an excellent meal, and she opened her eyes to the darkness.

She had used the Book of Destruction in this way, once before, in the autumn, when the forest had been livelier. That time it had been even more pleasurable. That time she had heard some of the mammals scream and yelp, squeaking their agony as they trembled and expired. There were fewer mammals now, though, in the cold of winter.

Sometimes the woman thought about using the book in a town or a city, where there were more than just insects and animals. She imagined what the screams would be like, but she wondered if it would all be too sudden, too quick. She wondered how to make the people know what was coming, so that she could feel their terror as she moved among them.

These were the things she thought about when she wasn't looking for books: how to make the world sing to her in pain.

The woman turned around and walked back through the quiet, dead darkness to the house, stroking the book she carried as if it were a pet.

And all around her, nothing stirred.

MEMORIES

The Shadow House

In a house lost to time, a house in nowhere, the Fox Library waited to be discovered.

The house had once stood on the banks of a loch in the northwest Highlands of Scotland, a Victorian lodge that had once been a home, and then a hotel, before it had been bought by Sir Edmund Fox in the early twentieth century.

"I need a place to keep my books," he had told the sales agent.

"It's a big house," the man had said, as the two of them had stood with their backs to the loch admiring the house.

"I have many, many books," Edmund had answered.

The house was an odd place, but not without its charm. It was a building full of narrow staircases and unexpected corners, tall windows that let in the light and afforded views of majestic sunsets. It had high ceilings and uneven floorboards and huge fireplaces that gaped like the mouth of some dragon. And after Sir Edmund moved in, it had books.

By the end of his life, books lined every room in his house, leaving space only for windows and doors and other less important features such as light switches and furniture. Books were everywhere, in tall bookcases along the walls and on shelves over doors, on side tables next to comfortable armchairs. But it was not ordinary books that had excited Edmund

Fox for most of his life. His interests had lain elsewhere: in the business of special books.

BORN IN THE LATE NINETEENTH century and raised in the upper classes of British society, Edmund Fox had yearned to escape what he saw as a tedious existence. He had started his adult life with the idea of becoming an explorer. In the course of his adventures in Southern Europe and North Africa in the early twentieth century he encountered stories of a special book that could transport the reader wherever they wanted to go. Some claimed the book was a relic of ancient Egypt, while others claimed it to be a product of witchcraft and devilry. Fox, who hated all things modern and scientific and who loved anything that suggested hidden, ancient knowledge, set about pursuing this item with considerable vigor. He followed leads and ignored dead ends all over Europe and North America, throwing family money away on any wild story and gossip. He found people who claimed to have seen the book, people who claimed to have used it, and most of these people were lying. But some were not. Some gave enough information to suggest or hint at a hidden truth behind the myths and mysteries.

In his early forties Fox invested his considerable family wealth in the establishment of a secret organization—the Fox Library—dedicated to finding this incredible item. Convinced of the book's existence, Edmund Fox made a deductive leap and concluded that there must be other such books and magical items, other wonders hidden from the rational world.

"One does not look at a dog and assume it is the only animal to exist," he famously proclaimed, on the evening of the first meeting held by his library's small group of members. "One reason is that there are other animals out there also, some we can see easily, some we can never hope to see. These books are the same. If we know that one exists, then others must too, and we will commit ourselves to finding them. The Fox Library will stand for my lifetime and beyond to preserve these wonders for all mankind!"

Fox's group of friends and collaborators—many of whom thought he was mad, but who enjoyed the drinks and the good company—cheered and banged the table, and the Fox Library thereafter set about pursuing magical books for the rest of Edmund Fox's life.

The Fox Library—the organization, rather than the collection of books—might have shriveled out of existence shortly after the death of its founder and benefactor but for one surprising development: The library actually found what it was looking for. Not the legendary book that had first caught Edmund Fox's attention, but another book, with similarly confounding and amazing abilities.

In the mid-1920s, only a few short months before Edmund Fox finally succumbed to the liver failure his prolific drinking had guaranteed, one of the library's most dogged investigators discovered the existence of a special book. Like all other similar books it was a slim notebook, just the right size to fit into an inside pocket and innocuous enough to be overlooked and ignored. The leather cover was colored in shades of dark gray and black that were discernible only in the right light, and the edges of the pages within the book were similarly painted, as if they had been sprayed with black ink. When it first came to the attention of Fox's investigator the book had been in the possession of a former British soldier who had been making a successful living as a jewelry thief across continental Europe. The soldier-thief had admitted to finding the book some years earlier in the neglected library of an estate house somewhere out in the English countryside. For years the man had carried the book with him, and during those years he had never once been caught while going about his burglary business, never once been discovered while engaged in even the most audacious of break-ins.

"I didn't believe it at first," he told Fox's investigator, over a few drinks in a French restaurant that overlooked the Bay of Biscay. The man was old now and had long since given up burglary. "Look at this, at what it says."

The man had opened the book and shown the investigator the first page. There were a few lines of text that Fox's investigator read as the man spoke.

"It says it is the Book of Shadows," he said. "It says that if I tear a page and hold that bit of page in my hand, then I go into the shadows and nobody can see me!"

The investigator nodded.

"What else is in the book?" he asked.

The man shrugged and flicked some of the pages, showing dense scribbles and ink blotches on many of them. For a moment the investigator thought he saw the text moving or shimmering.

"Just nonsense," the man said, cutting across the investigator's thoughts. "It doesn't matter about what's on the pages. It's what the book does! See, when I tear a bit of a page and hold it in my hand, the book starts to sparkle!"

"Sparkle?" the investigator asked dubiously.

"Like fireworks!" The man nodded. "Like a little cloud of colors. And while I have the torn bit of page in my hand, nobody can see me! Not until I let the bit of page go again, and then I come back. And you know what else? When I come back, there aren't any torn pages in the book. It's like it heals itself!"

Fox's investigator didn't know if he believed the man, but he paid for the book using the resources of the Fox Library, rewarding the man with a fortune to waste in the last few years of his life. Upon his return to the library the investigator experimented with the book, along with other members of the library staff. They examined the pages of text and the images that seemed to float in and out of focus, to appear and disappear. They studied the book's properties, noting how much lighter it seemed to be than it should have been. And they experimented with tearing bits of the pages, trying to make the book actually do what the previous owner had claimed it could do. It had taken some days, with different people trying repeatedly, until one of the staff members simply disappeared, and then promptly reappeared again, his hand open and a scrap of paper disintegrating in the air.

"That was strange!" the man exclaimed.

The other people in the room thought it was strange too, but their excitement quickly overcame any shock, and the book became item 001 in the catalog of the Fox Library. Soon enough, it became better known as the Book of Shadows.

It was the beginning of everything. The Book of Shadows was the validation of Edmund Fox's obsession, and the legitimization of the purpose of the Fox Library. Edmund Fox went to his grave knowing he had proven his doubters wrong, and bequeathing his entire and considerable fortune to the library, the running and management of which had passed to his niece and nephew by his youngest sister.

Over the decades of the twentieth century the Fox Library continued about its business, seeking and investigating special books, using Edmund Fox's country house on his Scottish estate as its base. It built a significant collection, seventeen books in total, and the Book of Shadows had been an ally in that work, a tool to be used by one or two of the investigators who were *able* to use it, whenever required. All of the books shared similar qualities to those of the Book of Shadows—similar size, similar dense text in unreadable languages and enigmatic sketches and scribbles, and similarly inexplicable weight. Some of the books had notes in the front, describing what they were or what they could do, but some did not, and the purpose and abilities of several of the books remained unknown, perhaps awaiting the right reader to unlock their mystery. It had been noted by the library how the contents of many of them seemed to change and evolve, as if the books were somehow alive, responding to circumstances, perhaps seeking just the right reader to reward with their riches.

During the darkest days of the Second World War, the Fox Library as an organization intentionally slipped into obscurity, deciding that its activities and possessions were better kept out of the light, but the library of special books remained hidden away within Fox's country house.

By the start of the twenty-first century Drummond Fox, the sole descendant of Edmund Fox's nephew, was the Librarian, the person responsible for looking after the collection of special books and for continuing the search for more. The quiet life in the Fox Library on the west coast of Scotland suited him. He loved books, special books or ordinary books, and he could pass weeks by himself reading or studying or trying to understand all that special books could do.

Occasionally he would venture out, and he made friends with other people from other parts of the world who each had their own special books. These were people who shared Drummond's interests, but also his perspective that special books should be kept safe, away from those who might use them for the wrong purposes. They were museum items, to be studied and understood, but to be used rarely if at all.

But then the world became a much more dangerous place. From nowhere a threat appeared, and when Drummond's friends were slaughtered in Washington Square Park and their books taken from them, he knew that it was no longer safe for the Fox Library to exist.

Drummond had traveled back to Scotland, the Book of Shadows his ally in his flight, and he had hidden himself away in the Fox Library, knowing that terror could follow him there. So he had used the Book of Shadows in a way it had never been used before: He made it so that the entire house in which the Fox Library was kept slipped sideways out of reality and into the shadows, a place impossible to reach. It became a house in nowhere, a house waiting to be visited and a library of books waiting to be opened and read.

The house still existed, with all of its books and furniture, its windows and its doors, but there was no way to reach it now, not in the shadows.

Unless, of course, someone could open one of the internal doors from a completely different place.

If someone had the Book of Doors.

Coffee in Lyon

They stood on the street catching their breaths and looking around.

They were alongside a broad river, tall trees leaning over toward the water like dancers in a line. The branches of the trees were bare but discarded leaves gathered along the edge of the curb in orange and brown drifts. It was dark, but dawn was coming, the night sky lightening in the distance, and Cassie could make out narrow buildings lining the far side of the river, painted orange and yellow and cream.

Drummond arched backward to stretch his spine, as if he had pulled a muscle when he had fallen through the door, and asked, "Where are we?"

"Lyon," Cassie said, some part of her mind that wasn't frozen in shock conjuring the words her mouth produced. "I was here years ago."

"I always liked France," Drummond said, speaking more to himself, as if he were lost in memories of happier times. Then he looked at Cassie, and at Izzy. "Great pastries here. Come on, we need to find food. We need to eat."

"It's still early," Cassie observed. "We might not find anything open."

"Let's try," Drummond said.

Izzy looked back and forth between the two of them. "That man was throwing people around!" she exclaimed. "How was he doing that?"

A cyclist zipped past, pulling a curtain of air behind him and glancing toward the noisy Americans with a frown.

"Come on," Drummond urged. He walked off before waiting for an answer and Izzy turned her stare on Cassie.

"Cassie, this is madness! That man . . . !"

Cassie nodded, trying to placate Izzy, but she was struggling to string together words. Instead she headed after Drummond. Izzy rolled her eyes unhappily but followed her.

They walked along the river in silence for a few minutes, passing through pools of yellow splashed by the streetlights and feeling the sharp edge of the winter breeze cut through to their bones. There were signs of the city waking up, a few other people moving along the streets, the headlights of cars cruising past, but they had to walk for a while until they found somewhere to get a hot drink. It was a small café just opening up for the day, a doorway of warm light and a woman maneuvering tables and chairs into place on the sidewalk, an awkward dance involving too many legs and music of clanks and scrapes.

"This'll do," Drummond decided. They approached and Drummond indicated at one of the tables as the woman retreated back into the café, and she nodded agreeably.

Drummond pulled out two chairs and gestured to Cassie and Izzy like a waiter, and then sat down on the opposite side of the table and turned his eyes to the river, his nose up like that of a dog sniffing the air. Cassie realized she was trembling, as adrenaline and shock coursed through her body. She looked at her hands, willing them to be still.

The woman reemerged from the café and greeted them with a singsong "Bonjour!" like a doorbell.

"Coffees?" Drummond asked, and both Cassie and Izzy nodded.

"Three coffees?" the woman said, slipping into English with the ease of someone used to tourists.

"I don't suppose you have any whisky?" Drummond tried.

The woman gave him a crooked grin and then pointedly looked at her watch. "Non, monsieur."

"Croissants?" Drummond asked instead. "We need to eat."

"Oui." She nodded and then disappeared back into the café with a smile on her face as if Drummond had amused her.

Cassie observed all of this as if it were happening very far away from her, happening to someone else. The world felt distant, and her mind seemed paralyzed. It played images for her: the bald man kicking the server's head, throwing furniture by magic, and her stomach flinched with each memory.

Izzy reached out for Cassie and gripped her arm, perhaps sensing what Cassie was feeling. They looked at each other, both of them seeking comfort after the terrifying experience they had just endured.

"Who was that man?" Cassie asked Drummond. Her voice sounded normal, betraying none of the shock that was vibrating through her limbs.

"Hugo Barbary," Drummond said. "He's an awful man. I'm sorry you had to experience that." He sighed, breathing regret into the air. "I really wish he hadn't been there."

Cassie nodded, accepting the apology, and found her gaze settling on Drummond's dark eyes. Their stillness calmed her.

"But who is he?" Izzy asked. "How can he get away with doing stuff like that?"

Drummond turned his eyes across the river, to the distance. "He's a book hunter."

"A book hunter?" Cassie asked. "What's that?"

Drummond squinted at her. "It's pretty self-explanatory, isn't it? He hunts books."

"He kicked that boy in the head," Izzy said. "It was so horrible. He didn't have to do that!"

The image flashed in Cassie's mind again as Izzy spoke, and she flinched and closed her eyes, trying to push it away. Had the boy died because of her? Would he still have been alive now if Cassie had taken Izzy somewhere else to eat? Guilt was a bitterness rising at the back of her throat. She tried to swallow it down.

"No," Drummond agreed. "But that's the sort of man he is." He shook his head. "That poor boy is just another victim of Hugo Barbary."

They sat in silence, each of them remembering what had just happened.

Then Drummond looked at Cassie and asked, "How long have

you had the book? Because you opened the door to here quickly. Easily."

Cassie shook her head slowly. She didn't want to answer questions. She didn't want to talk like ordinary people, like horrible things hadn't just happened.

The café owner reappeared with a tray of drinks supported by one hand. "Bon, three coffees," she said, setting the drinks down. "And three croissants."

"I understand," Drummond said to Cassie, as the woman disappeared back into the shop. Cassie met his eyes, full of skepticism, but her doubts melted away as he looked at her. He nodded once. "It's horrible, I know. I don't mean to appear callous about it." He pushed one of the croissants toward her, and then another toward Izzy. "You both need to eat," he said.

Cassie looked down at the croissant dubiously. Her mouth was full of the taste of guilt and fear. She didn't think she could eat.

"It helps," Drummond insisted, his voice quiet. "Trust me, I know. Right now you are in shock. Your body is pumping adrenaline. You need to eat, you need the energy. It will help you to recover."

Izzy was already eating—she was a woman who never needed encouragement to eat. Drummond did likewise, watching Cassie as he chewed, crumbs on his lips. Finally Cassie relented, lifting the croissant to take a bite. It was good: hot and buttery and flaky.

"Good," Izzy murmured.

"Isn't it?" Drummond agreed, obviously taking delight in Izzy's enjoyment. "I love croissants in France."

The three of them ate in companionable silence for a few moments, sitting in the apron of warming light on the sidewalk in front of the café. Drummond sipped some of his coffee and then relaxed back into his chair and closed his eyes.

"I'm sorry I met you both under these circumstances," he said. "It's not what I would have wanted. But maybe it's good."

"Good?" Cassie asked, raising an eyebrow. "I don't think there's anything good about what just happened."

"No, I don't mean that," Drummond said, opening his eyes. He shook his head at himself, as if he was annoyed that he was not communicating well. "I mean it's good you have seen how dangerous it is. You know you have to take the threat seriously."

"I never got my grilled cheese sandwich," Izzy murmured, as if she hadn't been listening. "Before that man came."

Cassie picked at croissant crumbs, realizing she did feel a little better. Her heart felt as if it had stopped racing, and her mouth was no longer filled with the bitterness of guilt.

"It was so violent," she said. "Why does he have to be like that?"

"Why does anyone have to be like that?" Izzy asked, her eyes drifting off to the view.

They were all silent for a moment and Cassie took the time to breathe and look around. The sky was slowly turning a deeper blue in the distance as night bloomed into day. All around them they could hear the sounds of the city waking up: delivery trucks and people talking and the clatter of cups and saucers from inside the café. It was all absurd, she thought. Ten minutes earlier she had been fleeing from violence and now she was enjoying a coffee and a croissant an ocean away. This is what the Book of Doors should be, she thought, travel and wonder and delight, not violent men throwing furniture around.

"I want to help you both," Drummond said. "But I know it's a lot. All that has just happened. What do I need to do so that you trust me? So that you let me help you?"

Cassie considered the question. It was a cold morning, but she was wearing her old greatcoat, and her woolen scarf wrapped around her neck, and she felt warm and cozy in the chair, with the coffee in her stomach and the taste of the croissant on her lips. She asked herself how she could feel cozy so soon after what she had just experienced, but she had no answer.

"You need to answer some questions," Cassie said.

"What questions?" Drummond asked. "What do you want to know?"

"The books," Cassie said. "Tell us about the books. What are they?"

"They're books," Drummond said, shrugging loosely. He took a sip of coffee and sucked his teeth. "We don't know what they are or where they came from. But people have known about them for a hundred years, maybe. They were myths and mysteries first, stories about people who could do unusual and incredible things, but eventually people realized it was the books. One book first and then another. And then over the course of the last century people began to understand that these books existed, that they could do things."

"But what *are* they?" Izzy pressed. "And don't say 'they're books.'"

"They are . . ." Drummond thought for a moment, trying to find the right words, his eyes rolling up to the sky. "They're magic," he said. He smiled as if embarrassed, his eyes sparkling, and in that instant, he was again handsome to Cassie. "I know how that sounds."

"Magic," Cassie said.

"I don't like the word," Drummond said. "It makes me think of bad variety acts. But there isn't a better way to describe it. Each book grants whoever possesses it an ability, a power. Whatever you want to call it."

"How many books are there?" Cassie asked.

Drummond shrugged. "Who knows? Some have been found, but there are probably others out there. There are rumors and stories about other books. Some of these stories will be complete flights of fancy, some will be based on truth. Like the Book of Doors. It's one of the books that has always been spoken about, but until now nobody seems to have ever actually proved it existed."

Cassie nodded, absorbing that and very aware of the weight of the Book of Doors in her pocket.

"Where did you get it?" Drummond asked.

"Hey, we're asking the questions," Izzy replied.

"Tell me about the book hunters and that man in the deli," Cassie said, ignoring his question.

"What can I say?" Drummond wondered. "The books are extraordinary items, in every sense of that word. People who know about them will pay a lot to possess them. The books change hands for fortunes. Or through bloodshed. Some people, the wrong kind of people, want them for the wrong kind of reasons."

"You said 'people who know about the books,'" Izzy said. "So only a few people know about them? How come it's not more widely known? This is crazy stuff. Magic is real and nobody knows?"

"You've answered your own question," Drummond said. "It *is* crazy stuff. It's magic. Those who know about it want it kept secret. It's power. They suppress all knowledge to keep the power for themselves."

Izzy gave Cassie a knowing look. "I told you," she said. "No wonder it didn't show up on Google. It's all being suppressed."

"What did you google?" Drummond asked, tilting his head to the side.

"I googled the book," Izzy said. "The Book of Doors. And you know what? There were no results. No hits at all."

Drummond pursed his lips thoughtfully for a moment.

"What?" Cassie asked, reading concern in his expression.

He hesitated to answer, and Cassie thought in that moment that he was trying to protect them. He was a man debating whether or not to reveal a worrying truth.

"What?" she pressed.

"It means people will know," Drummond said. "People will be looking for you now. They'll have traced your searches. They suppress all knowledge of the books. But they all watch for any signs that someone knows. When you googled 'Book of Doors,' flags would have gone up all over the world."

Cassie glanced at Izzy and saw the shock dawning on her face. "They can track me from internet searches?"

Drummond nodded. "Yes. I'm sorry. They have ways of finding you. Law enforcement could track you down, so these people definitely can. They are motivated and wealthy."

Izzy looked at Cassie. "I am so sorry, Cass, it's my fault. It's all my fault."

Cassie reached out a hand to touch Izzy's arm. "Don't worry."

"Who are 'they'?" Izzy asked. "You keep saying 'they.'"

"Different groups," Drummond said. "Book hunters and collectors. Governments."

"Governments know about this?" Izzy asked.

"Some." Drummond nodded. "Some people in some governments. But it's mostly private individuals."

"What sort of people?" Cassie asked. "Do I even want to know?"

"Terrorists. Warlords. Art collectors. Some of them are awful people, some of them benign. These books are like weapons and power: it's always the wrong people who end up possessing them. And they will want your book, Cassie. It's an incredibly valuable item, a book that people have been trying to find for over a century. Imagine what people could do with the Book of Doors." He dropped his eyes to his plate, the last few crumbs of croissant, as if wishing he could have another. "There's always someone happy to use a book for the wrong reasons."

"Like that man in the deli?" Izzy asked.

Drummond nodded. "He wasn't looking for you. He didn't find you because you searched the internet. I'm so sorry, it's my fault he was there. He was following me."

"How was he doing that stuff?" Izzy asked. "Throwing those bodies around?"

"He has a book," Drummond said. "More than one, probably, but he definitely has the Book of Control. That's what he was holding. It lets you control objects, move them around, throw them. Hugo Barbary is very good at using books, unfortunately."

"What do you mean he's good at using books?" Izzy asked. "Like, some people aren't?"

Drummond shook his head. "In principle everyone can use the books, but some people find it harder. Some people find using some books really easy, but they struggle with others. Some people, maybe like Hugo Barbary, are just naturally good with the books and seem to be able to use most books almost immediately."

"Why is that?" Cassie asked.

Drummond shrugged. "Who knows? Why do some people have perfect pitch? Why can some people draw, and other people can't? Everyone can try to play a musical instrument but not everyone can be a concert pianist. It's just humans, isn't it? But the point is, now that Hugo knows you have the Book of Doors he will almost certainly come after you. And where he goes, others will follow. Your lives are now in danger."

Cassie nodded slowly, responsibility and implications settling on her like a heavy duvet on a hot day, something she wanted to crawl free from.

"But who are you?" Izzy asked. "You've mentioned all these people, but we don't know who you are."

Drummond nodded. "Yes, I know. My story is a long one, and we don't have time to tell it now. I just need you to trust me. I am not like that man you saw."

"Well, that's a vague and entirely unsatisfactory answer," Izzy said, sitting back and folding her arms.

Drummond nodded, as if he agreed, but he didn't offer anything more. Instead his eyes flicked over to Cassie, and he asked, "Can I see it? Your book?"

Cassie said nothing, unsure how to respond, unsure of the risk.

"I'm not going to steal it," Drummond said. "I promise."

Izzy barked a laugh of skepticism.

Cassie met Drummond's eyes and held his gaze, trying to judge him and his intentions. Then she reached into her pocket and pulled out the book, Izzy watching her. She laid it on the table and pushed it over to him.

"It had a note on it when I got it," Cassie said, as Drummond examined the book. "A message from the person who gave it to me."

Drummond nodded, looking at the book with a frown. "Writing doesn't last in the books. It disappears after a time. Other than the writing that's in the book itself."

"Why?"

"Who knows?" Drummond said, his eyes narrowing in puzzlement as he looked at the Book of Doors. "Someone gave this to you?"

Cassie nodded.

"Who?"

"Just a man. I work in a bookstore. He gave it to me as a gift."

"What man?"

"It doesn't matter. He died."

Drummond's eyes flicked to her again, asking a question that Cassie didn't answer. He turned his attention back to the book, exploring it silently for a few moments, shaking his head slightly to himself like he was seeing something he couldn't believe or couldn't understand.

Then he closed the book and pushed it back across the table toward her. But his eyes didn't leave it. His eyes remained fixed on the book until it disappeared back into Cassie's coat.

"So what do we do now?" Izzy asked. "If dangerous people are going to be looking for us, can we go home? I have a job. I have bills I need to pay, I can't live in France for the rest of my life."

Drummond thought for a moment in silence, his fingers tapping the tabletop.

"I can help you," he said finally. "I can put things right for you if you'll trust me. I can make this all go away. But I need your help in return. I need you to let me do something."

"What?" Cassie asked.

"I need to destroy the Book of Doors," he said.

The Book of Memories

What?" Cassie demanded.

"We could sell it to you. How much would you pay for it?" Izzy asked, and Cassie threw her a sharp look.

"You're not destroying my book," Cassie insisted. "And I'm not selling it either."

Drummond nodded to himself. "I didn't expect you to just agree to that. It's a shocking request, I totally understand. The book is precious to you."

"It was a gift," Cassie said. "From a friend."

"I understand," Drummond said again. "All books are precious; believe me, I know. Particularly these books. But you really don't understand how dangerous that book is. I don't mean just to you and Izzy, I mean for everyone."

"How would you destroy it?" Izzy asked, ignoring Cassie.

"I'd burn it," Drummond said. "The books burn very easily. Probably because they are old."

"You're not destroying it," Cassie said again, her voice quiet. She once more felt herself trembling, as if the beneficial effects of the croissant were wearing off.

Drummond held her gaze for a moment, as if trying to judge the strength of her feeling. "There are other books," he said. "Maybe there is something else I could do for you, something I could swap it for?"

"Could you make our dreams come true, Mr. Fox?" Izzy asked, joking. "Could you make me rich and famous? Could you make me a film star?"

"You want to be a film star?" Drummond asked, like it was a possibility he was considering.

"What?" Izzy asked, shocked. "You're serious?"

"It's up to Cassie," he said. "What would your dream be, Cassie?"

The answer was immediate for Cassie, requiring no thought. "I'd like to speak to my grandfather again," she said.

Drummond tilted his head, not understanding.

"He died," she said. "Many years ago. But I don't think you can raise the dead, can you?"

"I'd like to be happy," Izzy said. "I know it's childish. If you'd asked me five years ago, I would have said I wanted to be a movie star. But now I think I just want to be happy. With someone I love and children, living somewhere nice. God, listen to me, I'm getting so boring."

"The young have the loudest dreams," Drummond murmured, more to himself. "Unfettered by life and reality."

Cassie and Izzy exchanged a glance. A young couple appeared then, scraping chairs and sitting down at the table beside them, and Cassie and Izzy shared polite smiles with them as the woman from the café appeared and gave her singsong "Bonjour!" greeting.

"Look, never mind our dreams," Cassie said. "What do we do about that man at the deli? You need to help us with that and then maybe we can talk about why the book is so dangerous."

Drummond nodded. "Okay, then," he said. "First, we need to go back to New York. There's a couple of things I need to do that will help you both, but we have to be in New York. Can we go, now?"

Cassie nodded. "Okay," she said.

"Let me pay for these," Drummond said, gesturing at the coffees. He stood up and disappeared into the small café.

"What do you think?" Cassie asked, once they were alone.

Izzy shrugged. "I don't know, Cass. I just want life to be normal again. That man in Ben's, he scares me."

"Yeah," Cassie agreed. Her brain forced her to see the bald man kicking the server again and once more, her stomach flinched. "Do you trust him?" Cassie asked, nodding sideways to the café, in the direction of Drummond.

"I don't *not* trust him," Izzy said. "He seems kind. And he's not tried anything suspicious so far. But you know what, Cassie? He's just one. That Dr. Barbary man is another. There will be more. That book you are carrying around, people are going to do awful things to get it. I told you, no good will come of it."

Cassie nodded. "Even though it was you who told the world about it by googling it?"

She regretted it immediately, the words coming out without her thinking. Izzy looked at her like she had been slapped. Cassie reached out to apologize with a touch, but Izzy turned away just as Drummond emerged from the café, and the moment passed.

"Let's go," he said.

THEY FOUND A DOORWAY DOWN a cobbled alley, an unlocked door that appeared to lead into a narrow passageway, and Cassie used the Book of Doors to step through it into her own bedroom in New York in the middle of the night. They shuffled around in the small space until they were all through the door from Lyon, and then Cassie closed the door, and the apartment was suddenly quiet. Cassie reopened the door as normal and led them through into the living area. It felt odd being back in the apartment, in their safe, comfortable home, after what they had seen in the last hour.

"So now what?" Cassie asked, switching on the kitchen light. "What's the plan?"

Drummond nodded as he began to pat down his jacket, as if looking for something.

"We need to do two things," he said, pulling out a book from inside his coat. "First of all, I need to show you the second book I have. And then I want to show you exactly what the Book of Doors is capable of."

"What second book?" Cassie asked.

"Hold this, please," he said, passing the book to Izzy. She took it in both hands and looked at it, eyes down like a nervous person reading a script. The cover of the book was light gray, like a rain cloud.

"My second book," he said to Cassie, "is the Book of Memories."

"What does that do?" Cassie asked.

"It can do a variety of things," Drummond explained. "It can help you forget things or remember them."

"Like if you've lost something and you're trying to find it?" Cassie suggested.

Drummond smiled. "A bit more than that. I used it once with a dementia sufferer," he said. "I brought her back for her family, just for a few hours."

"Wow," Cassie said.

Drummond nodded. "It was one of the best things I have ever done. They were so happy, for a while." He seemed to drift off for a moment, as if luxuriating in that happy memory. Izzy was right, Cassie thought, Drummond Fox seemed like a kind man. "It was great," he continued, his smile fading a little. "Until I had to take the book back from her, until she knew what was going to happen. That was . . . harrowing. I've never tried to help someone like that again."

Cassie thought about that. She thought about Mr. Kellner being able to know who he was once again, and then knowing that he would slip back into the dementia.

"How awful," she murmured.

Drummond nodded his agreement. "Yes, awful. But over the years the book has been used more to help people to forget."

"Why would you want to forget?" Cassie asked.

Drummond shrugged. "Think about it. Hasn't there been some awful trauma, some horrible thing that happened to you, that you'd rather forget about entirely?"

Cassie could think of such things, but she didn't know that she would want to forget them. They were part of who she was.

"Or you can make people forget things you want them to forget," Drummond added. "Tactically very useful for things like crimes and espionage. For people who want to have affairs and then make their lovers forget about them. For everything from the mundane to the malicious."

Cassie shook her head. "I don't see how it helps us with Dr. Barbary."

Drummond sighed. "It doesn't," he admitted. "But it helps Izzy."

He looked at Izzy and Cassie followed his gaze. Izzy continued to stare at the book in her hands and Cassie now saw that Izzy's face was lit up by the lights that were emanating from it, a swirling dance of deep reds and blues.

"I feel funny," Izzy said.

"Yes," Drummond said softly. "You will."

"What are you doing to her?" Cassie demanded, alarmed. She moved closer to Izzy and put a hand on her arm.

Izzy lifted her head—with some considerable effort, it seemed—and settled her eyes on Drummond.

"What's happening?" she asked.

"You are going to be fine," Drummond said, his voice gentle. Izzy was watching him as if trapped in his gaze. "I promise no harm will come to you. What I am doing, it is to protect you. You are holding the Book of Memories. I gave it to you, to help you forget."

"Forget what?" Cassie demanded, her thoughts racing. Panic was surging like a wave within her.

"The best thing that could happen to Izzy right now is for her to forget all about the Book of Doors."

Cassie looked down at the book Izzy was gripping, the colors it produced curling and swirling around it like smoke.

"It feels heavy," Izzy murmured. "The book feels heavy and warm." Her voice was like a child's as she turned her face to Cassie. "I don't feel right."

"You're fine, Izzy," Drummond said. "This is for your own protection."

"What is happening?" Izzy pleaded.

"When you let go of the book," Drummond explained, "you will forget about the Book of Doors, about everything that has happened over the last few days. The Book of Doors will be clouded and hidden in your mind."

"You can't do that," Cassie said, shoving Drummond roughly on the shoulder. "You don't have the right! Make it stop!"

"It's already done," Drummond said. "I'm so sorry, but I have to protect Izzy."

"I don't want to forget!" Izzy said, pleading to Cassie. "I don't like him changing my memories!"

"It's done," Drummond said again. "People like Dr. Barbary will keep coming. People worse than him. The only way to protect you is for you to know nothing about it."

"But he saw us together," Cassie exclaimed, not understanding how Drummond failed to see how important Izzy was to her. "He knows that Izzy knows."

"Yes," Drummond said. "But he saw me with you as well, and he's much more interested in me. It's me he will look for, not Izzy. And if he does find Izzy, he will see easily enough that she can't tell him anything. He will work out what I've done."

Izzy was crying now, but trying not to, gripping the book so firmly her knuckles were white. "What happens if I don't let go?" she asked.

"You will," Drummond said, speaking with the certainty of a man who had had similar discussions before. "You must. Eventually. You can't live your life holding a book. And the book will grow heavier and heavier and hotter and hotter as it takes more and more of your memories. You won't be able to hold on forever. Best to just let it happen."

Cassie was watching Izzy, hating the hurt in her expression, her own mind racing as she tried to contemplate navigating this new and dangerous world without her.

"You can't do this," she pleaded to Drummond, her voice a whine. "Please, Drummond."

Tears were in her eyes, she realized, and she hated looking weak in front of this man, but she couldn't stop them.

"Don't cry, Cass," Izzy said, even though tears were pooling in her own eyes. "If you cry, I'll cry . . ."

Drummond frowned at Cassie, an expression of surprise and regret, as if he hadn't expected this response. "But it's to protect her," he said, as if he didn't understand why Cassie was so upset. "It's to keep her safe, Cassie."

Cassie wanted to shout: *But what about me?* But she knew how self-ish that would sound.

She held Izzy close.

"What happens when she lets go?" she asked.

"Nothing," Drummond said, looking at Izzy. "You'll fall asleep and wake up tomorrow like normal, just like any other day. And then you'll have the urge to leave the city for a while, maybe visit family."

Izzy's shoulders were hitching up and down and she wrestled with the inevitability of what had happened to her, of what was to come. "I don't like my family," she said, between sobs.

"I'm sorry I blamed you for the Google thing," Cassie said to her, tears on her cheeks.

"What's the point in telling me now?" Izzy wailed. "I'm going to forget all about it."

"That's why I'm telling you now," Cassie said. "Because you're going to forget about it all, but I want you to know before you do, I don't blame you. I didn't mean what I said."

Izzy nodded distractedly, as if accepting what Cassie was saying but that it wasn't that big of an issue in the grand scheme of things.

"Can it be undone?" Izzy asked Drummond. "Can I remember again after I forget?"

Drummond shrugged. "I really don't know, Izzy. But would you want to know about all of this again? Isn't it better to not remember? Why would you want to remember something that will put you at such risk?"

"I'll help you," Cassie said to Izzy, even though she had no idea if it was possible or not. "I'll help you to remember, I promise," she said. "Once it's safe."

The two women met each other's gaze, and Drummond reached for the book.

"Let me help," he said.

"No!" Cassie snapped fiercely, standing in front of Izzy protectively.

Drummond's face fell. "It can't be stopped, Cassie," he said to her. "I'm sorry." He pushed her aside gently and reached for the book. "You're going to be fine, Izzy, I promise," he said.

Izzy turned her eyes to Drummond. "I fucking hate you."

"Fair enough," Drummond said quietly. "I'll pay that price if it keeps you safe."

Then the book escaped Izzy's grip and Drummond stepped away. Izzy gazed at Cassie for a moment with an expression that was both blank and confused, like someone with dementia, and then she simply crumpled at the knees, landing awkwardly on the floor between the end of the couch and the door to the hall.

"It's done," Drummond said, gazing down at Izzy.

Cassie took two steps toward him and slapped him hard across the cheek. "You had no right to do that!" she shouted, tears running freely down her cheeks.

Drummond rubbed his face where she had slapped him, his expression pained. He stood there silently, gazing at the floor, like a man who had intruded on some private moment and wanted to be anywhere else.

"You had no right," Cassie said again, more quietly. She looked at Izzy's sleeping face and felt her heart knot agonizingly. "Help me move her," she ordered Drummond.

They carried Izzy to her bed and then Drummond left the room while Cassie changed Izzy into her pajamas and covered her with her duvet. Izzy looked peaceful, untroubled by what had happened.

Drummond was waiting in the kitchen, pacing back and forth when Cassie emerged.

"I hated doing it," he said to her, before she said anything. "I hated misleading you both like that. But sometimes I have to do things I don't like to protect people. Sometimes I have to do things that terrify me to protect people. This is the life I have to lead."

He seemed angry; angry with himself for what he had done, angry at Cassie for her lack of understanding. He paced back and forth restlessly for a few moments. Cassie watched him, not forgiving him, but finding that the heat of her anger was dissipating. "Is she going to be safe?" she asked.

"Yes," he said.

"Why should I trust you?" Cassie asked.

"I don't know," Drummond admitted with a sigh of exasperation. "The best way to keep her safe is for us and the books we carry to be somewhere else."

Cassie nodded at that. "I need to rest. I'm exhausted."

Drummond watched her for a moment, obviously thinking about something.

"What?" she asked.

"I know you don't trust me. But I have somewhere we can go, if you will take us. Somewhere that will show you why this is all so important. And maybe I can tell you my story."

"What place?" she asked.

"My library," he said. "If I show you a photograph of the door, can you take us?"

The Fox Library, in the Shadows

Everything was gray and insubstantial, and Cassie thought that she was floating.

It had taken her a while to open the door. She had thought she was tired or stressed, but Drummond had told her that it would be hard, that she should keep trying.

"It's in the shadows," he'd said.

She'd tried again, holding the Book of Doors in one hand, Drummond holding up his phone and showing a picture of a grand room, a wooden door in the corner. Then she had felt it, had gripped something with her mind, something fragile that threatened to dissipate if she pulled too hard. She had waited a moment, and then had gently tugged, and the door to Cassie's bedroom had opened, revealing a monochrome room beyond, like watching a film on a black-and-white television.

"We go into the shadows now," Drummond said. "We cannot speak, but don't be frightened. All will be well soon enough."

He had stepped past her into the room, and Cassie had followed, hesitating only briefly.

It was silent and gray, and when she walked it felt like swimming. She closed the door, watching her arm as it left ripples in the shadows as it moved, and then turned to see something like the shape of Drummond waiting.

The shape turned and Cassie followed it, wondering if this was what it was like to be dead, to be haunting a place of the living.

They left a big space and floated into a smaller space. There was a suggestion of height behind them, of light, but the Drummond shape moved in the opposite direction, toward deeper darkness. Then a line of light appeared, white and expanding, and Cassie saw the shape that was Drummond standing there. Beyond him, she realized, it was *outside* but still in the shadows, and that Drummond had opened the front door of the building.

The shape that was Drummond compressed and she realized that he was bending over, picking something up. Then he straightened, and there was a gesture, like tossing a piece of rubbish, and a moment later color and substance spread into the world, like liquid spilling across a table. Light chased the shadows away, and Cassie felt a breeze on her face, the smell of fresh air. Suddenly Drummond was there, standing in a grand arched doorway with a backdrop of green trees behind him, leaves and branches waving in the breeze.

"Welcome to the Fox Library," he said. He turned away from her and walked out into the daylight.

CASSIE FOLLOWED DRUMMOND, HER FEET crunching on a gravel driveway as she stepped out of the house. She took a few steps and turned around to look at the building, standing next to Drummond as he gazed upward at his library, his hands in his pockets and an unreadable expression on his face.

The building was a large country house built of red sandstone, with dark gray roof tiles and ironwork and guttering painted in bloodred. The doorway they had just emerged from was an archway at the bottom of a tall tower that sat on the corner of the building, with windows high up that made Cassie think of a lighthouse. On either side of the tower the building stretched away to far corners, large bay windows on the ground floor revealing glimpses of bookcases and wood paneling, and on the upper floor dormer windows turned the roofline of the building into a jumble of peaks and valleys.

Behind the building, climbing up the side of a brown mountain in the distance, pine trees in shades of green were shimmering in the cool morning wind. Overhead the sky was gray but bright, and low clouds moved steadily across it, sailing on the sea of wind. Everything, it seemed, was moving. Everything except the library, which was solidly still, like some stone rooted to the core of the earth, permanent and immobile. But there was something welcoming about the place, Cassie thought, something to do with the proportions and the size, and its warm red sandstone face.

"It's beautiful," Cassie said.

"Yes," Drummond replied, smiling with a mixture of happiness and sadness. "It is."

Cassie turned. Off to her right, beyond the gravel moat, a smooth ribbon of tarmac led away through well-kept lawns before disappearing into the trees in the distance. The line of trees stretched right around behind where they were standing and for a distance in the other direction, creating a curtain around the library and its grounds. Down at a far point of the lawn Cassie saw that they were being watched, a deer standing in the shadows, perfectly still and gazing at them.

"Deer," she murmured.

Drummond glanced at her, and then toward where she was looking. "Yeah," he said. "Lots of deer in the glen. This used to be a hunting estate."

Cassie continued watching the deer. It flicked its ears and then turned and darted out of sight, back into the trees.

"We're about six miles away from the main road," Drummond said, even though she hadn't asked. "Everything between here and there belongs to the Fox Library. The whole glen, the mountains. It's a private road, so no one comes up it."

"You own a mountain?" Cassie asked, squinting at him.

He grinned, and Cassie liked that expression on his face. "Several, actually. It's not so unusual."

Cassie raised her eyebrows, disagreeing. "Where are we, though?"

"Northwest Scotland," Drummond said. "The Highlands."

Cassie nodded, and inhaled deeply, feeling the clean, cool air fill her lungs. Somewhere overhead a bird shrieked and shattered the silence.

"We're what, five hours ahead of New York?" Cassie asked. "How come it's light here? It should still be night, shouldn't it?"

"Time works differently in the shadows," Drummond said. "It's a little later than that. It took us a while to emerge from the shadows." He looked around, sniffing the air. "Early morning. Come, let's get in out of the cold. I want to have a look around and then I'll take you to the library."

SHE FOLLOWED DRUMMOND AROUND THE house for a few minutes, watching as he opened doors and wandered through rooms, touching furniture affectionately, nodding to himself in satisfaction as if pleased that everything was where it should be. There was a dining room and a lounge, a billiards room with a table lying under a heavy gray cover, and at one side of the house was an old kitchen with a large range cooker and a collection of pots and pans dangling from a rack overhead. Other than the kitchen, bookcases and bookshelves were everywhere. The rooms were all large, with high ceilings and dark wood paneling on the walls. Diagonal shafts of light cut into the gloom through tall windows, revealing dust motes that danced and spun as Drummond and Cassie's movements stirred the air. The rooms were full of silence and memory, the sweet smell of old books and the sharp tang of well-used fireplaces waiting to roar again. It was a place of wood and paper, of stone and glass; there was nothing digital, no flat-screen televisions or LEDs. It was almost as if the house had been born in another time and had existed undisturbed by modernity ever since.

In some ways, Drummond's house reminded Cassie of Kellner Books. Just like the bookstore, the house was full of books—no shelf was bare, no book alone and seeking company—but it was more than that. The house was full of warm corners and quiet places, pleasantly creaking floorboards and drafts of air coming from unseen gaps. The lighting was soft, and the colors muted and warm, interrupted only by the vibrant shimmering green of the trees outside when glimpsed through passing windows. It was a building that welcomed people who wanted comfort and silence, who wanted space to contemplate and to think. It had an air of formality but not stiffness, like a smartly dressed grandfather telling a rude joke.

As she toured the ground floor with Drummond, the two of them walking in silence, Cassie quickly concluded that she loved the library. It was a place she wanted to be, a place she could happily live if given the chance. As they returned to the hallway, lingering at the bottom of a grand staircase, Drummond said, "I've missed this place."

"I can understand why," Cassie said.

Facing them, on the middle landing of the staircase, a tall stained-glass window spilled light into the hallway. It made the space feel airy and open, despite all the dark wood and the heavy bookcases crowding in on them.

"Come on," Drummond said. "I'll show you the library."

He started up the stairs, and she followed him. "What was that with the shadows?" Cassie asked, as they climbed the stairs. "When we arrived, when it was like we were underwater and everything was gray."

"The library was in the shadows," Drummond said. "I hid it."

"Why? How?"

"We'll come to the why, I promise, because you need to know. As for the how . . . I used the Book of Shadows." He removed a book from one of his pockets and passed it to her as they reached the first landing and doubled back to climb to the upper floor. The book was dark gray in color and when Cassie opened it, she saw the text on the first page.

"'The pages are of shadows,'" she read. "'Hold a page and be of shadow too.'"

Cassie flicked through the pages and saw smudges of gray, like ink, and words and pictures that seemed to shift and change, partially disappearing and then reappearing. She watched it for a while as she climbed the stairs, amazed at this book that seemed alive.

"How does it work?" she asked, passing him the book back.

"You tear a page and hold the fragment in your hand. As long as you hold the fragment, you stay in the shadows. When I hid the library, I tore out a full page and left it inside the front door. And then the house slipped into the shadows. Nobody could reach it. Not without the Book of Doors."

Cassie considered that. "Couldn't you reach it with the Book of Shadows?"

"No," Drummond said. "I couldn't get back here. Not until now." He sighed and seemed wistful for a moment as he looked around. "It's been ten years," he said.

"Ten years?" Cassie asked, shocked. "You haven't been here for ten years?"

Drummond shook his head. "It was the price I had to pay to keep the books safe."

Cassie looked at him anew. What he had done to Izzy had made her hate him, if only for a few moments, but she saw now that he had paid a price too. To have been kept from his home, particularly a home as special as this place, she couldn't imagine. She wondered how difficult his life had been.

At the top of the stairs they reached a long landing with a thick carpet underfoot and several heavy wooden doors leading off. The walls between the doorways were covered in what looked to Cassie to be expensive wallpaper, a pattern of fine purple flowers against a pale cream backdrop. A second, smaller set of stairs led up to a higher floor, curving out of sight.

"In here," Drummond said. He crossed the landing and opened a door immediately opposite the top of the staircase, revealing a large bright room at the front of the house. A tall bay window framed the trees out front and the mountains beyond. This end of the house looked westward, away from the road, and even from the doorway to the hall Cassie could see a long body of water, flat and gray blue.

"What's that?" she asked.

"What?" Drummond said. "Oh. That's Loch Ailda."

The loch was surrounded by mountains on either side, brown and green and barren above the trees, and a fluffy straight line of mist hung in the cool morning air, halfway up the hillside. Cassie wasn't sure she had ever seen any landscape as beautiful.

The walls of the room were lined floor to ceiling with bookshelves, and the furniture was arranged on a large rectangular rug in the center of the floor—armchairs and side tables and a coffee table, all of these also piled with books. A large cast-iron fireplace was a wailing mouth at the edge of the room, and next to it a side table was piled with whisky bottles and tumblers.

"This is my library," Drummond said, his voice quiet as he ran his eyes around the room.

He reached out to the bookshelves by the door and brushed them with his hand lightly, an affectionate gesture. Then he walked over to the table by the fireplace and poured himself a whisky. He downed the measure in one and then sighed in satisfaction. "Whisky still good. Thank god. I might have cried."

Cassie was slowly pacing the length of the bookcase against the opposite wall, reading the spines, pulling out a book here and there with a curious finger. These books were old, she saw, antiques probably, the sort of books with dense, small text and a pleasantly sweet smell when you opened them.

She reached the large bay window and stood there, admiring the view.

"It's beautiful," she said, and then she turned around and faced the room. "And this . . ." She gestured with a hand. "This place is . . . it's just right. It's perfect. It's everything a private library should be."

Drummond frowned for a moment, considering that assessment. Then he nodded in agreement. "It's my home," he admitted. He smiled then, but it was a sad expression, and Cassie thought there were maybe tears in the man's eyes. "I used to spend all my time here. And then my friends, they'd come, and we'd just sit and enjoy our books. Or we'd drink and talk late into the night. There'd be music and food and we'd get the fire going. Laughter, lots of laughter. Meetings in the Fox Library, they were always my favorite times."

He shook his head, as if all of these memories were crazy, impossible, and wiped his eyes with the heel of his hand.

"It feels like a happy place," Cassie reflected, her eyes roving the bookshelves on the other wall. "To me at least. Safe and happy."

Drummond nodded, taking Cassie's words as a compliment, and poured himself another drink.

"Are the other special books here?" Cassie asked, inspecting the nearby shelves.

"They're here," Drummond said. "Not in this room." He walked over and handed her a tumbler with a measure of whisky. "Drink."

"I don't really like whisky," Cassie admitted, peering into the glass dubiously.

"I love it," Drummond replied. "My three favorite things in the world: whisky, cakes and pastries, and books."

Cassie coughed a laugh despite herself. "Cakes and pastries?"

He nodded seriously. "I'm not embarrassed by it. What's better than a good book and a slice of cake?"

"I suppose," Cassie said, peering at the whisky.

"You don't have to like it," Drummond said. "But drink it. It's good for you, just like the croissants in Lyon."

She debated for a moment, and then sipped the amber liquid. It roared down her throat and made her cough.

"It's like fire," she spluttered, handing him back the glass.

"I know," he said, grinning like she had given the drink a compliment. He placed the glass on the windowsill and they stood in awkward silence for a moment.

"I'm really truly sorry about Izzy," he said, his dark eyes watching her.

She nodded. "Okay," she said.

"You want to see the other special books?" he asked, and he looked excited, like a boy wanting to show off his newest toy.

She nodded. "I do."

"Okay," he said.

Drummond walked across to the bookshelf on the wall by the window, and then reached down the side of the bookcase. She heard a click and then the bookcase swung out on a hidden hinge, revealing a small doorway and curving stone steps within a tower.

Drummond gestured and smiled, twitching his eyebrows up and down. "Where else would I keep special books but in a secret room at the top of a hidden tower?"

UP THE STEPS A SMALL wooden door opened onto a large circular room with windows on two sides looking east and west from the house, toward the road and toward the loch. This was the top of the tower Cassie had seen from outside, she realized.

A single large desk sat in the center of the room on a square rug, with a chair pushed in on each of the four sides. The desk was laden with papers and pens. On the circular wall of the room Cassie saw a variety of things—maps with pins in, photographs that showed Drummond and other people looking happy around a dining table or seated in the library downstairs. There was an oil painting of the house in an ornate frame, a series of three small frames in a line displaying pressed flowers. Overhead a number of large light bulbs hung from cords at various heights from the rafters of the roof. Where the rest of the house had felt neat and tidy and ordered, this secret room felt cluttered, or *relaxed*. This space felt more lived-in than even the library at the bottom of the hidden staircase.

Cassie absorbed all of this, but her attention was drawn to small wooden cupboards that were dotted randomly around the circular wall of the tower, between the pictures and windows and maps. Each of the cupboards had a Roman numeral stenciled on the front in faded gold. There were twenty cupboards in all, and the arrangement and numbering made Cassie think of some strange advent calendar.

"This is the secret library," Drummond said, spreading his arms as he walked around the table.

"Those are the books?" Cassie asked, pointing at the cupboards.

Drummond nodded. He leaned against one of the windowsills. Cassie saw a set of binoculars sitting there. Drummond picked them up and then gazed out at the world, in the direction of the tarmac drive leading down to the trees. She wondered what he was looking for.

"You have twenty?" she asked, her eyes moving from cupboard to cupboard.

"No," Drummond said, placing the binoculars down again. "Not all of them are full."

He reached into his pocket and pulled out a key ring. He identified a key and then walked over to the cupboard hanging nearest him on the wall—number seventeen. He unlocked the cupboard and opened the door. Cassie saw a small shelf with a thin brass wire retaining frame. A single book leaned against the frame. Drummond picked it up and carried it over to the table in the center of the room. He placed the book down and then walked to a different cupboard on the other side of the room—number twelve. He repeated the process of opening the door and removing the book and placing it on the table. Both of the books were the same size and shape as the Book of Doors. He lifted his eyes to her, an invitation.

She approached and gazed down at the two books.

"What are they?" she asked.

"Examples," he said. "Two of the books from the Fox Library."

Cassie picked up the first book. It was light and insubstantial, almost weightless, just like the Book of Doors. The cover was a mosaic of many bright colors, like a floor covered in flower petals or confetti.

"What does it do?"

"That's the Book of Joy," Drummond said, moving back to the window. He folded his arms and leaned against the wall. "It lets you experience true joy. It removes all doubt and unhappiness and pain from your mind."

"Wow," Cassie said. She flicked through the pages briefly and saw texts and sketches in a variety of colors.

"It was sent to me by a friend in London," Drummond said, looking at the book in Cassie's hand. "For safekeeping."

Cassie nodded and returned the Book of Joy to the table. "And this?" she asked, lifting the second book. The cover was colored bright red and orange, angry tones.

"The Book of Flame," Drummond said. He shrugged. "Pretty obvious what that one does."

Cassie flicked through the pages, seeing similar text and sketches to what was in the Book of Doors, but this time the contents were scribbled in deep red ink, and the pages seemed almost browned in some way. As if they were wood, maybe.

"How many books do you have?" Cassie asked. "If not twenty, how many?"

"Seventeen," Drummond said.

"Seventeen?" Cassie gasped, her eyebrows shooting up in surprise.

"The Fox Library was the biggest single collection of special books anywhere in the world," Drummond explained. "The biggest I am aware of, anyway."

"What do the others do?" Cassie asked, her eyes skipping around the numbered cabinets. She was excited, thinking about all the wonders that might be possible.

Drummond shrugged. "Lots of different things. Some of them I don't know. They have never revealed their secrets. We know they are special books, because they have all the qualities—the weight, the text—but they are maybe just waiting for the right person to reveal what they are. But the other ones . . . well, they do lots of things. But that's not the point."

"What's the point?" she asked.

"The point is I need to protect them. That's why I am showing them to you. Imagine what would happen if these fell into the wrong hands? So much power here. And they are so important. I can't stand the idea that someone would just take them and use them like tools, like weapons." He pulled a face, as if he'd eaten something that tasted awful.

Cassie looked down at the book in her hand and then placed it back on the desk, alongside its sibling.

"They are so important, Cassie," Drummond said, his tone gentler now. "My friends, other people like me, we loved the mystery of them, what they could tell us about the world and creation. The history."

"The history?"

"They've been around for centuries, Cassie, some of them. Some of my friends, they were convinced that the existence of the books explained some of the mysteries of human history. Why some societies flourished while others with similar advantages did not. Why was Egypt so advanced so early? Why was it that China was responsible for so many important inventions? Why did Genghis Khan conquer so much of the planet? All those sorts of things. Even religious figures and miracles. Once you know of the existence of special books, it's impossible not to intertwine them with the big events in human history."

Cassie nodded, understanding. She didn't know much about history, but she could see the sense in what Drummond was saying.

He approached the desk again and picked up the two books. He returned them one at a time to their respective cupboards and locked the doors. "That's why they are so important. They have been part of the history of the world. They need to be studied and protected. Not used by idiots and thugs and psychopaths."

He slipped the key ring back into his pocket.

"I have a responsibility to protect them, Cassie. I didn't choose this life, but I take the responsibility seriously. That's why I put the house in the shadows, because there was a threat. That's why I need to destroy the Book of Doors, to keep them safe."

Cassie's insides jolted at his words. "What threat?"

Drummond shook his head. "Not now," he said. "You're exhausted. And if you're not, I am. And I haven't been home in a decade. I want to rest for a while."

Cassie said nothing. She was listening, but mostly she was thinking about the other books locked away in the cupboards around her. She wondered about all the miracles they could do.

"Come on," Drummond said, pulling her out of her thoughts. "There are rooms here. The beds will be made up. You can sleep for a few hours."

He led her back down the steps and into his library, closing the secret bookcase door behind them and sealing off the tower.

"Will it be safe to sleep?" Cassie asked. "You said you hid this place in the shadows . . ."

He waved his hand. "It will be fine for a few hours. The danger is very far away. It will be nice to be here again, just for a wee while."

She nodded. Despite the excitement of the secret tower room and the special books, despite how comfortable and inviting she found Drummond's house to be, how much she wanted to enjoy the experience of being there, he was right: she was exhausted. She turned around again and gazed out at the day through the large bay window. The clouds cracked at that moment and sunlight stabbed through, washing the hillside in brightness briefly. Then it was gone again.

"So I go to sleep. What happens then?" Cassie asked. Part of her didn't want to know. Part of her wanted to climb into bed and hide under the covers.

"I told you," Drummond said, walking toward the door to the hall. "I want to destroy the Book of Doors. But I know you don't want to do that. Until you do I need to keep you and the book safe. So I'll stick with you. Tomorrow, I'll show you why it needs to be destroyed, and I hope after that you'll agree with me."

Cassie pulled a face that said everything she felt about that.

"I know you don't trust me," he continued. "I know what I did to Izzy doesn't help."

"No, it doesn't," Cassie agreed.

"So I will do two things. Firstly, I will show you what the Book of Doors is capable of, so you really understand why it is so dangerous. And then I will tell you about the threat we face. I'll tell you why I had to hide this place in the shadows. But right now, let's find you a bed."

He opened the door to the hallway and gestured for her to follow. Cassie trailed behind, sad to be leaving the comfort of the library.

"What do you mean you'll show me what the Book of Doors is capable of?" Cassie asked. "I just took you from my apartment in New York to your house in Scotland. I know how to use it."

Drummond opened a door off the landing at the top of the stairs, looked inside for a moment, and then closed it again. "Not this one," he murmured. Then, to Cassie, "You're only scratching the surface."

"How?" she demanded. "How am I only scratching the surface?"

Drummond walked to the next door along the hall and opened it. "This will do," he said, stepping inside.

Cassie followed him into a large square room. A rectangular window looked out on the same landscape she had seen from other rooms, but viewed from a different direction. The hills seemed closer here, or maybe they were different hills. There was a large four-poster bed against the far wall, made up with bright blue linen the color of a summer sky. Yet again the walls were lined with bookcases, and there was an armchair at the foot of the bed, a side table next to it, and a footstool in front of the table. A small fireplace was set into the wall beside the armchair, a neat stack of logs piled on the hearth. Cassie could imagine a cozy winter evening in the room, the fire crackling as wind and rain battered the window, a pile of books and a hot drink on the small side table.

"Bathroom through there," Drummond said, gesturing toward a door on the opposite wall, by the side of the bed.

"It's lovely," she said, facing him. "But how am I only scratching the surface?"

Drummond shook his head. "Get some sleep first. I'll tell you when you wake up."

"No," she said, growing annoyed. "Tell me. I want to know."

He hesitated for a moment but saw that she would not sleep until he answered.

"You have a supercomputer," he said. "And you're using it to play *Space Invaders*."

"What does that mean?"

"'Any door is every door.' That's what it says at the front of the book."

"Yeah," Cassie said. "I know."

"No," Drummond said, shaking his head slowly. "I don't think you do. Doors don't just exist now, do they? Doors exist all through time, all through human history."

Cassie thought about that for a moment, and then, when she understood, her mind staggered backward, as if she had unexpectedly stumbled upon a huge canyon in the earth.

"People don't want your book just because they can travel around the world," Drummond continued, as Cassie's mind raced. "Anybody with money can jump on a private jet and be anywhere else in twelve hours. You said your dream was to speak to your grandfather again. I can't raise him from the dead, but you don't need me to. The Book of Doors is all you need."

Cassie blinked, trembling.

"You can open a door to the past, Cassie," Drummond said. "That's why people will want your book. Because it means you can travel in time."

The Book in Cupboard Six, and Discussions in the Fox Library

In the kitchen, by himself, Drummond Fox found some ice cream in the freezer. He set it on the counter to thaw a little and made himself a cup of tea. It had been ten years since he had been in the Fox Library, in his home, and the last time he had been there he had been running scared, having seen the slaughter of his friends.

Drummond sat at the counter, in a pool of light thrown by the hanging lamp, surrounded by darkness, and opened the ice cream. It had been half eaten, of course—ice cream had never lasted long in Drummond's home—but there was enough left to cheer him. He dug in and excavated a spoonful, letting it melt in his mouth.

"Shadow ice cream," he murmured to himself, smiling a little. The ice cream didn't taste like shadows, it tasted like a summer day—berries and sugar—as fresh as the day he had last eaten it. Things didn't spoil or decay or grow dusty in the shadows.

Drummond kept eating, not thinking about anything, just enjoying the taste, the buzz of sugar in his system. Eating had always been one of his pleasures, and it had kept him going over the last ten years, while he had been moving constantly. In the darkest moments, he would stop at a restaurant or a diner, surround himself with the happy noises of other people in their easy lives, and take his time over food. Those moments had been his respite, islands of peace in a stormy sea.

He ate his ice cream slowly, savoring it, and then returned the tub to the freezer. Then he picked up his mug, turned off the light, and carried his drink upstairs, through his library, and up the hidden staircase into the tower. He placed the mug down on the table and stood at the window for a moment, staring out at the familiar darkness. It was good to be home, good to be back where he felt safe and comfortable, even though he wasn't really safe, and he was struggling to feel comfortable.

Drummond walked to one of the small cupboards hanging on the wall—number six—and opened it. He removed the book that was within and carried it over to the table, placing it down next to his mug. He put his hand on its surface, stroking it gently, and then opened the book. The pages were full of dense text and sketches, as they always had been, but the very front page was blank. The book was obviously a special book, that was why the library possessed it, why it had been part of the collection for quite some time, but nobody had ever been able to read it, or to understand what it could do. The instructions on the front page of the book had never appeared for any member of the Fox Library.

Drummond frowned and then reached for another book, a leather-bound volume that sat on the corner of the desk. It was the register of the library's collection of special books. He turned to the relevant entry and double-checked exactly when the book in cupboard six had come into the possession of the Fox Library.

"'April third,'" he read. "'Nineteen-eighteen. Identified in Egypt, in excavations at Aswan.'"

He nodded. His memory had been correct. The book had been in the Fox Library for over a hundred years, safely locked away in cupboard number six. It had never left the library—there would have been an entry in the register—and indeed, the fact that the front page was still blank meant nobody in the history of the library had been able to read it.

Drummond shook his head, puzzling at the mystery.

Because the book lying in front of him was familiar. It was identical to the book Cassie had shown him in Lyon, the book she carried with her.

It was, Drummond was sure, the Book of Doors.

DRUMMOND SIPPED HIS TEA AND smacked his lips. Tea always tasted better after something sweet. In the background he heard the sounds of the house, the creaking of old timbers, the wind whistling through gaps, and somewhere below him Cassie was likely lying awake, coming to terms with what he had told her not too long ago: the Book of Doors could let her travel in time.

"Time travel," Drummond said to himself, stroking the book again.

Time travel had to explain it. If the Book of Doors could travel in time, it was possible for two versions of the same book to be in the same place and time together.

The fact that Cassie's book had the text on the front page said to Drummond that it had to be a version of the book from later in its own timeline. The version of the book on the table in front of him was younger.

He narrowed his eyes as he worked through the knot.

That meant that at some point in the future, somehow, the Book of Doors would be taken from the Fox Library and would somehow end up in Cassie's hands in the past, in New York City.

But how?

And when?

And why?

Drummond didn't know, but it worried him.

He had planned to take the Book of Doors from Cassie. After Barbary had shown up, he had wanted to get her and Izzy somewhere safe and then take the book from them. He almost had done it, when Cassie had let him look at the book in Lyon. But he had recognized it as one that should have been in the Fox Library. He had given Cassie the book back, because he had wanted her to bring him to the library so he could check.

"And it meant you could come home," he said, nodding at his own ulterior motive.

And here he was, the library as safe as he had left it, and the book he was sure was the Book of Doors had remained in its cupboard, untouched. He didn't know if it was reassuring or worrying.

He stood up and returned the book to cupboard number six.

He had to stay with Cassie until he knew the answer, he decided. He had to find out how she had come to possess the book.

He was surprised to find that the idea of staying with her was not unappealing; quite the opposite—if anything it cheered him a little.

"Why?" he asked the quiet room.

On the surface, the answer was simple: because he had enjoyed the time he had spent with Cassie and Izzy. After the deli, after Hugo Barbary, those few minutes drinking coffee and eating croissants in Lyon had made him happy. He had said much more than he would have expected, answered their questions more openly than was probably wise.

"Because you're lonely," he admitted to himself.

He missed his friends. He missed talking about the books. He was tired of being alone.

He nodded to himself as he came to terms with this truth. He returned to the desk and sipped his tea.

He was scared of the woman. He still had nightmares about that night in New York ten years previous, when his friends had died. He was terrified of what she would do if she got hold of the Book of Doors and used it to access the Fox Library, what she would do with all of the books. But he couldn't leave Cassie alone to face the dangers she was unprepared for. And he had to find out how she had gotten hold of the book.

"Some time travel jiggery pokery," he said, smiling to himself. Because that phrase had been used before in the Fox Library.

Drummond stood in the window, remembering a night with his friends in the library, and discussions about time travel.

"So, we have four categories," Wagner said, standing at the old blackboard like a schoolteacher, chalk in hand. Drummond was sitting in his armchair watching, holding a tumbler of whisky. Lily was leaning against the window, the dark night beyond her, her eyes closed as she dozed lightly after dinner, and Yasmin was sitting opposite Drummond, her cheeks reddened by the warmth

from the fire. She was nibbling on a piece of shortbread. Outside the night was full of wind and rain, drops being thrown against the window from the darkness, and in the room the air was warm, and the fire was crackling. It was a comfortable place to be.

"Four categories," Drummond said. "Run through them again."

Wagner nodded. "Books that affect the external reality of the physical world," he said, pointing his chalk at the left side of the blackboard. "Books that have an impact on the internal state of humans—Book of Joy, Book of Despair, Book of Pain, Book of Memories."

"Yes," Yasmin said. "Emotions and feelings."

Wagner hesitated, thinking about that. "Emotions and feelings," he said, and then scribbled those words at the bottom of the list, as if they were a potential alternative-category title. "Then we have what we are loosely calling the superpower books. Books that can give those who wield them superhuman powers."

"Is Lily asleep?" Drummond asked, peering across the room to her. Wagner turned to look briefly.

"Ja," he concluded. "Too much rich food. Lots to digest."

"I heard that," Lily mumbled sleepily, without opening her eyes.

"Book of Speed," Yasmin said, brushing crumbs of shortbread from her lips. "Book of Faces. Book of Shadows."

"Book of Control," Drummond said.

"Hugo Barbary's book," Lily said from the window, the name sounding like a swear word in her mouth.

"Ghoul," Yasmin agreed.

"And then the fourth category," Wagner continued. "Books that seem to have some sort of an effect on the laws of the universe."

Drummond stood up and stretched, and then took a few steps over to the blackboard.

"Book of Light," he said. "Book of Luck."

"Book of Light could be a superpower," Yasmin said.

Wagner bobbed his head back and forth as he debated that. "There are several books that could fit in more than one category. But I am a physicist. Light is a fundamental property of the universe, so I want to place it here, ja?" He smiled at Yasmin. "But we are making this up; this whole categorization might be an exercise in futility."

"Keep going," Drummond encouraged. He had no idea if there was any value in categorizing the books in this way, but he was enjoying it. "What other books play with the laws of the universe?"

They thought about the question for a few moments, the silence filled by the crackling of the fire and the scattering of rain against the windows.

"We don't know all of the books," Lily said, opening her eyes. She pushed herself off the window with a grunt and meandered across the room to sit in the chair next to Yasmin. "There are still books out there to be found. Maybe we will find a Book of Gravity or a Book of Time."

"The Book of Doors," Drummond said, and Yasmin and Lily both smiled at him. It was the story that started it all for the Fox Library, the mythical Book of Doors.

"If there really is a Book of Doors that would let you travel in time," Wagner agreed. "If you could open any door, that would be any door anywhere."

"There is a lovely English phrase . . ." Yasmin said, trying to remember the words. "Ah . . . yes . . . time travel jiggery pokery."

Drummond grinned at her. "Jiggery pokery" sounded funny in her accented English.

"If it exists," Lily said.

Drummond knew that Lily was unconvinced of the existence of a Book of Doors. "It is too much of a fairy tale," she had told him once, on his first visit to her in Hong Kong several years earlier. He had gone to Hong Kong with some notion of perhaps finding the Book of Doors. "Feels like something someone has made up."

"If you could travel in time," Yasmin wondered, "imagine what you could do. You could change history, change world events. Maybe it is better that such a book remains hidden."

"Nein," Wagner said, picking up his mug of coffee from the table. Wagner didn't drink alcohol, for reasons Drummond had never discovered. He seemed to exist solely on coffee and water. "I don't believe that."

"You don't believe what?" Drummond asked.

"That you can change history with time travel. I am a physicist. I understand the laws of the universe. I don't believe time travel would work that way. There is still cause and effect."

"Oh, you have to tell us how it would work, dear Wagner," Lily said. "Come, put the blackboard away and talk about time travel."

Wagner dropped the chalk into the holder on the side of the blackboard and returned to his seat. "Of course this is all conjecture, nobody will know until we do travel in time, but it seems to me that time is fixed. The past cannot be changed."

"Why?" Drummond asked.

"Look," Wagner said, crossing his legs, his elbow on the arm of the chair and his hand in the air, bouncing as he spoke as if emphasizing his words. "There are two ideas about time travel. There is the open model of time travel and the closed model, ja? In the open model, you can travel into the past and change events so that your present is consequently changed also. This is what you see in science fiction stories. You go back and do something and history changes."

Yasmin nodded. "But you don't believe that would happen."

"Nein," Wagner said. "Because the past is the past, events have already happened. If you go back and have any effect on the past, that will contribute to the present you already experience. This is the closed model. You cannot change events from what has already happened. If you go back and do something in the past, then that already happened in the past, and is part of history. It is part of what made your present be the present that it is, the present that you departed from when you went into the past."

"I am trying really hard to understand this," Lily murmured, her eyes narrowed slightly. "But I have too much rich food to digest and only so much energy."

"So you are saying you can't change events," Drummond said. "Even if we had a Book of Time, or the Book of Doors, if we tried to change anything in the past, nothing in the present would change?"

"That is correct," Wagner said. "Because it has already happened. The things you have done in the past have already happened, before the you in the now goes back to do them."

The three of them considered that in silence as Wagner sipped his coffee placidly.

Drummond felt his mind wrestling with the ideas Wagner was describing. He felt about three steps behind Wagner at the best of times, but now he was scrabbling and running to keep up with a man who was sauntering.

"But it is only a theory," Wagner said, shrugging amiably. "We will not know until we discover that time travel is even possible."

Lily's eyes had glazed over, and Yasmin was looking at the plate of shortbread as if wondering if another biscuit would be a bad idea or not. Drummond found himself still trying to make sense of Wagner's words.

"Have you ever thought of doing science to the books, Wagner?" Lily asked.

"Doing science to the books?" Wagner asked, amused.

Lily waved a hand. "You know, get them in a laboratory, examine what happens when they are used."

Wagner considered the question. "I have not," he admitted. "Perhaps I should, as you say, do science to the books." He looked at Drummond. "Perhaps if I could borrow one or two books from the library, we could run some experiments."

Drummond nodded. It was an interesting idea, and as far as he knew, nobody had ever conducted experiments on what the books were or how they worked.

"Has anyone heard anything from the Popovs?" Yasmin asked, already on to the next subject.

"The Popovs?" Lily asked, her eyes suddenly focused again. "The Book of Despair Popovs in St. Petersburg?"

Yasmin nodded. "I have a contact who told me a story that they had gone missing. Nobody has seen them or heard from them for some months."

"I hope not," Drummond said. "The Book of Despair could be very dangerous in the wrong hands."

"Ja," Wagner said, nodding, as he lifted his coffee mug.

"That's why I thought I'd ask," Yasmin said.

Lily was shaking her head. "We really should try to buy up all these books and keep them somewhere safe. I have nights where I lie awake and frighten myself with what might happen if the wrong people got more of the books."

"Like Hugo Barbary," Yasmin reflected.

"I have heard a story, actually, from a friend in America," Drummond said. "A story about a woman trying to collect all the books."

IN THE PRESENT, IN THE Fox Library, as Cassie slept below, Drummond stood at the window in his tower, the mug of tea in his hand and sadness smothering him as he remembered those days with his friends. He wished they had been more cautious, more attuned to the rumors and the stories they had been hearing. They had been naive, too ready to believe that the worst wouldn't happen.

And now his friends were dead, and he was alone. And he had to work out what to do next.

He sipped his tea and stared out at the dark, searching for an answer.

Matt's All-American Burgers (2012)

several hours after Drummond had revealed to Cassie what the Book of Doors could do, and more than a decade earlier, Cassie and Drummond stepped into Matt's All-American Burgers in Myrtle Creek, Oregon. Drummond had returned the Fox Library to the shadows, trying but failing to hide his obvious sadness at leaving his home once again, and then they had returned to the doorway they had come through the previous day, and Cassie had taken them into the past. Into *her* past.

They stood in the doorway of the diner for a moment, Cassie remembering a place she had known throughout her childhood, and then one of the servers greeted them and led them to a booth by the window.

"Where are we?" Drummond asked, gazing out at the dark green trees and the heavy gray sky.

"Oregon," Cassie said. Her voice sounded very far away to her own ears. She was struggling with reality, she realized, struggling with what she had come to do. "A town called Myrtle Creek. I grew up here. We used to come to this diner all the time."

The interior of the restaurant was designed to remind customers of an idealized 1950s that had probably never existed. There was lots of neon and chrome and red vinyl booths and a checkerboard floor. The pictures on the wall were full of optimistic young faces at barbecues or campfires.

"Is this place for real?" Drummond asked. "Tell me it's ironic, please."

"People don't come for the decor," Cassie said. "The food's real good." The televisions behind the counter were showing the sports network and news channels, events that were current for the customers but history for Cassie. She watched, hypnotized for a few moments, as a younger Barack Obama addressed a room, a crowd of faces gathered in rows behind him, and then she pulled a menu from the holder at the end of the table.

"Coffee?" the server asked, wandering over to them from a nearby table. She was a middle-aged woman who looked tired, giving out all the signals that she wanted an order and not a chat. Cassie remembered her, vaguely. "Coffee?" the woman asked again, and Cassie realized she had been staring.

"Yes," she said. "Coffee. Drummond?"

"Do you have any whisky?" he asked, and the server answered with a weary look. "Tea?" he tried.

"Coffee, tea," the woman said, and turned to walk away.

"Breakfast tea, with milk," Drummond called after her, and she glanced back without slowing her stride. "Boiling water for the tea, please, not just warm water."

There were only a few other people around them, but Cassie knew the diner would soon get busy with the lunchtime crowd. With people like her grandfather.

She turned her eyes to the world outside. The road that passed the diner was so familiar to her. She had traveled it thousands of times over her childhood. A few miles farther east was the house Cassie has grown up in. As she stared and remembered, lost in her thoughts, the first drops of rain spattered against the window, fat and round. The rain would fall all afternoon, Cassie knew. She remembered this day.

A crash of crockery pulled her attention back into the diner, someone dropping a cup, and then Cassie looked back across the table to Drummond, who was staring at the menu with a grimace.

"What's wrong with your face?"

Drummond gestured at the menu. "I've been traveling around this country for the last decade, and I am so tired of the food here," he said.

"Is it possible, at all, to find something to eat that isn't just meat between two bits of bread? Burgers . . . hot dogs . . . sliders . . . sandwiches? France is very good at cooking things. I wish I'd spent the last ten years in France."

He gazed out the window, lost in his thoughts.

Cassie watched him for a moment, unsure if she was annoyed or amused by his words, then she asked, "What will happen if I speak to him?" It had been one of the questions playing on her mind all afternoon and into the evening in Scotland, as she had lain awake in Drummond's luxurious bedroom, thinking about what he had revealed. "Will I change history? Or . . . I don't know, will something bad happen?"

"We talked about that once, my friends and I," Drummond said. "In the library. I remember a discussion about time travel." He shook his head. "In truth I have no idea. I studied literature at university, not advanced physics, and rather disappointingly the metaphysical poets don't have much to say about time travel."

He smiled, and she found herself smiling back at him, despite her nerves. When he was happy it cheered her, she realized.

"But my friend Wagner, he was a physicist," Drummond continued. "And he was certain that time travel couldn't change history. If we do anything here, now, then it creates the future as we know it, the future we exist in. It doesn't change our reality. Because it has already happened."

Cassie frowned. "So . . . if I speak to my grandpa here, now, then it always happened this way? I was always here in this time speaking to him?"

Drummond nodded. "I think so, I think that's what Wagner meant."

"Do you believe that?" Cassie asked.

Drummond shrugged loosely. "I don't know if I even really understood it, never mind believed it. But Wagner was a very clever man, and he would know better than most." His eyes dropped to the table for a moment, and Cassie thought that maybe he was thinking about his friend.

The server approached in the silence and placed their drinks before them. Cassie ordered whole-wheat toast and scrambled eggs even though she didn't think she could eat. Drummond ordered a slice of red velvet cake.

"When exactly are we?" Drummond asked, after the server left them.

"If I'm right, this is just over ten years ago," Cassie said. "August twenty-second in 2012, the very end of summer break."

Stepping through a doorway into the past had not been difficult for Cassie. It had been easier, in fact, than opening the door to the Fox Library in the shadows. She wondered if it was because the doorway to Matt's was a place she had known so well for so long.

"Why did you pick this day?" Drummond asked.

"I remember it clearly," she said. "I was out of town for a few days, camping with a friend and her parents." She pointed at the window, at the rain streaking the glass and the heavy clouds beyond. "This is the start of a three-day downpour. It's not something you forget when you're out camping. Everything was so wet. It was miserable. I've never been camping since."

"That doesn't answer the question," he pressed. "Why come today?"

"I'm out of town, so I'm not going to bump into myself, am I? And nobody I knew back here is going to see two of me around."

Drummond nodded, appreciating her train of thought. "I don't know what would happen if you met yourself," he said. He seemed distracted by that idea briefly.

"I can think of nothing worse," Cassie murmured. "I don't know who'd be the most horrified, the younger me seeing me dressed in all these thrift store clothes"—she gestured at her sweater—"or the me now being reminded of what I used to be like before . . ."

"Before what?" Drummond pressed.

"Just before," she replied, after a moment.

They sat in silence until their food arrived and then the silence kept them company as they ate, Cassie playing with her eggs more than eating them. The diner grew busy. Groups of men crashed in from the rain, chatting and laughing noisily; teenage girls giggled and whispered; and a young boy arrived with water-soaked comics and misery on his face. All around them cutlery clinked, and mugs and glasses thumped on tabletops. For a few minutes Cassie was distracted, happy even, imagining that the last ten years hadn't happened, that she could be back in the diner with her life spread out before her, a land of opportunity waiting to be discovered.

"Tell me more about how you got the book," Drummond said, dragging her reluctantly out of her own thoughts. She watched him dissect some of the red velvet cake and then spoon it into his mouth.

"Is that good?" she asked.

"Not bad," he admitted. "It'll keep me going. The book, who was the man who gave it to you?"

She thought about what to say, wondering why he was so interested in where the book came from. But then the door opened again and when Cassie turned her head, she saw her grandfather striding in from the storm, brushing a hand through his hair and shaking the rain off as he greeted the server with a smile that made Cassie's throat suddenly thick and sore.

And then he walked across the room behind the server to a table in the far corner and sat down.

Her grandfather.

Her wonderfully alive and healthy grandfather, the man who had died more than eight years before.

Izzy Out of Sorts

When Izzy awoke the following morning, at around the same time that Cassie and Drummond were leaving the library and traveling to Cassie's past, she felt immediately sure that something was wrong.

She clambered out of bed and stood in the middle of her bedroom, trying to place the source of her anxiety. It felt like the memory of a nightmare lingering, a sleep terror not yet shaken off. But she couldn't remember having had any dreams.

She had a shower, hoping it would wash off her malaise, but when she was done, she didn't feel any better. Had she been drinking the night before? She tried to remember, but the previous evening seemed elusive. She began to wonder if she had been drugged. Maybe she couldn't remember because someone had slipped something into a drink? Maybe the oddness she was feeling was some sort of aftereffect?

She got dressed for work, carefully checking herself as she did so without admitting to herself that she was looking for bruises or abrasions or other signs that something had happened to her. As far as she could see, as far as she *felt*, she was physically fine. Whatever was wrong, it was something more intangible.

As she headed out to work, she noticed that Cassie's bedroom door was ajar.

"Cassie?" she said, peeking her head around the door. The bed was tidy, like it hadn't been slept in. Cassie wasn't in the living area either. Izzy frowned at another anomaly. She couldn't remember Cassie ever not being at home overnight. It worried her.

She tried calling Cassie but got no answer, and for the first time she wondered if she was feeling strange because something had happened to Cassie. Maybe somebody had attacked or kidnapped her? Maybe Izzy's odd feeling was because she had heard it in her sleep?

She didn't know what to do. She didn't know if she was being hysterical, or if something was genuinely wrong. She wondered if she should call the police, and then she wondered what she could possibly tell them.

"I feel funny and I can't get hold of my roommate," she said to herself, and then pulled a face. They would look at her like she was stupid. They would joke about her being an emotional woman.

She called Cassie for a second time, and left a voice message: "Cassie, can you call me, please? I am worried and can't get hold of you."

As soon as she hung up there was a knock at the door, a jaunty *tap-tap-tap-tap*. She opened the door and saw two men there, an odd couple if she ever saw one. The man closest to her was Asian, short and compact, with high cheekbones and neat hair. He was handsome, Izzy noted. Behind him stood a giant, a man well over six feet tall and broad across the chest like some sort of cartoon superhero. He was white, with a frizz of curly brown hair on his head and a placid, watchful gaze. Both men were dressed in dark suits and raincoats, but the giant's tie was loose, his suit disheveled.

"Ms. Cattaneo?" the Asian man asked, with a smile.

"That's right," Izzy said.

"Do you mind if we come in for a minute and speak to you?"

They were police, Izzy realized.

"Is this about Cassie?" she asked.

The Asian man glanced over his shoulder at the giant and then looked back at her. "I'm afraid so," he said, with a pained expression.

"Oh god," Izzy murmured, hands going up to her hair. "What's happened? Is she all right? Don't tell me she's dead . . . I couldn't . . ."

The man raised a hand to try to calm her. "Better if we . . ." he started, nodding behind Izzy into the apartment.

"Oh god," Izzy said again, turning around and walking back inside. The two men followed her into the living area. The space felt crowded with the three of them, particularly with the giant standing just in front of the door, hands in his pockets.

"Ms. Cattaneo," the Asian man said. "My name is Azaki. The walking wall behind you is Lund. He doesn't say much."

"I don't care what your names are," Izzy said. "What happened to Cassie?"

"Can we ask you a couple of quick questions first?" Azaki asked.

Izzy was conscious of shadows moving and she realized the big man was walking away from the door. He squeezed between her and Azaki and went over to the window to peer out at the day.

"What questions?" Izzy asked impatiently.

"When did you last see Cassie? Had she reported any new friends or strange encounters recently?"

"Last night," she said, with more certainty than she felt. "I saw her last night. And then when I woke up this morning she was gone. And . . ."

"And what?" Azaki prompted.

"Shouldn't you be taking notes or something?" Izzy asked.

Azaki tapped a forefinger to his temple. "It's all up here. Don't worry, Ms. Cattaneo, this is not a formal interview. What were you going to say?"

"And I've just felt strange ever since I woke up, like something is wrong but I can't place it."

"Is it unusual for Cassie to not be home in the morning?" Azaki asked.

"Yes," Izzy said. "She normally works afternoons and evenings. She's a night owl. She's up late and sleeps late into the morning. She should have still been in bed."

"I see," Azaki said. He glanced at the other man, but the giant gave no response. "One other question, Ms. Cattaneo," Azaki continued. "Has Cassie brought home any new books recently? Or has she spoken about finding any interesting books?"

"Books?" Izzy asked, thoroughly confused. "Why the hell are you asking me about books?"

"Just answer the question, please," Azaki pressed.

Izzy thought about it briefly. "I don't know," she said. "Cassie works in a bookstore and she's always reading. She's always got new books. It's not something we talk about."

"She works in a bookstore?" Azaki said, as if this was interesting.

"Wait a minute," Izzy said. "I thought you were here to tell me something about Cassie. I thought she was in the hospital or dead or something?"

"Oh, we have no idea," Azaki said.

Izzy felt a jolt as a connection was made, a deduction drawn. "You're not the police," she stated, suddenly alert.

Azaki frowned. "Oh yes, we are, I'm sorry." He smiled apologetically and pushed both hands into his pockets as if searching for something, then one hand emerged with a badge that he held out toward her. She leaned in and read it.

"'Detective Azaki,'" she said.

"That's right," he said, putting the badge away again.

"Why are you asking about Cassie?" Izzy glanced over to the big man at the window. The man watched her, but there was no obvious threat in his expression.

"We are very keen to find her," Azaki explained. "We believe she may be in some danger because of a valuable item she has recently taken possession of. Does she have anything valuable, do you know?"

"Valuable?" Izzy said. "Cassie? I think you are mistaken. The only thing Cassie has is books and a bad fashion sense."

The giant coughed a laugh, a single *huh* that punched the air, and when Izzy glanced at him a smile was fading from his face. Azaki frowned in annoyance at the interruption.

"You said she was in danger," Izzy said. "What danger?"

"We think you might also be in some danger, Ms. Cattaneo," Azaki continued, sounding concerned.

Izzy felt her hand going to her chest in shock. "Why would I be in danger? I haven't done anything. What is it you're not telling me? Where is Cassie?"

"We really don't know," Azaki said sympathetically. He studied her for a moment, as if working something out. "Maybe it would be better if you came down to the station with us, just for a few hours. Just until we can find Cassie."

"The station?" Izzy said. "Are you arresting me?"

"No, not at all. Just for your own protection. I don't want to leave you worried."

"I don't like this," Izzy said. "You can't come in here and tell me I'm in danger."

Another knock sounded from the front door, this one a loud thump rather than the jaunty tapping that Azaki had done. Azaki turned his head toward the sound, and then nodded to himself. Then he smiled at Izzy.

"One second, please," he said. He hesitated a moment, and leaned in close, lowering his voice. "It will all be fine, Izzy," he said. "Just be brave."

As Izzy absorbed the odd message, Azaki gestured to the giant with a jerk of his head and the two of them walked out of the living area into the hall. Izzy wandered over to the window and stared down at the street, trying to create some sense from the crazy morning.

From the hallway she heard the apartment door opening. Then she heard a noise like a gasp or a yelp of surprise. And then there were two muffled thumps, and then two larger thuds, the sound of people hitting the floor, and Izzy froze.

The apartment door banged shut, and a moment later a third man appeared in the doorway, some sort of gun with a long tube on the muzzle in one hand and a bag down at his side in the other. He was a tall, bald man with round glasses. For some reason the very sight of him chilled Izzy to the bone.

"Hello again," he said, smiling at her like they were old friends. He glanced around the room like someone contemplating moving in. "Wow. What a fucking awful place. Is this all you can afford?"

Izzy wanted to say something, a question to help her understand, a scream for help, but she was frozen. She watched as the man slipped the weapon he was holding back into a holster on his hip, the end of the muzzle reaching down his thigh, and then he pulled his overcoat around to hide it.

"You and I are going to have a little conversation," he said, walking to her. He placed a hand on her shoulder and gently encouraged her down onto the couch. She could smell his cologne, a spicy, abrasive scent that was too strong or applied too liberally. "You are going to tell me everything you know."

"About what?" she asked. "Who are you? What did you do to the two detectives?"

He watched her for a moment, a very slight frown creasing his brow, and Izzy had the sense that he was drawing some conclusion.

"Very well," he said. "You know nothing."

He squatted in front of her, his knees popping audibly, and met her gaze. "We shall have to see if we can help you to remember."

He smiled, and it chilled Izzy to the core.

"Oh, don't worry," he said, seeing something of her thoughts in her expression. "It's going to be good. Really good."

Cassie and Joe (2012)

"That's him," Cassie said, speaking to Drummond but looking at her grandfather.

"You should go speak to him," Drummond said, making Cassie look at him. "It's what you wanted."

It *was* what she wanted, she realized. Her grandfather, Joseph Andrews, was studying the menu, as if he weren't just going to order the same thing he always ordered.

"Go on, then," Drummond said, his words touched with impatience.

She hesitated for a few moments more, watching her grandfather as he placed his order with the server. She knew what it would be: cheeseburger, home-style fries, and black coffee. It was what he always ordered at Matt's. Then the server left him, and he was alone. He patted his pockets and then pulled out his phone—an old Nokia, narrow and rectangular with a tiny screen and a small keypad that was revealed by sliding the top part of the phone upward. Cassie remembered how much she had been dazzled by the phone when her grandfather had first brought it home, even though it had already been a few years out of date at that point. It had seemed so futuristic to her, and seeing it now brought that memory back to life for her, her excitement bubbling in her stomach like a shaken soda bottle. Her grandfather placed the phone on the table next to him. From a different pocket he pulled out a battered old Stephen King paperback and settled back into his chair to read.

Cassie got up and walked across the room, her stomach spinning like a washing machine. She sat down opposite her grandfather without saying anything. He looked up from his novel and a series of expressions flitted across his face: the spark of recognition turning to confusion, a quick widening of the eyes in concern. Then he just stared, blinking once, his eyes running up and down over Cassie's face, seeing something familiar that looked different.

The server brought a coffee and left again, but Cassie's grandfather didn't even notice.

"Hi, Gramps," she said, trying to smile, trying not to cry.

He gazed back at her with an expression she had never seen before, the innocent, astonished look of a young boy on the face of a middle-aged man.

"Cassie?" he said, a hesitant whisper.

She nodded once.

"But, you look . . ."

"I look older," she said. "That's because I am."

He shook his head slowly, putting his book down on the table and sitting forward in his seat to study her.

He was a handsome man, Cassie saw now, something she had never noticed before. He was weathered from work and life, but he was handsome, with a square jaw and a full head of hair and dark blue eyes with crinkles at the corners. He had a broad chest and strong arms that had been developed over many years of physical labor. His hands were calloused and rough, with huge knuckles like bolts on screws, but they were hands that were capable of delicate work and tenderness. A craftsman's hands.

"When I was six," Cassie said, as she slipped her left arm out of her coat, "I fell and cut a wedge out of the skin by my collarbone." Her grandfather watched her, his expression blank and his mouth slightly open. She pulled down her sweater and T-shirt to show the scar that was still clearly visible by the strap of her bra. It had a round head with a tail fanning out, and to Cassie it always looked like a comet.

Cassie waited while her grandpa studied the scar. Then his eyes flicked to hers. He nodded once and Cassie slipped her arm back into her coat.

"One cheeseburger, home fries," the server announced, placing the food down. "You want anything, honey?"

"No thanks," Cassie said, without breaking eye contact with her grandpa. The server left them again and after a moment her grandpa seemed to remember where he was. He turned his eyes down to the food in front of him. He reached for his coffee and held it but didn't drink it.

"You should be camping with Jessica and her parents," he said.

"I am," Cassie said. "The me in this time. The younger me."

Her grandpa absorbed her answer, then sipped his coffee, frowning. "What is going on?"

"I don't know how to explain without sounding crazy," Cassie said, wrestling now with all the impossible and important things she had to say. Her grandfather was staring at her, as if he couldn't see her enough, as if there was not enough space in his eyes for all the seeing he needed to do.

"Just tell me," he said.

In those three words he reminded Cassie of everything he was and everything she loved. He was a man who listened and absorbed, a man who never made a quick judgment.

"I am from the future," Cassie said, feeling slightly embarrassed to even use those words. "It doesn't matter how or why, but I came back here to see you."

"I see," he said, watching her.

"Don't you want to eat your burger?"

"No," he said. "Not right now."

"Okay."

They sat in silence for a moment, looking at each other as the diners clattered and chatted around them.

"Do you believe me?" she asked. "About what I said?"

"I believe you are my granddaughter," he said, speaking slowly, considering his words. "And I believe you are older than the Cassie I said goodbye to yesterday morning. You are a woman. I can see that."

Cassie nodded. Her emotions were a waterfall within her, a vast and thundering waterfall that drowned out everything else, but her face revealed nothing.

"So?" Cassie said.

"What you say is as good an explanation as any," he said. "I can't think of anything better. Unless I am hallucinating. Unless you are not real."

Cassie reached out and put a hand on his. "Can you feel me?"

He nodded.

"I'm here."

She felt herself crumple in the center like she was made of paper. She felt herself falling into her core, all of the walls and defenses she had built up over the decade collapsing around her because he was here, and he was alive. Tears welled in her eyes no matter how much she willed them away.

"What is it, Cassidy?" her grandfather asked.

"Cassidy," she said, sniffing. "Nobody calls me that."

He was looking at her strangely now, the slight narrowing of his eyes like when he was doing calculations for some complex piece of woodwork.

"Why are you here?" he asked. "I can't imagine it was easy for you to get here, so why did you come here? Are burgers banned in the future or something?"

She laughed, a single, joyous bark, and then wiped her eyes on her sleeve, all the while conscious of how he was watching her.

"No," she said. "You can still get burgers. I just . . . I just wanted to see you, Gramps."

He nodded slowly and then looked down into his coffee. He lifted the mug and took a sip. "I'm guessing you can't see me in the future, then."

Cassie met his eyes, understanding the question, and then simply shook her head. He nodded, accepting her answer and all that it implied, and his eyes drifted away from her.

"Right," he said.

When he looked at her again, blue eyes running over her face, over her clothes, she could almost see his train of thought: *How old are you? How long do I have?*

"I wanted to tell you some things," she said. "Oh god, I've thought about this for so long, what I would say if I ever saw you again. All things I never got to say."

Her gramps spread his hands out. "I'm here, Cassidy. Just talk to me."

"I just wanted to thank you," she said after a moment, feeling the tears return to her eyes, the burning at the back of her throat. "You gave me so much, you gave me everything. You were the best dad I could have had. The best parents. And I'm sorry I never got to tell you."

He pursed his lips slightly, avoiding her eyes, awkward in the face of her open emotion. "I know, Cassidy," he mumbled. "I know all of that."

"I traveled!" she said, suddenly seized with the subject. "All over Europe!"

His eyes sparkled with interest, sunlight on water. "Yeah, where'd you go?"

"All over!" she said, bubbling with enthusiasm. "France and Italy and Great Britain. I saw all the museums and the works of art and the old buildings."

He shook his head slowly. Then, almost a whisper: "You are a beautiful woman."

"Gramps," she muttered, feeling uncomfortable herself now.

"I always knew you would be," he continued. "You look like your grandmother. I see a bit of your mother too, in your eyes."

Cassie said nothing to that, realizing that this was his moment to enjoy, his future he was staring at.

"I work in a bookstore," she said.

"Well, that doesn't surprise me. You love your books."

"I got it from you," she said. "Every night, after work, a book until bedtime."

"Yeah," he agreed.

She watched him, remembering features of his face she had forgotten—the crinkle of his eyes, the color of his hair—but she saw that he was becoming uncomfortable under her gaze. He glanced down at his food growing cold in front of him.

"Eat," she encouraged. "I'm so sorry, I'm interrupting your lunch break."

He gave her a disapproving look, but he lifted his burger and took a bite and started to chew, watching her all the while.

"I should tell you . . ." she said, the words coming out before she had thought about them, even though she knew this was always the point of the conversation. *If I can tell him about his illness, maybe he won't die.* But she hesitated, unsure how to raise it.

He frowned as he chewed. Cassie glanced over her shoulder to where Drummond sat in the booth, watching them without expression. He hadn't told her not to. He hadn't told her anything bad would happen. If anything he had encouraged her.

"Who's that?" her gramps asked, seeing the look.

"Nobody."

"Is that your boyfriend?"

"God, no!" she said, horrified. "Give me some credit."

"All right," he said, grinning and shrugging apologetically at the same time. "I don't know what passes for handsome."

She put a hand on his arm again, leaning into the table. "I need to tell you about what happens."

"What happens to what?" he asked.

"To you," she started, but he immediately shut her down.

"No," he said, his hand making a single, decisive swipe to the side.

"But—"

"No, Cassidy," he said, his voice firm. "I don't know where you've come from or what you know, I don't even know if I have a brain tumor or something and I'm sitting here talking to myself. But I know I am not supposed to know about the future. What you want to tell me, what I think you want to tell me, nobody is supposed to know that."

"But it might—"

"No," he said fiercely, and she felt like she was eight again when he caught her drawing on the new wallpaper with crayons. She hadn't liked the color of the wallpaper, so she'd tried to change it. She had never seen him so angry. At the time she hadn't understood how much money he had spent to make her room pretty for her, and that he hadn't really been angry, he'd been hurt that she hadn't liked it.

"I just . . ." she started, but everything she wanted to say, every justification felt weak. She was aware that tears were running down her cheeks, big fat bulbous drops that fell to her lap. "It was so hard. For you. And for me. And after . . ." She looked away, wiping her cheeks with the heel of her hand. "I miss you every day, all the time. You were all I had for all my life and then you were gone."

It was coming now, that waterfall of emotions bursting free.

"It's been so hard. It's a wound that won't heal and I spend my life alone, reading my books and staying in. Maybe if I can tell you things, maybe it will all be different and I can still be at home, reading in the workshop while you work."

The look he gave her was one of concern, but it was tinged with disappointment, she saw, and she heard how pathetic her own words sounded.

"Cassidy," he said. "What you are talking about, that's just life, no two ways about it, and you just need to get on with things."

Her brow creased in frustration. He didn't understand.

"You don't have a right to be happy, Cassidy. Look at me, look at my life. I lost my wife and my daughter, I work every day to put food on the table and just about manage to keep my head above water. But it's never easy. There've been times when I went hungry, when I couldn't pay the bills. Happiness is not something you sit and wait for. You have to choose it and pursue it in spite of everything else. It's not going to be given to you. And that stuff you are talking about, missing the house, missing me. That's just growing older. You think I don't miss your grandmother? I do. Every day, in every breath, every moment we would have shared together. But you have to let things go or it will eat you up. Let things pass."

"I don't want to," she said through her tears.

"Nobody does. But you have to."

It was his turn to reach across and hold her. His hand felt massive on top of hers, a huge, heavy shell.

"Even if you tell me whatever you want to tell me, even if it changes the future, you still have to live, Cassidy. You can't hide from the knocks and scrapes of life forever. I know you like to hide in books, and maybe that's my fault, because I like having you around all the time." He sighed quietly. "Maybe I should start making you go out and make more friends."

"No," she said, because it was the last thing she wanted.

"You hide away from reality. But that's not living. You know it."

She nodded even though she hated everything he was saying.

"So what now?" he asked a few moments later.

"I don't know," she admitted. She felt deflated. What had she been looking for when she had come to meet him? Had it made things better, or just made them worse? "I suppose I need to go."

Her grandpa considered that. "Is this . . . is this something you can do more than once?"

"I don't know," she admitted. "I don't know much. Sorry, it's really hard to explain. But . . . But I'd like to come back. I'd like to see you again if you don't mind."

He smiled, and it was like the first light of dawn after a bad night. "Why would I mind? Come again, anytime you want."

"It's good to see you," she said.

They stared at each other awkwardly. Then she asked, "Can I have a hug?"

He seemed surprised by the question.

"Please?" she asked.

"Of course, Cassidy. Of course."

They stood up at the same time and stepped around the table to hug. It was awkward at first, but turned into something more natural, more familiar.

"I miss you," she said into his shoulder.

"I know," he answered against her ear.

They separated and he held her at arm's length, running his eyes over her, a slight smile on his lips. "This is so unbelievable," he said, speaking more to himself than to Cassie.

He let her go, but the conversation wasn't over. "What's the future like?" he asked, a smile tugging the corner of his mouth.

She shrugged, unsure how to answer. "It's not so different from now," she said. "Just . . . you're not there."

His smile faltered.

"I'm sorry," she said, hating that she might have hurt him. "I should go," she added, although she didn't want to.

"I need to go as well," he said, suddenly distracted. He glanced at the table and picked up his phone and the Stephen King book. He pulled out some bills and left them by the remains of his burger and then held her gaze for a moment longer. "Be happy, Cassidy, please, for me?"

He held her shoulder briefly and she nodded.

"Maybe I'll see you again someday," he said. Then he walked away, through the door and into the rain.

Cassie walked to the window and watched as he hurried through the pouring rain and clambered into his truck. He sat there for a few moments, just staring straight ahead, not moving. He looked like a man in shock. Then he shook his head once, started the engine, and reversed out of the parking spot. He turned the wheel and pulled out onto the road, his taillights bright sparks of red disappearing into the gray.

Once he was gone, Cassie's emotions washed over her. She yanked open the door and ran out into the day. She stood in the parking lot, letting the rain pour down upon her, soaking her hair to her scalp, running down her back. When she looked up the sky was low and dark gray, a serious, heavy kind of sky.

"What are you doing?" Drummond demanded, emerging from the diner and narrowing his eyes to peer through the rain. "It's pouring down."

She ignored him. She walked across the parking lot toward the tree line without any idea where she was going or why, but she stopped before she got far. She dropped to her knees, splashing puddle water up over her jeans. She screamed and yelled into the gray day, distraught and destroyed at the loss of her grandfather again and needing to let it all out. The rain continued to beat down on her, like the world was crying with her.

What Izzy Forgot

Izzy watched from the couch as the man walked to the window and peered out at the street below. She glanced briefly to the door and the hall beyond.

"You won't make it," the man said, without looking at her.

She hadn't been thinking about running. She had been looking to see what had happened to the two detectives.

"Did you kill them?" she asked, astonished at how calm the words sounded when they came from her mouth.

"Yes," the man said, facing her. "I shot them both in the brain."

His answer made Izzy's mind stumble momentarily. It was an answer that was simply too massive to come to terms with.

"Who are you?" she asked.

"My name is Dr. Hugo Barbary," he said. "We met last night."

Izzy had no memory of the previous evening or of meeting this man. "What sort of doctor are you?" she asked, not because she was interested, but because she was trying to keep him talking.

"Oh, I am not a real doctor," he said. "I mean, I did go to medical school. But it was so boring that I didn't finish. I just call myself 'doctor.' But I was always interested in what makes people what they are. I always thought it was maybe hidden away among all the red wet stuff inside us." He patted his stomach.

He had an accent, Izzy realized, an unusual accent. He spoke English like a native, but his vowels were wrong.

"Is this about Cassie?" Izzy asked.

The man raised his head slightly, as if curious about why Izzy had asked that question.

"My roommate," Izzy said.

"What about her?" the man asked.

"She's not here. I don't know where she is," Izzy said. She didn't know why she was telling him these things.

"I want to know where the Book of Doors is," the man replied.

"The what?"

The man walked over, taking his time. "I want to know where the Book of Doors is," he repeated. He stood in front of Izzy, towering over where she sat on the couch.

"I have no idea what you are talking about," she said. The panic was starting to bubble, like a pot heating on the stove. She tried to remain calm, but she had no idea who the man was or what he would do. "Please don't kill me," she said, hating how pathetic she sounded.

"I don't want to kill you," Barbary said. "I mean, I might enjoy it. But it's probably not in my interests. You are an asset to me. When I find your roommate, she will want you to be alive, and that is to my advantage. If you are dead, I lose that."

Izzy absorbed his words, grasping for hope. Her heart was punching her rib cage like a boxer. A distant part of her mind reminded her of the nerves she had always felt before big auditions, how she had been able to suppress those, to give nothing away to anyone she engaged with. She knew she had to use that skill now, to show nothing of what she was feeling inside.

"But it is less important to me if you are whole or not," the man added. "If you lose a finger, or a limb, or your eyes . . ." He gestured vaguely at her body parts as he mentioned them. "So it is in *your* interest to keep me happy."

His words made her want to vomit, and her insides clenched suddenly.

"I don't know anything," Izzy said, clasping her hands together in her lap. "I promise."

The man nodded slowly. "I believe you," he said. "It's what you've forgotten that I am interested in."

"I don't understand," Izzy said, trying to smile. "I want to help you. I don't want to die, but I can't tell you what I don't know."

The man sighed. He seemed mildly annoyed, like a man who'd walked to a shop only to find the thing he wanted was out of stock. "I need to know what you have forgotten and if you can't remember, then I am going to help you."

"How can I remember what I can't remember?" she asked, panicking now. "I can't remember!"

The man put his bag on the floor and opened it. He reached in and pulled out a small notebook. The cover was a crash of purple and green shapes, like someone had tried to paint a migraine.

"This might help," he said.

"What's this?" she asked.

"Take it," he said, holding it out to her.

She looked at the book, up to the man's expressionless face, back to the book again.

"What is it?" she asked, more warily.

"Take it in your hands," the man instructed, speaking slowly like he was trying to make a stupid person understand something simple. He pulled back his overcoat to reveal the gun in its holster. "Or I will put a bullet in one of your joints."

Izzy took the book and as soon as she did, she felt her knuckles twinge, a twinge that didn't stop. It sustained and maintained, a low-volume screech grinding in her fingers. "Ow!" she exclaimed, looking down at the book. What she saw didn't make sense. The book, or the air around it, seemed to be pulsing, with deep red and green and purple colors emanating from between her hands. It made Izzy think of some sort of bizarre creature from deep in the ocean, flickering colorfully as it pushed itself through dark water. That thought was chased away as she realized the book seemed to be growing heavier and hotter, as the pain pulsed within her in time with the colors she was seeing. "This is the Book of Pain," the man said. "You can't drop it until I allow it. The pain you are feeling in your hand will steadily spread until it is in all parts of your body . . ."

As the man said this Izzy realized the pain was dragging itself up her forearm, like rusty nails being scraped through her veins. "Ow!" she said again, her body trying to flinch away from the book. She was an animal in a trap, and she felt tears bubbling in her eyes. "Make it stop!" she begged. The colors seemed to be pulsing more quickly now.

"Once it is in all parts of your body," the man continued, his tone completely indifferent to Izzy's pain, "then it will gradually grow worse and worse until all you are is pain. You will be nothing but a bag of torment. And then your heart will give out."

Izzy's shoulder was a ball of spikes, dry and crunchy, rotating against the socket. The book in her hands was so hot and heavy, the strange colors screaming in the air and flickering rapidly on her face.

"Nobody can hold the Book of Pain for long," the man said, the very sound of his voice agony in Izzy's ears. He squatted in front of her to watch her face, interested in what was happening.

The pain reached Izzy's neck and she screamed then, a howl that sounded very far away to her shocked mind. She knew that the man was speaking but she couldn't understand the words anymore. Tortuous fingers were creeping across her breasts and back, hot pokers burning through her skin. She rocked on the couch. Her bladder gave out and she urinated on herself but was not aware of it. The world was receding under the onslaught of pain.

"Pieces of your memory are sealed off from you," the man was saying, meaningless words, a foreign language in Izzy's world of torment. "The torture will open the doors, will reset your mind. I believe this to be true. You will remember, or you will endure until you die."

She screamed silently, her mouth and eyes stretched wide, unable to give voice to her misery. Her throat started to hitch as pain stretched into her arms, down to her hips. She saw no end, she saw no hope. She was incapable of conscious thought. She was desolate.

And then it stopped. The pain was gone in an instant and Izzy was lying on the couch in her own urine, blinking, her mind stuttering, and every part of her was gloriously free of pain. In that instant she had never been happier, never before filled with such joy.

"Anything?"

The man's voice shocked her, and she jerked away from it. He was squatting next to her, his dark eyes inspecting her through the lenses of his glasses, the book in his hands. She pushed herself up and away, as far away from the book as she could get.

"Do you remember anything?" the man demanded. "Has the pain shaken anything free in your little brain?"

Izzy tried to get away. She jumped up, but not thinking properly she ran toward the window, only realizing when she stood there that she couldn't go anywhere. She turned and the man was right behind her, crowding her, too close for her to pass safely. But she had to try . . . anything better than the pain . . .

"Do you remember, woman?" the man demanded again, angry now.

Her eyes were stuck on the book, the horrible purple and green thing that was the end of the world. She couldn't think clearly; all she could see was the book, all she could remember was the agony.

"Anything?" the man pressed, his voice rising. "Or do you need another round to shake up your tiny brain?"

"No!" she shouted.

She jerked to her left, trying to dart past the man, but he anticipated it and moved in that direction. She tried to course correct and twist in the opposite direction, but he was there too, and there was nowhere to go. She wanted to scream, she wanted to cry, but she was trapped.

"Hey!"

A voice erupted into Izzy's awareness, and Barbary twisted around in surprise just in time to meet a massive fist hurtling through the air toward him. Barbary was lifted off his feet, his head snapping sideways before his feet knew that he was moving, and he crashed into the TV unit and collapsed in a lump on the floor, facedown and his arms behind him.

Izzy looked at the giant, the man who had come with the Japanese man. There was blood running down one side of his face from a wound by his temple. He gazed at Izzy for a moment, breathing heavily. Then he glanced at Dr. Barbary, as if waiting to see if he would move, but the bald man lay still. The giant reached up and touched his hand to his own face. He winced slightly and then looked at the blood on his fingers.

"You are in danger," the giant said, his voice deep and round. To

Izzy his voice was like a warm embrace. "We are not police. That was a lie. But you are in danger here. Other people will come." He pointed to the man on the floor. "If he is not dead, he will keep coming for you."

"I don't know what's going on!" she wailed.

The giant nodded once, accepting that. "I am leaving now," he said. "The man I was with is dead."

Izzy nodded, as if this all made sense.

The giant seemed to hesitate, but then he said, "If you want to come with me, I will protect you. There's someone I can take you to who will keep you safe."

Izzy blinked, hearing the words but not really digesting them. Her eyes turned to the shape on the floor, to the purple and green book that had skidded away toward the kitchen when the man had been hit.

"Okay," she said, not thinking about it, just wanting to be protected.

The giant nodded and sighed, a sound of tiredness rather than annoyance. "Go and wash and change," he said. "Then pack a bag like you're not going to come back. And do it quickly before someone else appears and tries to kill us."

Old Friends in Bryant Park (2012)

They sat beneath the trees in silence, the rain pounding the earth and blurring the neon sign in the window of Matt's All-American Burgers.

"Shit," Drummond said.

She looked at him, her cheeks still damp from her tears, her body exhausted from her sobs. "What?"

"We ran out without paying," he said.

She watched him in surprise for a moment, and then a laugh burst from her mouth, a mixture of disbelief and amusement. "Are you serious?"

"What?" he asked.

She shook her head. "You're worried about a few bucks for some lunch? And me and Izzy were scared you were dangerous."

"I'm not a thief," he explained.

"You can still go back and pay," she said, wiping her cheeks with the back of her hand.

"Don't think my card from the future will work," he reflected glumly. "Probably should have thought about that before we ordered." He gave her a sidelong look. "How are you?"

"I'm fine," she said, warmed by his question, by his concern. "I mean I'm not. But I will be. This was the worst thing ever but . . . but it was also the best. It was life-changing." She gestured at the diner, shaking her head. "I spoke to my grandfather. I could speak to him again if I wanted, as many times as I want."

"If you have the book," Drummond said, his voice quiet.

"How could you destroy it?" Cassie pleaded. "There must be other ways to protect the books in your library. You want to destroy this book to protect other books—it doesn't make sense!"

Drummond thought for a while, his narrowed gaze peering through the rain. Then he asked, "Can I show you something? Can you use the book and take us somewhere else?"

"Why?" she asked.

"I said I'd show you what the Book of Doors could do, which I've done. And then I said I'd show you why I had to hide the library. I said I'd show you the threat. If you're willing, I can show you."

She held his gaze for a moment, and then nodded once.

IT WAS A HOT NEW York summer, the same year that Cassie met her grandfather, but a few months earlier. Cassie and Drummond were sitting at one of the tables in Bryant Park, shaded by the trees and facing the back of the New York Public Library. The heat was helping dry them off after the rain in Oregon. The heat felt good to Cassie. Like a warm bed on a cold day.

It was lunchtime and the office workers from nearby buildings were out drinking coffees and eating sandwiches, sunbathing on the grass. For Cassie everything she saw was familiar and forgotten—a place she knew well but dressed as it had been a decade before. The clothes were different, as were the shapes of the passing vehicles, and even the posters and advertisements, shouting about long-forgotten television shows and movies.

"So why are we here?" Cassie asked.

"I just want to see my friends again," Drummond said, sounding distracted. He smiled a sad sort of smile. "You saw your grandfather. I want to see my friends."

They sat in silence, because Cassie didn't think Drummond wanted to talk, not yet, and she was content to sit and reflect on the meeting with her grandfather. Already it was starting to feel intangible and dreamlike, as if it hadn't really happened. She wondered what he was doing now, how he was dealing with having met an older version of his granddaughter. And she wondered now about all those times she had been with him as the younger Cassie, all those days after that meeting in the diner. Had he looked at her differently? Had he spoken to her differently, in the knowledge of the woman she would become? She wished she had been more attentive as a teenager, maybe she would have seen something.

"There they are," Drummond said, flicking his head toward the entrance to the park from Forty-Second Street. Cassie saw two women walking toward a table in the sunlight and sitting down together. One of the women was Asian, short and stocky, and dressed in a bright red summer dress and white running shoes. She was listening intently to her companion, a tall woman with light brown skin and short white hair. She wore a pastel blue suit and blouse, with a multicolored scarf hanging around her neck and thick-framed glasses on her face. She was smiling as she was talking, like she was recounting some funny story.

"Who are they?" Cassie asked.

"That's Lily and Yasmin," Drummond said. "Lily is from Hong Kong. *Was*. Was from Hong Kong." He frowned as he kicked himself for his own mistake. "She ran a small luxury hotel on Hong Kong Island. Yasmin was Egyptian. She was a historian."

"So who are they? Are they book hunters?"

"No," Drummond said. "Not book hunters. Book hunters pursue books for profit, or to use the books for their own ends. But Lily and Yasmin, they were like me. Interested in the books, but wary of them."

"Wary how?"

"Like we had to be careful with them, just like any other precious item. Lily had two books herself. And Yasmin had three. And there, that man . . ." Drummond pointed to the other side of the park where a tall, skinny man with a lined face and spiky dark hair was walking. "That is Wagner, from Germany, the man I told you about earlier. He's a physicist."

"Was," Cassie said.

Drummond looked at her sharply. "That's right, he *was* a physicist."

"Sorry, I didn't mean it like that," Cassie said, regretting her words. "I wasn't trying to hurt you."

"I know," Drummond said, mustering a smile that showed he meant it.

Wagner was dressed in a light summer shirt open at the neck and light green corduroy trousers. He was carrying a backpack over one shoulder. "He had two books as well," Drummond continued.

The man joined the two women at the table. There were smiles and hugs and laughter and Cassie could see that these people were friends, that there was real affection there.

"Wagner inherited his books from his family," Drummond said, watching the group. "Just as I did. That's how I met them. At one time or another they had all come to me with questions about books, and I had spoken to them about some of the books in the Fox Library. We ended up forming a small group of like-minded people. And at least once a year, we would all meet to catch up, to discuss the world of special books, recent discoveries. All that sort of stuff."

"What, like a magic convention?" Cassie smirked.

Drummond acknowledged the joke with a glance. "Kind of," he admitted. "We'd spend hours talking about the books, theorizing about what the books could do."

"Like time travel," Cassie said.

"Right," Drummond agreed. "We'd have long debates about where the books came from, what the source of the magic was."

Cassie watched the group as Drummond spoke. The man, Wagner, was now listening to Yasmin's story, and after a moment both he and Lily laughed at whatever the punch line was, exchanging a glance with each other. They were happy, enjoying catching up like old friends after a long time.

"This is where it gets uncomfortable," Drummond murmured. "Uncomfortable and weird."

At the far end of the park, toward the back of the Public Library, Cassie saw Drummond, a younger Drummond, strolling toward the table. He was less gaunt than the man next to her, his body looked stronger and more filled out, and his hair was brown, with no strands of gray.

He was handsome, Cassie realized, a handsomeness that now seemed to appear only when Drummond smiled. Whatever had happened to him in the intervening decade had hidden away his natural good looks.

"There I come," he muttered. "God, is that what I look like when I am walking?"

"You look fine," Cassie said, and he threw a puzzled glance at her.

"Not like me, all lanky and clumsy."

"You look fine too," he murmured distractedly, and Cassie's cheeks warmed as if she was blushing. But Drummond wasn't looking at her, he was paying attention to what was happening in his past.

The three people at the table spotted the younger Drummond as he approached. Chairs were pushed back, and the group stood up to greet him with hugs and fond words before they sat down once again. They chatted together, laughing and smiling.

"I wanted to see this again," Drummond murmured. "For real. I have my memories, but reality is always better. I wanted to see us happy again."

"I get it," Cassie said.

After a few minutes the group of friends rose together and walked along the edge of the park toward where Cassie and Drummond were sitting. The pair ducked their heads slightly as the group passed, but none of them looked their way, caught up in their conversations.

"It was a great afternoon," Drummond said, following the group with his eyes as they headed out of the park at the southeast exit. "We walked for a while, just chatting, catching up. Wagner was talking about moving to a new university in the Netherlands. Lily was talking about politics and China and Hong Kong and what the future looked like. Yasmin was talking about retiring from her work. And her daughters, one of her daughters was getting married, I think. It was just normal chat."

"It sounds nice," Cassie said.

"It was," Drummond agreed. "It was and I miss it. I miss my friends."

"I miss my grandfather," Cassie replied, and they held each other's gaze for a moment, taking comfort in their shared sense of loss. Then Drummond turned his eyes back to his friends.

"We went for dinner, a restaurant down in SoHo. We had a private room at the back. We ate and we talked, and we told each other stories about books we'd learned of. We gossiped about book hunters, and the Bookseller . . ."

"The Bookseller?"

Drummond waved his hand as if the Bookseller was a distraction. "Lottie," he said. "Down in New Orleans. She sells books for those book hunters who are in the game for the profit. Kind of a middleman. She auctions them off. Makes a fortune off it. It was a long-running sore. It's like those people who trade on the black market in priceless artifacts. You ask any archaeologist, and they'll have strong views on it. So we bitched about her for a while."

Cassie waited, sensing the end of the story was coming.

"It was late when we left the restaurant, and we walked back north together, heading to our hotels. We were going to meet again the following day and we were discussing that, what we would do, where we would go. And then . . . and then we got to Washington Square Park. It was quiet, and the day had turned strangely cold. Not like now." Drummond gestured to the blue sky above them. "I remember a mist suddenly coming down, almost freak weather. And then a woman appeared across the park."

"What woman?" Cassie asked.

"I don't know her name," Drummond admitted. "I just call her 'the woman.' I had never seen her before this day, I had no idea who she was. I still don't. But she knew who we were, and this day was the day she made herself known to us."

"How?" Cassie asked.

Drummond didn't answer. Cassie wasn't sure if he hadn't heard, or if he didn't want to say any more.

"How?" she asked again, placing a hand on Drummond's arm to get his attention.

"They all die today," he said, his face serious. "Wagner, Lily, and Yasmin. The woman kills them. I was the only one who survived, and she's been hunting me ever since."

Cassie's eyes widened in shock. "Why?"

"Because she wants the Fox Library," he said. "This is why I hid it in the shadows. After this day, after I saw the woman for the first time. It was . . ." He seemed to struggle to find the right word. "Devastating," he said after a moment. "Awful."

"What . . . ?" Cassie hesitated, wanting to know more, but not wanting to know. "What did she do?"

"I can show you, if you want," Drummond replied, his eyes darkening. "If you really want to know why I have been running for ten years, why the Fox Library is in the shadows, why we must keep the Book of Doors from her, I can show you."

"How?"

Drummond pulled a book out of his pocket. "The Book of Memories, Cassie," he said, holding it out to her. "I can show you my memories of this day." Cassie stared at the offered book for a long time, and it felt as if the whole world receded into the background. She knew Drummond wanted her to see; that was why they were there. She knew it would be awful, but a part of her wanted to share Drummond's burden, to help him not be alone.

She reached out and held the book and suddenly Bryant Park was gone, and Cassie was looking out of another person's eyes.

Izzy and Lund

"I remember it, but I don't," Izzy said, watching the footage of Cassie at the door in their apartment with the Venice street beyond her. She had found it when checking her phone for her movements for the last day or two. "It's like a dream, you know? When you remember it, but it doesn't seem real?" She shook her head once, watching until the footage was cut off with the sound of her own voice. She pressed Play again and watched it once more. It was hypnotic. "How does it work?" she asked. "Is it like science or magic?"

Receiving no answer to her question she lifted her eyes. Lund sat across the table from her, a bowl of chicken noodle soup in front of him, the spoon on its journey to his mouth. He held half a bread roll in his other hand. It looked tiny.

"Will it come back to me? Will I remember it all?" Izzy asked.

Lund swallowed the soup and his eyes flicked up to Izzy's, then down to the bowl again. "Don't know," he said.

"I mean, I think I remember most of it," Izzy continued. "Whatever that man did, all that pain . . ." She waited while a shudder vibrated through her. "It shook some things loose. I know what happened. But I don't remember *experiencing* it. If that makes sense?" She stared at her reflection in the window. She knew she was prattling. She was nervous, in shock maybe, and she couldn't stop herself. Outside it was late morning, the street throbbing with traffic and people. They were in a diner somewhere in Midtown, a large, spacious place on the corner of a block, a place Lund had picked.

Two hours after they'd arrived they were sitting in the same booth and Lund was finishing his third meal, the bowl of chicken noodle soup having come after a cheeseburger with fries, then an omelet. Izzy hadn't been hungry, she'd been too shell-shocked to eat, but she'd ordered a grilled cheese sandwich and a coffee anyway. By the time the food had been served the memories were already starting to come back to her. She had let it happen, not forcing it, feeling like this was a process of getting back to normal, of feeling more like herself than she had all day. The process helped distance her from what had happened, from the pain, from the bald man who had tortured her.

"You don't say much, do you?" Izzy said now, reflecting on how few words the giant had spoken since they had left the apartment.

Lund lifted his bowl and slurped the last of his soup. "Nope," he agreed, wiping his mouth with his napkin. He placed the remaining half of his bread roll in his mouth and chewed, watching Izzy without expression.

"You look like a cow," Izzy observed, but there was no cruelty in it.

He smiled around his chewing.

"What are we waiting for?" Izzy asked, suddenly impatient.

"You're not waiting for anything," Lund said. "You can go if you want. I'm not forcing you to wait."

"Okay, what are *you* waiting for?" she asked.

"A message," Lund said. Izzy waited for him to elaborate but it didn't come. She slumped back against the booth, defeated.

"Do you think Cassie is okay?" she asked.

Lund shrugged. "Don't know." He was watching the world outside, the passing traffic, the buildings across the street. He seemed content to just wait.

Izzy checked her phone again. There were no messages, no calls. "I haven't heard from her. It's not like her. What if that man got her?"

"If that man had her, he wouldn't have come for you," Lund observed.

Izzy accepted that reassurance gratefully. "Yes," she said. "You're right. I hope she's all right."

They sat in silence for a few moments, and Izzy remembered something else, another moment uncovered: Ben's Deli, with Cassie, and a man.

"There was a man," she said suddenly. "With Cassie and me . . ."

Lund watched her with interest.

"I think . . . I think he was the one who made me forget," she said.

Lund waited.

"It was an unusual name." She murmured to herself, as she struggled to remember. "Drummond," she said finally, relieved. "He said he was trying to protect me." More of the memories came back to her. She remembered Cassie talking to her, telling her that she would help her remember, and her love for Cassie washed over her like a wave of warm water. "She's okay," she concluded, suddenly feeling brighter. "She's with that man."

Izzy sipped some of her coffee, feeling better with the world now that she knew Cassie would be safe. "So what do I do now?" she wondered. "I can't go back to the apartment. But I'm supposed to be at work today . . . oh god, work. They're going to fire me." She dropped her head into her hands. Everything was madness, it seemed, and she craved boring normality.

"I don't think you need to worry about work anymore," Lund said.

"What?" she asked. "Why not?"

"You're gonna be rich," he said.

"What?"

Lund pulled out his phone and checked it again. He nodded, then typed something and put his phone back into his pocket. "We are waiting for the Bookseller," he said, as if that explained everything. "The man who was with me, Azaki, he had a contact who sells those magic books. I have his phone." Lund patted the phone in his pocket as he spoke. "I told her we have a book and I want to meet her. I am waiting for her to reply."

"I have no idea what you're talking about," Izzy exclaimed.

Lund reached into a different pocket and removed a book. Upon sight of the purple-and-green cover, Izzy flinched, and her stomach somersaulted. She looked away.

"We have this book," he said. "It was lying there on the floor where that man dropped it. So I took it while you were packing. It's not the book Azaki was looking for, but the Bookseller will still be interested in it. We sell it to her, and we'll be rich."

Izzy tried to make sense of his explanation. "Wait, what? I don't understand. Why would I be rich?"

"These books," Lund said. "They are priceless. People pay a lot of money to own them. Like, stupid amounts of money. Why do you think Azaki was looking for it? Just one book can set you up for life. That's what we were looking for." Lund thought for a moment, gazing down at the book. "He probably had other books," he reflected. "Man like that probably had a few of them in his pockets. Maybe I shoulda checked. But being greedy is what gets people killed."

"I'm sorry about your friend," Izzy said, remembering the Japanese man then, realizing she hadn't given him a second thought since stepping over him on the way out of the apartment. "God, he's still lying there in my apartment. What if people think I killed him?"

"He wasn't my friend," Lund said. "Not really. But he was a nice man. Kind."

"Can you put that away?" Izzy said, nodding at the book. "It's making me ill."

Lund returned the book to his pocket and turned his eyes to the world outside, just waiting again.

"So why would I be rich?" Izzy asked once more.

"The book," Lund said. "We sell the book, you get half the money."

"Why would I get half the money?"

Lund blinked, like she was being purposefully obtuse. "The book came from your apartment. It was used on you. It's not the book Azaki was looking for. I was just in the right place at the right time to see it. It's only fair you get some of the money. We'll split it. Half for me for connecting you with the Bookseller. Half to you."

"You're saying all this like it's totally reasonable," Izzy muttered. "Why wouldn't you just take the book and take all the money? It's not like I can stop you, is it? You're the size of a house."

"I said I would look after you," Lund said, as if that explained it.

"Was going to split the money with Azaki anyway. How much money do I need? I don't have expensive tastes."

"How . . ." Izzy hesitated. "How much money are we talking about here?"

"Enough money you won't need to worry about work anymore," Lund said. "Just think of it as compensation for all that has happened to you."

Izzy shook her head in disbelief.

"Besides, I have something else," Lund said, pulling out a different book. This one was black, with a complex design in fine gold lines on the cover. "This was Azaki's," Lund said. "The Book of Illusion. He could make things out of nothing."

Izzy frowned. "What, like the police badge he showed me? That wasn't real, right?"

"Right," Lund said. "He just held the book in one hand in his pocket and imagined it. I saw him create a cathedral in the desert a few days ago. Something like a badge was nothing for him."

Izzy's eyebrows shot up skeptically, but before she could say anything Lund pulled his phone from his pocket once more to read a message.

"Time to meet the Bookseller and make your fortune," he said. "She is in the city."

The Memories of Drummond Fox (2012)

W here did this mist come from?" Drummond asked as they approached Washington Square Park. He was conscious that he was feeling a bit tipsy. But he was in a good mood; it had been so long since he had been away from home, so long since he had been in New York, and so long since he had been with his friends.

"Freak weather," Wagner said, walking alongside him. A few steps behind, Lily and Yasmin were arguing about some obscure point of Egyptian history that Drummond had lost the thread of.

It had been a good meal, a long, luxurious event that none of them had wanted to end. They came together so rarely, but Drummond wondered if the meetings would be as good if they happened more often. Would they enjoy each other as much if they met more frequently? He knew these were the uncertain thoughts of an introvert, and he pushed them away in an attempt to live in the moment.

"What's the plan for tomorrow, gentlemen?" Yasmin asked, appearing between Drummond and Wagner and slipping her arms into theirs as they crossed the street.

They had another full day together, and the plan had been to do some work, whatever that meant. In the past they had discussed the potential to bring all of their books together into the Fox Library, to create a combined collection, perhaps on some new premises. It was something they toyed with from time to time, but Drummond never said much in those conversations, not wanting to give any of his friends the impression that he was trying to take their books for himself.

"I think we should just eat some more," Lily said. "I know all the good places in Chinatown. I can get us a good deal."

Drummond smiled at that. The way he was feeling right then, he'd be happy just to eat and talk and enjoy his friends. It was nice to be distracted from his worries, from the stories he was hearing of the book hunters becoming more violent, more aggressive. He worried about the future, about his friends and the books falling into the wrong hands. Sometimes he just wanted to hide away in his house in the middle of nowhere, close the doors and forget about the world.

"We should probably try to do some work," Wagner suggested, as they crossed the street into Washington Square Park. "But I am thinking of opening a restaurant when I retire, so that counts as work for me."

"Very good point," Lily agreed seriously.

"I am getting too old to eat this much," Yasmin complained. "I am getting fat."

"Please," Lily spluttered. "I could fit three of you in my dress."

The mist seemed thicker in the park, Drummond thought, as if this was where it was coming from. The first itch of unease tickled the back of his mind, but it was a distant thought, softened by the alcohol he had been drinking all evening, and he was distracted by Lily asking him, "Have you heard the rumors about a book that's been discovered in the Australian Outback?"

"No," he answered. "Where? What book?"

Lily shrugged, and then shivered as if suddenly feeling the cold. "I thought it was supposed to be hot in New York this time of year. I should have brought a coat."

"Who's that?" Yasmin asked.

Drummond looked ahead and saw a woman standing motionless in front of them, not too far away. She was a beautiful woman, Drummond saw, young and slim, wearing a white summer dress that was a bright light in the mist. The woman smiled as they all looked at her, bowing her head slightly.

"Hello?" Wagner asked, but Drummond felt that tickle growing stronger.

He knew, he already knew something was wrong.

The woman said nothing, but it seemed to Drummond that the mist was growing thicker around them, swallowing them and separating them from the city outside the park.

"Is she doing this?" Yasmin asked.

"What?" Lily asked.

"The mist," Yasmin said. "Is the woman making this mist?"

"Yes," Drummond said, because he saw it in her face.

"Who are you?" Yasmin asked loudly. "And what do you want?"

The woman in white smiled and everything was silent for a moment in the misty darkness. Drummond heard his own heart pounding in his ears.

And then sudden, shocking action.

The woman moved in a blur and in a second she was next to Lily, to the side of Drummond. Before Lily had a chance to react the woman had pressed a book into her hand and Lily immediately crumpled to the ground with a gut-wrenching wail.

"Lily!" Drummond gasped, shocked at the sound of her pain.

The woman in white looked at Drummond, then to Yasmin next to him and to Wagner just beyond, choosing an adversary. The corners of her mouth twitched up, like she was enjoying herself, and she dropped her head slightly to look at them from beneath her brows. Behind her, on the ground, Lily rolled over and started to beat her own head on the tarmac, violently lurching up and throwing her head down again.

"Lily!" Drummond cried again. His beautiful friend was like something from a nightmare, rivulets of blood running down her face, her teeth bright white and bared in agony.

Drummond took a step sideways, trying to get past the woman to help Lily. The woman ignored him as Wagner and Yasmin spread apart.

"Who are you?" Yasmin demanded. "Do you know what you are doing? Do you know who we are?"

No answer came. As Drummond hurried toward Lily, he saw

Yasmin nod once and close her eyes. This was how she used the Book of Light. A bright yellow glow appeared, framing Yasmin like an outline.

"I will blind you," she said, as much a warning to her friends as a promise to the woman. As Drummond turned away light erupted behind him, like a star exploding. He crouched down by Lily, her face damaged and broken, the book grasped tightly to her chest.

"Let me help," he said, reaching for the book.

Lily rolled away, her eyes wide, white holes in her red face, her mouth a shocked O of horror and pain. She shook her head through her agony.

"Please!" Drummond begged, horrified by his friend's torment and desperate to help.

Lily shook her head once more, a stern message: *You can't help me! Whatever is happening, it will happen to you too.*

Drummond became aware of the light suddenly dimming behind him, and when he looked, he saw the space where Yasmin had been was now a cloud of dense fog and mist, like the weather had suddenly gathered around her and was containing the hot, white light.

"Oh god," he muttered, scampering backward.

A little farther away Wagner and the woman were circling each other, as if in the first few steps of some sort of ballroom dance. Wagner was wary, Drummond could see, undoubtedly shocked by how quickly and how easily the woman had incapacitated two of his friends. The woman appeared relaxed, that same coy smile playing at the edges of her lips, her hands clasped behind her back.

Drummond was paralyzed, wanting to help his friends but not knowing how to. None of them were fighters. They carried only books that could be used to defend themselves if needed, not to attack. Drummond carried only the Book of Shadows, which granted the ability to disappear and slip away.

He looked at Lily again. Her wailing had turned to whimpers, obscured by the blood that was in her mouth, the mess she had made of her own face as she continued to beat it on the ground. If Lily had a book, Drummond didn't know where it was. Yasmin was lost in the storm that engulfed her, the Book of Light struggling with the darkness. He could see her moving, pacing, and trying to escape, but the cloud moved with her, coiling like a snake.

"I don't know what to do, don't know what to do," he gabbled, helpless and terrified. He was a child alone in his bedroom when the monsters came to visit, a child with no parents to chase the monsters away.

Wagner's panicked eyes glanced to Drummond. There was a message there, a bravery: *Protect the books!* And then Wagner turned his gaze back to the woman. Drummond reached for the Book of Shadows, ready to vanish into the night. Before he could do anything, a grunt punched the air. Drummond saw Wagner down on one knee, clutching his chest. The woman stood immediately in front of him, having moved in the blink of an eye, one hand on Wagner's shoulder. Wagner grunted again and gasped, his face agonized, and he collapsed onto his side and jerked a few times as if having a fit.

Then he was still.

"No!" Drummond cried, his stomach vaulting. He turned away and vomited, half-digested dinner splattering onto the concrete, even as Lily's whimpers still sounded in his ears.

When Drummond faced the woman again, she was still standing over Wagner, as if watching as the last of life left him. Blackness fell over Drummond like a cloud, despair and terror gripping him and paralyzing him.

The woman ran her eyes around the park, Lily now lying unconscious but still trembling, the roiling cloud that was swallowing Yasmin's light. Drummond saw an expression cross the woman's face, a flicker of anger and hatred, like a light switched off and on again, and his blood seemed to hesitate in his veins for a second, his heart stuttering and then racing. He had seen evil, he knew, absolute inhuman evil, and it was dressed in the skin of a beautiful woman.

The storm where Yasmin stood collapsed in on itself suddenly, like an explosion in reverse, and there was a scream of agony, a horrifying crunching of bones like a butcher cutting through the breast of some animal with a cleaver, and a squelching of blood and tissue, and then the scream was suddenly cut off. The mist dissipated, releasing Yasmin's battered body. She dropped to the ground as liquid in skin, all of her bones crushed to powder.

"No!" Drummond yelled to the sky, unable to stop himself, seeing what had become of his brilliant, funny friend. This woman, this incarnation of evil, had turned her into meat, had taken away from Yasmin all that had made her special. Drummond's eyes filled with tears as his stomach somersaulted and his bowels trembled with fear. He shoved a fist into his mouth and bit it, trying to silence the scream that was building in his chest.

The woman walked to the mess of skin and gristle that had been Yasmin and she reached down and retrieved the Book of Light. She inspected it for a moment, and then she turned to look at Drummond.

"Drummond Fox," she said, her voice low and husky. It was almost a whisper, almost a tease.

Drummond wanted to scream. He wanted to run. He wanted to stay perfectly still and hope that she wouldn't see him, even though she was already looking directly at him. In his pocket, a trembling finger searched desperately for a page of the Book of Shadows.

"Give me the Fox Library," the woman said, walking casually over to where Lily lay in her own blood. She looked down at Drummond's friend for a moment and then jumped up into the air and landed heavily on Lily's stomach with both feet. Air and blood exploded out of Lily's mouth.

"Stop it!" Drummond yelled reflexively, flinching away in horror. "Fuck!"

The woman looked at him over her shoulder, still standing on Lily's stomach. "Give me the Fox Library," she said again, with a tone suggesting she was losing her patience.

Drummond shook his head, his eyes flicking to Wagner's prone body, the mess that had been Yasmin, Lily's bloodied and broken shape. These had been his friends, the people he had loved. These had been people who had never hurt anyone in their lives. They had been magnificent and funny and *so* alive, and now they were not; they were full stops at the end of a beautiful poem.

He backed away, hating that he was leaving his friends, but knowing that they would want him to survive, to keep the books from this woman. In his pocket his fingers finally found a page of the Book of

Shadows. In front of him the woman stepped off Lily and wiped her shoes on the tarmac. Then she turned to face him.

"Give me your books!" she screeched at him, her face suddenly a twisted mask of fury.

Drummond tore the corner of the page and disappeared into the shadows just as the woman moved in a blur to the place where he had stood moments before.

As he hurried away out of the park and onto the street, he saw her looking around and searching for him.

He fled, running from images that would haunt him forever, weeping in the shadows for his friends and the ghastly things the woman had done to them.

The Bookseller (1)

They met the Bookseller in the lobby bar at the Ace Hotel, just off Broadway at West Twenty-Ninth Street. Izzy had been to the bar before on a double date not long after she had first arrived in New York, and the place hadn't changed in the intervening period. The space was large, like it had once been a bank, with broad white pillars dividing it and holding the roof high above them. Wood paneling ran around the walls and the bar was lit by table lamps and bulbs hanging high above. When Lund and Izzy entered it was early afternoon, and there was a low, comfortable hubbub of people passing the time and catching up. Izzy waited next to Lund as he searched the space with his eyes, before settling on a figure sitting in the far corner.

"Wait here," he said.

"No," Izzy said. Lund looked at her, assessing her, and didn't argue. He headed toward a woman sitting by herself at one end of a leather sofa. She looked up when they drew near, and Izzy saw that she was beautiful. She had the dark skin of an African American, with large eyes and high cheekbones. She was bald, and large, colorful earrings hung from her ears. She was dressed in an expensive gray suit with a crimson blouse that was buttoned low enough to reveal cleavage and she had spectacles on a chain around her neck. She was sitting with her legs crossed and Izzy saw expensive heels on her feet, of a similar color to the blouse she was wearing. She had a cocktail on the table in front of her.

The woman looked at them for a moment. "Help you?"

"Azaki is gone," Lund said simply.

The woman absorbed that for a moment, her lips pursing slightly. "And you are?"

"Lund," Lund said. "I was with him." He tossed Azaki's phone onto the couch next to her, and her eyes flicked down to it.

"The bodyguard," the woman said.

"A bald man shot and killed him," Lund said.

"A bald man," Lottie said.

"Tried to shoot me too," Lund continued, pointing at the wound on the side of his head. "But he missed. Which is incredible given I am much bigger than Azaki."

"Dr. Barbary," Izzy said. "That was his name. Hugo Barbary."

The woman sighed, and then gestured to the seats across from her. Izzy and Lund sat.

"You must be Izzy," the woman said. She glanced at Lund, who nodded in reply.

"Yes," Izzy said hesitantly. "How do you know?"

"You are a beautiful woman, Izzy," the Bookseller said, ignoring the question. "You must get told that all the time."

"Not often enough," Izzy replied. She waved a hand over her own head while looking at the Bookseller's scalp. "I like the bald. I could never pull that off."

The Bookseller grinned in response. "Oh, I like you," she said. "Which is good, because I have promised someone that I will keep you safe."

"Who?" Izzy asked. "Who have you promised?"

"Doesn't matter," the woman said. "For now. You won't have long to wait."

"It does matter," Izzy argued. "I want to know what's going on."

"All that matters is that you will be safe. That is what I asked Azaki to do, and that, I assume, is why Mr. Lund brought you to me."

Izzy looked a question at Lund.

"It's not the only reason we're meeting," Lund said to the Bookseller.

Lund removed the Book of Pain from his pocket and slid it across the table to her.

"Mmm," the Bookseller murmured. She lifted her glasses and slipped them on. "This is not the Book of Doors."

"Pain," Lund said simply, and the woman's eyes flicked up in surprise.

"Lovely," she said. "I've heard rumors about this and Hugo Barbary."

Lund made no comment. Izzy watched as the woman turned the book over in her hands, and then opened it.

She looked at Lund. "You took it from Hugo Barbary, then?"

"Does it matter?" Lund said.

"Usually, but to annoy Hugo I will make an exception."

"Can you sell it?" Lund asked.

"Of course." The Bookseller smiled. "Always. Even when the world is going to shit, people still want to buy special books. Is that what you want?"

"Yes," Lund said. "You can buy it from us, give us the money, and then sell it."

"No," the Bookseller said, pushing the book back across the table. "That's not how it works. I do not take possession of the book. I act on your behalf. I sell it for you. You need to wait for the money."

Lund glanced at Izzy, back to the woman.

"She will be safe," the Bookseller said. "If that is why you are so keen for the money."

"How does it work?" Lund asked.

"We will have an auction," the Bookseller said. "Book hunters from around the world will be invited. It will be quite the occasion. I already have a venue and arrangements in place. I was expecting to auction the Book of Doors, but we can certainly sell this."

"When?" Lund asked.

"Midnight, tonight."

"So quick?" Lund asked.

"People make time for my auctions," the Bookseller said. "They are rare events, Mr. Lund, but high value. People will come. Nobody is more than twelve hours away, and they can send a proxy if they can't come personally. And believe me, the sooner you sell it the better for you, for all of us. Having one of these books just draws attention."

"How much?" Lund asked.

"Straight to the point with you, isn't it? Well, obviously, I cannot preempt the auction, but a book like this . . ." She bobbed her head back and forth. "Twenty, twenty-five easily."

Lund nodded.

"Twenty what?" Izzy asked.

"Million," the Bookseller said.

Izzy felt the blood drain into her feet and the world tilted for a few seconds. She reached out a hand to steady herself on the side of the chair.

"My fee is forty percent. Usually I'd take thirty, but Hugo Barbary makes this more dangerous. Is that acceptable?"

Lund shrugged. "Whatever."

She stood and brushed herself down.

"It's a shame about Mr. Azaki," she said to Lund. She lifted her cocktail and downed it in one gulp. "I liked him a great deal."

Lund nodded in agreement.

"But the world moves on and these are tumultuous times. We must adapt and persevere. And that's much easier to do when you have lots of money, believe me."

"I believe you," Izzy said.

"Now, you will both come with me," the Bookseller instructed.

"What?" Izzy asked.

"It's nothing sinister. But since I've gone to the considerable expense of arranging an auction, I want the merchandise to be safe. If you want me to sell your book, you will stay with me for the next twenty-four hours. No contact with the outside world, no secret messages to potential bidders. None of that. It is no reflection on you, I hope you understand. I am a careful woman."

Lund looked at Izzy, asking a question.

"I don't know," she said. Then she looked at the Bookseller. "But I think I like her. I like her much more than the bald man. I'm okay going with her if it means we'll be safe."

"Safe as you'll be anywhere else," the Bookseller said. "Come on."

They walked out of the hotel together and climbed into a car that was waiting for them.

Stranded

Cassie gasped in terror and fell forward out of the chair onto the ground in Bryant Park. A young couple passing by turned her way, but Drummond gave them a smile that was both reassuring and apologetic. "She's okay, just a bit lightheaded."

He helped her back into her seat as the couple continued on their way.

"Do you see?" Drummond asked. "Do you see why we have to keep it from her?"

"That poor woman, Lily . . . what did she do to her?"

"I don't know," Drummond admitted. "But if I had to guess, I would say it was the Book of Despair."

"The Book of Despair," Cassie repeated.

Drummond nodded. "It was owned by a family in St. Petersburg, in Russia. It was kept in a church, of all places—perhaps because a church is where people go when they are in despair. But we'd heard stories, before this night, before she attacked us, that the family had gone missing, and nobody knew what had happened to the book. I didn't know if I believed them or not, there were always stories of books going missing, books being found. But the woman took it, and she killed the family. I don't know this for sure. But I feel it."

Cassie shook her head.

"Lily was such a bright, vivacious woman," Drummond said. "She loved her food, and she loved to show people Hong Kong, her island. When she laughed, she laughed with her whole body." He shook his head slowly. "To do that to her, to make her despairing to the point that she wanted to end her own life in the most horrible way . . ."

"She saved you," Cassie said with certainty. "She knew that if you tried to help her, you would also be affected by the book."

Drummond hesitated, unsure. Cassie saw that he wanted her to be right, that that was how he wanted to remember Lily.

"I believe it, Drummond," she said. "I believe she saved you. I could feel how guilty you were that you didn't do more."

He looked away, his eyes on the ground as if embarrassed that so many of his inner thoughts had been revealed in his memories.

Cassie put a hand on his shoulder. "You don't need to feel guilty, Lily didn't want you to die like she did. I didn't know her, but I know that. I *saw* that."

Drummond nodded, accepting her words. "Thank you," he said quietly, avoiding her gaze.

A sudden wave of emotion—terror and horror—washed over Cassie as the memories forced themselves back to the front of her mind: the image of evil passing across the woman's face as Drummond had watched, the brutal crunching of bones before the bloody remains of Yasmin fell to the cold ground. She dropped her head between her knees. "It was so horrible," she murmured. "I wish I hadn't seen . . ."

"I'm sorry," Drummond said. "I carry those memories with me. I know how awful they are. I was *there*. But now you know why I want to keep the library from her, why she should never have the Book of Doors."

"But to destroy it?" Cassie asked, looking up at him. "Is it the only way?"

She could see the question tormented him, as if she had given voice to what was in his own mind. "What happens if that woman gets to the Fox Library, if she gets all of the books?"

Cassie shook her head, eyes on the ground.

"It's what she wants," Drummond continued. "It's what she was seeking even back then. She'll be stronger now. It's been ten years. And she's still looking, still gathering books."

Cassie looked up at him.

"I've heard the stories," he said. "I still speak to people in the book world, from time to time. She's been systematically hunting down book hunters and other collectors, taking their books from them. Everyone who meets her and who lives—and there aren't many of those—they say the same thing. She asks where I am. And she asks about the Fox Library. Everybody knows she wants all of the books, but nobody knows why. Nobody knows who she is or where she came from. And nobody knows what she will do when she has them all."

"Why don't you stop her, then?" Cassie asked. "Instead of destroying my book, destroy her! Use the books you have against her rather than hiding them."

Drummond flinched back, as if stung. He opened his mouth, trying to come up with an answer, then closed it again.

"I . . ." he struggled. "I'm not a fighter, Cassie. I sit in quiet buildings and study books. What am I to her? You saw her. She's deadly."

Cassie shook her head, disagreeing with his assessment. "You stood up to that man Barbary, back in the deli. You defended Izzy and me . . ."

"I only did what I had to do, to get away, to protect you and Izzy and to keep the book from him."

"It's not different," Cassie said. "We need to stand up to the woman and keep the books safe from her."

Drummond coughed a laugh into the air, disagreeing. "It *is* different. Hugo Barbary is just a man, and he terrifies me. But the woman . . . the woman is worse. You've seen."

Cassie wrestled with it, knowing he was right, but knowing she couldn't let the Book of Doors be destroyed. She had to think. She had to work out what to do. She stood up.

"We need to go back, back to our own time," she said.

Drummond looked up at her, disappointed.

"I just want to see my friend, Drummond," she said. "I need to clear my mind. I can't . . . I can't deal with this right now. I want to make sure she's all right."

"Okay," he said. "Okay."

"You've lost your friends, and I am so sorry for that," Cassie said, her voice softening. "But Izzy is still alive. After what I've just seen, I want to check how she is."

Drummond nodded. "I understand," he said. "Let's make sure she's safe."

They walked out of Bryant Park in silence, heading east along Forty-Second Street, bumping and jostling with the lunchtime crowds. The city smelled of hot metal and concrete and the air was thick and grimy. They found an underground parking garage and wandered down the ramp into the cooler air, looking for an out-of-the-way door. Cassie reflected that she was getting good at finding the right sort of doorways now, the quiet doorways that nobody looked at or noticed. Those places were made for the Book of Doors. She found an entrance to an internal fire escape staircase.

"This will do," she said.

"Leave the door ajar," Drummond said. "Just in case someone is there. We need an escape route."

Cassie nodded at him and then opened the door to reveal the hallway of her apartment.

"What's that?" Cassie asked, peering at the floor close to the front door. "Is that blood?"

The two of them took a few steps and looked at the sticky red puddles marking the wood. Cassie's heart beat a tattoo of panic.

"Yes," Drummond said, his voice flat. "Blood."

"Izzy!" Cassie gasped. She darted passed Drummond and into the living area. Everything appeared normal at first glance, but as Cassie's eyes danced around she spotted things that weren't right. She saw a mess, the TV stand collapsed and broken. She thought she could smell urine in the air.

"Oh god!" she muttered, turning where she stood, hands in her hair.

She saw furniture and belongings toppled out of place, a stain on the couch cushions, the man hiding behind the door lurching toward her.

"Fuck!" Cassie yelled, as Hugo Barbary lunged for her, his face a sneer of anger.

"What?" Drummond called in surprise from the hall.

But Cassie couldn't answer, because Hugo Barbary's big hand was around her neck, squeezing breath and rational thought from her. She batted at the hand ineffectually. Cassie wasn't short, but she was shorter than Hugo Barbary, and his arm was thick and solid like a tree trunk. He pulled her close and she saw that one side of the man's face looked swollen and red.

"I'll take this," he murmured close to her ear, as his free hand dipped into her pocket and removed the Book of Doors.

Cassie slapped harder at the arm, but her brain was shouting at her that she couldn't breathe, that the book really wasn't that important.

"Thank you kindly," Hugo said, just as Drummond appeared in the doorway.

"Wha . . ." he started. "Aw, fuck," he finished.

"Mr. Fox," Hugo preened, taking a few steps away from the door. "How nice to see you again. I have your lady friend and her book."

To Cassie, still stuck in Hugo's grip, still struggling to draw breath, his words started to sound almost dreamlike, as if they were being heard by someone else.

"What are you going to do, Librarian?" Hugo asked. "Are you going to go into the shadows and run away again, like the last time?"

Drummond wavered, eyes flicking back and forth between Cassie and Hugo, indecision in human form.

"Coward," Hugo spat.

And then Cassie kicked him between the legs, as hard and heavily as she could manage, hoping it was enough.

The man gasped and squeaked and dropped her, his face flushing red as she staggered away.

She moved toward Drummond and the two of them backed out of the room to the hall, even as Hugo gathered himself, as he forced his way forward, his eyes fixed on them.

"I've had enough pain for one day!" he muttered.

"Come on," Drummond urged Cassie, as if he knew what Hugo might do.

"What did you do to Izzy?" Cassie demanded, her voice a hoarse whisper. "Where's my friend?"

They were moving toward the door to Cassie's room, still the door to the past, their escape route. Hugo saw what was through the door as he stepped toward them, his eyes lighting up.

"Quite marvelous," he said. Then he looked at Cassie. "Perhaps I killed your friend because she annoyed me," he said.

"No," Cassie said, refusing to believe him. To believe what he said would be the end of her, she knew; she would shatter like dropped crystal.

"He's lying," Drummond said.

"Am I?" Hugo countered. "Why would I?"

"It's who you are," Drummond answered.

"Either way, this is tiresome."

Cassie looked at the Book of Doors in his hand, and then realized, in an instant, it wasn't the Book of Doors.

"You, I have more business with," Hugo said to Drummond.

Then he looked to Cassie, just as the book in his hand sparked into life, pouring purple and red sparks into the gloomy hallway.

"You, I am done with."

Cassie felt herself jerked upward and backward, and she tumbled through her bedroom doorway and into the past. She heard Drummond shouting "No!" and then she felt rough concrete as she rolled along the ground in the parking garage.

She landed awkwardly, a tangle of legs beneath her, and then Dr. Barbary stepped into the doorway. He glanced around, appreciating that Cassie was now in a different place, and then he smiled at her.

"Goodbye," he said simply, as Cassie scrambled to her feet, moving so slowly.

Barbary closed the door, the slam echoing around the parking garage like a thunderclap, and Cassie was alone, in the past and without the Book of Doors.

PART
3

ECHOES IN THE PAST

Alone in the Past

Cassie was alone amid the noise and light, a solitary figure among the tourists and traffic in New York City.

She was sitting at the top of the TKTS red stairs in the heart of Times Square, sweating in the warm evening, her greatcoat folded on her lap, the hat and scarf tucked into its pockets. On all sides electric lights screamed at her, forcing her mind into a protective huddle and making her want to run away somewhere dark and quiet. But she couldn't think of anywhere else to go. She was stuck in the past, with no money and no friends and no way to get home. Times Square was illuminated all night, and there were always tourists. It was safe, at least. Noisy and bright and jarring, but safe.

"Why would anyone want to go to Times Square?" she said to herself, remembering something Izzy had said a lifetime ago, before the world went crazy: "The only people interested in Times Square are tourists and terrorists."

Tears came again, quiet, defeated tears brimming in her eyes, and the lights of New York City blurred in her vision.

"Oh god," she wailed to herself.

Cassie had been through difficult times in her life. Her grandfather's illness and his death, and the dark weeks that followed when she had been truly alone in the world for the first time. But even in those days she had never felt as alone as she did now, as helpless.

"What am I going to do?" she asked herself, wiping her tears with the sleeve of her old pullover.

After her bedroom door had slammed shut upon her, Cassie had waited in the parking garage for a while, hoping that it would open again, hoping that Drummond would come for her. But as the minutes and then hours had ticked by her hope had dimmed. She didn't even know if Drummond could use the Book of Doors. Maybe no one could, other than her.

She had been too numb to panic straightaway. With her hope extinguished she had wandered up out of the parking garage into the hot New York afternoon. She had walked aimlessly for a while, her mind strangely silent, as if it had just checked out for the day. Streets and people and traffic had buffeted her, and then she had found herself on a bench in Central Park, watching dog walkers and joggers, and she had tried to think rationally about her problem, to find the obvious solution that was just a few logical steps away.

But there was no solution. She had no money. She was alone. Any ID she was carrying was dated from the future and would likely be useless in the past.

The panic had bubbled up like rapidly rising floodwaters, threatening to drown her. She had gripped the arm of the bench, trying to steady herself, hyperventilating while all around her New York went about its business and pointedly ignored her.

She was alone. More than ever.

Now, several hours later, as the lights of Times Square tried to hold back the coming darkness, Cassie's mind had emerged from the hole it had slid into and tried to help her.

"Think about the positives," she told herself, as a young Japanese couple posed for photographs in front of her. She saw them debating whether to ask her to take their photo, but they took one look at her tearstained face and went to a middle-aged man a few steps farther away instead.

"It's warm," she told herself, nodding. "It's summer. You're not going to freeze to death."

She patted the coat on her lap. If she needed to, she could stay on the steps all night. She would be safe, and she would be warm.

"You're not in any immediate danger."

She nodded again, trying to emphasize the positives to herself.

"Great. So you're not going to die immediately."

That was it. That was all she had.

CASSIE SAT ON THE STAIRS all night, strangely scared to move, as if moving would make it all real, as if it meant she would have to deal with it all. The city never really went to sleep, certainly not in Times Square. The lights blinked and buzzed, and there were always taxis streaming by, always tourists, even though their numbers thinned in the small hours of the morning. And then it all started to come to life again, the traffic grew heavier, the noises grew louder, and Cassie realized she had dozed sitting up. Suddenly she was awake again, panicked and blinking and trying to remember why she was in Times Square alone.

Then she saw an advertisement for a film that was ten years old, and it all came crushing back upon her, the panic, the fear, and she had to get up, she had to move, just to stop the despair from swallowing her again.

She needed the toilet, and her mouth was dry, so she walked down Seventh Avenue to Penn Station, letting herself be pushed by the tide of commuters on their way to or from work. Inside the station she used the toilet, trying her best to ignore the shouted, aggressive conversations that seemed to echo around her, and hurrying away as soon as she was done, before someone tried to speak to her. She found the water fountain and drank until she was satiated, washing the taste of the city air out of her mouth.

She wandered the corridors of the station, smelling the bread and hot dogs, not yet feeling hungry but knowing it was coming. Knowing she had to do something if she was going to survive.

She saw a homeless woman, bulging plastic bag in each hand and many layers of clothes covering her body, and saw her own future. She saw herself becoming anonymous and forgotten, one of the people hidden beneath the surface of New York, a loner who told crazy stories about being from the future.

Suddenly Penn Station was suffocating, a trap she couldn't escape from, and panic rushed her back out into the warm morning air. She walked north again, because her mind seemed to panic less when she walked, and she found herself back at Bryant Park, where she and Drummond had sat the previous day to watch the younger Drummond and his friends.

Cassie took a seat at a table and tried to relax. All she wanted was a bed. Her apartment. And Izzy.

"Oh no, Izzy," she said, remembering what Hugo Barbary had said to her, before he had pushed her through the door: *Perhaps I killed your friend because she annoyed me.*

She dropped her head into her hands.

What if it was true?

What if that man *had* killed Izzy?

Cassie's insides were a stormy sea, roiling and tempestuous, her whole being in disarray like she had never known. The world blurred around her again as tears bubbled up. She tried to wipe them away, but more kept coming, her breaths hitching as she wiped and wiped, until her cheeks were raw. But there were still more tears. The tears were endless.

When she was spent, when she was an exhausted shell devoid of all hope, she asked herself who could help her. She couldn't survive on her own. She thought about who she knew in the past.

Her grandfather—a continent away, and even if she could get to him, would he help her? What could he do? He had his own Cassie to look after.

Izzy would be somewhere in New York City, but Cassie didn't know where. And the Izzy of ten years ago didn't know Cassie. Why would she help her?

Then she thought about Drummond Fox. She had hoped the Drummond Fox from the future would come back to rescue her, but surely he would have arrived by now? He had known where she was. She couldn't rely on him.

But what about the Drummond Fox of the past? The Drummond Fox of ten years ago?

It felt like an idea, an opportunity. For the first time since her bedroom door had slammed shut on her it felt like a possible way forward.

Cassie stood up and let her feet carry her around Bryant Park, her gaze turned inward as she nurtured the idea, and her hope, like a fragile plant.

If she could find Drummond Fox, she could tell him about the Book of Doors and all that happened in the future . . . he would believe her, she was sure.

She felt a sudden rush of adrenaline as she realized that the Drummond Fox of the past was in the city . . . she and *her* Drummond had watched him the previous day, in Bryant Park . . .

And then her hope drove itself over a cliff as she realized that Drummond Fox was gone. The previous evening he had seen his friends killed by the woman—Cassie had seen it herself, she had *been* there, in his memories. Drummond had fled the woman and the massacre of his friends. He had started his ten years of running and hiding, of living in the shadows. She had no way of knowing where he would be until ten years in the future, when she and Izzy would see him on the rooftop bar of the Library Hotel.

"No," she said to herself, as these truths made themselves known. She stopped walking, forcing other people to step around her. She didn't hear the annoyed words, she didn't see the irritated glances thrown her way. She was lost in her own thoughts.

Drummond Fox couldn't help her.

She waited for her mind to respond, to come up with an alternative.

If she couldn't find Drummond Fox, and there was nobody else in the past who could help her, she had to help herself. And there was only one way that she was going to get back to her own time.

"I have to find the Book of Doors," she said to herself, her voice quiet, as she realized this was the answer she should have thought of twelve hours earlier.

But where to start? Where to find such a book?

The answer was simple: start with the man who had given it to her.

She had to find Mr. Webber.

CASSIE WAITED FOR MR. WEBBER outside his building. It was late afternoon when he emerged, and at first Cassie didn't realize it was him. This was a Mr. Webber with darker hair and fewer years in his bones.

She caught up to him before he reached the corner. "Mr. Webber!"

The man stopped to look at her. Cassie saw a polite smile, curiosity and caution in his expression.

"Mr. Webber, it is so good to see you," she gushed, her emotions suddenly overflowing. "You have no idea. Please, I need your help." Her words were a torrent; twelve hours of fear and anxiety and panic poured out of her because she saw a face she knew, even if that face didn't know her. "I'm so sorry, I know you don't know me, but I need help and you are the only person I know."

Mr. Webber's brow creased, his eyes flicking up and down over her face as if he was trying to place her.

"I need the Book of Doors. You give it to me in the future; I don't know why, but you did. But I got stuck here in the past and I need it to get home and I can't think of anyone else to help me, oh god . . ." She put a hand to her head. Her brain told her she was rambling. It told her to think about what she must look like to a man who didn't know her. She forced herself to breathe, to calm. "I know this sounds crazy, I know what I must look like."

"You need help?" Mr. Webber said, nodding kindly.

"Yes!" Cassie said. "Yes! I need help, please . . . the Book of Doors. I need to use it, just once."

Mr. Webber nodded slowly. He threw a glance sideways, to the bustle and noise of Second Avenue. "I'm afraid I don't know what that is. But you look like you could use a hot meal and a drink, is that right?"

Cassie hesitated, not sure where this turn in the conversation was leading.

She watched as Mr. Webber pulled a few notes from his pocket and passed them over to her, pressing them into her hand.

"Get yourself some food and a drink. There is a women's shelter in Midtown, I think. They will get you some help. I'm sorry but I can't do any more."

Cassie watched as Mr. Webber hurried away, as he threw one worried glance over his shoulder to see if the madwoman was following him or not.

Cassie stood there dumbly for a few minutes, the notes crumpled in her hand, the uncaring city churning around her.

The Fabulous Tale of Cassie Andrews

Cassie did the only thing she could think of doing: She went somewhere familiar, somewhere she could think. She went to Kellner Books. After the hot, sticky city streets, stepping through the door into the bookstore was a relief. The store looked the same, even if the books were different and she didn't recognize any of the staff. It was somewhere safe, somewhere comforting. Cassie found the old armchair in the back corner of the room and sat down, a random book in her hand as if she were reading, just trying to wrestle her racing mind into submission.

She sat there for a while, her mind slowing but her despair stubbornly present, listing her personal failings.

Why had she gone back to the apartment?

Why had she not seen Hugo Barbary in the living area? Was she stupid or blind?

Why had she left Izzy behind when she had gone with Drummond?

"Oh no," she muttered, her stomach dropping as she remembered the blood on the floor. Where was Izzy?

Someone at a nearby bookshelf glanced over at the sound of her despair, and Cassie tried to smile away their concern. She couldn't stay there forever, she knew. It would be dark soon, and she had nowhere to go. The thought of spending another night in Times Square by herself was bleak. Was this what her life would be?

She thought of the shelter Mr. Webber had mentioned. Should she go there? There might be a bed at least. Food.

Then she remembered the notes he had pressed into her hand, and she was suddenly aware of her rumbling, empty stomach. She had walked miles in the course of the day, just trying to keep calm, and she hadn't eaten since the diner with Drummond, when she had met her grandfather. She needed food. She smiled weakly as she remembered Drummond saying the same thing to her in Lyon, and she realized she missed him. She had known him for only a day, and she missed him.

She forced herself to her feet. She put the book back on the shelf and headed through the store to the coffee bar at the front. She bought a large chocolate muffin and a large coffee and then sat at one of the empty tables, suddenly self-conscious that she might smell after her night on the streets of the city, hoping the other customers wouldn't notice.

She picked at the muffin, trying to linger over it, savoring every mouthful like it was her last meal. With her stomach full, and coffee in her veins, she started to feel more rational again, able to strengthen the walls of her mind against her raging emotions.

She sat there, gazing out to the front of the shop and the street beyond, not trying to solve all of her problems, not trying to fix the impossible. She just sat and was calm and quiet.

And then the door to the street opened, and Mr. Webber walked into Kellner Books.

HE DIDN'T NOTICE HER, NOT at first, and she didn't draw his attention. He went to the counter as he always did and ordered his coffee. Cassie noticed that he had a book under his arm now, a book he hadn't been carrying earlier on the street.

She watched Mr. Webber take his seat, three tables away, and she knew that his appearance in Kellner Books was her last chance. He was the route to the Book of Doors. She had to make him believe.

She watched him read and sip his coffee for a few minutes, trying to think about the best approach, trying to think about how to make him believe her at least enough to have a conversation.

Then she got up, carrying her drink with her, and walked over to sit down opposite him. When he looked up from his book his expression cycled through several emotions: surprise, shock, wariness.

"Thank you for the money, Mr. Webber," she said. "That was very kind."

That disarmed him, she saw. The wariness subsided.

"I got a drink and some food, and I really needed that." She smiled. "I think I was a bit hyper when I spoke to you earlier. I'm sorry if I worried you."

He shook his head, starting to end the conversation politely before Cassie had said what she wanted.

"Let me say one thing," she said. "And then, if you want me to, I'll leave you alone, I promise. One thing only."

Mr. Webber pursed his lips briefly, considering it. "I'll admit, I am puzzled how you know my name, miss."

"Please," Cassie said, feeling her eyes close with the effort of remaining calm. "Please let me tell you just one thing."

"Okay," he said. "What do you want to tell me?"

Cassie nodded and felt whole worlds of hope and despair pivoting on one moment, on one sentence.

"When you were in Rome, when you were younger," she said. "You stayed at a guesthouse near the Trevi Fountain. The woman who owned the hotel came into the room to give you coffee and found you naked."

Mr. Webber absorbed that with a blank expression, and then he sat back in his chair, his brow creased, and he stared at Cassie for a long time.

"Who are you?" he asked.

"My name is Cassie," she said.

"I've never told anyone that story. No one. Nobody can know that. How do you know?"

"You told me," Cassie said. "We're friends. That's how I know your name. That's how I know where you live. I was waiting for you earlier. It's how I know you come here regularly to sit and read your books. I know you love *The Count of Monte Cristo*."

"But how do you know these things?" Mr. Webber asked, shaking his head. "We've never met."

"No," Cassie agreed. "That's the hard bit, Mr. Webber. I'm from the future. We meet in the future and become friends. And I don't expect you to believe that because . . . well, it's outrageous, isn't it?"

Mr. Webber was watching her, and she could see that he was having some sort of internal debate, wrestling with conflicting facts.

"I'm not dangerous, Mr. Webber," she said. "I'm just stranded here, alone and with no money and no friends that can help. You are the only person I know who might be able to help."

Mr. Webber took a sip of his drink. "I don't know if I believe you," he said. "What you're saying . . . it is too fabulous, too crazy."

She nodded sadly, her eyes dropping to the table. Of course he wouldn't believe her. Why would anyone?

But he didn't chase her away. When she looked up again, he was still watching her.

"I can't work out how you could possibly know about Rome," he said, but he was speaking more to himself. "I have told *nobody* that story. I have never written it down. If this is some sort of scam or confidence trick . . . I can't possibly see how you would know that. And I've already given you money today. What reason would you have for speaking to me?"

"It's not a scam," Cassie said quietly.

They sat in silence for a while.

The store had quieted and now there were only a few other people browsing, a young couple sitting at one of the other tables with their heads close together and giggling. The day was trundling along, evening turning to night, and Cassie felt her heart sink as she contemplated stepping out of the comforting familiarity of the shop and back into the lonely evening.

"Do you have a phone?" Mr. Webber asked, interrupting her thoughts.

"What?" Cassie asked.

"A phone," he said. "A cell phone. Everyone carries a phone these days."

"Yes," Cassie said, automatically patting the pockets of her coat.

"Let me see it, please," Mr. Webber requested, extending a hand.

"Why?" Cassie asked.

"If you want me to believe you, if you don't want me to get up and leave right now, let me see your phone."

Cassie contemplated the request for a moment and could see no downside. She dug out her phone and passed it over.

"Unlock it, please," he said, handing it back to her.

Cassie typed in the code and gave it back and waited a few moments as Mr. Webber inspected the device, flicking the screen, his eyes moving as he read. Then he put the phone down on the table, his hand resting on it, and he stared silently at the tabletop.

"What?" Cassie asked, when she could stand it no more.

"It's from the future," he said, his eyes flicking up to her. "I am not the Luddite I like to pretend I am, I have my own phone." He reached into his pocket and removed an iPhone, a much earlier predecessor of the phone Cassie owned. "What you have there is obviously much more advanced."

"I won't even be able to charge it for five years," Cassie reflected miserably.

"And the web page that was open in the browser," Mr. Webber continued, shaking his head slowly. "It was dated several years into the future. It's impossible."

"Yes," Cassie agreed. "It is."

Mr. Webber sighed then, a heavy, weary sound. Then he pushed the phone back toward Cassie and she returned it to her pocket.

Mr. Webber sipped his coffee and leaned back in his chair. "I've been alone most of my life," he said. "For a long time it was just me and my mother, but then she died, and I was alone." His brow creased, as if he was wrestling with something he had been struggling to understand. "I don't really know why I've always been alone," he reflected. "I would very much have liked to have had more friends, someone to love. But my working life was spent traveling around a lot, and I worked unsociable hours. It was hard to meet people, and if I'm honest I think it was easier to just not try after a while."

Cassie listened, wondering where he was going.

"So I spent my life by myself, and when you're by yourself you get very good at watching people. I pay attention. I have no conversation to distract me, no worries about my friend or my partner, no drunken nights to recover from. I've become very good at reading people. And the problem I have is I don't think you are crazy, my dear. I don't think you are trying to con me, even though everything you say is ridiculous. I cannot reconcile these things."

"I'm sorry," Cassie said, and Mr. Webber nodded, accepting the apology. "If I haven't scared you off yet, can I at least tell you my story?"

Mr. Webber nodded. "Okay," he said. "Tell me your story."

So Cassie told her story, leaving out Mr. Webber's quiet death, and Mr. Webber listened without comment, occasionally sipping from his coffee, or shuffling in his seat.

When she was finished, Mr. Webber didn't say anything for a while. His long fingers tapped his coffee cup, and his eyes settled on the table between them.

"It's crazy," she said, feeling the need to reassure him that she knew everything she had just said was unbelievable. "I know it is. But it's all true."

"I don't know if it's true or not," Mr. Webber said. "But having seen your phone . . . and with what you've said you know about me, it's easier to believe than it might have been. But if it is true . . ."

"Yes?"

"It falls down on one crucial point."

"What point?" Cassie asked.

"This magical book you say I gave to you."

"The Book of Doors?"

"I do not possess it," he said. "I have no idea what it is, and I have no idea how I could give it to you in the future."

Cassie shook her head, struggling to believe him. "It must come to you," she insisted. "Sometime in the next ten years it must come to you. Otherwise you couldn't have given it to me and none of this could have happened."

Mr. Webber shrugged. "Perhaps. But I don't have it now. And I cannot help you get back to your future."

Cassie felt herself physically shrink in defeat. "But what am I going to do?" she wailed, more to herself than to Mr. Webber. "I can't be stuck here."

Tears again, horrible, bitter tears filling her eyes.

"Well, you'll just have to wait, dear," Mr. Webber said, and she saw concern in his face, as if perhaps he thought he had made her cry.

"I can't wait!" Cassie exclaimed, as panic frothed within. "I need to get back. I have no money, no house; what am I supposed to do here, stuck in the past?"

Mr. Webber thought about it for a moment before answering. "You are trying to solve everything at once," he said. "Why not solve one problem at a time? You need somewhere to sleep. You will think more clearly after a good night's sleep."

"Where will I sleep?" Cassie asked. "Homeless shelters?"

Mr. Webber shook his head, sighing. He turned his head to gaze to the street. And then he looked back at Cassie. There was another debate within him, Cassie saw; he was being pulled in different directions. Then he nodded, a decision made.

"My apartment isn't far from here," he said, then he caught himself. "But you know that, don't you, my dear?"

Cassie nodded through her tears.

"I have a spare room. You are welcome to sleep there until you make sense of your situation. You cannot stay long, but perhaps until you work out what to do. A day, two at the most. Will that help?"

Cassie blinked and wiped away her tears. "You mean it?" she asked.

"I am not sure I do," Mr. Webber admitted. "But it would be wrong to leave you in such distress. I have the means. But only for a night or two, this is a stopgap measure. Understand?"

"I promise," Cassie said, even though she had no idea how her situation would be any better in two days' time.

Mr. Webber finished his coffee, and together they walked in silence out of the bookstore.

The Passing of Days

Over those first two days, Cassie didn't really settle in Mr. Webber's apartment. She felt as if he would eject her at any moment. She tried to be helpful, offering to make drinks, to go to the store, to help him tidy. Sometimes he took her up on her offer, but she could see that it made him uncomfortable, as if perhaps he was worried that she was trying to make herself so helpful that he wouldn't throw her out. And over those two days he asked her to tell her story again, and he would quiz her on details, inquire about facts he didn't understand. He never seemed entirely satisfied by what she said, but Cassie couldn't work out if it was because he didn't believe the tale, or because he was failing to pick holes in it.

On the evening of the second night following that meeting in Kellner Books, Mr. Webber came out of his bedroom after a nap to find Cassie running her fingers along one of the bookshelves.

"I love your collection of books," she said. "I always wanted a library like this, a place I could just sit by myself and read."

Mr. Webber sat in his chair and let his eyes wander over his books. "Yes," he said. "So did I. And now I have it."

He smiled at her, like he had detected a kindred spirit. And then they spent the evening discussing books, the books they had read and wanted to read, the books they liked and disliked. Cassie made them both tea and then, a little later, a sandwich each, and they kept talking. Mr. Webber liked talking about books; it was how they had first connected when Cassie had started work at Kellner Books all those years later.

On the third day Mr. Webber didn't ask her to leave. He didn't tell her that she could stay, but he didn't ask her to leave. Instead, over breakfast, he asked her, "How can I help you get home?"

She looked at him with unbelieving eyes, and he responded with a dismissive wave. "I am not saying I believe. But I am happy to play along. What can I do to help you get home?"

So she recounted the thoughts she'd had on that first, wretched night alone in New York. She told him about trying to track down Drummond Fox, but how impossible that would be.

"Because he's hiding now," Mr. Webber said. "From this lady who wants the books."

"Correct," Cassie said. "That's why I came to you. Because you give me the Book of Doors."

"Which I don't have," he said.

"No," she said, poking miserably at her breakfast yogurt with a spoon.

"Well then, that is what we will do," Mr. Webber said. "We will search for your Book of Doors. Perhaps that is how I come to have it in the first place? Because you make me look for it?"

Cassie thought about that, feeling hope dawning. "Yes," she said, warming to the idea. "Yes, maybe you're right! That would make sense!"

She thought about Drummond telling her about time travel when they had been waiting in the diner—about how you can't change the past, you can only make things happen.

"Maybe this *is* how you get the book!" she agreed.

So they started searching for the Book of Doors together, and days became weeks and weeks became months.

Over those first few months with Mr. Webber, when she wasn't looking for the Book of Doors, Cassie kept to a comfortable routine. She would wake up first and have a light breakfast and then she would walk the city in the morning, either looking for leads or just stretching her legs. She lost weight and gained conditioning, becoming fitter than she ever had. Then she would return home for lunch, out of the heat in the warmest part of the year, and she and Mr. Webber would share coffee and pastries, or a sandwich, sitting in the window surrounded by his books. They would discuss strategies for locating the book, rare bookshops to check, libraries to visit, and Cassie would update him on what she had found. Most days Mr. Webber would head out in the afternoon—"for my constitutional, my dear, I must keep my old limbs moving or I'll waste away"—and Cassie would clean the apartment, read books while sitting in the window, or watch television. Sometimes she would lounge on the sofa and dream about the Fox Library, that wonderful, peaceful place that was so comforting in her memories. And she would think about Drummond Fox, the man who was handsome when he smiled, and she wondered what he was doing in the future. She hoped he was safe. She hoped she would see him again.

In the evenings she and Mr. Webber would eat dinner together and then read in a companionable silence or discuss books. If the weather was pleasant, they would walk together to a nearby restaurant or coffee shop. Sometimes they would take a cab to Central Park and spend the evening in the golden sunlight. Months rolled by and Cassie found herself celebrating Thanksgiving and Christmas and New Year's, just the two of them, a simple, improvised family.

During this time, Mr. Webber was incredible company. He asked for nothing from Cassie except companionship. He would listen whenever she wanted to speak, usually offering wise advice, and he wouldn't impose upon her with his own conversation when she wasn't in the mood for it. She learned all about him, about his lonely childhood with an overbearing mother; about musical gifts that had been recognized at a young age—"I was a prodigy, don't you know? Not precocious, but definitely prodigious!"—and then his career as a concert pianist and composer. She learned that he had made his fortune not from playing piano around the world, but from composing theme tunes for a handful of popular television series in the 1990s.

"It was so ridiculously well paid," he told her one day, as they strolled around SoHo. "Especially when the shows were syndicated. And the show that paid me the most, it was the most ridiculously simple tune. Just four notes, like a ringtone, something recognizable. Those four notes earned me more money than all the other music I composed combined and bought me that apartment and many of my books."

Months turned to years.

In the summer the city was occasionally unbearable, the air thick with pollution and the smell of stewing garbage. The subway was an oven, with people sweaty and flushed and irritable. In autumn, cool air would come, and people would wrap themselves up in scarves and coats, anticipating the bitter chill of winter, those cold winds that would race along the canyons of concrete. And then the cycle would start again, warmth creeping into the streets of the city, flowers and trees blossoming, the black and white of winter turning into the Technicolor of spring. And through these changing seasons, and all the work searching for the Book of Doors, Cassie found herself afflicted with a low-level anger, a permanent impatience. She knew what lay ahead of her and was desperate to get back to it. It was a book she hadn't finished reading, a meal half eaten. But toward the end of the second year Cassie felt the flame of her impatience dimming, as she succumbed to the comfort and contentedness of her routine.

"I am starting to get comfortable here," she admitted to Mr. Webber one evening. "I am starting to like it. I don't know if I am hiding from my problems or just waiting for them to arrive. I really want to find the Book of Doors, but part of me doesn't. Part of me doesn't want to go back to all of that danger."

Cassie was still searching for the Book of Doors, but with less commitment than during those first few months. It was almost a hobby now, something she did when she felt inclined, an occasional activity rather than an all-consuming obsession.

"Why can't it be both?" Mr. Webber asked. They were sitting at the kitchen table eating ice cream, and Mr. Webber licked his spoon and dropped it into his bowl. "Or why can't it be neither? Why does it have to be anything?"

Cassie shrugged, not understanding.

"Stop trying to think about things," Mr. Webber said. "I know that sounds crazy. I am firmly of the view that more people in this world could use their brains more often, but my dear, if anyone needs to think less about things it is you. All you do is think and worry. We could heat the apartment with the energy your brain is constantly using. You have to just live, be in the moment. Either you will find the Book of Doors or you won't. Either way you will get back to where you came from. It doesn't need to fill up every moment of your life between now and then. You are allowed to just enjoy your life. You are viewing this period of your life as an agony, but you can choose to see it as a gift."

She thought about his words, drawing lines in the melting ice cream pooling in the bottom of her bowl.

"I have to find the book," she said to herself. "I have to get back. I don't know what I'd do if I don't."

"I do, my dear," Mr. Webber said. "You would endure. You are young, and the worst that is going to happen is you travel to the future by living it. You are safe here, you have nothing to worry about. At the very worst you will have a few years planning for what happens when time finally brings you back to where you left off. That's not the worst fate, is it?"

Cassie continued her search, but she was chasing ghosts and memories, myths and misunderstandings. She found bread crumbs, references to magical books, names without explanation or description—the Book of Mirrors, the Book of Consequences, the Book of Answers—and she had no idea if these were real books or made-up ones. She tried to research the whole world of special books, but it all seemed so hidden and mysterious, pointless even, like trying to build sandcastles on the beach when the tide is coming in.

One night, lying alone in the small bedroom after another day where she had discovered nothing, Cassie found herself staring at the old wardrobe by the side of the room, the small pile of books on the windowsill, and she had a sudden flashback to the first time she had been in Mr. Webber's apartment, the day after his death.

She remembered the wardrobe of clothes that she was now looking at, the paperback books that were now on the windowsill. She had thought they might have belonged to a lover or a relative. But they were *her* books and *her* clothes—they always had been.

It was so shocking to her, that memory, that realization, that she sat up on her bed, her mouth wide open.

There had been many clothes in the wardrobe, and more books on the windowsill than were currently gathered there.

Cassie shook her head as she understood then that she would be with Mr. Webber for a while yet.

"I'm not going to find the Book of Doors," she admitted to herself.

After that, she stopped looking.

DAYS AND WEEKS AND MONTHS and years.

Time moved on, and gradually Cassie came to accept that her only way home was to travel there minute by minute, day by day. She settled into her life and routine and let the days pass her by, knowing that she would not get back sooner than time would allow.

The Other Cassie

I saw you today, my dear," Mr. Webber said, as he eased himself into his armchair. To Cassie he looked troubled, or perhaps distracted. "Not you," he clarified. "A different you."

It had been almost four years since Cassie had met Mr. Webber in Kellner Books, since she had been pushed through a doorway from the future. Four winters, four springs, and now into another summer. During those years Mr. Webber had indulged Cassie's story, even though it had seemed to her that he had never entirely believed it. The expression on his face as he lifted his feet onto the footstool suggested that something had changed.

"You saw me?" Cassie asked. She was standing in the kitchen, a dish towel in her hand. She had been cleaning, one of the things she did to make herself feel like she was contributing. She had been living at Mr. Webber's expense, and it bothered her hugely, but she had struggled to find any way to make money as a refugee from the future.

"You were younger," he said, his eyes drifting off to the window next to him. It was late summer, and the air was dense and hot. Mr. Webber was red-faced and sweating from his walk. The window was open a crack in an attempt to stir some of the thick air in the apartment, but it made the room noisy with street sounds. "Not that you're not young now, of course. But you looked even younger."

Cassie was leaning on the counter, thinking back on her life and her movements. Over the last few years she had regularly joked with Mr. Webber that he would see she was telling the truth when he first met the younger version of her in Kellner Books. That date of her first day of work had become almost totemic in its importance. But Cassie had forgotten that she had been in the city for some time before starting work, and she'd been in Kellner Books often during those days.

"In the bookstore?" she asked.

Mr. Webber nodded. As he often did Mr. Webber had taken himself out for a walk in the afternoon, a circuit around several city blocks that would take him past the bookstore. He would stop for a drink—an iced coffee on hot days—and to browse or to read whatever book he was carrying with him. Cassie had a similar routine, left over from the days she would search for the Book of Doors, but she would walk in the morning, as if they were taking turns to be out of the apartment. She would cover greater distances than Mr. Webber. Often she would take the subway to a distant part of the island, or over to Brooklyn, and she would walk her way back over several hours. Her mind would be filled with the same thoughts, the same ideas, inspected and polished like rare gems. How could she get back home? How could she have been so stupid to have been left in the past? When would the Book of Doors appear in Mr. Webber's life if they didn't search for it? What happened to Izzy and how could she protect her friend? What was Drummond doing and was he worried about her?

"Of course," she said, remembering the younger version of herself. "I came to New York about this time. It was early summer this year." She walked over to the window and leaned against it, her hip on the sill and her eyes on the street below. "I was staying in hostels," she said, remembering the six-bed dorm in the hostel down in Chelsea, the shared facilities and the other tourists. "I hated not having my own space."

She looked at Mr. Webber and saw that he was studying her closely, like it was the first time he was seeing her.

"I almost had a heart attack," he said, without any trace of humor. "It was you, right there in the bookstore. I almost spoke to you until you turned around and I saw your hair was different. It was much shorter."

Cassie smiled grimly. "I kept it short when I was traveling. Nothing worse than long hair when there's a risk of head lice."

"You smiled at me when you passed me today," he said. "Do you remember? Can you remember seeing me?"

Cassie searched her memories from those days when she had first arrived in the city. It was a jumble of images and smells and noises, days filled with excitement and potential and the optimism of opportunity.

"I don't," she said. "It's a long time ago . . ."

"It was today."

" . . . for such an incidental moment."

"I never really believed you," he said, narrowing his eyes slightly, one hand going to his chest as if checking that his heart was still pumping. "I know we've spoken about it, and I've met you in those conversations as an equal. But every time, in my head, I'm saying to myself that you are obviously crazy or deluded. And I am waiting for the punch line or the revelation or the truth."

She watched him, saying nothing, not admitting that she knew all this.

"But it's true, all of it is true."

"Yes," she said simply. "It always has been. I am from the future, but I am stuck here until you get the Book of Doors."

"The Book of Doors," he said, murmuring the words to himself, his eyes slipping sideways to stare at the world outside.

"Shall we have some tea?" she asked, because Mr. Webber always liked to drink tea when he came back from his walks.

"Yes," he said, fumbling for a smile. "That would be nice."

Cassie returned to the kitchen feeling a little lighter, feeling as if Mr. Webber would be more of an ally now, rather than just a polite host. But her mind was also troubled by the thought of the younger version of herself being in the same city. As she made the tea, she wondered what would happen if they met. She wondered what she would look like to herself. She wondered if she could go see her younger self somewhere, to see what other people saw when they looked at Cassie Andrews. She remembered Drummond Fox seeing the younger version of himself in Bryant Park and how he had been struck by the experience.

"What are you going to do now, Cassie?" Mr. Webber asked, as she carried the tea over to him.

"Well, right now I am going to have tea with you," she said, and he smiled as she sat on the windowsill again.

"I mean in general," he said.

She shrugged. "I'm going to do what I've been doing for the past four years," she said. "I am going to live and wait. I know that I will be here for some time. Either the Book of Doors will appear, or I will live long enough to arrive back to the future I left."

"You are no longer actively seeking the book, are you?" Mr. Webber asked.

She looked away, an admission.

"Why?"

She equivocated. "I just realized that I am going to be here for a while. Some things started to make sense."

Mr. Webber nodded as if he understood, but she knew him well enough now to know that he saw she was hiding something.

"Have you thought about what happens if you don't find it? If it doesn't appear?" Mr. Webber asked.

"I've thought about little else," Cassie muttered. "It keeps me awake at night."

Mr. Webber sighed. "I've enjoyed having you here, Cassie," he said, looking into his cup. "It's nice not to be alone. It's nice that there's life in this old apartment. After those first few days, I didn't care that you were crazy or delusional."

"So kind," she said, smiling.

"But now I know that what you say is true." He shook his head. "I can't just sit by and take advantage of you like that."

"You're not taking advantage of me." Cassie laughed. "Mr. Webber, I don't know what I would have done if you hadn't come along. I was homeless and penniless."

"Nonetheless," he said. "I am getting something from this. I am using you for company."

"I think the word you are looking for is 'friendship,'" Cassie said.

"I cannot let you persist, trapped in this place like this," he continued, as if he wasn't really listening to her. "We must find your book. This crazy, wonderful book. I will help you however I can. No expense spared. We start now. Tell me what we should do, and I will do it if I can."

He beamed at her happily, and in the future Cassie would always remember this moment, sitting on the windowsill with the cup of tea in her hand, surrounded by the sounds of the city and seeing Mr. Webber in his chair, his wall of books the backdrop behind him. It was how she would always think of him, keen to help and beaming with the enthusiasm of a little boy.

"Okay," she said. "But I don't think trying to find the book is what will help now."

"Well, what do you think will help?"

She sighed. Her mind had been going in a different direction recently. "I need to think about what to do when I get back to where I left. Whether we find the book or not, I need to be ready to face what I'll find there. To help my friends."

"Okay," Mr. Webber said, nodding seriously. "And what do you need?"

The figure of Dr. Barbary loomed large in her memories, intimidating and terrifying. What could she possibly do against such a man, with his books and powers? And what about the woman in Drummond's memories, that terrifying, beautiful figure? If she did get back, she would have to be ready.

And what about Izzy? How could she help Izzy?

And Drummond . . . why did she keep thinking about him?

"I don't know," Cassie admitted. "But I'll think about it."

WHEN THE ANSWER CAME TO her—a possible answer, rather than a certainty—it came completely out of the blue. Cassie was out for one of her usual walks. It was a cloudy day, several months after her conversation with Mr. Webber, and she had stopped for a coffee in Bryant Park. As she sat there sipping her drink, she remembered the conversation she'd had with Drummond as they'd watched his friends meeting on the day they would die. Cassie found herself thinking through those conversations with Drummond, several years in the past now, and she remembered a detail she had forgotten, a fact that gave her a jolt of adrenaline and made her sit up straight and spill her coffee.

She examined the fact, and the idea that slowly developed from it, looking for flaws and weaknesses. She saw none. She saw only possibility.

A possible way to meet Dr. Barbary on a more equal footing.

But then it didn't matter, because Mr. Webber told her that he had found the Book of Doors.

The Book of Doors Discovered

What?" Cassie asked.

She had just returned from a walk. It was autumn, almost winter, and the days were dark and blustery. She was standing just inside the doorway, pulling off her greatcoat, and Mr. Webber had hurried to meet her, his eyes bright.

"I've found the Book of Doors," he said. He was almost hopping with excitement, barely able to stand still.

"What?" Cassie asked again. All thoughts in her mind had stopped dead, like a car hitting a wall.

"Come, sit," Mr. Webber urged. He pulled her over to the couch and then explained. "Ever since I saw that other you, the younger you, I've been searching. Ever since I really started to believe."

"Uh-huh," Cassie said.

"So I sent out emails to all of my contacts, all of my book friends."

"You have book friends," Cassie said, a statement, not a question.

"Rare book collectors. People who go to book auctions. I like first editions." He gestured at the shelves that surrounded them.

"Uh-huh," Cassie said again. She was trying very hard to feel nothing. To be skeptical.

"I just got an email this morning from my contact Morgenstern. He's a collector in Toronto."

"What did you tell them? When you sent out your email?" Cassie's mind was catching up with the conversation and was ringing alarm bells at the thought of an email going out to lots of people talking about magical books.

"Oh, nothing revealing," Mr. Webber said. "I just described the book as you described it to me. I said it was sometimes called the Book of Doors. I said it had indecipherable scribbles in it, and sketches."

"Right," Cassie said. She was conscious her knee was bouncing nervously. "So Morgenstern in Toronto . . . ?"

"Yes!" Mr. Webber said. "He said he found it. Or he thinks he did. He was in Eastern Europe on holiday, and of course what do book people do? We go to every bookshop, we peruse every village fair. We are always looking for books."

"He found it?" Cassie asked in disbelief.

"Look!" he said. He reached over for his laptop, sitting on the coffee table, and turned it so that she could see the screen. He opened an attachment to an email and displayed an image, and Cassie's heart stuttered. "Is this it?" Mr. Webber asked.

Cassie leaned in close to the image. It showed a book in a man's hand. She could only see the front of the book and the spine.

"And this," Mr. Webber said, clicking to a second photograph. This showed the inside of the book, pages with scribbles in black ink. The image did not have the resolution to reveal the text in enough detail, but Cassie felt her heart leap up and run a lap of victory in her chest.

"It might be," she said, forcing herself to be calm.

"This might be it!" Mr. Webber exclaimed. "This might be when I get the Book of Doors. This might be when you can go home!"

MR. WEBBER HAD ARRANGED FOR his friend to come to Manhattan that evening. "It's a short flight," he said. "I'll pay, I'll put him in a nice hotel. He'll come for that. He loves the finer things in life."

Cassie wasn't even listening. She was pacing the room, unable to sit still. It had been over four years since she had been stranded in time, and now it felt she had no time to prepare.

"I need to find Izzy," she said, nodding to herself. "That is all that matters. If I get the book, and I go back earlier, maybe I can take her from the apartment before Hugo Barbary even arrives."

She was conscious that she was rambling to herself. After a moment she stopped and saw Mr. Webber leaning on the kitchen counter and watching her. His face was serious.

"What?" she asked.

He smiled, but it was an expression of sadness. "I am really delighted for you," he said. "I truly hope this is the Book of Doors and you are able to go home."

"But?"

He sighed. Whatever he was about to say was hard for him to admit, she saw.

"I am going to miss you, my dear. If you go home, then you leave here."

Cassie didn't know what to say to that. She held his gaze for a few moments.

"Oh, Mr. Webber," she murmured.

She walked over to the kitchen and hugged him from behind.

"I'll miss you too. Until we meet again."

He patted her hands on his chest and she felt him nod.

"I think I will take a nap, until we leave. Wake me, will you?"

He pulled away and headed to his bedroom, and Cassie thought that maybe he was embarrassed to show how upset he was.

"Oh, Mr. Webber," she said again, quietly.

THEY MET MORGENSTERN IN THE Champagne Bar in the Plaza Hotel. He was a large man, with long flowing hair and thick-framed spectacles. He was wearing an expensive suit, with a cravat around his neck.

"Morgy!" Mr. Webber exclaimed, gripping the man's hand and shaking it.

"Webber!" Morgenstern replied, and then he gave Cassie a slow look up and down.

"Ah, this is my research assistant, Ms. Andrews," Mr. Webber said.

Morgenstern nodded and gave Cassie a quick smile but didn't offer his hand. He gestured to the seats next to him and they all sat. The

Champagne Bar was filled with the murmur of conversation and the tinkle of light background piano music.

"Such a pleasure to be able to have a night at the Plaza Hotel," Morgenstern said to Mr. Webber. "So kind of you to put me here."

"Well," Mr. Webber said. "It was the least I could do."

Cassie's eyes were fixed on the package on the table. It looked like a book wrapped in brown paper. A book about the size of the Book of Doors.

"Mmm," Morgenstern said. "It makes me wonder why this book is quite so important. You fly me down here at short notice. Put me up in this lovely, lovely place." He gestured at the room around them, just as a waiter appeared at his shoulder. "Champagne for my friends," Morgenstern said, and the waiter scurried away again.

"Well," Mr. Webber said. "We don't know if there is anything special about this book at all, do we? That is why you are here, so we can ascertain if it is what I am looking for."

"And what is it?" Morgenstern asked.

"Is that it?" Cassie asked, interrupting the flow, pointing at the package on the table.

Morgenstern sighed, a sound of annoyance. Cassie's eyes flicked to Mr. Webber and he gave her a reproachful look, all but saying: *Let me do this.*

"Who is this girl?" Morgenstern asked.

"Now, Morgenstern," Mr. Webber said, pulling himself up slightly in his seat. "You are here at my expense, as my guest. Let's not be rude to my colleague. Show us the book so we can determine if it is what I am looking for or not. If it is, you will be very richly rewarded, I assure you."

Morgenstern made a big deal of thinking about it, pouting slightly as he sipped his champagne, and then waiting while the waiter placed two more glasses on the table, and poured drinks for both Cassie and Mr. Webber.

Cassie wanted to scream. She wanted to swipe everything off the table and send it shattering to the floor. She wanted to grab the book and tear the paper from it. She wanted the Book of Doors.

"Very well," Morgenstern said sulkily. He pushed the book toward Mr. Webber with one delicate finger.

"Where did you say you found it?" Mr. Webber asked, as he picked up the book to pass to Cassie.

"Romania," Morgenstern said, watching as the book changed hands. He sipped his champagne and Cassie tore the paper off the book quickly, drawing the gazes of some of the people sitting around them.

She saw the leather cover of the book beneath the paper and her heart fluttered and her hands shook. It looked like the Book of Doors, and everything around her faded into the background: the noise, the people, Morgenstern's chatter, and Mr. Webber nodding politely as he watched what she was doing.

She tore off more of the paper, revealing the spine, and still it looked like the Book of Doors.

"Is it . . . ?" she murmured to herself.

More paper torn, and then the wrapping fell to the floor between her legs like autumn leaves, and Cassie was holding a book . . . *the* book . . .

She grasped the edges with trembling hands and opened it hurriedly, desperate to see those sketches, the scribbled words.

She saw text, a jumble of black ink.

"It's full of complete nonsense," she heard Morgenstern say, his tone dismissive, and she had never wanted to slap anyone more.

And then her eyes settled on the text and made sense of it, and her breath stopped in her chest and the whole world seemed to freeze.

She saw text she didn't understand, but she recognized the letters. She saw sentences that were obviously written by a human hand, perhaps in Romanian or some other European language.

"Maybe . . ." she murmured, a desperate plea.

She flicked to more pages, looking for images, sketches, for things that she knew were inside the Book of Doors.

And then her heart plummeted as disappointment opened up a vast chasm in front of her. She stared numbly at the book that was not the Book of Doors and she hated everything and everyone in the world.

"Cassie?" Mr. Webber asked, his voice puncturing her thoughts like a pin to a balloon.

When she looked at him and shook her head, there were tears in her eyes.

IT TOOK CASSIE DAYS TO get over the disappointment. Mr. Webber apologized several times, and every time she waved it away, because he had nothing to apologize for.

"It was hope," she said. "You gave me hope for a few hours and that was nice."

Still, Mr. Webber seemed pained by her low mood. When they spoke about it a few days later, over dinner in the apartment, she told him why he should not feel bad.

"It was devastating," she said. "In that moment. But it made me realize how much I want to get back home. It made me realize I need to start thinking about that. I had an idea, a few weeks ago, a memory of something Drummond Fox said to me. I want to work on that."

"A way to find the Book of Doors?" Mr. Webber asked.

She shook her head. "An idea about something I can do so that I am ready when we catch up with my present. So I am ready to deal with the dangers waiting for me."

Mr. Webber nodded slowly. "Okay," he said.

In the following months she began a slow process of investigating her idea, looking for a person instead of searching for a book. It took her almost six months to make the contact she needed to make, and then another few months of discussion, two people cautiously figuring each other out. She discussed things with Mr. Webber often, testing her thoughts and idea with him.

Almost a year after her epiphany in Bryant Park, nearly five years after she had first arrived in the past, Cassie took a long journey by herself. She had a meeting and a discussion and made a deal. And then she returned back to New York and the apartment that had become her home.

"Well?" Mr. Webber asked, when she arrived.

She nodded. "It's done. Now we just have to wait."

The Final Goodbye to Mr. Webber

In the ninth year of her life with Mr. Webber, Cassie's mind turned toward the inevitable future that was now barreling toward her. For so long it had seemed so far away, and too long to wait, but now it seemed that she didn't have enough time to get ready. What had felt like an eternity looking forward felt like a moment looking back.

Mr. Webber had grown weaker and frailer over the years, a process so gradual and sneaky that Cassie hadn't even noticed until one day when he had struggled to get out of his chair, smiling with embarrassment at his frail knees. Cassie had looked at him, seeing how skinny he now was, how loose the skin was around his neck. His face was still smooth and youthful, his hair full and white, but his hands were increasingly weak, his naps longer, and Cassie knew that his time was running out. The knowledge that these were the last days of his life, his last Thanksgiving and Christmas and New Year's, his last spring, saddened her greatly. She had to hide her emotions around him, terrified that she would reveal something he shouldn't know.

She found herself thinking about her grandfather again, and that conversation in Matt's. She had tried to tell him about his health, but he had refused to listen. She didn't know if it would have made a difference, but looking at Mr. Webber she knew, somehow, that there was nothing she could do to change what would happen to him. He was a man who had lived his life to its natural conclusion.

"Oh, the light is fading for me, Cassie," he said to her one evening, without any real sadness. "But that's okay. It comes to us all, and I have lived a charmed life, all things considered."

"Please stop talking like this," she scolded him. "You're fine. You still have your mind, you're still able to get out and walk around and go to the bookstores. You're still reading, aren't you?"

"I am not complaining, Cassie, I am just being realistic."

Cassie busied herself with work in the kitchen that didn't need to be done rather than engaging with the subject.

Mr. Webber had become her friend, perhaps the best friend she had ever had. He had been stability and security and a bedrock of kindness and compassion when she needed it most. It was unbearable to her that he wouldn't be in her life anymore. She had already grieved for him once as a casual acquaintance; she dreaded that she would have to grieve for him again as a dear friend.

In the summer of the year of Mr. Webber's death, the year when the other Cassie would receive the Book of Doors, Cassie realized she had to leave Mr. Webber. She told herself it was because she had to prepare for what was to come, but she knew it was because she couldn't bear to be with him.

She told him, one evening, when the city had grown quiet and dark, when they were sitting together in his living room, a radio on in the kitchen playing Baroque music in the background.

"I need to go," she said.

"I know," he said simply. "Your past is almost your present again." He smiled, enjoying his wordplay.

She nodded.

"I never did get the Book of Doors, did I?" he said. "I don't suppose it matters now if I do. Not much value to you being able to jump forward a few months."

"No," Cassie agreed.

The question of the Book of Doors remained a puzzle. How had Mr. Webber ended up with it to give it to her in the first place?

She sighed.

"What is it?" he asked.

"It's passed so fast. Ten years. It's felt like no time at all. But I remember coming here that first night, thinking it was so long, it was forever."

"I can say the same about life in general." He smiled a bit sadly. "Take a little advice from me. Don't waste your life hidden away in your own mind. Make the most of the time you have, otherwise before you know it, you'll have no time left."

"I know," she said.

"And I want to say one other thing, while we're being all emotional here. I want to thank you for being with me these last ten years." He reached out for her, and she held his hand. "It has truly been the best ten years of my life." He was smiling, but she saw there were tears pooling in his eyes. "I am so pleased that you could be my friend, it has meant so much."

"Me too," she said, tears in her own eyes.

"But don't worry," he said, releasing her and sitting up straight. "I will keep looking in on you at Kellner Books. We can still be friends, you just won't know how deep that friendship is, not yet."

Cassie smiled and nodded, knowing that he would not be looking in on her for very much longer.

"You know that story, about your first day in Rome and the woman coming into your room when you were naked?"

"Mmm."

"You told that to me several times over the years when I saw you in the bookstore," she said. "I always thought you were forgetful, but you're not, not at all. Had you told me that story several times because you wanted me to remember it? Because it was the thing that made you believe me when I told it back to you that first day I was stuck here?"

He smiled. "She saw me in my entirety, you know!"

SHE LEFT MR. WEBBER'S APARTMENT for the last time in early winter. She had a bank account with some money he had given her, some of the clothes she had accumulated over the years in a bag, and the phone that she had brought with her into the past, freshly charged using a charger she had bought as soon as the right type had become available. She hadn't switched the phone on yet, not knowing if that would interfere with the other version of the phone the other Cassie carried. She didn't want anything to change the events that had led her to where she was.

"Well, I'm ready," she said, Mr. Webber standing by in the kitchen. They both nodded, suddenly awkward. Then she stepped close and hugged him. "Thank you," she said.

"No," he said. "Thank you."

They released each other after a moment.

"Don't worry," he said. "I'll take a walk later today. I'll head around by Kellner Books and see the other you there. And in a few months, once this is all over, maybe you can come see me again? No reason for the friendship to end, is it? We will be living in your present then."

"No," she said, trying to smile.

"I look forward to hearing all of your adventures," he said, leading her to the door. "All about your magical books. Meanwhile, I'll keep myself busy. Plenty of books to read."

"There are always books to read," she agreed, as she stepped out into the hallway.

"I am thinking of going back to an old favorite," he told her. "I might read through *The Count of Monte Cristo* one more time."

Cassie smiled at him as her heart broke a little. "Such a great book," she said.

"Yes," he said. "Yes, it is."

She hugged him again, a hug that seemed to last forever but which wasn't long enough.

"Go now," he said. "Go do whatever you need to do. I will see you soon."

She kissed him on the cheek and then walked away without looking back, her final goodbye to Mr. Webber.

From the apartment she walked through the city to Penn Station. She had a ticket for a train ride south, and a meeting in a few days' time. It would be a short meeting, she knew, and then she would be heading straight back north to New York.

The Bookseller (2)

For the second time in her life, Cassie met Lottie Moore, the Bookseller, in New Orleans. They met, as had been agreed several years earlier, at ten at night in Café Du Monde on Jackson Square. When Cassie arrived Lottie was already sitting at one of the outside tables, under the green-and-white awning, with coffee and beignets on the table in front of her. The night air was thick and warm like a rich stew, and Cassie was sweating.

"I had wondered if you would show up," the Bookseller said, as Cassie sat down next to her. "I had begun to wonder if I had imagined the whole thing."

"I wasn't sure you would be here either," Cassie said. There were other people sitting around the tables, despite the lateness of the hour: young people taking a break from their drinking and partying, a couple of tourists finishing the night with coffee and beignets. Out on Decatur Street an old Black man was sitting on a stool and playing a battered tuba, brassy notes punching holes in the dense night air. Every now and then the tuba would stop and he'd sing a few lines of lyrics in a nasally, scratchy voice, cutting through the background noise like a knife.

"Much better at this time of night," Lottie explained, as Cassie looked around. "During the day it's full of tourists. I prefer it when it's not so busy, when I can get a seat, and nobody is trying to hurry my coffee. I can't live without this place. This coffee, these pastries. This is life."

A middle-aged Chinese woman shuffled over to the table and scowled a question at Cassie, inviting an order. Cassie asked for a café au lait.

"So you believe me, then?" Cassie asked, once the server had left the table.

The Bookseller nodded. "Well, all the things that you said would happen, happened. So you were either from the future or you're psychic. Or a very good guesser. Either way it was worth another conversation. And I did like you that first time we met, five years ago. You have an energy I enjoy."

"I've never been accused of having an energy before, but I'll take it." The server returned to the table and placed a coffee down in front of Cassie.

The Bookseller took a bite of a beignet, spilling powdered sugar over herself. She brushed it off. "You should eat one," she instructed. "You're too thin."

"I've never been accused of that either," Cassie said, but she took a beignet and ate it in a few bites. It was delicious. It made her think of Drummond and the croissants they had eaten in Lyon. She would be seeing him again soon, she knew, and that created a buzz of excitement in her stomach she didn't quite understand.

As she chewed, she watched a gaggle of barely dressed young women totter along the street toward the busker. As they drew near him they started dancing in the street to the sound of his tuba, whooping and laughing and drawing a blast of a horn from a car trying to pass.

"You said you would help me," Cassie said to the Bookseller, licking sugar off her fingers.

"You remember our agreement?" the Bookseller asked.

"I do. You will send someone to protect my friend."

"Izzy," the Bookseller said, and Cassie was impressed the woman didn't need to check a note or be prompted to remember the name. "I remember."

"She's important to me," Cassie said. "I want to make sure she is safe."

"I understand. Tell me where and when."

Cassie took a sip of her coffee and then brushed some sugar from her lap. "I'll send you an email closer to the time with the details. Give me an email address."

The Bookseller nodded.

"I left her asleep in bed," Cassie explained, turning her eyes to the street again. "Someone needs to watch and make sure she is okay. And then, in the morning, when she's up, take her somewhere to keep her safe."

"Understood."

"And I want to borrow whatever book you have that will help me with Dr. Barbary."

The Bookseller said nothing for a while, looking into her coffee cup, rotating it on its saucer. Cassie listened to the tuba, to the chatter of tourists at nearby tables talking about the Garden District and cemeteries and how bad the gumbo had been.

"What you are asking," Lottie said, pulling Cassie's attention back to her. "It's not a small thing. You understand?"

Cassie shrugged. "What I'm giving is not a small thing either."

"If it really exists," the Bookseller said.

"You know it does, otherwise you wouldn't be here. We're past this already, and I have to get back to New York."

The Bookseller smiled. "I do like your attitude, girl," she said. "So self-confident."

"That's something else I've never been accused of," Cassie murmured. Beyond the sound of the tuba and the chatter in the café, Cassie heard a bell ringing somewhere behind her, maybe from a boat on the wide Mississippi. She didn't know if boats cruised so late at night. She imagined it would be lonely, out there in the dark.

"So tell me this," the Bookseller said. "If you manage to recover your book from Hugo Barbary, why don't you just travel back in time and stop him from throwing you into the past? Why don't you just make it so that all of this didn't happen?"

Cassie smiled. She and Mr. Webber had spent many nights discussing time travel. "I don't think time travel works like that," she said.

"Somebody once told me that you can't change the past, you can only create the present you live in."

"That makes no sense."

"Once you've done a bit of time travel, you begin to see," Cassie said. "Things always turn out the way they happened. I don't think I could stop that happening to me. And more importantly, I don't know if I would want that now."

"Oh?" the Bookseller asked.

Cassie shrugged. The first few months stuck in the past had been hard for her. She had never known despair like it. But after that, in the years that followed, in all the time she had spent with Mr. Webber, she had been happy. She had built a friendship with Mr. Webber, and it had been a special time in her life. She wouldn't change that now, she wouldn't sacrifice those memories. "It doesn't matter," she said. "That's not what I am here for."

The Bookseller raised her hand and gestured to a man sitting across the café from them. He was a tall white man with pale skin. He walked over and handed a briefcase to Lottie.

"This is Elias," she explained. "He is my bookkeeper. In the sense of a man who keeps books safe, not an accountant."

Elias gazed at Cassie without expression. There was something intense about the man's gaze, and in a different light and without an introduction he would have been creepy.

Lottie put the briefcase on the table, pushing cups and plates aside, and then unlocked it using a key on a chain around her neck.

"I own one book that I will never sell," she said. "It has been in my family for three generations. It is the book that allows me to live the life I live. It has kept me safe from book hunters and other people over the years. Without this book I am exposed. It is not a risk I take lightly."

"I will return it to you as soon as I have the Book of Doors," Cassie said.

"You will give both books to me," Lottie said.

Cassie nodded reluctantly. "That's the deal."

"If you do not," the Bookseller said, "there is nothing in this world that will stop me from finding you and killing you. Do you understand?"

"I do," Cassie said.

"Uh-uh." The Bookseller shook her finger at Cassie, like she was telling her off. "Don't say it without thinking about it. I am not Hugo Barbary. I am not some stupid man with an ego. I am a professional and people only cross me once."

"I understand," Cassie said.

The Bookseller held her gaze for a moment, reiterating the message. Then she turned the briefcase around on the table.

The book inside the case was the same size as the Book of Doors—as all the special books, Cassie assumed—but this book had a pure white cover, like fine porcelain or crisp cotton.

"It's beautiful," Cassie said, remembering how wonderful these special books were, despite all the unhappiness they had brought to her. "What does it do?"

"Take it," the Bookseller said.

Cassie removed the book from the case and held it between her hands. It was so light, like holding a cloud. The surface was very slightly textured, like the rough softness of a bandage.

"This is the Book of Safety," the Bookseller said, her eyes stuck on the volume between Cassie's fingers. "If you have it with you, no harm will befall you. No one can hurt you. You cannot be injured." The Bookseller shrugged. "It will keep you safe."

Cassie took a breath and then opened the book, remembering the thrill of discovery, the thrill of magic in book form.

She smiled as her eyes scampered over the text in the Book of Safety, because she knew that Hugo Barbary wouldn't be a problem.

Out on the street, the busker stopped playing his tuba, and sang his words into the thick, dark night.

The Quiet Death of Mr. Webber (2)

Cassie returned to New York, the Book of Safety tucked away within her coat pocket. She stayed in hotels for a few days, keeping out of sight, keeping to herself.

After dark on the third day, with a chill in the air, Cassie left the hotel where she had been staying and she walked the city until she reached Kellner Books. The snow was coming, she could feel it in the air, and she pulled the collar of her coat up around her neck. She stood across the street, in a doorway to the side of the sushi restaurant, and she watched her younger self through the window of Kellner Books. She watched that younger Cassie on the day her life had changed.

She couldn't see the tables at the coffee bar from the street, but Cassie knew that Mr. Webber was already in there, drinking coffee and reading *The Count of Monte Cristo*.

Then she saw the other Cassie leave the counter at the front of the store, a stack of books under her arm. The snow started to fall, and somewhere in the shop she was speaking to Mr. Webber, talking about Dumas and Rome.

Cassie felt something on her cheek, and she thought it was a snowflake, but when she reached up with a finger, she felt tears.

The other Cassie reappeared in the window of the store, gazing out at the night in wonder as the snow started to come down. Somewhere behind her, Mr. Webber was dying quietly.

For the second time she was with Mr. Webber—or near him, at least—at the end of his life. She wished she could have been with him, holding his hand, keeping him company in his final moments. She had wanted the same with her grandfather, but she had been asleep, exhausted from caring for him over many days. The fact that she had missed that moment still burned her in her core.

In the window of Kellner Books, the younger Cassie got up and hurried out of sight.

Cassie stepped out of the doorway and walked down the street. She found another doorway to shelter in and watched as the paramedics came, and then the cops, and as they left minutes later. And then, not long after, younger Cassie stepped out of the store and locked up, swallowed in her greatcoat and wrapped in her burgundy scarf and bobble hat. She walked along the street and stopped directly in front of the doorway where the older Cassie was watching. She saw her younger self take the Book of Doors from her pocket and open it to examine briefly. Then the younger Cassie shook her head, slipped the book back into her pocket, and wandered off toward her life and adventures.

Older Cassie wiped the last of the tears from her face as she watched her younger self be swallowed by the snow.

"No more tears," she told herself.

This was the night that Cassie first traveled with the Book of Doors.

In a few days' time she would return to her apartment with Drummond Fox to find Dr. Barbary waiting for her, to throw her back into the past.

This time she would be waiting too, ten years older and ready for him.

PART
4

A DANCE IN A
FORGOTTEN PLACE

A Meeting in the Fox Library: On the Nature and Origin of Magic (2011)

During what was to become their final meeting in the Fox Library, in the year before three of them would die in New York City, Drummond Fox and his friends discussed the origins of magic.

It was a spring day, a world full of color, and the sunlight streamed into the dining room and sparkled on the glassware and cutlery. Drummond and his friends were enjoying a sumptuous lunch he had arranged to celebrate their presence.

"So are you going to tell us what you learned?" Drummond asked, looking at Wagner.

It was why they had gathered that weekend. Wagner had come to return the books he had borrowed for his experiments, the studies the four of them had talked about during their previous meeting. Lily and Yasmin had traveled to Scotland to hear all about the experiments and the details of what Wagner had learned.

"Ja," Wagner answered, sawing at his roast lamb with his knife. "I will tell you everything I learned," he said. "I can tell you in one word: nothing."

The others around the table shot glances at each other.

"Nothing?" Drummond queried. "Nothing at all?"

"Nothing," Wagner said.

"Nothing?" Lily demanded. "I flew over from Hong Kong for nothing? Do you know how much flights cost from Hong Kong, Wagner?"

Wagner smiled, knowing Lily was joking. "By all scientific measures, the books appear entirely normal."

"Did you try using one?" Yasmin asked. "You know, with the light and everything." She waggled her fingers, as if to convey magical happenings.

"Ja." Wagner nodded. "The light was not detected. Not visible other than to human eyes, it seems. There were no particles I could capture, nothing to weigh or measure. It is as if the magic is not subject to scientific interrogation." He lifted a finger. "This is most unusual."

"Is that an understatement?" Yasmin wondered.

"Ja," Wagner said. "Quite so."

They ate in silence for a few moments, digesting that disappointing news.

"It seems to me that the colored light the books produce *is* the source of the magic," Lily said. She speared half a roast potato with her fork and held it in front of her as if assessing it. "The color *is* the magic, I think. It only appears when the magic is happening. The book is always there, but the color is only there when there's magic."

Wagner was nodding as Lily popped the potato into her mouth. "Ja," he agreed. "Like some universal force that we simply have not understood."

"And which you couldn't detect with your experiments?" Drummond asked.

"Exactly," Wagner said. "It may not even be that mysterious, once we understand it properly."

"So you're saying it is like electricity or gravity?" Yasmin asked, frowning.

Wagner shrugged agreeably. "It *could* be. We thought these things were magic also, until we understood them properly."

"Electricity would have seemed pretty amazing to someone who knew nothing about it," Drummond agreed. Outside, beyond the tall windows at the end of the dining room, pink and white blossoms blew across the lawn.

"Maybe it is not a force from this universe," Wagner continued. "Maybe it is something seeping through from another reality. A different reality. That is why we cannot understand it. Or from some part of the universe that lies behind our own. Some underpinning place that is the source of all matter and reality."

They considered that, chewing over the big ideas as they chewed over their lunch. This was what Drummond enjoyed most about his meetings—it wasn't that answers were always found, it was that questions were asked and considered and enjoyed. No idea was scorned or dismissed, all thoughts were valid. His friends were people who knew more than he did, who understood different things, and sometimes it felt that only together, with all of their different perspectives, could they come to any conclusions.

"But why books?" Lily wondered after a while. "Why is it books, and these books in particular, that can channel or contain this force? The magic?"

"That is a good question," Wagner replied. "One I do not know the answer to." He forked a chunk of lamb into his mouth and chewed. "This is very good lamb, Drummond. Very good."

Drummond dipped his head, acknowledging the compliment.

"Books are a specifically human item, aren't they?" Yasmin said. "It's not like we find books in the natural world. Dogs and cats don't write books."

"I would read a book written by a dog," Lily commented, and Wagner grinned.

"But what I mean," Yasmin continued, "this magic, this force we don't understand yet, it must have been *put into* the books somehow. Or if it is fragments of another universe as Wagner suggests, how did the walls crack, and why did those fragments end up in books?"

"I've always thought it was a person," Drummond admitted. "Maybe centuries ago, someone who was able to make these magical books. They channeled something or found something, and then over the centuries the books traveled and were dispersed around the world."

"One person did all of this?" Wagner asked, frowning. "One person made all of these books?"

"Someone who loved books." Drummond nodded, aware but not self-conscious that this was a silly and romantic notion.

Lily was nodding. "Yes," she said. "Only someone who loves books could create the special books. They are too beautiful to be an accident."

"I agree," Yasmin said. "It is not an accident that the magic is in books. I don't know if it was a person who made them, or if that person loved books, but the magic is in books for a reason."

"Ja," Wagner agreed. "These books, they share so many similar features, as if they are from a set. It feels like they have been made through the same process. Perhaps by the same human hand."

"Or a nonhuman hand?" Lily asked.

Drummond grinned. "What, an alien?"

"A god?" Lily suggested. "History is full of gods, just like human stories are full of magic. Maybe there were gods at one time too. Maybe these books are relics or artifacts from some supernatural being."

"It is all hypothesis," Wagner said, shrugging. "I do not know. We may never know. Certainly 'doing science' to the books did not help us."

Lily smiled at Wagner's echo of her words from their earlier meeting.

"What I know is that I have homemade Bakewell tart to follow this," Drummond said. "And that is a supernatural experience in itself."

The group laughed, and conversation moved on, to rumors of newly discovered books, to mutual friends that hadn't been heard from for some time, and to the stories of the beautiful woman who was traveling the world looking for books.

Barbary's New Books

What a bitch that woman is," Barbary said conversationally, as Drummond picked himself up from the floor. Then he grinned. "Always better when it's just the boys, isn't it? Nobody to get offended by a harmless joke."

"What did you do, Hugo?" Drummond asked. "Did you push her back through the door? She'll be stuck in the past!"

Barbary grinned devilishly. "You seem to be confusing me for someone who gives a fuck."

Barbary flicked his wrist and Drummond felt himself immediately yanked up into the air. He hovered upright a foot off the floor. The Book of Control, held down by Barbary's side, effervesced with light.

"You should know that I have had a very bad day," Barbary said. He waved vaguely at the side of his face and Drummond noticed for the first time that it looked swollen. "My eye is bloodshot. Some fucking ape slapped me like I was his wife. And you know what else he did?"

Drummond watched, unable to move, all parts of his body tense. His mind was racing, trying to work out how to escape, trying to work out what Cassie would be doing, trying to work out what Barbary was going to do to him.

"He stole my fucking book!" Barbary yelled in fury, spittle spraying out and hitting Drummond on the face.

"You just stole Cassie's book," Drummond observed. "You don't exactly have the moral high ground, Hugo."

Barbary removed the Book of Doors from his pocket and inspected it. "Ah yes, the Book of Doors." He flicked through the pages. "What fun I could have with this. It's not a spectacular-looking thing, is it?" He studied the cover of the book. "Pretty ordinary. But a fabulous prize."

Drummond moved suddenly, aiming to grab an arm or Barbary's neck, but the man was expecting it. Barbary jerked his hand and Drummond's arm froze in midair, meeting resistance as firm as a wall.

"There's no point," Barbary said, his tone almost sympathetic. "I anticipate anything you might do. But you do remind me that you are carrying your own books, aren't you?"

Barbary flicked his hand twice and both of Drummond's arms were pulled out to his sides, a mockery of a crucifixion. Barbary pushed him through the air into the living area and positioned him so that he was hanging in front of the window.

"Isn't it awful," Barbary said then, gesturing at the living area and kitchen behind him. "It's like some fucking depressing modernist play from the 1990s. Do people actually live like this?"

Barbary didn't wait for an answer. He placed the Book of Doors on the floor and then reached into Drummond's inside pockets, his big hand scampering like a spider until he found and removed the Book of Memories.

"Very nice," he said, inspecting the book. "This is the Book of Memories, I assume." Drummond didn't respond. Barbary gripped the book by the back cover and let the pages spill open so he could inspect them. "Very nice." He put the book on the floor and reached into Drummond's pockets again, more spidery fingers, and removed the Book of Luck and the Book of Shadows. "Lovely," he said, admiring the golden cover of the Book of Luck. "What is this one?"

Drummond refused to answer, staring over Barbary's head. Barbary shrugged. "No matter. Time will tell." He placed the two books on the floor with the Book of Memories and the Book of Doors. Down by his side his Book of Control continued to pulse with color.

"Quite the treasure trove," he said. "Maybe I could start building my own collection to rival the woman's? What do you think, Drummond? Which monster would you prefer? Me or her?"

"Oh, you, absolutely," Drummond said.

Barbary tilted his head, interested. "And why is that?"

"Because she's terrifying, and you're a fool. I wouldn't lose any sleep over you, Hugo."

Barbary cackled as if this was a fabulous answer. "Well, let's see if we can do something about that, shall we?" He looked at Drummond, as if actually trying to decide which torture to inflict upon him. "It's such a shame that some gorilla of a man stole my Book of Pain. I would have enjoyed making you tell me all your secrets." He sucked his teeth for a moment as he considered his options. "Maybe I can still have some fun without the book . . . maybe I can make you talk the old-fashioned way. What do you think? How would you feel about some light torture?"

Barbary's thoughts were interrupted by a single chiming noise from his pocket. He removed his phone and studied it for a moment.

"That bitch," he muttered.

"What?" Drummond asked.

"That fucking Black, bald bitch."

"The Bookseller?" Drummond asked.

"She's selling my book," Barbary said. "That Jap and his ape must have been working for her."

Barbary stood for a moment, hands on his hips and his eyes off to the side of Drummond, as if he was making plans or working out how to respond.

"Well, I'll have to kill her," he said, like this was the self-evident conclusion.

"The Bookseller?" Drummond asked again, his eyebrows raising skeptically.

"Her, and any other fucker that tries to take my books. I still have the Book of Control," he said, lifting the glowing, pulsing book he held by his side. "Shouldn't be hard."

"She doesn't allow books into the auctions," Drummond said. "You know that."

"No, I don't know that," Barbary muttered. "I've never been to one of her auctions. But that just makes it easier. No books, nobody else has an advantage. I'll just shoot them all instead." He flipped back his overcoat to reveal the gun on his hip. "Maybe I'll shoot you first just to shut you up."

Drummond tried to shrug where he hung in the air. He really didn't care anymore. It was interesting how little room he had for fear when his body was full of exhaustion. "Get on with it then, man, please, for the love of god."

Drummond heard a noise then, the scrape of a key, the front door opening. Barbary heard it a moment later and turned to face the hall just as a woman stepped into the living area.

Not just a woman—this was Cassie.

A different, older Cassie, with a mission in her eyes.

"Hello," she said. "I've waited a long time for this."

The Book of Safety

The room was silent for a moment, as Barbary stared at her. Behind him, Drummond hung like a crucified man in midair, backlit by the window. Cassie's stomach twisted in delight and excitement when she saw him. It had been ten years and he looked bedraggled and worn out.

Concentrate!

Barbary's book was glowing by his side, as he held Drummond aloft.

"You," Barbary said, narrowing his eyes to inspect her. "You look different."

"Give me my book," Cassie said. She wasn't interested in a conversation about what had happened to her.

Barbary laughed. "Fuck off, bitch. I've started my own collection. I've got your book, and I've got his." He pointed at Drummond behind him, and then crouched down to pick up the books at his feet, slipping them into his pockets one at a time.

Cassie took a few steps toward him, and Barbary's eyebrows jumped up in surprise, a smile of delight stretching across his face. "Mr. Fox," he said, speaking over his shoulder. "Your young lady has become rather bold. What are you going to do, dear? Are you going to scratch me and pull my hair?"

"Cassie," Drummond said, the word a warning.

"You can't do anything to me," she said.

"Oh?" Barbary said. "Well, I am excited to test that."

He moved his arm suddenly and Cassie was yanked forward into Barbary's outstretched hand, his fingers around her neck as he lifted her off the floor, his face pressing close.

"You know, one of the worst things that ever happened was when all you women started thinking you were equal to us men." Cassie could smell spicy meat and sweat, Barbary's aroma, and she wanted to gag. "Sometimes I wish I lived back in the 1970s when the natural order was still in place. Life was so much simpler then. I could just give you a slap and send you away to make my dinner and nobody would even blink."

He grinned at her, but then his mouth curled suddenly into a furious grimace. "You need to be taught a lesson, girl, just like the olden days." Behind Barbary, Drummond dropped to the floor as if forgotten. Almost simultaneously Barbary twisted at the waist, judo-like, and threw Cassie down. Her body thumped audibly, and she felt the vibrations through her chest, but there was no pain.

The Book of Safety was protecting her; she felt its warmth through her clothes, and no harm could befall her. The reality of that truth was sunlight breaking through clouds in her soul.

"Stupid bitch," Barbary muttered, as he stepped over her and stuck his head into the hallway as if to make sure nobody else was there. By the time he turned around again Cassie was on her feet. He blinked in surprise.

"Have to do better than that," she said to him.

Then she raised the gun that she had taken from his holster when he had pulled her close. She had never fired a gun before, and this gun had a long tube on the muzzle that she assumed was a silencer, but she didn't think it would be difficult to use. Barbary was a big shape, and he was very close. She pulled the trigger and there was a muffled thump and at the same time, it seemed, Barbary was punched backward at the shoulder into the hall.

"Get the books," Drummond muttered behind her, pushing himself up from the floor.

Cassie approached the hallway as Barbary was sitting up, one hand on his shoulder.

"You shot me!" he exclaimed, apparently outraged.

"Give me my book," Cassie demanded.

"Fuck off," Barbary said again. He jerked his hand and Cassie shot upward, the small of her back thumping into the top of the doorway painlessly.

"You can't hurt me," she said to him. "But I can hurt you."

She lifted the gun again and pointed it at his head.

His fingers flicked, and this time Cassie was thrown backward into the kitchen, crashing to a stop against the stove.

"Maybe I can't hurt you," Barbary said, reentering the room. "But I can keep you out of my way."

Cassie fired again, slightly wide over Barbary's left side. "Can you keep bullets out of your way?"

He hesitated, debating with himself as she pushed herself to her feet, never once moving her eyes from him.

"Can you stop lots of bullets?" she asked. "Or do you think I'll get one into your guts sooner or later?"

He stared at her venomously, seeing the stalemate. She could see his mind working, trying to find a way out, but she didn't want to give him the time to come up with a plan.

"Give me my book," she snapped. "Before I put a bullet through that space in your head where a brain should be."

He didn't move and she could see how he didn't want to give her what she wanted. He was furiously trying to do anything but that.

Out of nowhere, moving with surprising speed, Drummond leapt up from the floor, pushed off from the couch with one foot, and vaulted into Barbary from the side while he was distracted. The two of them crashed into the wall by the door, a tangle of limbs and anger, shouting and grunting, and the Book of Control slid out of Barbary's grip and flew across the room. They wrestled briefly, collapsing onto the floor with Barbary on top, punching Drummond repeatedly in the face, grunting and muttering as he did so.

"Stop," Cassie said simply, approaching him from behind and placing the cold mouth of the pistol against the back of his fat neck.

Barbary froze, a fist in the air.

"Get up," Cassie said, pushing the gun against Barbary's neck. The man clambered up and Cassie backed away out of his reach, waiting as Drummond pulled himself up off the floor. His face was a mess of blood. He reached over and picked up the Book of Control from where it had landed. It was a dull gray item with a textured surface, like cross-hatching.

"Give us the other books," Drummond said to Barbary, wiping his eyes with his sleeve. "All of them."

Cassie kept the gun pointed at the bald man as he stared at them from beneath his brows, his lips a sneer.

"Really bad day for you," Drummond said. "Losing both of your books. None of the books in your pockets can help you now, not against the Book of Control and a gun. Give them back to me and I'll let you live."

Barbary exhaled heavily through his nose and then reached into his pockets and removed the books one by one, tossing them across the floor—the Book of Luck, the Book of Memories, the Book of Shadows, and finally the Book of Doors.

"You might as well kill me now," he said. "Because if I am still alive, I will come for you. And I will keep coming for you."

"I don't really want to kill anyone," Cassie said, bending to pick up the Book of Doors, her heart singing as she held it again for the first time in ten years. "But I don't really want to be looking over my shoulder for you for the rest of my life either."

She thought for a moment while Drummond opened the Book of Control and smiled grimly as he looked at the first page. "'Control,'" he read, turning the book around to show Cassie. The word "control," block capital letters etched in thick black ink, was the only thing on the otherwise blank page. "Not exactly poetry, is it?"

Cassie grunted and Barbary stared furiously.

Drummond held the book for a moment, his brow knitted in concentration. The book started to glow in his hands and a moment later the couch moved a few inches away from the wall, scraping across the floor.

"Not so hard," Drummond said to Barbary, as the glow diminished and the air cleared. Then, to Cassie, "What do you want to do?"

"I know what I want to do," she said. She walked into the hallway and closed her bedroom door. "Put him in here when I open the door."

Drummond nodded once, understanding, and the Book of Control started to glow once again. Cassie pushed open her bedroom door to reveal a bustling street in New York, traffic streaming by, pedestrians in clothes that came from another time. Drummond moved his hand and Barbary was thrown forward and through the door, tumbling out into the gloom.

Cassie watched through the doorway as he picked himself up.

"Let's see how much you really like living in the 1970s!" she screamed at him, releasing ten years of anger and pain. She slammed the door on him as he looked around, realization dawning.

DRUMMOND COLLAPSED ONTO THE SOFA as if suddenly exhausted. She gave him some paper towels from the kitchen and waited while he tried to mop the blood from his battered face.

"You look different," he said finally, and she thought he was trying to avoid her eyes. "You seem different."

She said nothing, standing in front of the window with her arms crossed. It was so strange for her, being back in the old apartment after a decade.

"What happened to you?" he asked.

"It's been ten years," she said. Her voice was quiet, not angry, not shouting. She was drained of fury.

Drummond stared at her in shock.

"Ten years," she said again, as if needing to make sure that he heard.

"How . . ." Drummond started, but then he stopped himself, as if perhaps realizing that there was no point to any questions. He swallowed once and she saw him reordering his thoughts. "You've waited ten years?"

She shrugged. "There was no other way."

He absorbed that for a moment, then asked, "Where did you send him? Barbary?"

"I did to him what he did to me," she said. "I've sent him into the past. He was so keen to live in the 1970s so I put him back there. Let's see how he likes it."

"What if he comes back?" Drummond asked. "You did."

Cassie thought about that for a moment.

"I had to live through ten years and that was hard enough. He'd have to live through fifty years. How old would he be now? Ninety?"

Drummond shrugged.

"If he lived that long," Cassie said, "I don't think he'll be any threat to us."

Drummond patted his damaged face some more. "I'm sorry," he said finally.

Cassie nodded. "It wasn't your fault," she said.

He looked at her. "Are you sure?"

She sighed. "I don't know, Drummond," she said. "It's just good to see you after all this time."

After a moment he nodded, accepting that. He studied Cassie quietly for a few seconds, his eyes moving slowly over her face, obviously seeing how changed she was.

"I can't believe it's been ten years for you," he said quietly. "How have you survived? How did you keep going?"

"I had help," she admitted. "I'll tell you about it sometime. But right now we need to go to Izzy. I haven't seen her for a decade and I really, *really* want to see her again."

"I don't know where Izzy is," Drummond admitted. "I don't know what happened to her. I'm sorry."

"I do," Cassie said.

Drummond looked a question at her.

"I struck a deal," she said. "With the Bookseller. She gave me the Book of Safety so I could deal with Barbary. And she promised me she would send someone to look after Izzy."

"Barbary talked about a Japanese man," Drummond said. "Probably Azaki. And whoever he was with."

Cassie shrugged. She didn't know the details.

"In exchange for what?" Drummond asked. "What deal did you strike?"

Cassie held up the Book of Doors. "In exchange for this. I'm sorry, Drummond, but if you want the Book of Doors, you're going to have to buy it from the Bookseller first. I promised I'd give it to her if she kept Izzy safe."

The Forgotten Place

In a forgotten place on West Twenty-Seventh Street, Izzy watched the book hunters arrive for the Bookseller's auction as the minutes of the day slowly crept toward midnight.

She was on a mezzanine level in a space that had once been a bar, a floor above the art deco lobby of the former Macintosh Hotel. At the front of the lobby the once grand entrance was now shrouded with plywood, sealing it off from the world. A single door had been cut into the boards, and as it opened a gaunt old man with white hair and leathery skin stepped through. His eyes were cruel and judgmental, Izzy thought, and he looked as if everything he was seeing was just as awful as he had expected it to be. He was a man who liked to be disappointed in things.

"Who's that?" she asked.

"That is Pastor Merlin Gillette and two of his awful children," the Bookseller said. "I don't mean that only some of his children are awful. They all are. But today he brought only two of them."

The man had been followed into the lobby by two younger adults who looked like twins, one man and one woman. Both were tall and thin and blessed with flowing and lustrous blond hair.

"They look like a shampoo advertisement," Izzy observed. "For Nazis."

All three of the new arrivals were dressed in gray suits, the men were wearing ties, the daughter a crucifix on a chain around her neck.

"What is he pastor of?" Izzy asked.

"Oh, some crazy, rich Pentecostal church from South Carolina," the Bookseller said. "They think the special books are the work of the devil and that they should be destroyed. Because the only special book that anyone needs is the Bible." The Bookseller rolled her eyes. "They're awful people, but pretty harmless in the grand scheme of things. Unlike some of the other people who'll be here tonight."

They watched in silence as the pastor and his progeny were patted down and then directed through the lobby and out of sight beneath the mezzanine.

"Where are they going?" Izzy asked.

"The ballroom," the Bookseller said. "I'll do the auction in there. It's big enough that nobody has to stand too close to anybody else. That's usually for the best at these things."

The Bookseller seemed distracted, anxious even, like someone having to tolerate small talk before a job interview.

It had been hours since Izzy had first met her in the lobby of the Ace Hotel. After their meeting the Bookseller had taken them across town to the unspectacular redbrick building on West Twenty-Seventh Street. From out front the place had looked derelict, with graffiti-covered hoarding sealing it off from the street, like it was under some sort of renovation. The Bookseller had escorted them inside through the same small door that Merlin Gillette had just arrived through, and into the gloomy lobby. Izzy had marveled at the space, a cathedral of faded gold and rosewood, black and white carpets, and art deco lettering above the reception desk. Huge mirrors hung on the walls, some of them cracked or the glass missing entirely. It was a forgotten place, a hotel from the past, crumbling in the darkness.

"What is this place?" Izzy had asked, turning a slow circle in the cavernous lobby as the Bookseller had flicked a switch to release a breath of weak electric light into the space.

"It was a hotel once," the Bookseller had said. "The family that built it lost all their money after the war. They were paying down their debt for decades, keeping this place mothballed in some crazy hope they might reopen it one day. I bought it from them twenty years ago. It's useful to have my own place in the city, somewhere off the books."

The Bookseller had led Izzy and Lund up a grand set of stairs to a large room on the second floor, a space that appeared to have been two rooms knocked into one and then modernized compared to the rest of the property. There were leather couches and a large flat-screen TV, a kitchen, and a bathroom with expensive gray stone tiles and a walk-in shower.

"Wait here," the Bookseller had said. "There's food and drink in the kitchen. The place is empty but it's safe. Feel free to wander around. I don't care. But don't leave the building. Not until the auction is over."

Izzy had slept for a few hours, her dreams a cocktail of forgotten memories and terror and the background noise of the TV program Lund was watching. She'd eaten some noodles that she'd found in the cupboard, and then had grown impatient and restless. So she'd gone for a walk through the hotel, wandering long gloomy corridors through stagnant air where the memory of cigarette smoke and perfume still hung. The plaster on the walls was cracked in places, the stained-glass ornamentation dull and lifeless in the gloom. She opened bedroom doors at random and found variations on a theme of decay and dereliction. There were old worn armchairs and heavy drapes layered with dust, glass ashtrays with ancient cigarette butts, now curled up and desiccated. Some rooms had beds, some were empty. In some the carpets had been lifted and the drapes removed, leaving a dusty wooden shell, while others appeared almost frozen in time.

After walking aimlessly for a while, Izzy had crossed the staircase the Bookseller had led them up earlier that day, the column of empty space flooded with light from the glass skylights high above, and had arrived at the mezzanine level and the bar. It was a large space, with armchairs and tables so dated they were almost fashionable again, and the bar was long and wooden, off to the side, with a display of bottles on the wall behind. Glass ashtrays were piled up on one corner of the bar, as if they had been collected in one evening and then left there ever since. To Izzy they looked like some sort of scale model of a futuristic building an expensive architect might produce.

She had been exploring the collection of bottles behind the bar when the Bookseller had appeared without her noticing.

"What are you doing?"

Izzy had started in surprise as the Bookseller stared at her.

"I'm bored," she said. "I took a walk. Why don't you fix this place up? It would make a fortune."

"Too much work," the Bookseller said. She walked over to the balustrade to watch the lobby below.

"More work than finding and selling magic books?" Izzy asked skeptically.

The Bookseller had smiled to herself but said nothing.

Izzy had stood next to her and watched as a group of men in dark suits and wearing weapons in holsters had gathered in the lobby by the front door. One tall man with pale hair and a briefcase in his hand had taken up position behind a table just inside the door, and then Merlin Gillette and his awful children had arrived.

Once the pastor was out of sight Izzy pointed at the tall man with the pale hair and the briefcase, who was waiting by the door. "Who's that?"

"Elias," the Bookseller said. "My bookkeeper. All special books are surrendered on entry. Elias looks after them and returns them when people leave. It's best for everyone. Look, are you sure you don't want to wait back in your room or something? I'm not looking for company right now."

"No, I'm fine," Izzy said.

"It was more of an order than a suggestion."

"I know," Izzy replied. "But I'm not your employee."

The Bookseller sighed in annoyance, and then thumbed over her shoulder to the bar behind them. "Any of that still drinkable?"

Izzy shrugged.

"If you insist on being here, bring me something that looks like it won't kill me."

Izzy found a few vodka bottles that were unopened and a couple of glasses that she dusted clean with her blouse. She opened a bottle, sniffed it experimentally, and then poured a couple of inches of vodka in each glass.

"Straight vodka," she said, handing the Bookseller one of the drinks. She held out her glass and the Bookseller tapped it with her own, then they both sipped. "Strong," Izzy said, twisting her face at the taste.

"It's fine," the Bookseller said. She swallowed it down like it was water.

They watched in silence and Izzy understood that the Bookseller was assessing her audience, like a performer about to work the crowd. Izzy studied the people as they arrived, the bidders with all of their money. All of them desperate to get hold of the thing that had tortured her only hours before. She remembered those moments of agony, the helplessness, the despair, and her stomach churned. She wondered what the successful bidder would do with the book. Would they inflict that experience on others? Could she take millions of dollars from someone who might use the book in the way it had been used on her? She bit her nails nervously, surprised at how conflicted she felt.

"That's Okoro," the Bookseller said, pointing to a large Black man who had just stepped through the door. "Very dangerous. He's a mercenary and an assassin. Probably runs drug gangs in West Africa as well."

The man took a book from his pocket and handed it to the Bookkeeper. It disappeared inside the briefcase.

"What's that?" Izzy asked.

"He has the Book of Matter," the Bookseller said.

"What does that do?"

"Lets him control matter. Change solids into liquids, liquids into gases, that sort of thing. I am sure he is keen to add the Book of Pain to his collection. The Book of Pain would be very useful to a man like Okoro."

Izzy sipped the last of the vodka and contemplated returning for a top-up. She wanted to keep a clear head, but she also wanted to drink, to soften the sharp edges of this strange world she now found herself inhabiting.

"Ah, the representatives of the president of Belarus," the Bookseller said, nodding at two old white men as they entered. They looked like tired office workers at the end of a long day. "What they would do with the Book of Pain." She clicked her tongue and shook her head once.

"Don't you care who it goes to?" Izzy asked.

"It's an auction," the Bookseller said. "Highest bidder wins."

"I know how an auction works," Izzy muttered in annoyance. "That's not what I mean, and you know it."

"Girl, if I'd known you were going to be so talkative, I would have locked your door."

Izzy waited.

"No, I don't really care who it goes to," the Bookseller admitted, after a moment. "I can't. Not if I want to conduct an honest auction. I can't play favorites."

Izzy waited some more, feeling that the Bookseller's answer wasn't yet complete.

"But yes, I suppose I'd much rather the books went to people who won't use them to make the world a worse place. But at the end of the day I am a businesswoman, I'm here to make money, and the money I'm paid for selling these books, I can use it to make the world a better place. That's what I can control."

"And how do you do that?" Izzy asked. "How do you make the world a better place with all of the money you earn?"

The Bookseller gave Izzy a sidelong glance as if reassessing her, and then looked back to the front entrance, not answering.

"Mmm, thought so," Izzy murmured.

More and more people filed in, most of them flunkeys and supporters of the people with money, and most of the people with money didn't have their own books to offer up. In total it seemed only three books had been surrendered to Elias. In addition to Okoro's Book of Matter, a well-dressed middle-aged woman had surrendered the Book of Health ("That's Elizabeth Fraser. She's English. And she's over a hundred and twenty," the Bookseller said. "That book keeps her young. Doesn't stop her being a complete bitch, though.") and a middle-aged Hispanic man in a gray suit and turquoise shirt surrendered the Book of Faces. "That's Diego," the Bookseller said. "Spanish or Portuguese, I think. He specializes in industrial espionage, as far as I know, but straightforward assassinations are not beneath him. He lives in California like a film star. The Book of Faces can make him look like anybody, man or woman. Very useful for someone in his line of work."

"So there are only three books," Izzy observed. "Three books for all these people?"

"That is the reality of special books," the Bookseller explained. "Most people who know about them have never even seen one. More people want them than can have them. They are the ultimate rare and precious commodity. The perfect item for sale at auction." The Bookseller checked her watch. "You should go," she said to Izzy. "Go find that mountain of a man and bring the Book of Pain to the ballroom downstairs. We'll start the auction at midnight exactly. I want you both in the room so I can keep my eyes on you."

"Keep us safe, you mean?"

"Yes," the Bookseller said, looking into her empty glass. "That's what I mean, of course."

Izzy returned to the room where she had spent the afternoon and she found Lund standing at the kitchen counter with the Book of Illusion open in front of him. He looked up in surprise when she arrived, his hand moving quickly to cover the book.

"Are you trying to hide that?" she asked.

He shrugged. "Just seems to me it's better that people don't know when you have one of these books."

She nodded. "Lots of people arriving. The auction's gonna start at midnight."

He nodded.

"What are you doing with the book?" she asked.

"Trying to learn how to use it," he admitted. "Can't seem to get it, though."

"I think Cassie used the Book of Doors almost immediately," Izzy said. "Like, without even trying."

"Huh," Lund said, sounding disappointed.

"Why do you want to do illusions?"

Lund thought about the question for a moment, then answered, "Why wouldn't I?"

Izzy thought that was a good answer. "Can I try?"

Lund shrugged. "I'm going to the bathroom."

As he wandered away Izzy lifted the book gently, feeling the texture of the leather, the smoothness of the thin veins of gold. It felt slightly warm to her, like it had been sitting on a radiator before she'd picked it up. The book was a beautiful thing, black and gold and luxurious. It looked like it had been produced by Fabergé, or some other high-end jeweler famous for intricate detail with precious metals. Izzy opened the book and saw sketches in black ink, pages of scribbles. The book felt odd in her hand, heavier than she expected it to be. She closed the book and turned it over, inspecting the cover as if she might find something to explain the weight. As she was doing that Lund returned from the bathroom, and almost simultaneously the door to the hall opened suddenly.

Izzy slipped the Book of Illusion into her hip pocket, out of sight, as one of the Bookseller's security team, bulky and solid in his black clothes, peered in at them both with a serious face.

"The Bookseller has requested that you join her," he said. "Do you have the item?"

Lund pulled the Book of Pain from his pocket. Izzy avoided looking at it.

"Good," the security man said. "Let's go. The auction is about to start."

The Ballroom at the Macintosh Hotel

The ballroom at the Macintosh Hotel was one of Lottie's favorite places. It was a grand square space with a giant art deco chandelier hanging from the center of the ceiling, like someone had captured the sun in a glass wedding cake. Tall rectangular mirrors were lined along the wall, interspersed with doors leading to the toilets or the kitchens or back offices, and wall-mounted lamps. The carpet around the edges of the room looked like a wiring diagram, with black and white lines and geometric patterns, and in the center of the room was a large square dance floor, the wood now scuffed and warped after years of neglect. It was still an impressive space—Lottie had loved it from the moment she'd bought the hotel—and she could easily imagine it as it had been a hundred years in the past, with rich white people in stiff suits and elegant dresses, swirling around the dance floor in a haze of cigarette smoke and alcohol, a jazz band in the corner, double bass notes punching the air rhythmically.

The ballroom was faded now, with cracked plaster and water damage to the ceiling in one corner, but it still had atmosphere; it still conveyed grandeur and elegance, even in its disheveled state.

As Lottie walked through the large double doors from the hotel lobby, her customers, groups of people and individuals scattered around the space, turned to watch. For a moment she felt like the bride arriving for the first dance, but she pushed the childish fantasy away and focused on acknowledging everyone she thought mattered, throwing a glance or a nod at those who were dangerous or rich or both. Normally she was more confident at the auctions. Normally she had the Book of Safety. This time she would have to brazen it out, at least until Cassie arrived.

If she arrived, Lottie told herself.

Lottie didn't think Cassie would leave her friend, but she hadn't gotten to where she was in life by always thinking the best of people.

At the far end of the ballroom, on a raised platform where the wedding party would sit, or the band might play during dances, a lectern had been placed. Lottie stepped up and stood behind it, gazing down on the crowd of people. She saw impatience, calculation, outright hostility, and she ignored it all.

"Ladies and gentlemen," she said. "Welcome to this auction."

"Enough of this circus," Okoro shouted from the left side of the room. "You have taken my book from me, and you have poked and prodded me. How much of this indignity must I stand?"

Lottie stared at the man without expression. She said nothing. She was scared of Okoro, but she firmly believed that dealing with people like him was just like training a dog. You had to make sure it knew who was in charge, even if it could bite your head off.

"I didn't force you to come, Mr. Okoro," she said evenly. "You are free to leave." She raised a hand and gestured toward the door at the back of the room. "We will wait until you have departed."

It was a risky strategy, trying to embarrass him into submission, but Lottie knew two things. First, she knew that Okoro really wanted the Book of Pain. She recognized the hunger in his expression. And second, she knew that when she had bought the Macintosh Hotel she had made some modifications to the structure of the building. The mirror on the wall immediately behind Lottie was a door to a panic room which in turn led to a secret corridor and an exit on the rear of the building. If anything happened that the pair of security men who were in the ballroom with her couldn't handle, Lottie only had to retreat three steps through the mirror, and she would be safe. She would have preferred to have been carrying the Book of Safety, but even without it she felt she was in control. Even Okoro couldn't reach her before she could flee.

"No?" she asked Okoro. The man crossed his arms and glared at her. "I would very much like you to stay with us, Mr. Okoro," she said, throwing him a bone of respect. "The more the merrier, right?"

"Get on with it, then," Okoro muttered.

"Yes, come on," Pastor Merlin Gillette shouted, his voice nasal and sharp-edged like the engine of a dirt bike. "Get on with it, woman!"

"We will get on with it," the Bookseller snapped, firing the old man a warning look. "At my leisure. I will take no more interruptions from the floor. If you want to speak you raise your hand. Is that clear?"

The audience stared back silently.

"Ladies and gentlemen, for those of you who have your own special books, I thank you for handing them over to Elias." The Bookseller gestured to the back of the ballroom, where Elias stood in the doorway, the briefcase in his hand. "As is customary, the Bookkeeper will now depart to a safe location elsewhere in the hotel. He will return once the auction is over, and any special books will be returned to you upon your departure."

Elias nodded and then left. Lottie said nothing for a few beats, letting the crowd watch him go. At the same moment the security man she had sent to retrieve Izzy and Lund appeared, with the two of them trailing behind. He led the giant and the girl around the edge of the room.

"Now," she said. "Down to business. You are here tonight to bid for ownership of the Book of Pain."

She gestured to Lund as the big man arrived at the front of the ballroom and he stepped up onto the platform next to her, towering over her. He passed her the book and she held it aloft, like a preacher with the Bible. All eyes fixed upon it. Lund stepped down again and walked back to the side of the ballroom to stand next to Izzy.

"This is the Book of Pain. The cover is colored purple and green," she said. "I can confirm its authenticity and good condition." She opened the book at a random page and held it up so that everyone in the room could see the contents. "Whoever possesses the Book of Pain is able to cause considerable suffering and agony in others," Lottie said.

"It is the devil's work, if ever I saw it!" Merlin Gillette croaked, ignoring Lottie's instruction to raise a hand before speaking.

In response to the remark Elizabeth Fraser, the woman who had come with the Book of Health, raised a hand, and Lottie nodded at her to speak.

"The Book of Pain will also remove pain from others," she said, her voice a surprising and pleasing alto. "It is the power of relief, as much as it is the power of suffering. It is no devilry. That is the comment of a man with a superstitious and underdeveloped mind."

A few people sniggered. Merlin Gillette turned to face the older woman where she stood, a few feet behind him.

"I'll show you an underdeveloped mind, you witch!" he shouted.

"You already have, young man," Elizabeth said mildly.

Gillette's daughter restrained him, whispering something in his ear, and the man turned back to the front.

"That's enough!" Lottie called, sounding sterner than she felt. This sort of friction before the bidding always helped. It was the fight before the lovemaking. "You will all behave, or I will have you removed."

Merlin Gillette threw her a mutinous glance but said nothing.

"Let us try it out," someone called from the back of the crowd.

The call was answered by Okoro. "Yes, let us try it on someone to prove it is real."

"No," the Bookseller answered, her tone firm. "Nobody is using the Book of Pain at this auction. It is authentic. If you do not trust me, you do not have to bid and you are free to leave before we start."

She waited. Nobody moved. The hall was silent.

"Very well," she said. "Now we can get on with the auction. The currency is US dollars, naturally. Raise your hand to bid. We will assume increments of five hundred thousand dollars unless you specify otherwise. The bidding will continue until we have a successful bidder. Money will be transferred immediately and once received by my bank, the Book of Pain will be released."

The audience shuffled and readied itself, people throwing glances around and trying to judge the appetites and wealth of opponents. In the mirrors around the edges of the ballroom, reflections of the audience did the same.

Then Lottie asked, "Who will open the bidding at fifteen million dollars?"

Nobody moved, nobody bid. The event that everyone had been waiting for, the moment, had arrived. Like wary boxers, nobody wanted to throw the first punch.

"Fifteen million dollars!"

The bid came from the back of the room, a woman's voice, shrill and piercing. It was one of the twins from Shanghai. There were rumors they were antiquarians or art collectors. There were also rumors they really worked for the Communist Party.

"Thank you, Ms. Li," the Bookseller said. "The auction is underway."

THE AUCTION PROCEEDED, BIDS COMING slowly at first, cautiously, but then the energy changed, the confidence and determination growing, and the price for the Book of Pain climbed steadily higher.

"We have twenty-two million," Lottie called. "Any advance?"

She expected more. None of the serious people had bid yet; they were waiting for the amateurs to finish playing around.

"Twenty-five million."

It was Okoro, standing with his arms folded and a scowl on his face.

Lottie nodded, acknowledging the bid, and then repeated the figure to the room.

"Twenty-six," a man shouted in heavily accented English.

"Twenty-six," Lottie said. "To the man from Belarus. Any advance?"

The bidding seemed to pause, the energy lapsing slightly as people took a breath, considering their wealth and weighing it against their desire for the book. Lottie knew it wasn't over yet. Okoro was scowling at the Belarusian. Diego, the Spaniard, was leaning against the side wall as if he was bored, but Lottie could see he was ready to pounce at the last minute. The twins from Shanghai were whispering to each other and Merlin Gillette's children were both whispering to him. People were working out their tactics.

"Any advance on twenty-six million dollars?" she asked, leaning on the lectern with her elbows.

"This is going on too long," Diego suddenly announced, pushing himself off the wall. "Thirty million dollars and let us be done with it!"

"Thirty million dollars," Lottie said, as people threw murderous glances at Diego. Before she could search the gathered faces for further bids there was a boom from a nearby room, a thunderous clap that shook the walls.

Everyone turned their heads toward the sound. Lottie looked immediately to one of her security team. He had one hand to his ear and a frown on his face like he wasn't hearing what he expected to hear. He glanced back at her and shook his head once: *Don't know.*

"Thirty million dollars," Lottie said again, raising her voice. She was determined to complete the auction. Even if Cassie didn't turn up with the Book of Doors, she could take enough of a profit from the Book of Pain to get out of the business for a while.

Another boom sounded, this one closer, and then a third. People started muttering, moving away from the walls and glancing around to see what everyone else was doing.

"Please," she called. "Just give us a moment."

A figure walked into the doorway to the ballroom, at the opposite end of the room from Lottie. She watched, and other people turned that way too.

"Stop!" Lottie called. "Who are you?"

He was a tall man, dressed shabbily in an old raincoat, a cowboy-style hat on his head. He advanced into the ballroom, walking slowly with a limp like he had a weak leg.

"Who are you?" Lottie demanded again, her voice full of indignation and authority. The man came to a stop just inside the room and then lifted one hand to remove his hat and toss it off to the side. The face revealed was withered and weathered, many years older than it should have been, gaunt in the cheeks and sagging around the jowls, but Lottie recognized it.

"My name is Hugo Barbary," the man shouted, the voice a thin, reedy croak. He extended his arm and pointed an automatic handgun at her, the muzzle a huge, gaping hole of dreadful possibility. "Now give me back my fucking book, you bitch!"

Pain in the Forgotten Ballroom

"You have no place here," Lottie said, sounding calmer than she felt. She was shocked at Barbary's appearance, but she covered what she felt with a shield of annoyance. "You did not advise of your attendance."

"Do I look like I'm in the mood to send a fucking email?" Barbary screeched. "You stole my book! I'm not here to buy it off you. I've waited fifty years for this!"

"You are embarrassing yourself," Lottie replied, confused by his words but ignoring the confusion. She was aware that the other people in the room were looking at Barbary, looking at her, trying to predict how the confrontation would go. "Walk away now, before I make you."

Barbary smiled, soft wrinkled skin stretching to reveal stained teeth. "I've been waiting for so long, Bookseller. Hiding and waiting for this day." He giggled like a child. "I know all about your secret room behind the mirror, Bookseller."

Lottie flicked her eyes to the leader of her security team, a signal he was waiting for. The man and the two other members of his team—including the one who had escorted Lund and Izzy—ran at Hugo Barbary from two sides of the hall. None of them were quick enough. Hugo pivoted on his heel, shot twice, and then turned and shot again, and all three men fell to the floor as they were running, bullet holes in their foreheads. "I still got it!" Barbary cackled to Lottie. "Now you have no men with guns."

Lottie was aware of the girl Izzy gasping off to her side, stepping backward as if trying to escape. Barbary caught the movement as well and turned his attention in that direction. Lottie saw Lund step in front of the girl and in that moment she decided that she liked the big man.

"You," Barbary spat. His face was a tight knot of fury and grizzled hatred. He limped forward, lifting the gun toward Lund. "You stole my book."

"Is somebody going to do something about this fool?" Merlin Gillette called out. "What kinda circus you running here, woman?"

Barbary swung his arm and shot Gillette through the center of his forehead, sending drops of blood and brain matter spattering onto the mirror behind him like lava spat out of a volcano. Gillette's two children screamed and shouted and collapsed down next to his body. Seeing now that nobody was safe from this interruption, other people in the room started to move, circling away from Barbary as he limped across the floor. Lottie saw a couple of people run out of the room, heading away through the lobby. Many of the other people, she knew, would be having their own internal debates between self-preservation and getting their hands on the Book of Pain.

All the while Barbary advanced toward Lund.

"I am going to kill you first," Barbary muttered. "Just to put me in a good mood."

Lund gazed at the advancing figure without expression and the Bookseller wondered why he wasn't more scared.

Before Barbary could reach the far side of the room Okoro charged him, his head low, but Barbary spotted the movement in one of the mirrors and pivoted awkwardly away.

Okoro connected with Barbary and the two men collapsed to the floor in a knot of limbs and fury. The gun fired once, the bullet going wide and shattering one of the mirrors on the left-hand wall, creating a shower of glass. Lottie glanced over to Lund.

"You," she said. "Pull him off."

Lund blinked once and then looked at the wrestling men. He took a few steps and then heaved Okoro off the older man.

"Get off me, you fool!" Okoro shouted at Lund, brushing down his expensive suit once he was on his feet. Lund turned his attention to Barbary and gripped the old man's wrist, pulling his gun from his fingers as he pulled the man to his feet.

The Bookseller stepped down from the platform and approached them. Barbary looked up at her defiantly, his face wrinkled, gray stubble dotting his cheeks.

"What happened to you?" she asked, genuinely interested.

"You have my book," he spat. "They stole it." He jerked his chin toward Lund. "Is this what you do now, Bookseller?" he asked. "Steal books to order and then sell them at a profit?"

"I am not going to dignify that with an answer," Lottie said, but she could feel people considering the question, her customers watching her with narrowed eyes. "And frankly, you must have lost your mind to think you can come here and disrupt one of my auctions like this, all by yourself with a handgun." She took his gun from Lund and inspected it like it was a joke. "With this? You didn't think I could handle an old man with a gun?"

Barbary grinned as he looked at her from beneath his brows.

"What?" the Bookseller asked. "Why are you smiling?"

"You're right. I would have lost my mind to do that. But I have been waiting for a very long time for this moment. I have had years and years to prepare, Madame Bookseller. Years and years to plan what I would do."

Barbary waited a moment, making sure what he was about to say would be heard.

"I've had time to know where to look for your bookkeeper during the auctions. Time to know how to get all the books he was carrying."

For Lottie, the ballroom tilted for a moment, and Barbary showed his teeth in a sneer.

Barbary dropped down suddenly, as if losing the strength in his legs, and Lottie watched Lund release him. But the man didn't collapse to the floor. Instead, he touched the dance floor with one hand, as his other hand reached into the large pocket of his overcoat. Almost immediately Lottie felt the floor beneath her feet soften. She glanced down in shock and hurriedly backed away a few steps, seeing Lund do the same. As she watched, the wooden dance floor rippled like the surface of a swimming pool around Barbary. The man appeared to be crouching on a circle of solidity, as if he were standing on a column just submerged below the surface. Other people similarly backed away, creating a wide circle around the old man.

"Mr. Okoro," Barbary shouted, pulling the Book of Matter from his pocket, throwing sparks and color into the air as it pulsed. "Your book is fabulous fun!"

Before Okoro could reply, before he could run to attack once again, Barbary lifted and dropped his hand rapidly, and the liquid floor bulged up six feet and rushed to the ballroom door, a wave racing to shore, and all of the people standing there, and Merlin Gillette's body, were tossed up and thrown roughly against the ceiling. As the floor dropped away beneath them as quickly as it had risen, becoming solid once again, people and plaster crashed back down in a tumult of groans and clatter.

In the bedlam, Barbary dashed forward and snatched his gun back out of Lottie's hand. "I'll take that."

Lottie offered no resistance, her thoughts slow with shock and surprise.

"You know, I am much, much older," Barbary was saying. "I've had a holiday in the past, courtesy of that bitch with the Book of Doors, and I am fifty years older than when you stole my book."

"Cassie?" Izzy asked.

"Shut up," Barbary snapped. He turned his eyes back to Lottie. "I am ninety-four years old, but I am starting to feel much like my old self. It must be one of these other books I took off your man. The Book of Health, is it? The Book of Vim and Vigor?" He barked a laugh, delighted and triumphant. "I probably couldn't even have shot those men without the benefit of this book! I feel like I haven't felt for years!"

He pointed the gun without much care and fired jubilantly, the shot ricocheting off the walls.

"Fine," Lottie said suddenly, and Barbary's expression dropped in surprise. "You want this?" she said, showing him the Book of Pain. She saw how his eyes caught on it, like clothing on a barb. She watched his expression fall away to leave only naked hunger, all of the anger gone, all of the fury.

All of the pain, she thought, and then she remembered what Elizabeth Fraser had said a few minutes earlier.

"You can take it," Lottie said, extending her hand and the book toward Barbary. The book that was full of dense and angry text, scribbled images of screaming faces and sharp weapons.

The old man reached out and gripped the book, but before she released it, Lottie said, "I'll take all your pain away."

Barbary's eyes widened in surprise, and color spilled out of all sides of the book. A moment later he crumpled at the knees, one hand still holding the book, Lottie still holding the other edge. They were two people holding a firework between them, the book a connection, and through the book Lottie could feel all of the man's pain. She could feel his physical trauma, the ache in his bones and his left leg, in the old bullet wounds that riddled his body. But below and beyond that, deeper in the pool of Hugo Barbary's consciousness, she could feel the *other* pain, the spiritual and psychological pain that made him what he was. It swam there in the depths, curling and turning out of sight.

Lottie thought about pulling that pain away from Barbary. She could feel the strands of it and began to tug. It was fibrous and tough, and resisted her as she tugged on it, like a tangle of hair in a shower drain. She closed her eyes and concentrated, bringing the pain to the surface, collecting it together and giving it form to remove it, to cleanse the wound that was his soul.

Barbary was on his knees before her, screaming, shocked by the sudden gathering of all of his pain.

Lottie kept pulling, strands and strands of darkness and agony, of bitter fury, dragging them from this man's soul, bringing them up to dissipate and vanish in the light. She opened her eyes and saw Barbary's upturned face looking back at her, wide, clear eyes, the eyes of a terrified child. She met that gaze, she held it, and she continued wrenching the darkness to the surface.

"I free you from your pain," she said, her teeth gritted.

She was aware of movement, something rising just beyond her

peripheral vision. And then, before she could finish her surgery of Barbary's soul, the contact was broken, and Barbary was sent tumbling across the floor, Okoro wrestling him.

Lottie gasped at the break of the connection and stumbled backward. Arms caught her before she fell and she craned her neck to see Lund behind her, steadying her.

"Mr. Okoro!" she yelled. Some of the people, the younger and fittest, were starting to pull themselves up from the floor, from where Barbary's wave had dropped them. Others lay dead or seriously injured—Elizabeth Fraser, without her Book of Health, among them. But Okoro had been the first to his feet. "Okoro, stop!"

Okoro and Barbary were wrestling on the floor, Okoro throwing brutal punches, Barbary holding his hands up defensively, obviously still dazed by what Lottie had done to him.

"Take it!" Barbary spat, pulling the book from his pocket again and tossing it away. "Take your fucking book!"

The Book of Matter skidded across the dance floor and came to a stop on the worn carpet.

Immediately Okoro was up on his feet, pursuing his prized possession, Barbary forgotten. He stalked across the floor and picked up the book, dusting it down and slipping it into his breast pocket. And then he turned his eyes to Lottie.

"I will take the other book now," he said, holding out a hand as he walked toward her.

Lund stepped between them, looking down on Okoro from a foot above him. He said nothing. He just stood there, motionless, staring at the man. Lottie didn't know why the big man felt the need to protect her, but in that instant, she was grateful to have him between her and Okoro.

"You want to play with me?" Okoro asked, unperturbed. "I've killed big men before."

Things were out of control, Lottie knew, but she still had the Book of Pain. People's attention appeared to be on the confrontation between Lund and Okoro. Barbary lay on the floor gazing up at the chandelier as if dazed, and Izzy stood behind Lottie, cowering against the wall and trying to appear small and insignificant. Lottie thought it was perhaps

time for her to make an exit. There could be another auction, on another day.

She started backing away, heading toward the mirror behind the
podium.

Then the door on the far wall opened, beyond Lund and Okoro, and
Cassie and Drummond Fox stepped into the ballroom. Behind them,
through the door, was a different place entirely, a room in a different
building.

Seeing them arrive like that was astonishing, even to Lottie. She felt
her mouth drop open and she was aware that everyone else in the room,
even Okoro, had stopped to look.

"It's the Librarian," someone said.

Cassie and Drummond stood there, absorbing the bedlam of broken
bodies and blood. Then Cassie's eyes settled on Izzy, and Lottie heard
Izzy call Cassie's name.

In that moment Hugo Barbary pushed himself up from the floor.

"Hugo," Drummond muttered, upon seeing him. "Again."

Lottie saw him throw a pointed glance at Cassie.

Hugo swung his gun around to aim it past Lottie to Izzy behind her.

"Give me back my Book of Control, Librarian," Barbary said. "Or I
will put a bullet through the pretty face of your friend."

Barbary looked at Cassie.

"And I'll take the Book of Doors as well, for good measure."

Too Late Arrives

All eyes turned to Cassie as everyone in the room absorbed what they had heard. Even Okoro turned away from Lund and gave Cassie a calculating look.

"Did you hear me?" Barbary said. "Give me the fucking books."

But then his face changed. It crumpled somehow, collapsing in on itself in a storm of emotions and doubt. His free hand went to his head, and he grunted.

"What did you do to me?" he demanded of Lottie, staring through pained eyes at her.

He gathered himself, recommitted to the threat, and pointed the gun again.

Lottie saw Lund glance in the man's direction, then back at Okoro in front of him, and she realized that he was trying to work out where the greatest danger was. Or maybe he was trying to work out who to protect, Lottie or Izzy.

"I took your pain away," Lottie said. "Or most of it. Before we were interrupted."

Barbary grunted again but watched through narrowed eyes as Cassie walked a wide circle around him, moving toward Izzy.

"I will kill her!" he shouted, but it sounded to Lottie that he was trying to convince himself. And it looked to Lottie that there were tears in the old man's eyes. She wondered if in trying to fix him she might have broken him.

"Just put the gun down," Lottie said, her voice honey.

Okoro took one step to the side and Lund took one step to match him, maintaining his position between the man and Lottie.

"What did you do to me?" Barbary asked again, this time more of a plea than a demand. "Why don't I want to . . . ?"

He couldn't finish the sentence. There was a blur of movement that Lottie noticed too late, and Diego was dashing toward her, taking the opportunity of her distraction to aim for the Book of Pain. He didn't reach her. Before he was within six feet he was yanked up into the air as if pulled by the collar of his expensive suit jacket and thrown backward against the wall by the ballroom door. Another mirror shattered, and Lottie looked to see Drummond dropping his hand and staggering backward as if shocked at what he had just done, as if surprised at how easy it had been to kill a man by throwing him across the room.

Lottie expected Barbary to respond, but the man seemed lost in his own thoughts, trapped in a puzzle in his own mind, his gun arm limp by his side now.

"Cassie?" Izzy's voice came from behind Lottie, uncertain.

Lottie saw that Cassie's attention was on the center of the room, where Okoro and Lund were still facing off, and Barbary had dropped to his knees. Drummond was watching the other people who were still milling around on the fringes of the room, waiting to see what would happen, waiting for the auction to restart.

Lottie was contemplating that: Maybe the worst was over. Maybe she could still make a sale. Or maybe two, with the Book of Doors now also present.

"What am I?" Barbary asked, lifting his eyes from the floor. "What was I?"

He looked around in confusion, but then certainty returned to his eyes, and he lifted the gun again.

"Drummond!" Cassie shouted. She darted back to the door they had come through moments earlier and pulled it open. Drummond moved his hand again and Barbary was lifted off his feet, the gun falling from his grip and tap-dancing on the wooden floor. "Go back to the past, you fuck!" Cassie shouted, as Drummond jerked him across the room and through the doorway. Lottie could see another, different place beyond the doorway, a sunny street, and then Cassie swung the door again and it slammed shut. The room seemed to exhale as one, the threat gone.

"Mr. Okoro," Lottie barked. "Do you want to continue posturing, or shall we get back to the auction, now that our interruption has been dealt with?"

Okoro didn't react.

"Most of the other bidders are incapacitated or worse," Lottie said. His eyes flicked to hers, understanding the subtext: *You'll probably win.*

Okoro looked like he really wanted to fight Lund. Like he had something to prove.

Men are so childish when you get down to it, Lottie thought, some of them at least.

"Fine," he said, pulling his shirtsleeves out from the cuffs of his suit jacket. "Let us continue."

The crowd rearranged itself around the room, people eyeing each other nervously, as Lottie stepped back up on the platform. Drummond Fox stood off to one side, near the door he and Cassie had come through, and Cassie had crossed the room to embrace Izzy. The two women stood together against the other wall, speaking in low voices. Lund stood a little way in front of Lottie's podium, like he had taken on the role of her security team. As she watched he kicked the gun that Barbary had been using off to the side of the room, out of the way.

"Let us recommence. The last bid was with the Spanish gentleman." Lottie gestured to Diego, unconscious or dead, in the corner of the room. "Who seems unable to continue. So we will revert to the preceding bid, which was twenty-six to the man from Belarus."

A series of quick bids followed, as if people were keen now to be done with the whole thing. The twins from Shanghai bid twenty-seven, and then Okoro raised it to thirty. The Belarusian bid thirty-one and Okoro counterbid at thirty-two.

It was warming up nicely for Lottie. As the bids continued, she debated with herself whether it was the right time to also auction the Book of Doors. It would mean she could be done with the whole thing once and for all, take all of her money and get out of the world of special books before it was too late. But she also wondered whether conditions were right to get the optimal price for the Book of Doors. Many of the richest bidders were either no longer alive or able to bid. Perhaps a separate auction, in a week or two, would draw more interest and a bigger crowd.

"Thirty-four!" It was the Indian man from England. He hadn't bid yet. His tactics had obviously been to wait until the auction was peaking and then swoop in. Okoro gave the man an annoyed stare, like he had no right to be entering the bidding at such a late stage.

"Where is the smoke coming from?"

The question came from the far end of the room, from one of the Shanghai twins. Lottie peered that way and saw that the people in the distance were less clear, like the air was thicker there and obscuring her vision.

"It's not smoke," Drummond said, sounding alarmed. He pushed off the wall and hurried across the floor toward Cassie. "It's mist."

Lottie frowned, not understanding.

"Give me the book!" Drummond demanded of Cassie. "Quickly."

"What is this?" Okoro demanded.

The far end of the room was a gray wall now, the people there just indistinct shapes floating in the mist.

And then the mist parted, like curtains on a stage, and a woman was there, a beautiful woman in a layered black skirt that looked like crow's feathers and a white bustier top. Her hair was jet back and slicked back from her head, and she seemed to be wearing smoke-effect makeup around her eyes. She was carrying a black purse, hanging by a strap from the crook of her elbow, and in one hand she held a book that was pulsing with gray light. Her head was up, her eyes traveling around the faces that watched her arrival.

"It's the woman," someone said.

Lottie sighed, almost too tired now for fear.

She had meant to get out of the business before it was too late. One or two last sales and then be done with it.

But it seemed she had pushed her luck too far.

It seemed that too late had arrived.

Death in the Ballroom

When Lottie had continued the auction, Cassie hugged Izzy furiously, holding on to her like a shipwreck survivor clinging to a rock in the vast ocean.

"I've missed you so much!" she exclaimed, her heart full and tears brimming in her eyes. When she pulled back Izzy looked shocked by the emotion, and then she studied Cassie's face.

"What . . . what happened to you?" she asked. "You look . . . different."

Cassie shook her head dismissively. "It doesn't matter. I'll tell you, but I've missed you. I thought you were dead."

Izzy shook her head. "I . . . well . . . a lot has happened." She nodded to the tall man who was standing in the middle of the room. "Lund helped me. That man Hugo, he was in the apartment, but Lund helped me."

Cassie nodded and then hugged Izzy again.

It was too much. It was ten years of agony and uncertainty and emptiness, but Izzy was there. Cassie smelled Izzy's soap, a smell so familiar it made her feel like she was back in the apartment, living their quiet, unspectacular lives, before all of this madness. In that moment Cassie *yearned* for that simple life with an ache in the center of her being.

"I am so sorry for everything," Cassie murmured in Izzy's ear. "I am sorry all of this happened. I should have listened to you. I should never have used the book."

They were interrupted then by Drummond Fox, running up to them, making them both flinch in surprise, his eyes wide and panicked. "Give me the book!" he said to Cassie. "Quickly!"

Cassie read the fear in his eyes and looked behind her as the woman emerged from a cloud of mist like some sort of god or demon. Cassie had seen this woman before, in Drummond's memories. It had been more than ten years now since she had lived that memory, but it had stayed with her.

The room seemed to adjust around the woman's appearance, people shuffling into different positions, whispering to each other. And then the Black man who had been fighting with Hugo took a step toward her in the middle of the room.

"So you are the crazy white lady everyone is so frightened of?" he asked, breaking the silence and giving the woman a dismissive look. "You don't seem so scary to me, woman."

"Mr. Okoro," the Bookseller said, a caution.

"Give me the book," Drummond said to Cassie, his voice low. "I'll take it into the shadows."

Cassie shook her head at him.

"I owe it to the Bookseller," she told him, but even as she said it, her feelings betrayed her. She didn't want to give it up. She had only just recovered the Book of Doors after ten years. She wasn't going to give it away so easily, not unless it was absolutely necessary.

In the center of the room the woman's eyes moved from face to face, and then seemed to settle on Drummond, where he stood near Cassie and Izzy.

"Who's that?" Izzy asked. Cassie just shook her head, not taking her eyes off the woman.

"How about I turn your blood to stone?" Okoro sneered at the woman, removing his Book of Matter and holding it by his side, his body turned away from the woman to shield the book. "And you drop dead right here? Or I turn the air in your lungs to liquid and you drown?"

Cassie watched as the woman's eyes slid back around to settle on Okoro. The look she gave was of a mother to a misbehaving child. The woman shook her head at him once, and then, in an instant, the mist returned, curling rapidly back into the room to fill the space, drawing curtains down between each person.

"Move!" Drummond hissed, a disembodied voice close to Cassie's ear. Cassie was holding Izzy's hand, a firm grip that kept them connected through the mist, and she felt Izzy tugging her away toward the far end of the room.

"That won't work on me!" Okoro shouted from somewhere behind them, his voice cutting through the panicked chatter of the other people in the room. Almost as soon as the mist had appeared Cassie saw a pulse of indistinct light through the gray air, and the mist became water, a swimming pool that crashed down to the floor and sloshed against the sides of the room.

Ahead of them, Cassie saw that Lottie was already retreating from the platform, the mirror behind her opening to reveal a passageway. Izzy looked back at Cassie as they scampered, pointing at the escape route, and Cassie nodded her agreement. She checked behind her and Drummond was following a few feet away, his face and body soaked with the water that had just fallen around them. Farther back drenched people were retreating out of the ballroom, throwing nervous glances over their shoulders at the woman and Okoro slowly circling each other in the center of the dance floor.

Izzy pulled Cassie in the opposite direction. "Cassie, come on!" she pleaded, heading toward the Bookseller's secret passageway.

In the middle of the room, Okoro screamed, "Time to die, witch," and Cassie couldn't help herself, she had to turn to look, she had to see if the man *could* kill the woman.

The woman closed her eyes, and immediately there was a burst of light, shimmering on the puddles and drips of water on the wall and mirrors, and everyone who was left in the room flinched away. Cassie staggered backward, pulling her hand free from Izzy's to throw it in front of her eyes.

"The Book of Light!" Drummond shouted, and Cassie remembered the Egyptian woman from Drummond's memory. The woman was using Drummond's friend's book.

The light was blinding, even with her head turned away and her hands in front of her eyes. Cassie tumbled sideways against the wall, reaching out with a hand and feeling the damp plaster, the cool of the mirror.

"Izzy!" she called, as she stumbled onward, using the wall as a guide.

An inhuman scream sounded, a high-pitched squeal like air being released from a tire under too much pressure. The light seemed to grow more intense for a moment, and then it was gone, a memory only in Cassie's eyes.

She blinked and looked around, chasing distortion from her vision. In the center of the room there was a puddle of blood and bone in a fancy suit. The woman stood just beyond it, gazing down at the mess that had been Okoro. She raised her eyes slowly to Cassie, the gaze of a cat that had just left a dead animal on the doorstep: *Look what I have done.*

Cassie's stomach did a somersault and she turned away and spattered vomit onto sodden carpet at her feet. When she looked to the back of the room she saw Izzy reaching the Bookseller's secret exit just as the mirror slammed shut.

"No!" Izzy yelled, banging the mirror with a balled-up fist. As Cassie gathered herself, the big man who had been standing in front of the platform—Lund, Izzy had called him—reached Izzy. He stood next to her protectively, his eyes scanning the room in search of danger.

He loves her, Cassie thought, the idea coming from nowhere but feeling certain, and that cheered Cassie in some small way.

"No!" Izzy yelled again, banging the mirror. Cassie watched the big man take her hand and pull her away, along the back of the room to the other side of the dance floor. And then Cassie felt herself yanked around and Drummond was in her face.

"Give me the book!" he demanded, more panicked than angry. "We can't stop her!"

Cassie flicked her eyes over Drummond's shoulder to the center of the room. The woman was bent at the waist and reaching a hand into the red mess that had once been Okoro. Cassie heard a wet squelching sound and her stomach somersaulted again.

"Oh god," she muttered. It was like a nightmare. Even after confronting Hugo Barbary in the apartment, she wasn't ready for this.

The red mess on the floor still pulsed weakly, as if some desperate remains of life existed there still. When the woman withdrew her hand, it was holding a book: the Book of Matter. A smile of satisfaction spread across the woman's beautiful features.

There was a sudden crack, like dry wood snapping, and the few people still in the room yelled in surprise at the sound of the gunshot.

Behind the woman, the Spanish man Drummond had thrown across the room earlier was pointing the gun that Hugo Barbary had dropped at her back.

"Give me all of the books!" the man demanded. He fired a second shot up into the ceiling above him, and the woman turned her head to look at him over her shoulder.

"Give me the book!" Drummond demanded of Cassie again, gripping her arm.

Cassie shook her head. She couldn't. She looked toward the door that they had come through on the opposite side of the room. And then she looked along the wall and saw Lund leading Izzy in that direction as well. If Cassie could get there, they all could flee.

"Let's go!" she said to Drummond, pulling away from him roughly, and pointing at the door. "Now!"

Another shot fired in the center of the room, and Cassie ducked reflexively, glancing toward Izzy in a panic. Izzy met her eyes and Cassie saw fear there. Cassie pointed at the door and Izzy nodded, and then tapped Lund on the shoulder to convey the message.

In the center of the room the woman faced the man with the gun, and Cassie saw her top lip curl in annoyance as she lifted the Book of Matter up by her side. It was her new toy, Cassie realized, a new thing to play with.

The man with the gun saw something in the woman's eyes, and as Cassie watched he seemed to decide that the books were perhaps not that important after all. He backed off, the gun in front of him defensively, moving slowly at first. But the woman advanced upon him, the Book of Matter starting to glow in her hand.

"Fucking die, woman!" the man shouted, firing again as he backed away. The bullets seemed to go right through the woman, cracking a mirror on the opposite wall, near where Lund and Izzy were creeping toward the door.

Then the woman darted suddenly, speeding across the floor toward the man in a blur.

Another bullet punched a hole in the wall and the Spanish man started to scream as the woman fell upon him, snarling like an animal. The door, the escape route, was just steps away. Izzy and Lund were only a few feet farther along the wall, so close. Cassie saw both of them turning instinctively to the source of the scream as it pierced the air.

Cassie was about to say something to Izzy, to shout a direction, but then a stray bullet gouged a hole in Lund's shoulder, and he was thrown backward against the wall with a grunt.

Then a second bullet exploded Izzy's skull, splattering a part of her brain on the mirror behind her and sending her tumbling to the ground.

Cassie heard another anguished scream, a bird of despair taking flight, and a moment later she realized it was her own voice.

She collapsed to her knees on the dance floor. Izzy was lying below a smear of blood and brains on the wall, her mouth wide in shock, her one remaining eye open as if surprised.

"Izzy!" Cassie screamed, her vocal cords stretching and tearing. She screamed again and her hands went to her cheeks, her nails digging into skin, the noise coming from her mouth not a word, just a shriek of pain.

She felt hands on her, someone trying to pull her to her feet, but it didn't matter, nothing mattered, she had endured through years to find her friend again, but Izzy was dead. Her beautiful friend, her warmth and her humor and her love, destroyed in an instant. A vast and endless nothing where moments before had been Cassie's everything.

Cassie shrieked again, unable to fully relieve herself of the agony that was filling her up.

The bright light came, a sun exploding in the room, white and cleansing. Cassie heard the clicking of a trigger, the man still trying to fire the gun long after the rounds were all used up.

Cassie didn't care anymore; she was suffering and loss and pain in human form.

Izzy was gone, because of her, because of the choices she'd made.

Cassie wanted to be gone too. She wanted nothing more of this horrible world.

She found herself running, fleeing toward the door in the wall just as she had always run from her troubles, tears streaming from her eyes and deadly light chasing her.

Cassie disappeared through the doorway, wanting to be nothing, wanting to be nowhere.

THE NOTHING
AND NOWHERE

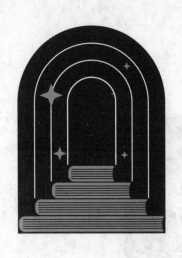

She was nothing and nowhere. She was only thoughts and memory in the silence beyond reality.

Nothing existed here, in the nowhere and everywhere; nothing *could* exist. Not anything alive, certainly not anything human, and the thoughts and awareness that had been Cassie moments before wouldn't have existed either, but for the fact she had been carrying the Book of Safety with her. Some essence of that remained, refusing to let Cassie dissipate into nothingness, binding her into existence.

She was nowhere and everywhere. Her thoughts hung idle and stagnant, existing but only barely. All that there was, was thought, a single thought forming slowly over an endless age. The thought of being. But this thing that was, this thing that had once been Cassie, was shocked and insensate, stretched over the nothingness beyond creation.

Then an image: a woman.

Izzy.

Izzy!

Her face shocked and damaged, vacant.

In the nothing and nowhere, many colors exploded, a rainbow screaming, and a deep, buzzing bass note vibrated and shook all consciousness, a huge foghorn blasting through unreality.

After that, all was silent again. The shock of that image of Izzy sent the consciousness scuttling back into the darkness like a frightened creature. The consciousness tried to hide, to exist no more. But it was an impossibility to exist without thought. Even to desire not to think was to think.

Thoughts formed unbidden, memories and emotions and images, all the things that form a human.

The consciousness turned away from these things but had nowhere to turn to and nothing to hide behind. It had only thought.

These thoughts that troubled it were distant things at first, like something on a faraway shore, something definitively there, but uncertain and indistinct. The consciousness ignored these things, but soon felt drawn to them. Over time it became less afraid. It reached out to these things—these memories and emotions—because thought needed something to think about.

There were sensations first, and the consciousness remembered sensations. A different type of thought, a thought with substance, a doorway to the external world.

Oil and wood, the dampness of a rainy day.

Then sounds, the buzz of machinery, the rhythmic scrape of sandpaper.

And then the light and texture of an image, a memory: a man at a workbench. A tall man, broad across the chest, his face focused on his work.

And the consciousness remembered the sensation of touch: the feel of the pages of a book between fingers. The luxurious flexibility of young muscles, strong limbs.

The man at the bench looked at the consciousness—at the thing that had been Cassie—and the consciousness felt something else then: a sudden blossoming, like a vast meadow of flowers springing into vibrant life all at once. This was beautiful and comforting, as colorful as the rainbow scream but not terrible and terrifying. This was joy, and the consciousness delighted in this.

The consciousness felt something then, something beyond thought. It felt herself, the personality that had been Cassie, the wants and desires, fears and delights. And the consciousness wanted more like the meadow of joy.

Another image appeared then: a warm day, sunlight on her face and a breeze tickling her cheeks. Her eyes were shaded by a hat, the brim flapping in the wind, and she could smell the rough salt of the sea in the air. She was a young woman again, facing the Mediterranean from a high cliff, a white cathedral behind her. Somewhere out on the breeze a seagull squawked into the sky, the noise carrying to Cassie—because that was her name, she knew, Cassie—where she stood on the cliff.

The colors came again, the weave of reality, the meadow blossoming, a rainbow across the sky in her vision, but this time the foghorn was a major chord, bright and lively, rather than a rattling scream of pain.

Cassie remembered the joy she had felt in that moment on the high cliff, the freedom and the opportunity, and the foghorn sounded its major chord again. This was not something to run from. This was the thrill of human emotion, of sensation, of life.

A darker memory erupted into her thoughts, a gate-crasher at a pleasant party: a gloomy room with the tortured figure of the man that had been her grandfather, now emaciated and weak, fading and fading. The house that she had grown up in, the only home she had ever known, transformed into a place she no longer wanted to be. What had once been cozy and homey was claustrophobic and suffocating, and the walls and bedclothes all reeked of sweat and blood and pain. It was a house of death, and it was here that her grandfather had died, alone, while Cassie had slept in a chair, exhausted by the care she had been giving.

Cassie, in the nowhere, remembered the quiet horror of what her house had become, and the foghorn sounded once again, an angry sound, atonal and brutal, and her consciousness trembled. The rainbow scream too came once again, more vivid and terrible, screeching the agony of this memory, and Cassie, the consciousness, scuttled away, curling into herself to forget and hide.

When she dared to emerge again, her consciousness unable to stop itself from floating to the surface, the memories and emotions came more quickly. Faster and faster, each one an eruption of light and noise, all human emotion and memory streaking out into the nothing and the nowhere behind reality. She was creating things, Cassie realized, creating by remembering and by being; all of reality was changing. Cassie's memories and pain, her despair and her joy, her escape and her fear, made the unreality tremble and shake. All of these emotions, all of these memories, the building blocks of personality and humanity, were too much for Cassie's consciousness to contain.

Out here in the nothing and nowhere, floating as thought, she was powerful. Cassie's consciousness, in the nowhere and everywhere, used the rainbow scream, used that energy of creation, to hide away her emotions and memories, the fragments of her life that had destroyed and made her and destroyed her again. They were too much for her, so she would put them somewhere else.

Where else would she put all these things, but in books? Where else could she lock away all of her emotion, but in the place where all of life's joy and delight were to be found? And as she created these books, these special books, born in the nowhere and everywhere, each one created from her memories and emotions, from the fragments of her reality, she threw them out into the world, propelling them away from her, scattering them throughout reality and time, their pages full of languages old and new, known and unknown, images and words, the language of everywhere.

This she did for an age, time having no meaning in the nowhere and everywhere, and only once she had exhausted of all of her agonies and delights, once all of her special books had been thrown out into reality, once she was empty, she rested, at peace.

The consciousness that had been Cassie and which was becoming Cassie again slept—or entered the state that was closest to sleep in the unreality. When she awoke—or entered that state closest to wakefulness in the nowhere and everywhere—there was more Cassie than consciousness. Cassie in the nowhere didn't panic, she was just aware that she was somewhere else, somewhere that was nowhere.

She had come to this place through a doorway that she had opened, trying to flee reality and the awfulness of what she had done.

As she remembered her terrors now, there was no screaming rainbow or blossoming meadow; there was no foghorn. There was only memory.

She knew she had to go back. Her consciousness couldn't exist in this place.

And just as some essence of the Book of Safety had remained and had kept her alive where no life should exist, some essence of the Book of Doors remained with her. And as Cassie thought about returning a doorway appeared, a featureless rectangle distinct from the nothingness by virtue of its somethingness.

The doorway was the only thing, and it drew her toward it, drew her toward something that Cassie realized was light.

Drew her back into reality and out of the nowhere and everywhere.

A PLAN IN
FIVE PARTS

The Woman, After the Auction

After the auction in New York City, the woman drove home, thirteen hours through the night along roads that started out empty and dark, and which grew busier as the morning light came and the day crawled around to lunchtime and afternoon.

She was satisfied, a sensation she rarely felt. For a while, at least, she was satiated. She had taken another book to add to her collection, the Book of Matter. She would enjoy experimenting with it, as she had with all of her books, testing what it could do and how she could use it on other people.

She drove with relative silence in her mind, enjoying the satisfaction, replaying some of the moments from the auction. The pain and the suffering were what she enjoyed the most. She liked to see agony on the faces of other people, and she preferred it when the agony lasted, when it was more than a fleeting moment.

She had seen Drummond Fox again, and that had delighted her, but once again he had evaded her. She knew she should have been furious about that, but she was not. Instead she felt reinvigorated. She had proof, now, that the man still lived, and she had more books. And she would collect more books in the coming years. Time was running out for Drummond Fox, she knew. She was circling irrevocably closer to the Fox Library. Nothing could stop that now. If anything, she enjoyed knowing that the experience would be prolonged. She hoped that she appeared in his nightmares.

As the woman crawled along the road to her cabin she saw, to her disappointment, another vehicle parked up in the gravel drive. It was a large utility truck, parked facing the property, with two men, one of them sitting on the hood, the other standing in front of him. There was music thudding from the truck's stereo, insistently kicking noise into the quiet woodland afternoon. They were laughing as she approached, and then they noticed the car and they interrupted their conversation to stare. Both men were holding cans of beer, and one of them, the one sitting on the hood, took a casual sip as he watched the woman come to a stop. He was tall and thin, with fair hair and wearing a Kiss T-shirt that looked to have been washed more times in its life than he had. The other man was shorter and fatter, like he ate doughnuts for breakfast, and dressed as if he had just gotten off work at a gas station or was planning to go to work later.

Both men watched as the woman climbed out. She wondered if they had come here before. She was away often. Maybe it was the place they came to drink and hang out when they were bored. She closed the car door and looked at them, feeling the cool, thick air of the afternoon, the damp of the surrounding woods. They stared back at her, both of them running their eyes up and down her body, exchanging a glance. The taller one, the blond one, had a hungry, mean sort of look. He was a type the woman had come across before. There were lots of his type in small towns across the world.

"Hello, darling," he said.

She said nothing.

"This your place?" he asked, nodding at the house.

The woman nodded without expression.

"We ain't doing no harm, just having a few beers," he said. "Right, George?"

"Yup," George agreed, nodding, but he was less sure of himself. George was just going along with his friend.

The woman held the tall one's gaze for a moment, saying nothing.

"That's a nice dress you got, lady," he said.

The woman walked to the house without replying. She unlocked the front door and opened it, the hinges calling out into the day like a bird. She looked back at them over her shoulder and then left the door open as she stepped inside. It was an invitation.

They joined her soon enough, switching off the truck and hurrying into the house.

Their mistake. If they had simply left, she wouldn't have pursued them.

She waited for them just inside the house, standing primly with her purse on her arm by the basement door. When they arrived, clattering clumsily over the threshold, expressions like dogs at feeding time, she opened the basement door and walked ahead of them down the old wooden stairs. As the two men joined her at the bottom of the stairs, they looked around cautiously. The tall man saw the mattress in the corner and nudged the other man with an elbow. They saw no danger here, only opportunity.

The woman decided that she wanted to try out the book she had taken from the Black man at the auction—the Book of Matter. She had to experiment to understand its potential. How fortuitous two men had fallen into her lap.

She gestured at the tall man to come farther into the room. And then she gestured for him to get down on the floor.

"What, here?" he asked, throwing a smile at his friend. "On the floor?"

The woman nodded, and the man happily complied, dropping to the concrete floor beneath the swinging bulb and lying on his back.

The woman looked at the other man over her shoulder and gestured him toward the mattress in the corner. He looked scared, she thought, but he nodded obediently and shuffled past her.

"I hope you are ready, miss," the man on the floor said, leering up at her. "You ain't never had nothing like me!"

As the woman stared down at him, the man gestured with both hands, encouraging her to join him. She squatted down, one hand on the cement floor, the other reaching into her purse to hold the Book of Matter. She directed her will toward the floor, softening it into liquid matter beneath the man. Then she pressed on his chest with her hand. He didn't realize at first, he was still smiling for a second or two, wondering what she was doing, glancing down at her feet as if maybe she was removing shoes. Then he noticed that he was sinking. His expression changed, incomprehension dawning, and the woman loved it.

"Hey, wait . . .

He flailed in the soupy concrete, but found no purchase, and his flailing only made him sink faster. And then the concrete was rising around his face, covering his legs, and he went quiet as he panicked and tried to extricate himself, fighting to survive. As she watched she saw his eyes growing wide and white as the concrete swallowed him.

And then his eyes were gone, and only his lips and nostrils and the fingers of one hand protruded, and the woman made the concrete solid again, hardening it around his skinny body with a creaking sound. She watched with interest for a few minutes as the man's lips flapped and smacked, the light still swinging back and forth over him, shadows growing and shrinking as he struggled for air, as his lungs tried to inflate within his crushed chest. She wondered what he was thinking, suffocating in the darkness.

Then the smacking stopped, the ragged breaths running out, and the visible parts of the man's body were still.

In the corner of the room, on the mattress, the other man was pulled into a ball and whimpering. When the woman looked at him, he went quiet. His hands were clenched in front of his mouth like he was trying to hide, his eyes wide and terrified.

"Please," he begged, tears in his eyes. "Please don't kill me. I'll do anything. We wasn't gonna do anything to you."

The woman didn't even hear the man's words. She approached him, holding the Book of Matter by her side, and recalling what the Black man had said, about filling her lungs with water or turning her blood to stone. The woman was interested in the idea of transmutation of a living being. She was interested in the terror that someone would experience as their very matter was changed into something else. So she tried it out. She decided to make the man's cells liquid.

She squatted down again, reaching forward with her hand to place it gently on the man's leg. In her other hand the Book of Matter began to grow heavy and started to glow in the gloom, throwing colors into the corners of the cellar. The woman directed her will as the man on the mattress watched in horror. She wanted his cells to become liquid, and almost immediately she saw his face slacken.

She heard a gurgle and then the man's skin started to drip away from his bones like a syrup. He gurgled something again and the woman realized that he was perhaps trying to say something, perhaps trying to scream in terror.

She pushed her will further and the man's organs and even his bones turned to thick liquid, collapsing down in on themselves like a chocolate sculpture melting in the heat.

The thing that had been the man was now a pink frothy soup puddling on the old mattress and dripping off the edge onto the floor. The woman withdrew her hand and wiped the residue on the mattress while all around her color drained out of the world, the Book of Matter dormant again.

She stood up and inspected what she had done, as the soup trembled. She thought she heard another gurgle, maybe a final, despairing scream of terror from the puddle on the mattress.

Then she thought she heard another noise, or detected something else in the air, and the woman's mind was suddenly silent. She looked to the stairs, to the other man swallowed by the concrete, searching for what could have disturbed the air. It had been an odd moment, something she had never felt before. But so brief . . . and then gone.

She frowned, staring into space, listening intently. But there was nothing there. Just the two dead men, or what was left of them.

The woman walked over to the safe in the corner. She unlocked it and withdrew the books from her purse, the three she had taken with her to the auction and the Book of Matter, a new prize to add to her collection. Then she closed the safe again and walked away. She pulled the cord to switch off the light and headed up to her room to wash off the smell of the city.

Reality, Again

Cassie fell back into reality, out of the light of nothingness and into the darkness of somethingness.

Not absolute darkness, though; there was a suggestion of light here. As she lifted her head and her eyes readjusted to reality she saw less darkness to her right, more darkness to her left.

The ground was soft beneath her hands and knees . . . soft and damp.

"Carpet," she said, the word a dead bird falling to the floor in the flat acoustics of the room.

She was in a large space . . . and the light seemed more discernible now, off to her right. There was a doorway, and beyond that vague shapes were visible.

Cassie stood up on unsteady legs and stumbled backward against solidity. A wall. She reached out and felt a handle, a door. Smooth coolness . . . a mirror.

And she remembered, then.

She remembered the ballroom, and the mayhem.

And Izzy.

The memory punched her in the gut and made her gasp, and she fell to her knees once again.

"Izzy," she wailed.

Her friend. Her beautiful friend who drank wine from mugs and slept in Cassie's bed when she was cold. Gone. Everything she was, destroyed in an instant.

Cassie lay on the damp floor and made herself hollow from crying.

After an age, when she had no more tears left to cry, when she was numb with grief, she made her way to the doorway, and she could see light coming from nearby, a staircase with skylights high above. She found switches and tried them with her shaking hand, and lights flickered on behind her in the ballroom.

It was as she had remembered it. Large and square, shattered glass all over the floor from the mirrors and the chandelier. There was dampness in the air, and she remembered the mist that had turned into water. She saw black stains of mold, running along the bottom of the wall by the carpet, but there were no bodies. She had dreaded turning on the light in case Izzy had still been there, lying with her blank and shocked single eye. But someone had removed the corpses. Cassie wondered where Izzy now lay. Was she in some anonymous grave with the other bodies? Alone and forgotten for eternity?

She pushed those cruel thoughts away, unable to open her mind to such possibilities.

As she walked back to the far side of the ballroom, to the doorway she had just tumbled through, she wondered idly how much time had passed. She stopped and stared at the wall by the side of the doorway. This was where Izzy had fallen, she knew, but there was no blood on the wall here.

Cassie ran her eyes around the rest of the room. There were marks on other areas of the wall, blood from other victims, bullet holes. Whoever had taken the bodies hadn't cleaned the room. The dampness in the carpet spoke to that. There had been no effort to tidy up and repair all the damage.

But why had Izzy's blood been cleaned up?

Cassie frowned and rubbed her head, wondering if maybe she was misremembering. A seedling of hope poked through the dry earth of her heart, but she refused to water it. She knew what she had seen. Nobody could survive such an injury.

She walked out of the ballroom, leaving the mold and the damp and the memories of mayhem behind her, and found herself in a lobby space. She walked through it to what appeared to have been a grand entrance at one time, but all of the windows and doors had been boarded over. There was a single doorway cut into the wood, but it seemed to be locked from the outside. A padlock maybe, on a thick bolt. Cassie rattled the door, but it didn't budge.

She stood there for a moment, surrounded by silence, and didn't know what to do. She was struggling even to have a conscious, directed thought.

"Think, woman," she muttered.

She patted her pocket then and discovered that she was still carrying two books. It seemed that whatever she had carried with her, whatever she had been wearing, had survived the place she had been.

She stopped, her brow knitted as she contemplated that place, thinking about it properly for the first time since having returned.

It was nowhere, a place no person should exist. It was somewhere outside creation, some different universe or reality. But she had survived.

"Because of the books," she said. "The Book of Safety."

She had survived and come back, from a different place, a different reality. It was the place the books had come from, she knew. It was the place the *magic* came from.

All that magic, and Izzy still gone, she thought bitterly.

Cassie remembered the Bookseller then. She remembered the woman fleeing through the mirror when the violence started, shutting off Izzy's escape.

"Coward," she muttered to herself.

And she remembered Drummond, using the Book of Control to protect her, and her bitter heart warmed slightly. She wondered what had happened to him. She found she was worried for him.

And she remembered the woman. The monstrous, beautiful woman who had done awful things with the books.

With *her* books.

Because Cassie knew now that the books were hers. Created by her in the nothing and nowhere.

The books were hers. And she couldn't let the woman continue to use them. She wouldn't allow it.

CASSIE USED THE BOOK OF Doors and stepped through one of the doorways in the ballroom and into the bedroom in the apartment she had shared with Izzy. It was a sunny day, she saw, a bright clear day beyond the window by her bed.

She hadn't been in this room for over ten years, and in some ways, it felt that more time than that had passed again while she had been in the nothing and nowhere.

She shrugged off her clothes, not caring about anything anymore, and slipped into bed, closing her eyes and pulling the comforter over her head to shut out the world.

She slept.

WHEN SHE AWOKE SHE FELT more like her old self, whatever that meant, and then she remembered that Izzy was gone, and her insides dropped away into a bottomless pit.

"Oh, Izzy."

She sat up, feeling heavier and emptier than she could ever remember, the bedclothes gathering around her waist. She sat there for a long time, trying to come to terms with the idea that Izzy's light and life were no longer in the world. She gazed out the window. It felt as if a few hours had passed. There was still daylight outside, but night was coming. She could hear the reassuringly normal sounds of the city: traffic, car horns, people shouting. So wonderfully mundane.

Her eyes moved around to the bookcase at the bottom of her bed and landed on Mr. Webber's edition of *The Count of Monte Cristo*. She smiled sadly to herself, remembering happy times over the past decade.

Why was she surrounded by so much sadness?

She forced herself up, had a shower, and then dressed in fresh clothes, taking a few minutes to enjoy rummaging through the wardrobe and drawers she hadn't seen for a decade. It was such an oddly simple delight. Once she was dressed she slipped her two books into her pockets, ensuring they were always with her.

She padded through the apartment to the door to Izzy's room. She stopped a moment before entering, taking a deep breath to settle her roiling emotions. The room smelled of her friend, a mixture of soap and shampoo and perfume, the scent hanging in the air like a memory. All that remained of Izzy, and that too would slowly disappear over time.

Cassie felt her emotions bubbling again as she stepped around the room. Her eyes caught on the pictures and postcards taped to Izzy's wall—pictures of Izzy and Cassie over the years, at Kellner Books, on that awful trip to Florida. There were postcards from her parents—more because they were places Izzy wanted to go than because she wanted to keep the messages. And there were cuttings from magazines, images of models in expensive clothes that Izzy had particularly loved.

Cassie ran her hand along the top of Izzy's chest of drawers, where she had kept all of her makeup and toiletries. It felt empty now, like some of her things had been taken, and Cassie frowned, wondering again if she was misremembering.

She took a few moments to open Izzy's drawers, the built-in wardrobe, and all the while she was growing more and more certain that some of Izzy's belongings were missing. Where was the wool sweater Cassie had bought her two Christmases ago? Where were her favorite leggings? The black jeans? Where was the small box of jewelry Izzy had kept in the drawers by her bed? Had they been burgled?

Cassie walked back to her own bedroom and dug around in the clothes she had shrugged off earlier. She found her phone and switched it on.

She waited impatiently for a few seconds as the phone ran through its start-up procedure. Then it was on, and Cassie gasped as she saw three things in quick succession.

First, it was early March; months had passed since the events in the ballroom.

Second, she had received a voice message from Izzy's phone, in the days after Izzy had supposedly died.

And third, for the past three months, someone had been sending Cassie text messages every few days, each message containing only a picture of a door, and every door different from the last.

Beach Fires at Night

On a beach at dusk, on the West Coast of the United States, Lund built a fire. He had bought wood and kindling from a hardware store in town, as well as an old-style plastic cigarette lighter that he used to start the fire.

"Let me see that," Izzy said, as she approached, a bag in one hand. He tossed the lighter over the fire to her and she caught it as she sat on the sand. "I used to have one of these when I was younger. I tried smoking for a while," she explained. It felt like the start of a story, but she didn't say anything else, and her eyes drifted off into the fire.

The Pacific Ocean murmured ahead of him, and the wind caressed Lund's cheek as he stared out at the dark sky. It was March, but it was a warm evening, with little chill in the air.

They were quite far north now, out of California and into Oregon, but the weather had been kind to them over the last week or so. They were in Pacific City, a gathering of holiday homes and RV parks over three or four streets that ran along the length of a stretch of golden sand and a wide bay. It was a place of tourists, local and foreign, a place where a couple of travelers could blend in easily enough.

"I got some chips and some Coke," Izzy said. She slipped the lighter into her pocket and passed him a bag of chips. "Hope that's okay."

"Yup," he said.

The fire was going well now, licking the logs, and he saw the glow reflected in Izzy's face as she stared into the flames.

They were killing time, he knew. Ever since the ballroom and New York, they had been moving around just to stay hidden, killing time until something happened. He didn't know what they were waiting for, but he was happy to keep waiting. They had traveled south and west first, riding Greyhound buses on long stretches, deciding where to go next at each stop, and eventually they'd ended up on the West Coast in California. They'd stay in one town for a few weeks, until both of them had felt the need to move, suddenly suspicious that something was coming for them, fearing a shadow on the horizon growing nearer. For the last while they had been making a slow crawl up the coast, along the Pacific Coast Highway, hitch-hiking or bumming rides from people they met in bars.

He looked at Izzy. She sat with her arms around her knees and her face to the Pacific. Her hair was tied up behind her head, the breeze playing with it. She was beautiful, and so unselfconscious about it.

Lund had liked her from the first moment he'd seen her, from the joke she'd made to Azaki about her friend's bad fashion sense. He'd wanted to be with her ever since, and she'd seemed happy to have him around. It was nothing more than that, and she seemed so lost in her own thoughts much of the time that it had never seemed right to suggest anything more. Not that Lund expected to talk his way into her affections. He didn't have the words for that. But he was happy to just be with her, to be trusted by her, and he was happy to wait to see what else she might want, or not. He had nowhere else to be.

Satisfied that the fire was now self-sustaining he lounged back in the sand, stretching his legs out and leaning on one elbow. He could feel the warmth from the flames on his face. The fire chatted in crackles, while the sea whispered and hushed, and Izzy was silent. Behind them, a row of holiday apartments stood at the edge of the beach, and he could hear the burbling of conversation from the people sitting on their balconies, watching the night with glasses of wine and warm blankets around their shoulders.

Lund opened the bag of chips. He ate for a while, studying the stars scattered across the sky.

"Pretty," he said, gesturing vaguely above him.

Izzy didn't seem to hear him. She was thinking about her friend, he knew. It was what had occupied her mind ever since they had fled from New York. The friend had disappeared through a door in the ballroom, and nothing more had been heard from her. On a couple of occasions he had tried to broach with her the possibility that her friend was gone for good, but Izzy had been unwilling or unable to entertain that, so he had stopped saying anything. Now he just waited. She had to work through what she was missing and what had happened to her friend in her own time.

"Eat," he said, tossing the bag of chips across the sand to her.

Izzy glanced down at it, and as she did her head moved, and Lund saw a figure farther down the beach. There were other people out on the sand, sitting around fires like Izzy and Lund, couples strolling hand in hand, and even a group of young children racing around and screaming, but the figure stood out from this background noise, because it was alone and motionless. And it appeared to be looking toward Izzy and Lund.

Izzy grabbed a handful of chips and then saw that Lund's eyes were staring past her.

"What?" she asked, turning her head.

The figure down the beach moved then, a few steps toward them, her face lit up by another fire.

"Cassie?" Izzy asked, a whispered question.

Lund pushed himself off the sand to sit upright.

The figure drew nearer, and Lund saw that Izzy was right.

"Cassie!" Izzy shouted, jumping up and throwing her chips aside.

The two women ran to each other and embraced.

Lund turned his eyes back to the fire, thinking that the thing they had been waiting for had finally arrived. He was surprised to find he was disappointed about that.

"I THOUGHT YOU WERE DEAD," Cassie said. She was seated across the fire from Lund, and the flames were painting pictures on her face. Izzy had introduced them as Cassie had sat down.

"Thank you for looking after her," Cassie had said to him, as she'd shaken his hand.

He'd shrugged, said nothing, and then she'd simply nodded and sat across the fire from him. The two women talked for a few minutes, both of them seemingly forgetting that he was there. It wasn't an unusual experience for him; despite his size, Lund made little impact in social situations. He disappeared into the background. He was an outsider, always living slightly off to the side of everyone else.

"I know," Izzy said. "That's why I left you the message. I couldn't stand the idea that you thought I was gone."

She reached across and held the other woman's arm for a moment.

"What happened?" Cassie asked. "How did I see you die?"

Izzy shrugged and then looked across the fire to Lund. They had spoken about it often, particularly over those first few days. Or Izzy had spoken about it, and Lund had listened, offering a word or two now and then.

"I don't know, if I'm honest," Izzy said. "The best we came up with is it was the Book of Illusion."

Cassie frowned. "The Book of Illusion?"

"It creates illusions," Izzy said. "Makes people see things different from how they are." Izzy turned to Lund, as if asking for help.

"Izzy had the Book of Illusion in her pocket," he said.

"Where did you get it?" Cassie asked.

"From me," Lund said. "From a friend of mine. I was trying to use it in the hotel before the auction. It ended up with Izzy. When things started going to hell, all the bullets flying and everything else, Izzy was terrified. We think, maybe, some part of her was able to use the Book of Illusion to protect herself after I was shot. Like it made her appear dead so nobody else would do anything to her."

Lund's shoulder still ached, particularly when it was cold. But the bullet that had caught him in the ballroom appeared to have gone right through, just below his collarbone. It had bled for a few days, and had hurt like a bitch for a few weeks, but after a couple of months he had been able to get through the day without painkillers. That arm felt weaker now, in certain movements, but it hadn't affected his life.

"So, what, it conjured an injury and a dead body?" Cassie asked.

"I thought I was going to get shot," Izzy said, gazing into the fire. "After I saw Lund, I just imagined getting a bullet through the brain."

"That's what I saw," Cassie said.

"It protected her," Lund said. "After you disappeared through the door, the woman turned her attention to the man you were with."

"Drummond," Cassie said.

"He disappeared, like smoke or something," Lund said. "I was watching. I was just lying there playing dead, hoping she didn't notice me among all the other bodies. After that man—Drummond— disappeared, she didn't even look at me. Or Izzy. Or anyone else. She just walked away."

"She didn't know you had the Book of Illusion," Cassie said to Izzy. "If she had known, she would have taken it off you. Probably killed you."

Izzy nodded. She smiled guiltily. "You should have seen his face when I sat up a minute later."

Lund looked into the fire, letting her enjoy the moment.

"It was like he'd seen a ghost," Izzy said.

Lund smiled to himself. He'd just been happy that she was alive.

"He babbled nonsense for a bit, until I got through to him that I wasn't a ghost. That I was alive."

Izzy spoke about how they had gotten out of the hotel after that. How they had returned to the apartment she had shared with Cassie, because she hadn't known where else to go. They had dressed his wound as best they could, and then Izzy had gathered some things and they had left, heading to the bus station for the first bus to anywhere else.

"Didn't know where we were going," she said. "We just didn't want to stay where we were. I was scared she would come for us."

Lund saw Cassie nod at this.

"And I didn't know what had happened to you," Izzy continued. "But I wanted to make sure you could find us. So everywhere we stopped I sent you a photo of the door. I didn't know if you would come, but I hoped . . ."

"How did you find us here?" Lund asked. "On the beach?"

"I asked at the motel. They said you were still booked in. So I just wandered out from the motel, followed the noise and the activity. Where else would you go in a town like this, in the evening?"

"I'm so glad you're here," Izzy gushed, reaching forward to hug Cassie again.

Lund sipped his Coke, letting them have their moment.

Lund listened for a while as Cassie told Izzy about her ten years in the past. It sounded unbelievable, but he had seen so many unbelievable things he was no longer incredulous.

"So, what," Izzy asked, frowning, "you're now eight years older than me?"

"That's right," Cassie said. "Old and sagging and gray. I am your future."

"Where did you go?" Lund asked, somehow feeling like he wanted to cut across their happiness. He didn't know why he felt that way. "From the ballroom? Where have you been all this time?"

Cassie didn't answer immediately. Her eyes glazed over as she stared into the fire, and then her brow knitted briefly. "I went somewhere else," she said. "I was nowhere, a place where humans don't go."

"What do you mean?" Izzy asked.

Cassie shrugged. "It's hard to explain. When I thought you were dead, I just wanted to run away, I wanted to be nothing, nowhere. So I opened a door, and I went there. To . . . nothingness." She shook her head. "I don't even really remember it. It's like dreaming, maybe . . . you know you had a dream but as soon as you wake up it fades away."

Lund could make no sense of it. He glanced across the fire and saw Izzy studying Cassie.

"And then, at some point, I realized I wanted to come home. A doorway appeared and I stepped through it. And here I am."

Izzy nodded slowly. "Well," she said. "Wherever you were, I am glad you came back."

"Maybe I'll tell you more about it someday," Cassie said. "If I ever understand it myself."

"What are you going to do now?" Izzy asked.

"I don't know," Cassie admitted. "But I don't want to spend my life running away from that woman."

Izzy threw Lund a glance. That was exactly what they had been doing.
"Who is she?" Izzy asked.

"No idea," Cassie said. Izzy looked back to Lund and he shrugged.

"Are you going to try to stop her?" Lund asked, drawing Cassie's eyes
to him. She watched him silently for a moment and then shrugged too.

"I don't know," she said. "I haven't thought that far ahead yet. I was
focused on finding Izzy first."

"We'll help," Lund said, and now both women looked at him.
"Whatever you want to do, we'll help."

"Since when do you speak for me?" Izzy asked, but there was humor
in the question. Lund thought that maybe she was pleased with what
he had said.

"Sorry," he offered. "I mean, I'll help. I can't speak for Izzy."

"Thank you," Cassie said, smiling at him. "I appreciate it."

"You're not alone, Cassie," Izzy said, reaching forward again. "You're
with friends now."

LUND FETCHED SOME MORE DRINKS and chips from the store a few
streets back from the beach. He took his time, letting Izzy and Cassie
have a few minutes alone. When he got back the beach had grown quiet,
and the wind from the ocean had a sharper edge. He played with the
fire for a bit, coaxing flames and warmth from it, and passed beers to
Izzy and Cassie.

"Where are you sleeping?" Izzy asked.

"I'll get a room at the motel," she said. "Or if there are none, I'll go
somewhere else. I have the book."

They were quiet for a few moments, just the sound of the waves and
the crackling of the fire.

"What did you do with the book?" Cassie asked, her eyes on the
flames. "The Book of Illusion?"

Izzy looked at Lund.

"We buried it," he said.

"We didn't think it was safe to keep it on us," Izzy said.

"Did you use it again?" Cassie asked Izzy. "Did you work out how
to create illusions?"

Izzy shook her head. "Maybe I can only do magic in times of certain death. Remember what Drummond said when we were in Lyon? Some people can learn to use books."

"Yeah," Cassie said.

"Maybe I can learn to use the Book of Illusion," Izzy said. She looked into the fire. "Not sure I want to, though."

"We need the book," Cassie said. "If the woman thought you were dead it means the illusions work on her. Maybe we can use an illusion to defeat her."

"We can go dig it up," Izzy suggested.

"Is it far?" Cassie asked.

"Yeah," Lund said. "It's far."

"How far?"

"It will take a few days to get there, unless we get a car of our own."

"We don't need a car," Cassie said. "We just need a doorway nearby."

Lund sipped his beer and shook his head. "No doorways nearby," he said. "Your book will only get you so far. We thought of that. Just in case someone else got your book."

He saw her nod, appreciating how careful they had been.

"It's getting cold," Izzy said. "And everyone else is leaving. Shall we head in? I don't like these empty places when there's nobody else around."

"City girl at heart," Cassie murmured.

Lund jumped up and killed the fire by kicking sand over it.

"You coming?" Izzy asked Cassie, as Lund pulled her up.

"I'll be a while," she said. "Need to do some thinking."

Izzy hesitated.

"I'm not going to disappear again," Cassie said. "I promise."

"You better not," Izzy muttered. She nodded her head at Lund and led him away up the sand.

Lund looked back once and saw Cassie sitting there by herself, staring out at the dark sky and the ocean beneath it.

The Shadow in the Sand

"You can come out now," Cassie said to the wind. "We're alone."

Nothing happened for a moment, and Cassie began to wonder if she was wrong. But then Drummond Fox materialized off to her side, as if stepping out of a pocket of darkness. He looked the same, the same clothes, slightly disheveled, but he seemed thinner to Cassie, his eyes darker.

He walked over to her, hands in his pockets, kicking sand before him, and dropped down next to her.

"Hi," he said, meeting her eyes.

She smiled at him.

"Good to see you again," he said. He smiled back at her and then looked off toward the dark ocean. "How long has it been this time?"

"This time it felt quick for me," she said. "Were you listening to the conversation?"

Drummond nodded. "You went somewhere you can't explain."

"I can explain more than I said to Izzy," Cassie admitted. "It was where the magic comes from." Drummond looked at her, interest sparking in his eyes like a match in a dark room.

"Really?" he asked.

She nodded. "I am sure of it. I *know* it. I shouldn't have been able to survive, but the Book of Safety protected me. It was somewhere else, somewhere outside of this reality. But there were colors there sometimes, like when the books are doing their thing."

Drummond digested that, biting his lower lip absently. "I'd like to hear all about it. Everything you remember."

She nodded. "I'd like to tell you. All about the place . . . and . . . other things." She wanted to tell him about the books, about the fact that she had made them all, but it felt too big, too much to deal with right then. "There are other things I can tell you, in time."

He watched her for a moment, hands clasped around his knees, perhaps trying to work out what she was getting at. "Okay," he said. "I'd like to hear. Anytime."

She nodded and it felt like a promise.

"Have you been following them around all this time?"

Drummond nodded. "They are not very good at hiding," he reflected.

"To be fair, he's about ten feet tall," Cassie said.

"And Izzy is not the quietest person I have ever met," Drummond said, a playful smile tugging at his cheeks. "I know she's your friend. But she's noisy."

"She is," Cassie agreed happily.

"But I like her," Drummond said, looking at Cassie seriously. "Izzy is smart and she's kind and she's been loyal to you this whole time. I like her a lot, Cassie."

Cassie felt her core warming at Drummond's words, and she wanted to hug him.

"Lund is harder to read," Drummond continued, oblivious to the effect his words were having on her. "But he seems devoted to Izzy. Together they make quite a pair."

"I'm glad she had someone," Cassie said, looking over her shoulder as if she could still see Izzy and Lund in the distance. "I'm glad she wasn't alone."

"Yes," Drummond agreed.

"How have you survived?" Cassie wondered. "You've been alone this whole time."

"It's not so hard. I've been alone for ten years. When you use the Book of Shadows you become . . . insubstantial. So I can go places. I can ride in cars or at the back of buses and nobody knows I'm there. And when they stop, I just find an empty room nearby and sleep there."

"Why?"

He looked at her.

"Why did you follow them?" she clarified.

"Because I knew that if and when you came back, you would go straight for her. She's your anchor to your old life. You lost her for ten years, didn't you? You barely said ten words to her in that ballroom. My best chance of reconnecting with you was sticking close to her."

Cassie's stomach felt funny, squirming and unsettled, as Drummond watched her, and she felt like a schoolgirl on a first date. She had to look away from him.

"I'm glad you were with them," she managed to say, her voice shaking only slightly. "And I'm glad you waited around long enough for me to reappear."

They sat in a companionable silence in the darkness, the stars rotating above them and the waves crashing rhythmically. Somewhere behind them, down the street in Pacific City, a woman yelped in delight and a man's deep laugh followed. People living ordinary lives, happy lives.

"Can you do that with other people?" Cassie wondered. "Follow them around like a shadow?"

"I suppose so," he said. "Why?"

"Just wondering," she said.

"You're going to try to stop her," Drummond said, drawing Cassie's eyes to him. "The woman."

"I think so," Cassie admitted.

"And what does 'stop her' actually mean?" Drummond asked. "Take her to the police? Take her books? Kill her?"

"I don't know," Cassie said. "And I don't know how I'm going to do it. But someone once told me to imagine what she might do if she got all of the books."

Drummond grunted.

"You once said you wanted to destroy the Book of Doors so she can't get to your library," Cassie said. "If we can stop her, somehow, then the library can come out of the shadows again. And maybe the books can still do some good?"

Drummond didn't say anything. His face was expressionless as he faced the sea.

"I'd love to go back to the library," Cassie said, reaching across to put a hand on Drummond's arm. "I'd love for it to be out of the shadows for good. But I need your help. I can't do it without you."

Drummond thought about that for a few moments. Then he gave her a sidelong look. "Admit it, you just want me for my mountains."

She laughed, throwing her head back and tossing her amusement to the wind, and she felt free and happy for the first time in years.

IZZY AND LUND GREETED DRUMMOND coolly at first, when Cassie brought him to their room.

"I found him," Cassie said. "Wandering along the street."

Izzy's eyebrows rose skeptically. "Really?"

"Book of Luck," Cassie said. "You remember how we bumped into him in Ben's Deli?"

"Hello, Izzy," Drummond said. "Last time we spoke you said you hated me."

"Did I?" Izzy asked. Then, pointedly: "I don't remember, do I?"

"Yes, I'm sorry about that," Drummond said, walking over to her. "Really, truly, I was only trying to keep you safe."

"Not sure it worked," Izzy murmured.

"You're still here," Lund observed. Izzy scowled up at him, not appreciating his interjection.

The tension seemed to ease then, as Cassie and Izzy chatted. Lund switched on the TV and lay on one of the two double beds, his legs dangling over the edge of the mattress, watching as some handsome newscaster bellowed at him about world events. Drummond slumped into an easy chair by the door and stared at the screen. Cassie saw this, and thought he seemed grateful for the distraction.

"Anyone hungry?" Cassie asked after a while. "I'm starving."

"You can order pizza," Lund suggested. "There's a takeout menu on the table."

Izzy called the pizza place, and when she asked if anyone wanted drinks, Cassie said, "Do they do whisky?" and Drummond looked at her in surprise. She smiled back at him, unable to stop herself, and the corners of his mouth twitched and then his eyes crinkled in amusement.

THERE WAS NO WHISKY, BUT they ordered a pizza and soft drinks and cookies and sat around in an easy silence waiting for it to come. Cassie and Izzy sat beside each other on the second bed, their backs to the wall. After a while Izzy started speaking, wondering how Cassie could find the woman, how she could take her books or otherwise beat her. Cassie joined in, and she could see that Drummond was listening. The pizza came and they took slices and drinks and returned to their places. The conversation continued, and Lund turned down the TV so they could talk without distraction. They spoke about the woman and her abilities they had seen, trying to itemize the books she might have.

"What does she want?" Izzy wondered.

"She wants the books," Cassie said.

"She wants the Fox Library," Drummond said. "She told me. The first time I met her." He picked pepperoni from his slice of pizza and discarded it into a garbage can next to the chair.

"Don't waste that, man," Lund muttered.

"What's the Fox Library?" Izzy asked.

So Drummond explained and told her how he had hidden it.

"You have seventeen books?"

He nodded as he chewed, and Cassie found herself remembering that library she had visited all those years ago. It remained in her memory as a special place, despite the turmoil and uncertainty of those days since, a place she wanted to visit again. A place, perhaps, where she wanted to stay.

"Could we use the Fox Library as bait?" Izzy wondered. "Lure her to it?"

"I wouldn't want to lead her right there, even as part of some plan," Drummond said warily. "It's too dangerous."

"Well, a fake one, then," Izzy said. "Lure her there and trap her or something?"

"Lure her and trap her," Drummond echoed, skepticism hanging from every word.

"I don't know. But at least I'm thinking."

"What about an illusion?" Cassie wondered. "We can get the Book of Illusion, right? Could we create an illusion of the Fox Library, something she'd believe?"

"That's right, she believed the illusion of me being shot in the ballroom," Izzy offered. "So illusions work on her."

Cassie looked at Izzy. "Could you use the Book of Illusion to make a library?"

Izzy scoffed. "I don't even know how I did the thing in the ballroom. No, I don't think I could do that, even if I wanted to."

Cassie looked at Drummond. "You seem to be able to use every book that comes your way. Could you use the Book of Illusion like that? Could you make her believe she was in the Fox Library?"

"What are you going to do if I can?" Drummond asked. "Because I don't think getting her somewhere is the hardest part of the job here. We can get her to come somewhere. But she's still going to have her books. You need to be able to deal with them."

"It's a start," Cassie said. "Someone once said to me that I don't need to solve all problems at the same time. Let's do it one at a time. Could you create that sort of illusion?"

Drummond sighed and thought about it, taking a swig of his drink. "I've never used the Book of Illusion," he said. "Even if I could use it, I'm not sure I'd want to gamble on it in these circumstances. And besides, if you are facing the woman, you probably want me to be free to do other things."

Cassie nodded, feeling deflated.

"Azaki could do it," Lund said, and everyone looked at him.

"What?" Cassie asked.

"Azaki could do it. I saw him create a cathedral in the desert. I am sure he could make a library."

"Who's Azaki?" Cassie asked.

"Doesn't matter," Lund said. "He's dead."

"When? What happened to him?"

Lund explained about traveling with Azaki, about coming to New York, and what had happened in Cassie's apartment when Hugo Barbary had shot them both. Cassie glanced a question at Drummond.

"I was in the apartment shortly after that," she said. "We both were. I didn't see any body of a Japanese man."

"No," Drummond agreed.

"I saw blood in the hallway, but no body."

Lund thought about that for a few moments, his expression blank.

"You thought I was dead as well," Izzy observed. "Maybe Azaki isn't dead either. Maybe it was an illusion."

Lund frowned, the most expressive Cassie had seen him all evening.

"Tell me all about Mr. Azaki," she said. "Was there ever a time when you were traveling with him when he was alone?"

"Why?" Lund asked, suspicious.

AFTER THE PIZZA AND THE talk about Azaki, Cassie realized that her relationship with Izzy had changed forever when she went to her own motel room to sleep, late in the night. Izzy said that she would stay in the room she had with Lund, but she walked with Cassie across the parking lot to the opposite side of the motel.

"You're getting on okay with him," Cassie observed, trying to make the comment light despite the pain she felt.

"He's nice," Izzy said. "I know it's hard to tell because he's so . . . I don't know, quiet, right? But he was there when I needed him. And he doesn't lie. He is what he is. I like being with him. I think he likes me too."

"Of course he does," Cassie said. "He'd be crazy not to."

Izzy smiled at that. "We're okay, right?" she asked, reaching for Cassie's hand.

"Of course," Cassie said, smiling. "We'll always be okay, even when things change."

"You've been away ten years, for you," Izzy said, her expression serious.

"But not for you," Cassie said. "It was just a few months ago for you."

"I don't know how you survived," Izzy reflected quietly.

"I told you, I made a friend," Cassie said. "I was okay. In a strange sort of way, I needed it."

"You do seem different," Izzy said, studying Cassie's face closely in the darkness. "More sure of yourself, maybe."

"I'm still me," Cassie said, and knowing what Izzy was getting at, she added, "We're still friends and we always will be. I know I don't deserve it because of how I've ruined your life with this . . . this madness . . ."

"Oh shush . . ."

"But we will always be friends, if you want it."

"I do," Izzy simply said. She reached out for Cassie and hugged her. They stayed like that for a few moments and Cassie felt at peace. The tension she had been carrying with her for years released her from its grip, if only briefly. "Now, go get some sleep and we'll meet for breakfast in the morning. Deal?"

"Deal."

"You can even bring that miserable Scotsman if you want."

They had left Drummond dozing in the chair in Izzy's room.

"He's not so bad," Cassie said. "He's been looking out for you guys these last few months."

Izzy was surprised by that. "Really?"

"Yes," Cassie said. "He was following you guys, making sure you were okay."

"Huh," Izzy said, turning her head to look back toward her room, as if she was reevaluating things. "Maybe I'll go make him a coffee or something, then. Just to be nice."

"You do that."

They smiled at each other.

"I love you, Cassie," Izzy said, the words offered without any embarrassment or awkwardness.

"I love you too, Izzy," Cassie said.

Izzy nodded once and wandered back across the parking lot and into her room.

When she entered her own room Cassie found she was lonely and in need of company. So she opened the door again and returned to her old home, to see her grandfather one last time.

Home (2013)

Cassie went home. To the place, to the person.

It was many years before, and almost a year after she had met her grandfather in the diner with Drummond. She stepped through a doorway onto the porch of her house, back in Myrtle Creek. It was night in late summer, and she could hear the buzz of insects. The air was moist and cool, and she could tell from the smell of damp earth that it had recently stopped raining.

Cassie walked along the porch and sat on one of the old wooden chairs at the corner. She could see her grandfather's workshop from there. The light was on, the window of the workshop glowing like a lantern in the dark night. She could hear banging and movement, her grandfather tidying up for the night after Cassie had gone to bed. Or gone to her room, because Cassie didn't always go to sleep when she went to her room. She would sit up late, reading, long after her grandfather had turned in. But Cassie's room was on the other side of the house, with a window that looked out on the trees. And that other, younger Cassie would be in another world, caught up in the lives of the characters in whatever book she was reading.

After a few minutes the light in the workshop switched off and her grandfather emerged through the large front door. The workshop had been a garage once, before her grandfather had converted it, but it still retained the same door. Her grandfather locked up and then walked across the yard to the house, his head down, his arm swinging by his side. Somewhere off in the woods a bird called in the night, a lonely but somehow comforting sound, and her grandfather looked in that direction as he stepped up onto the porch. And then he looked the other way toward where Cassie was sitting, and he stopped in his tracks. She faced him and their eyes met.

He was thinner than when she had last seen him, she was sure. He was within a year of his diagnosis now. The cancer was already inside him, changing him. Eating him. She wondered if he felt it. If he knew.

He walked along the porch, the wood creaking under his weight, and he sat down next to her on the other chair. There was a small table between them, and Cassie remembered how they would sometimes sit out there together and drink bottles of Coke, particularly in the summer, when it was warm and light. But it was dark now, and the only light came from the kitchen window behind them.

"I thought it was you," her grandfather said. "I mean, the other you. I thought you'd gotten out of bed."

"No," Cassie said, her voice low. "I'm still there. Probably reading."

"Yup," her grandfather said. He was studying her closely again. "Maybe it's just the light, or maybe it's my eyes, but you look older."

"I am," she admitted. "It's been ten years for me, since I saw you in Matt's."

"Wow," he said. He relaxed back into the chair, and it creaked with his weight. Together they gazed out at the drive, the main road a short distance away. A truck passed in the silence, heading south toward Myrtle Creek. Then her grandfather spoke again. "I'd decided I'd imagined the whole thing," he said. "Meeting you. I'd decided it had to be a dream or . . ."

"Or what?"

"I don't know. *Something.* Because anything made more sense than this. But here you are again."

"It wasn't a dream."

"I know," he said.

"How are you?" Cassie asked. "How are you feeling?"

He took a moment before replying, and his answer seemed guarded somehow: "Fine. Same as always."

She wanted to tell him he looked thin. She wanted to tell him to go to the doctor, but she knew he didn't want to know. And she knew that she couldn't change the past. Too many things that she now was and now knew were connected all the way back to what had happened to her grandfather. It was a chain that couldn't be broken. Time travel didn't work that way, she knew.

"Why are you here?" he asked.

"I don't know," she admitted. "I just wanted to feel like I was at home again. That I still had a home."

He said nothing to that. Then he reached across and put a hand on hers.

"I have to do something hard and scary," she said. "I think maybe I just wanted to remember what it was like before there was anything hard and scary in the world, before I do it."

"Life is full of hard and scary things," he said. "Sometimes you know you are going to face something hard and scary." He nodded and Cassie thought he was talking to himself as much as to her. "But you have to get on with it. No point bitching and moaning. Get it done."

She smiled sadly. "Very pragmatic," she said.

"What else can you do?" he asked, and he seemed annoyed, with her, with the world. "Because if you stop you admit the bad stuff has won, don't you? All you can do is keep going. Refuse to be beaten, even when you are beaten. The bad stuff only wins if you let it. I refuse to be beaten, Cassie. I refuse."

She had never seen him like this, she realized. This was the side of him he had always kept from her. This was the bitterness and the anger at all that life had done to him.

"I refuse, and so should you." He jabbed a finger at her. "Whatever you need to do, you get it done and you move on. Put it behind you and survive."

"Yeah," she said. "That sounds good."

They sat in silence again. Cassie was surrounded by the sounds and smells of her childhood, and it comforted her, the closest thing she could get to a mother's hug.

"Stay there a minute," her grandfather said. He got up from the chair with a grunt and wandered along to the door to the house. He disappeared inside, and Cassie heard him moving about in the kitchen. When he reappeared a moment later, he was carrying two bottles of Coke. He passed her one and she took it as he sat back down next to her. "Let's have a drink," he said. He used the bottle opener on his key ring to open them, a couple of quick *tsks* in the quiet night, and then they tapped their bottles and Cassie took a slug of the drink. The fizz and the sugar shocked her awake.

"Is this the last time I'm gonna see you?" her grandfather asked, peering into his bottle.

"I hope not," she said. "I hope I'll see you again."

He nodded at that and then smiled at her. "Good," he said. "It's good seeing you like this. Older, I mean. It's good talking to my granddaughter as an adult, not as a child."

"It's good talking to you as an adult," she agreed.

"So talk," he said, lifting his bottle to sip from it. "No need to rush your drink. If you're a time traveler, you can go back whenever you want, right?"

"Right," she agreed again, smiling.

"So enjoy your drink and tell me something about your life. I want to know what the future is like."

She thought about it for a moment, and another two cars passed on the road out front, traveling in opposite directions toward each other, like medieval jousters, their headlights lancing the night.

"Okay," she said, and she spoke until she was finished with her drink, telling her grandfather a tale about a magical book that could open doors to anywhere, and her grandfather listened with the wide eyes of a child enraptured by a story at bedtime.

A Plan in Five Parts

The next morning, after the night of pizza and drinks and chat, Drummond sat on the ground in front of his motel room, facing the parking lot and thinking about what kind of man he was. For a long time he had been a man who had run and hidden, because that had been the right thing to do. He was still certain of that—he could not have fought the woman, not ten years ago, and not since.

Not on his own.

Now it felt as if he had friends again, people he shared a cause with. He told himself he was reading too much into one night, into pizza and drinks, but he hoped he was not. He wanted friends. And he wanted people to help him. Because it was too much on his own.

It was a beautiful day, the sky above bright blue; it felt warm already, and Drummond enjoyed the sensation of the air on his face. He enjoyed just watching people coming and going, the traffic out on the main street. And then he saw Cassie emerging from the door to her room across the parking lot, and she smiled an acknowledgment, and walked toward him, and he enjoyed that too.

"What are you doing?" she asked, sitting on the ground next to him.

"Just enjoying the peace and quiet," he said. "Thinking about what we need to do."

"Yeah," Cassie agreed, her eyes narrowing as she gazed into the parking lot. She ran her hands through her blond hair and pulled it back behind her head into a ponytail with a hair band.

"I think we should all go get breakfast," Drummond said, and Cassie looked at him. "You and me, Izzy and Lund. We should sit together and eat, just like we did last night."

"Why?" Cassie asked. "I'm not disagreeing. Just wondering why you're suggesting it."

"Two reasons," he said. "Because I like it. I like the company. I like all of you, and it's been a long time since I've enjoyed being around other people."

"Okay," Cassie said.

"And second, because we need to make a plan."

He looked at her.

"You're already thinking about it," he said. "That's what last night was all about, the questions about Azaki."

She shrugged. Not disagreeing. "I got very good at thinking about the long game when I was in the past," Cassie said. "I got good at planning things out."

"I'm good at surviving. And I know the woman better than any of you. And Lund and Izzy know things also."

"Yeah."

"If you're going to make a plan, we do it together, over breakfast."

She smiled, and it seemed to Drummond that she was relieved somehow. "Okay," she said. "I'd like that."

They sat together in silence, enjoying the warmth of the morning. It was going to be a beautiful spring day, a day that would make you believe nothing was wrong in the world. It was a perfect day to chase away doubts and fears and to plan for the impossible.

WHEN IZZY AND LUND EMERGED from their own room a short while later, they spotted Drummond and Cassie sitting on the ground.

"They have chairs, you know," Izzy joked.

Cassie jumped up first. "Where's good to get breakfast around here?" she asked, as Drummond clambered to his feet. "We're going to have breakfast together and plan our next moves."

Izzy glanced at Lund, who nodded once.

"Pancakes," he said.

"Brilliant," Drummond said.

IZZY LED THEM TO A pancake place a short walk away, a big barn of a room with large windows looking out over the beach and the Pacific, and long wooden tables with cutlery in mugs and a few other tourists dotted around. They ordered pancakes and bacon and coffee, and Drummond interrupted Izzy to ensure he got tea instead, and then they drank and ate and listened to Cassie and Izzy reminiscing about a road trip they had once taken to Florida to visit Izzy's cousin.

"Two days on Greyhounds. Worst experience of my life!" Izzy laughed.

"Even after everything I've been through over these last ten years," Cassie said, smiling. "That trip is still the worst thing that happened to me."

It was good, easy conversation, and Drummond felt at home. But there were decisions that had to be made, and when he suggested to them that they had to get down to business, he felt like the adult telling them to do their homework.

Their plates were taken away and their drinks refilled, and then they got to working out a plan. Cassie had a few ideas, thoughts she had been nurturing since the previous evening. She laid them out and Drummond added to them, identifying problems and risks. Izzy asked questions and Lund listened. And then Lund asked a question, and they realized the plan wouldn't work and they started again.

They discussed for over an hour, as tourists came and went, as Drummond's tea grew cold, and then they talked for another hour as they walked along the beach, refining and revising the plan. It was difficult and complex, a plan in five parts, involving the Bookseller and Azaki (who was perhaps dead) and a risky trip for Drummond to follow the woman. And all of it, if it worked, would culminate in them having to face the woman.

"No matter if it all works, she's still going to be dangerous," Drummond cautioned, as the four of them stood on the beach, squinting in the sunlight. The waves were roaring in front of them, birds calling high above. "We might be planning our own demise."

Izzy didn't look happy at that. Lund was inscrutable as always. But Cassie shook her head.

"I don't think so. I think we can beat her."

"What are you going to do?" Izzy asked. "Are you going to kill her?"

Cassie hesitated. "I hadn't thought that far ahead," she admitted. "I'm not a killer."

"No, you're not," Izzy said sternly. "So what do we do with her if we get her? We can't take her to the police."

Drummond was gazing out to sea. He knew the answer to the question. He had decided what they had to do that morning, before speaking to any of them.

"We kill her," he said, and all three of them looked at him. "She's evil. You can't just deal with her. She won't stop." He looked at Cassie, knowing he had to get her to agree. "You saw what she did to my friends," he said, and to his surprise he heard his own voice tremble with emotion. A distant part of his brain said: *Wow, you're really on edge.* "You saw in my memories."

Cassie nodded.

"You saw what she did in the ballroom. She wasn't killing because she had to. She could have taken the books, and nobody could have stopped her. She killed because she wanted to. And she did it in the most horrible ways because she gets off on it. Tell me I'm wrong."

Cassie looked away to the distant horizon. A little way down the beach a couple of kids yelped and screamed as they chased each other around the beginnings of a sandcastle. It was all so normal, so happy.

"We kill her," Drummond said. "We commit to that, or we don't even start. Because there is no point. No halfways. We do it properly, and only then will we be free. Only then will all of this"—he gestured at the people around them—"be safe."

"I'm down with that," Lund said. "Kill her."

Izzy looked at Lund in surprise, her face creased with conflict. Then she looked at Cassie.

"Cassie?" she asked.

And Cassie nodded, not moving her eyes from the horizon. "Yeah," she said. "We do it properly."

Izzy nodded reluctantly. "Okay," she said.

"Good," Drummond said. He waited for a few minutes, letting the decision settle, and then he said, "Let's get started, then, shall we?"

The Plan, Part One—Azaki's Story
Antofagasta, several months earlier

Not for the first time in his life, Azaki was feeling like shit. The illusion in the desert had been as much for him as it had been for the old woman. He'd felt like he'd defrauded her somehow, offering her something she desired, something she had needed, that he knew he was never going to be able to give her. The things he did just to find special books were starting to weigh upon him.

"Beer, please," he said, as he reached the bar. The bartender nodded at him and pulled out a bottle from the fridge behind the counter. Azaki charged it to the room and settled on a stool. The bar wasn't busy, just enough people to generate sufficient background noise to be pleasant. "To Miss Pacheo," he said to himself, tapping the air with the top of the bottle before taking a swig.

He didn't know how much longer he could keep going, but he couldn't stop. He was scared, he knew. Scared of the woman. She was killing people like him and taking their books. He had heard of her, through acquaintances, other book hunters he met in bars. They told stories of the massacre at Washington Square Park in New York, other book owners disappearing. What sort of person could do that so ruthlessly? What sort of person wanted all the books?

Azaki just wanted to find one more book. He'd sell it through the

Bookseller and take his millions and go hide somewhere. Get away from it all.

He sipped more of his beer, looking at his own face in the mirror behind the bar.

Of course, he had a book that he could sell. His own book.

He shook his head at his own reflection: *Don't even think it.*

The Book of Illusion was his. He wouldn't sell it. Not ever.

He felt a tap on his shoulder and saw Lund in the mirror, towering over him.

"I thought you were going to the room," Azaki said, without turning around.

He liked Lund. The man was quiet, low maintenance. He was the perfect bodyguard. But Azaki didn't need him sitting on his arm all night.

A woman's voice answered: "He's a different Lund."

He turned around and saw a pretty blond woman standing next to Lund. And then he saw that Lund looked different. A change of clothes, his hair longer.

"What's going on?" he asked.

"Best we talk somewhere more private," the woman said.

Azaki looked at Lund and the big man nodded.

They moved to a table in the corner of the room, away from anyone else.

"So what's going on?" Azaki asked.

The woman withdrew a book from her pocket and placed it on the table. For a moment Azaki wondered if Lund had found a book, and his heart leapt at the possibility of escape. But he realized almost immediately that he was wrong.

"Okay," he said. "What's that?"

"You need to listen to her," Lund said.

"It's the Book of Doors," the woman said. "My name is Cassie. We've come from a few months in the future to save your life."

Azaki blinked, absorbing that, and then looked at Lund again.

"You're from the future?"

Lund nodded, and then said, "Like I said, you need to listen to her. Because some serious shit is going to go down in the next few months."

"You need to go to New York," the woman said. "The Bookseller is going to call you at some point over the next few days and tell you to go there anyway."

"Why?" Azaki asked.

The woman bobbed her head. "It's a bit difficult to explain. Because I asked her to. In the past. It doesn't matter."

Azaki smiled, because it was ridiculous.

"Stop smiling," the woman said. "This is serious. I'm trying to save your life here."

"Why?" he asked. "Why do you want to save my life in the future?"

"Because we need your help," Cassie said. "To stop the woman."

Azaki stopped smiling, because it didn't seem so ridiculous anymore, and he listened as Cassie told him about his future, and about the plan she had in mind.

"Is it possible?" she asked.

Azaki considered the question for a moment. "It's possible," he said. "Hard, but possible. I'll need some time to practice."

New York, several days later

When Azaki answered the door, he had one hand in his pocket holding the Book of Illusion, and he created the illusion that he and Lund were six inches to the right of where they actually were.

Hugo Barbary was there, just as Cassie and the other Lund had told him, but Azaki was still surprised at the truth of what he had been told. He was staring straight down the barrel of Barbary's gun. Or he would have been if he had been six inches to the right.

Barbary fired and Azaki dropped to the floor, keeping his hand in his pocket and creating the illusion that he was dead as he lay facedown, a bloody wound to his head. Barbary fired again and Lund dropped, just as Azaki had been told he would.

He lay still for a while, listening to Barbary torture Cassie's friend Izzy in the other room. If he hadn't already known that she was fine, he might have tried to intervene. Or maybe he would have quietly gotten up and left, he didn't know. He didn't think he was any sort of hero, but he had never really been required to test himself in that way. As his father had once told him as a child: "The best defense to any punch is to not be there. Run away, boy. There is no shame in surviving."

He heard Lund getting up after a few minutes. The big man came over and checked on Azaki but saw only a corpse, bleeding out on the floor. Azaki heard him sigh, as if he was sad that Azaki was dead, and in truth that made him a little happy. Then Lund stood up again, surprisingly quiet, and a few moments later Azaki heard Barbary hit the floor when the big man smacked him, and he cheered inwardly. Then he heard Lund talking, and Izzy passed him in the hall to enter one of the rooms, gathering a bag of clothes. While she was doing that Lund came back to Azaki, and this was the bit that was risky. Or it would have been, if Azaki hadn't already been told by future Lund that the big man hadn't noticed anything when he'd taken the Book of Illusion from Azaki's pocket. Azaki had taken his hand out of his pocket and pushed it under his body, leaving his pocket open. Lund already believed Azaki was dead, and he was rushing, and he didn't notice that the side of Azaki's head had miraculously healed.

Then Lund and Izzy left, hurrying from the flat before Barbary awoke.

Azaki waited a minute or two, ensuring they wouldn't return, even though Lund had been very clear on that point, and then stood up and brushed himself down.

He felt strange without the Book of Illusion in his pocket. It had been with him for over twenty years. It was his most precious possession. Already he was impatient to get it back.

He took a few steps along the hall and looked into the living area. Barbary was there, lying in a mess against the far wall. Lund had hit him hard.

"You fucking deserved it," Azaki muttered. "You're such an asshole."

He left the apartment as it was, knowing he had to be gone before Cassie arrived with the Librarian. He was clear on the chronology.

Now he had to wait.

Tonight there would be an auction, and the woman would appear and cause mayhem.

Lund and Cassie's friend would flee, taking the Book of Illusion with them. They would travel south with the book and hide it along the way.

Azaki knew where they would hide it. He had been told, back in the bar in Antofagasta. He would be there to collect it as soon as they left.

The desert, south of Las Vegas

Azaki had taken a room at the Rio Suites in Las Vegas, just passing time for a few days. He had flown straight from New York to Vegas, a journey of five hours. He had landed at Harry Reid International Airport even before the auction had started back in New York. He had settled into his room and was on the bed in his underwear, eating an overpriced room service burger, at the time people were bidding on the Book of Pain. And shortly after that Lund and Cassie's friend Izzy, and the Book of Illusion, would be on a Greyhound heading west. Azaki knew they wouldn't arrive in town for another three days yet, but when they did, they would take the cheapest room they could find in Circus Circus, off the Strip, and the following morning they would hire a car and drive south on Interstate 15 for half an hour until they had reached Highway 161. From there they would travel west until they found a dirt track road running north through the desert, parallel with the power lines. Lund would stop at the third power line pole, walk ten paces west into the desert, and bury the book in a plastic bag beneath a shrub using his good arm, the other arm in a sling.

"Your strides are bigger than mine," Azaki had pointed out, when Lund had described where he'd buried the book, during their conversation back in the bar in Chile.

"Count fifteen, then," Lund had said. "The shrub is obvious. It was all by itself, directly in a line with the third pole."

Azaki hoped it was as easy as that.

On the day that Lund buried the book, Azaki was waiting at the Starbucks just off the cloverleaf beneath Interstate 15. He got there early and sat at the window. He was there watching as Lund and Izzy drove past just after ten in the morning, Izzy at the wheel. And he was sitting in his rental car waiting impatiently when they drove back in the other direction half an hour later. He watched them follow the road up onto the interstate and head back north to Las Vegas. They would stay there another couple of nights, debating whether they had done the right thing leaving the book out in the desert. Lund had told him this, as if he had felt guilty for discarding Azaki's prized possession. Right then, as he raced along the highway to the road by the power lines, Azaki was willing to forgive Lund. Assuming he found it, of course.

He found the road with the power lines.

And he found the third pole and parked the car, seeing the tracks of Lund's car stop in the same place.

He even saw Lund's boot prints in the sand, walking away from the car tracks. He followed them and saw the bush Lund had told him about days earlier. He dropped to his knees, the hot sun beating on his back, and dug with his hands until he felt cold plastic.

Through the plastic, the book felt warm. It felt familiar. It felt like home.

He unwrapped the book eagerly, like a child with chocolate, and smiled when he saw the black-and-gold cover.

It was beautiful, as beautiful as it had always been but more so because he had been without it.

He pushed himself up again and stood for a moment, just feeling the book. Then he gazed out into the desert, narrowing his eyes against the glare. The wind blew dust and sand against his cheeks.

He closed his eyes and, holding the Book of Illusion, light and color spilled out between his fingers. Azaki painted pictures in the sky, vast sculptures of sand, swirling and swarming around him, as if he were standing in the eye of a storm. And then the sand became solid shapes, serpentine creatures circling him and hissing and yelling. He felt these beasts, he heard their cries, the illusion absolute.

Sometimes Azaki liked to flex his muscles just for his own entertainment.

He painted the serpentine creatures in colors, red and yellow and blue, and then they changed from sinuous, writhing forms into dancing lights, one of his favorite illusions. Lights in the desert, a rainbow without rain. All of this conjured by Azaki, like an athlete testing his muscles after the offseason.

His gift, the gift of the Book of Illusion, was still there.

He let the lights fade in the sky, and the glowing colors around the book faded as well. And then it was just him and the hot, dry sun.

He walked back to his car.

He had to head back north, he knew.

He was needed, to help deal with the woman.

He had told them he would help, he had promised, because they had saved his life by telling him about Barbary.

A voice in his mind—his father's voice, perhaps?—told him he should run. There was no shame in surviving. It bothered him all the way back to Las Vegas, and it bothered him all the way to the airport.

By the time he was on the plane, the voice had shut up, and Azaki felt oddly at peace.

The Plan, Part Two—The Bookseller

Cassie met the Bookseller for the third time at midnight in Café Du Monde in New Orleans, but this time the Bookseller had not expected her.

Cassie had visited on three different evenings in quick succession, opening a door from a hotel room across the country, and stepping out into Café Du Monde. On the first night it had been warm and wet. Cassie had waited for an hour past midnight, but the Bookseller hadn't appeared. On the second night it had been warm and dry, and Cassie had waited for longer, but the Bookseller hadn't appeared again. On the third night in New Orleans—the same evening for Cassie—the Bookseller was already there when Cassie arrived. She was sitting at the same table where Cassie had met her previously, coffee and beignets in front of her and a faraway look in her eyes. The Bookseller didn't even notice Cassie until she pulled out a chair and sat down opposite her.

"Hello," Cassie said.

The Bookseller regarded her without expression.

"I wondered if I'd see you again," she said. There was no anger in her words.

"How have you been?" Cassie asked, although she didn't care. In the Bookseller's time it was just over two months since the auction. Cassie had traveled back in time.

"I've been peachy," the Bookseller said. "Considering my auction turned into a mass murderer's wet dream. Considering that animal Barbary killed my only real friend. Considering I didn't even sell the fucking Book of Pain. All in all, it's been a good few months."

Cassie listened without comment.

"What do you want?" the Bookseller asked.

"Well, I want three things," Cassie said. "First, I want a coffee and a beignet, because someone once told me they were good, and she was right. Second, I want the Book of Pain. And third, I want your help."

The Bookseller's eyebrows rose in disbelief, but she waited until a waitress came and took Cassie's order before saying, "You want my help? You've got some nerve to ask for my help."

Cassie blinked, not understanding. "Why do I have some nerve, exactly?"

"You still have my Book of Safety. You never returned it to me. Or the Book of Doors."

"Ah well," Cassie said. "I couldn't give you the Book of Safety, could I? Because you ran away before I had the chance."

The Bookseller's mouth formed a tight line of annoyance.

"And I'm not going to give you the Book of Doors, because you didn't deliver on your side of the deal. You wouldn't have seen it, because you ran away, but Izzy got a bullet in her brain from some man when he was trying to fight off that woman."

The Bookseller looked away, her eyes flicking back and forth like she was watching a tennis match. The waitress returned and Cassie took the coffee and the plate of beignets.

"Relax," Cassie said. "She didn't die. But you wouldn't have known, because you ran away."

"All right," the Bookseller snapped. "You made your point. I ran away. I did what I had to do to survive. And if I hadn't run away that woman would have gotten another book for her collection."

Cassie took a bite out of a beignet. It was as good as she remembered.

"Not that she needs any more books," the Bookseller said, speaking more to herself now. "The things she did. The speed. The ferocity. Did you see what she did to Okoro? I mean, that man didn't take a breath in his life that didn't ruin someone's day, but nobody deserves to die like that."

"He wasn't the only person who died," Cassie said. "At your auction."

"Don't you think I know that!" the Bookseller snapped bitterly. "I've thought of nothing else. I was trying to get out of the business, and I just invited disaster down on my own head. Well, no more. I am having nothing more to do with those damnable books."

"Found religion?" Cassie asked, raising an eyebrow skeptically.

"Your question presupposes I ever lost it. Don't sit there in judgment on me, young lady. You know nothing about me, nothing about my life. I am not apologizing for anything I've done."

"I didn't come for apologies," Cassie said. She took a sip of coffee. It was dark and bitter, a perfect dance partner for the sweet and buttery beignet.

"Yes, you said. Coffee and beignets and help. What help do you think I can give you?"

"Where is the Book of Pain?" Cassie asked.

"It's somewhere safe," the Bookseller said. "I'll give it back when I receive the Book of Safety."

Cassie nodded to herself. The offer wasn't a surprise. She waited while a group of loud young men wandered past, singing some sports song, leering at Cassie and the Bookseller briefly before moving on.

"Fucking tourists," the Bookseller muttered. "Destroying this town. The Book of Safety is mine. You have no right to keep it."

Cassie smiled to herself as she took another sip of coffee, thinking she had every right and that the Book of Safety was more hers than it had ever been the Bookseller's.

"I have no wish to keep it from you," Cassie said. "But if you want it, you need to help me."

"Help you what?"

"I am going to stop the woman."

The Bookseller stared at her for a moment, then laughed in disbelief. She folded her arms across her chest. "You have some balls, girl, I will give you that. You want to stop her? You and your Book of Doors?"

"I don't just have the Book of Doors," Cassie said. "And it's not just me. But there are some things I don't have that you can provide me."

"What would that be?"

"I need another auction. I need to get her attention. She came the last time you had an auction. Have you wondered how she knew?"

The Bookseller shrugged. "It's not exactly a secret. I send a notification to everyone. The more people who know, the more come."

"She didn't strike me as the type of woman with lots of friends."

"Mmm, well. She's probably taken phones from some of the people she's killed. She would have gotten the notification from those phones when we sent it out."

"So she'll get a notification again, if you have another auction. Particularly if she wants the books."

"What books?" the Bookseller asked, and despite everything she had said, Cassie saw a spark of interest there.

"The Fox Library," Cassie said, and the Bookseller's eyebrows shot up in surprise.

"You found it?"

"I know where it is," Cassie said.

"And you're going to use that as bait? Are you out of your tiny white head? You're going to give her the opportunity to add that to her collection?"

"I need to be sure she will come," Cassie said. "It's the biggest prize."

The Bookseller shook her head. "You're putting me off my beignets."

"You don't need to be there," Cassie said. "You just need to set the time and the place and send the notification when I tell you. We'll do the rest."

"We?" the Bookseller asked. "Who's in your gang? Your friend Izzy, who would talk the handles off a door? Or the big man? Or Drummond Fox, who would run away from his own reflection?"

"You think the worst of people," Cassie said.

"I've had a lot of experience of people letting me down," the Bookseller said.

"You seem much more . . . brittle than the last time we spoke," Cassie observed.

"Brittle," the Bookseller said. Then she smiled a tight smile. "Nobody's ever accused me of that before."

"You help me out, I'll give you back the Book of Safety. You have my word."

"Oh well, if you give me your word . . ."

Cassie ate her second beignet, taking a moment to enjoy the surroundings. There were a few other people at the café: a middle-aged couple who looked like tourists, a couple of young women who looked worse for wear, like they were trying to ward off a hangover with coffee and sugar. The waitresses stood at the counter, speaking to each other in low voices.

"Okay," the Bookseller said, finally. "When do you want to do this nonsense? And where?"

"Don't know when yet," Cassie admitted. "But I know where. I want to do it the same place you did the last one."

"My hotel?" the Bookseller asked. "In New York?"

"Why not?" Cassie said. "It's a hotel. It's got lots of doors."

The Plan, Part Five (1)

In a forgotten place in New York City, Cassie waited for the woman.

The ballroom still smelled of damp, despite it having been months since the auction, and a few weeks more since Cassie had tumbled back through into reality from the place she had been, the place where she had created the books. And it was a mess still, with shattered mirrors and glass all over the floor, bloodstains on the walls. The chandelier overhead was a fragment of its former self, the light it threw much reduced and struggling to reach the corners of the room. They had lit candles and placed them around the edges of the room, just to provide a bit more illumination, and the candlelight danced and flickered. The ballroom was a place of shadows now, of hidden corners and menace, no longer the glittering domain of dance and laughter.

Cassie sat cross-legged on the platform at the end of the room, in front of the mirror that led to the Bookseller's panic room and escape route, reminiscing about the years she had spent with Mr. Webber as she waited. It had seemed like an ordeal, at the start, a punishment maybe, but now she remembered those days fondly. She would always carry them with her as a time when she had felt safe and protected, when she had been able to enjoy the simple things. She wondered then if experiences were always better in retrospect, in reminiscence. Was it possible to truly enjoy something in the moment?

She thought of Izzy and all that she had put her through. Cassie felt so guilty about all of that. A few hours earlier, in the dead time as they waited for the woman to arrive, Cassie had sat with Izzy in the hotel bar, surrounded by empty glasses and bottles, the detritus of their last few days in the hotel.

"I don't want you here," Cassie had said, not meeting Izzy's gaze. "I can't put you at risk."

"I know you're older than me now, but you're not the boss of me," Izzy had said. "I'll go where I want. And I want to be here."

"It's not your fight. I put all of this on you. You were the one telling me to stop."

Izzy had shrugged. "You're right. But I'm still not going anywhere. I'm not your friend just because you always do what I say. And I'm not stopping being your friend because of all that's happened."

"Will you do it to help me, then?" Cassie had asked, and Izzy had narrowed her eyes suspiciously as Cassie reached into her pocket and passed her a book. "I need to make sure she doesn't get hold of this. This is the Book of Safety. If she has this, nothing can stop her. Will you take it somewhere else and keep it safe? That way, if something happens to us, at least I'll know she'll never get it."

Izzy had taken the book and had run her hand over the cover. "Why don't you give me the other books too?" she had asked. "If you want to keep them safe from her, give me all of the books."

"We need them," Cassie had said.

"Not all of them. Not to defeat her."

Cassie had said nothing.

"Or are you just giving me this to keep me safe?" Izzy had asked.

Cassie had accepted that Izzy wouldn't leave her. "Will you just keep the book on you?" she had asked. "Please? For me? I'd never forgive myself if anything happened to you. Please?"

Izzy had nodded, finally. "But nothing's going to happen to you either, okay? We'll get through this."

Sitting in the ballroom, waiting for the woman, Cassie hoped Izzy was right.

A noise pulled her wandering thoughts into focus, and she lifted her eyes to look straight ahead to the far end of the ballroom. The sound she had heard had been a door opening and closing, she was sure. The sound of someone arriving.

Cassie sucked in a breath nervously, her heart beating rapidly. "Someone's here," she said to the room. They were all there with her—Drummond and Izzy, Lund and Azaki—all of them hidden, made invisible by another of Azaki's illusions. Cassie took some comfort in the knowledge that she was not alone. She hoped it might help, if it came to it.

She dropped her head onto her hand, her elbow on her knee, her face purposefully expressionless while her stomach performed gymnastics.

She waited and nothing happened for a few moments. The building felt suddenly very quiet, as if the walls themselves were holding their breath.

Then the mist came, tendrils curling and poking into the ballroom like serpents. They gyrated into a wall of mist, separating the ballroom from its entrance, and then parted like curtains, just like the last time the woman had arrived, and she stepped through the gap and onto the dance floor. Once again, she was wearing her layered black skirt and white bustier top. The skirt pooled around her feet and made it look as if she were standing in a puddle of shadows. In one hand she was carrying a small purse by the straps, so it dangled down at the side of her leg, and she was holding the Book of Mists in her other hand.

The woman ran her eyes around the room and then settled them on Cassie.

"You need to get a new trick," Cassie said, gesturing toward the wall of mist churning behind the woman.

The woman stared back, no expression on her face.

"Wondering where everyone is?" Cassie asked.

She jumped up from the platform and took a few steps forward to face the woman across the dance floor.

"There's nobody else here," Cassie said. "Just me and you. Nobody was going to come to another auction here, not after the last time."

The woman's chin lifted slightly, her eyes narrowing.

"I set up the auction to get you here," Cassie said.

The woman had the watchful, wary expression of a cat that had just seen a dog it didn't know.

"You don't say much, do you?" Cassie observed, and she was surprised to find she was angry with this woman, despite her fear. "But I know you can speak. It's just for show, isn't it? Just to make people think you're scary?"

The woman's mouth twitched at the corners, not quite a smile but perhaps a recognition of Cassie's analysis.

"Everything about you is affected. Even that mist when you come in the room. Like you're Dracula or something."

The woman adjusted her stance, moving her weight from her left foot to her right.

"You are everything that's wrong with this world," Cassie continued. "You have all this magic at your fingertips and what do you use it for? To cause pain and suffering. That is all you can think of to do, when there are so many amazing and wonderful things you could do instead."

Cassie could almost feel Drummond willing her to shut up, to get on with the plan, but she couldn't stop herself. She was venting years of frustration and despair.

"I pity you," Cassie said. "I feel sorry for you."

The woman's expression seemed to relax then, all emotion gone, just a blank mask.

"How lonely it must be, to hate everything," Cassie said, shaking her head slowly.

The woman's expression hardened, her mouth tightening into a line and her jaw muscles clenching.

"What are you going to do?" Cassie asked. "Are you going to crush me or skin me or burn me with your light?"

The woman lowered her head, a predator preparing to pounce.

"Go ahead," Cassie said, as her heart raced with adrenaline and fear. "Take your best shot."

The Plan, Part Three—
Drummond and Cassie in the Shadows

The hardest part of the plan, the part that Drummond had feared the most (other than the final part), was following the woman to find out what they needed. In the hours before, by himself in the hotel, he'd paced his room restlessly, debating whether what they were doing was right or not. He'd felt the moment barreling toward him, but his indecision kept him trapped there, facing something he wasn't sure he wanted to do.

It was Cassie who came for him, knocking on the door to his room a few minutes before they had agreed to meet in the hotel bar. When he opened the door, she was standing there by herself, beautiful and disheveled in the big old coat she always wore, her hair pulled back from her face.

"Are you ready?"

"No," he admitted.

She nodded and her eyes slipped off to the side. "Me neither."

They stood in awkward silence for a few moments and then Drummond spoke. "Best get started, then, before we both lose our nerve."

He found he wanted to be braver than he was. In a silly, schoolboy sort of way he wanted to impress Cassie, this woman who had been through so much because he hadn't been able to protect her when Hugo Barbary had attacked, or when the woman had come for them in the ballroom months before.

"Yep," she agreed.

They walked together through the hotel to the bar, where Izzy and Lund and Azaki were hanging out, chatting and fidgeting with nervous energy.

"You doing it, then?" Izzy asked, standing up to greet them. Cassie nodded once. Drummond watched as the two women met each other's gaze.

"Be safe," Izzy said to Cassie, pulling her into a hug. "I know you're older now, but you gotta listen to me, otherwise I'm going to kick your butt."

Cassie grinned over Izzy's shoulder, and then the women separated, and Izzy looked at Drummond.

"I'll kick your butt too if anything happens to her."

"I know," Drummond said, trying to smile.

"Okay," Cassie said, nodding, trying to hide her apprehension. "Let's do this."

They walked to the first room along the corridor from the bar, and Cassie used the Book of Doors to open the door, revealing what appeared to be another corridor in the hotel.

"Through there is just before the auction," she said to Drummond. "Just before she attacked. Far enough away from the ballroom that nobody should see us."

"Right," Drummond said. He held out his hand and Cassie looked at it in confusion.

"I'm going to take us into the shadows now," he explained. "You have to hold my hand."

"What? I didn't hold your hand the last time, when I took us to your library."

"That was different," Drummond said. "The library itself was in the shadows. We went there together. I am taking myself into the shadows. If you come with me, we have to hold hands. And you can't let go, do you understand?"

"What happens if I let go?" Cassie asked.

"You will fall out of the shadows," Drummond said. "You will fall back into the real world." He shook his head seriously. "Please do not let go, not when we are anywhere near the woman."

"Hold his hand, Cassie," Izzy called from behind them. "Hold it like it's your favorite book."

"Shut up!" Cassie muttered.

Drummond watched her hesitate, staring at his hand as if it were something strange and slightly scary. Then she reached out and their fingers intertwined. Her hand was cool and smooth, and Drummond felt himself shiver unexpectedly—delightfully—at the contact. Their eyes met, and Drummond thought that Cassie felt it too. She looked a little embarrassed, just as embarrassed as Drummond felt.

"So sweet, the two of you," Izzy said behind them, mischievous and grinning.

"I told you to shut up!" Cassie barked.

"Ready?" Drummond asked.

Cassie gulped visibly and then nodded.

"Remember, we can't talk, I won't be able to hear you. Just stay together, whatever happens."

She nodded, understanding.

They stepped through the doorway and into the past, closing the door behind them. Drummond pulled them into the shadows, and suddenly everything was gray and dreamlike, and he felt that familiar, pleasant sensation of floating through unreality.

THEY DRIFTED THROUGH THE HOTEL, through insubstantial walls and forgotten rooms, down to the ground floor where people were moving about, bulbous, noisy shapes in this unreal world. Drummond was used to seeing what humans looked like in the shadows, but he realized Cassie was not. He looked at her, next to him, and saw her eyes were wide and astonished. He tugged gently on her hand and she turned her head toward him. He flicked his chin: *Okay?* She nodded once and turned her eyes back to the scene before her.

They stood together, hand in hand, at the side of the ballroom and watched the events they remembered, but this time seen as if underwater, in monochrome shades, and with the sounds muffled and echoing. They watched people scream and die, and they watched the Bookseller flee. They watched the woman destroy Okoro, and then Diego with the gun. They saw Izzy's illusion, and they watched as Cassie screamed in shock and horror, at the moment she thought her friend had died, and then saw her flee through the doorway. Drummond watched his earlier self, saw him panic, saw his eyes darting about, and then that earlier, cowardly Drummond dissolved into nothingness, into his own shadows.

HE FELT A GENTLE TUGGING. Cassie pointed and he followed her finger to see the woman, the devastating angel, as she walked out of the ballroom. Drummond hurried after her, Cassie scurrying alongside him, her hand in his, and he put his free hand on the woman's shoulder, gripping her and then letting himself be carried with her as she moved through the lobby. They didn't need to run anymore. He looked at Cassie and she understood, lifting her feet from the floor. They were carried with the woman out into the New York night, trailing behind her like a cape tossed by the wind.

She took them to a car. Drummond and Cassie sat together in the back seat holding hands like shy lovers as the woman drove for hours through the night. At one point Drummond looked over and saw that Cassie's eyes were closed, as if she was sleeping. She looked so peaceful, he thought, even as they journeyed with a nightmare creature. He let her sleep, wondering what sort of dreams she might have in the shadows, and watched the world roll by. The drive was silent. There was no radio, no music. Just the rumble of the engine and the woman's eyes in the rearview mirror, flicking up occasionally to stare through Drummond to the road behind.

WHEN THE CAR STOPPED CASSIE was awake. She looked at him, wide, worried eyes in the shadows, and he tried to squeeze her hand, tried to reassure her even though he was bristling with his own terror.

Drummond melted sideways out of the car, pulling Cassie with him. There were woods all around, and a house, and noise and light: another vehicle. Cassie and Drummond floated behind the woman, watching mutely as she invited the two men into her house. Cassie tugged Drummond's arm to get his attention and when he looked her way, she gestured urgently at the men.

What do we do?

Drummond shrugged and then shook his head with sorrow. *Nothing.*

Cassie tensed and pulled both her hands up to her face, pulling Drummond's hand with her, until he resisted. She gave him a fierce look, and he could only nod: *I know.*

He led her through the walls of the house, following behind the two men as they descended into a basement.

Drummond positioned himself and Cassie at the side of the stairs, and waited, his stomach overfull with dread like he'd just finished eating too much. There was a buzzing in his ears that he realized was his own blood pumping faster and faster around his body.

The woman directed one of the men to a mattress in the corner, and the other to lie on the cold concrete floor. That man had hungry eyes, Drummond saw, hungry eyes that were blind to the threat. He thought he was in control. He thought this small, beautiful woman was no danger to him.

And then the incomprehension, the panic, as the floor swallowed him. Drummond forced himself to watch, forced himself to see every horrible second as the man fought and struggled. He watched the woman and the joy in her eyes at the suffering she was creating. Drummond made himself watch because it was a bulwark against any reservations he had about what they planned to do. This was who she was. This was why they had to stop her.

Cassie tugged his arm as if trying to flee, but he held her, looking at her and shaking his head sternly: *We need to know. We haven't finished what we came to do!*

Drummond Fox, doing what had to be done, no matter the cost.

He hated himself as Cassie tried to turn away, turn her back on what was going on.

Then the man in the floor was nothing more than smacking lips and flared nostrils struggling for oxygen. Drummond watched as the lips fell still, as the man died in his tomb of concrete, and he held Cassie close, her face to his chest, their hands still clasped together awkwardly between their bodies.

The woman walked over to the mattress and Drummond took a few steps forward to watch. Not because he wanted to. Because he had to.

Cassie lifted her eyes from his chest and looked that way, just as the man on the mattress shook and melted into foamy liquid, as his gurgled screams bubbled horribly in the shadows.

Cassie shook her head and pulled away, using her free hand to attempt to pry Drummond's fingers from her own. She was shouting silently into the shadows: *No! No! No!* And Drummond could see she was terrified and traumatized, her eyes flicking back to where the woman was inspecting the liquid mess that had moments before been a man.

Drummond tried to pull her back to him, tried to catch Cassie's attention, but she was panicking like a terrified animal, her eyes wide and wild. She started thumping his chest with her fist, desperate to be released.

Then the woman stood up.

And she looked directly toward them.

Drummond's heart stopped. It was all he could do not to release Cassie's hand and flee himself.

Feeling something, seeing the change in Drummond, Cassie stopped and followed his eyes to where the woman stood. And suddenly she was still too, as if they had just seen a predator, the whole world frozen, waiting to see what would happen.

THE MOMENT PASSED, AND THE woman turned away. Drummond looked at Cassie and saw that she was crying, shadow tears pouring from her eyes, but the panic appeared to have abated. She was watching the woman and pointedly not looking at the mattress.

As the woman walked to a corner of the basement Drummond took a few steps to follow. The shadows and the gloom lifted enough for him to make out what the woman was doing. There was a safe here, in the corner of the room. They watched as the woman opened it and revealed three books inside. She removed books from her purse and placed them inside alongside the volumes that were already there. Drummond tried to peer through the gloom to make out what books she possessed.

Then she closed the safe, stood up, and walked straight past them. The sound of her heels on the stairs as she ascended back into the living area of the house was a slow metronome, and it felt like forever before the woman was gone, the door to the basement closed behind her.

Drummond looked at Cassie. She was gazing at the safe. When he tugged her hand, it took a few moments for her to turn her face to him. She looked traumatized. She had the hollowed-out expression of someone on the news, some eyewitness to a horrible event.

Drummond pointed at the safe and flicked his chin, asking the question: *Enough?*

She considered the question blankly for a moment, and then nodded. She had seen enough. More than enough.

The Plan, Part Four—Azaki and the Books

You know the problem with Lund," Azaki said, waving his glass around airily.

"No," Izzy said. "But do tell."

"The problem with Lund is he thinks being quiet all the time makes people think he's stupid." Azaki stared at Lund, who was watching him from across the table. His brow was dropped slightly, as close to a scowl as Azaki had ever seen him come. "What he hasn't realized is stupid people aren't usually quiet. Stupid people are usually the noisiest people in the room."

"Oh god," Izzy muttered. "What does that say about me?"

Azaki peered at her for a moment and then laughed. "There's always an exception to the rule. Because you are definitely not stupid."

"Just loud," Izzy said happily.

"Certainly loud," Azaki said, toasting the air before sipping his drink.

They were in the mezzanine bar in the Macintosh Hotel. The hotel gave Azaki the creeps. He hated it, particularly at night when he'd tried to sleep. It was an empty place, rooms full of melancholy and memory. But of all the places in the hotel, the mezzanine bar was the place where he was most comfortable. Since meeting up with Lund and the others a few days earlier, he had been most relaxed when sitting in the bar with Lund and Izzy.

It had been strange, meeting Lund and Cassie again, so long after seeing them in Chile. For Lund and Cassie, when he met them in Bryant Park, it had been only a few hours since that last meeting. They had stepped through a doorway in Oregon to Chile, and then had stepped back after persuading him of his future. And then they had stepped through another doorway, alongside Izzy and Drummond Fox, to New York, to rendezvous with Azaki as promised.

They had spent the first night at a bland tourist hotel in Midtown, and while there Cassie had visited the Bookseller in the past and had persuaded her to let them use the Macintosh Hotel, a place the Bookseller apparently owned. Azaki had been quite excited when he'd heard about the place, but he had been disappointed when they'd walked across town and through the hoardings into the old building.

But getting to know Izzy had cheered him up over the last few days. He enjoyed spending time with the woman. Lund was a comfortable companion, like a quiet, peaceful room where you could relax. Izzy, in contrast, was the best party you'd ever been to—vivacious and funny and beautiful, and he loved being around her. Cassie had a kind way about her, beneath all the worry and quiet. And Drummond Fox was a revelation to Azaki, much warmer than he had ever imagined, and with a sense of humor that seemed to emerge when he was more relaxed.

On that first night in the Macintosh Hotel, Azaki and Izzy had gone out to get supplies. Mostly alcohol, but some food as well. Since then they'd spent most of their time in the bar, just talking, drinking, trying to ignore their nerves and their fears. Sometimes Cassie would join them, often distracted and distant. Drummond would come and drink quietly, but obviously listening to the chat, like he wanted to be around people but without any need to participate. Azaki understood that.

"I didn't realize you knew how clever I am," Lund said now, and Azaki stared at him in surprise.

"I didn't say you were clever," he said.

"That's right," Izzy agreed. "He didn't say you were clever."

"I just said you weren't as stupid as you want people to think you are."

Lund considered that for a moment, then said, "I wish I was clever enough to understand the distinction."

"You're very dry," Azaki said, peering at him. "It's impossible to tell if you're joking or not."

Cassie and Drummond had appeared momentarily, and they'd all watched them disappear through the door into the past.

"That's it, then," Izzy said, once they were gone. "It's happening."

"Yeah," Azaki agreed, and he realized he was nervous. The next bit was down to him. He put his glass down on the table.

Cassie and Drummond returned almost immediately. The door opened, they tumbled through, and Cassie slammed the door shut behind them again. Azaki was alarmed at the look on Cassie's face. Her eyes looked hollow, her skin blanched.

"Well?" Azaki asked. He realized he was clenching and unclenching his hand rapidly in his pocket, a nervous tic he'd always had as a kid.

Cassie walked past him and dropped onto one of the sofas in the bar.

"I need a drink," Drummond said. "Where's the whisky?"

"Behind the bar," Izzy said, but her eyes were on Cassie. She sat next to her friend on the sofa.

"Bring me one!" Azaki called, as Drummond walked over to the bar. Drummond raised a hand in acknowledgment.

Cassie seemed to be gathering her thoughts.

"What happened?" Izzy asked, obviously sensing that something was wrong.

Azaki exchanged a glance with Lund, who flicked his eyebrows up and down once.

"Doesn't matter," Cassie said. "We saw the woman. We followed her home. We were with her and . . . She killed two men while we were there." She shook her head. "It was horrible, Izzy."

Izzy looked pained. She held Cassie's hand.

"What did she do?" Azaki asked. He couldn't stop himself. He was scared and wanted as much information as possible.

Cassie lifted her face to regard him. She seemed miles away. "She turned a man to liquid," she said. "I think . . . I think he was screaming as she did it. But it sounded like a gurgle because he was all liquid. Oh god . . ."

She dropped her head into her hands. Azaki crossed his arms, pacing the floor restlessly.

"I've never been more sure of what we're doing," Cassie said, speaking through her hands. "She's evil."

Then she looked up at Azaki.

"But we found where she keeps the books. It's a safe in a basement, in a house somewhere south of here."

"So you can take them?" Azaki asked.

"I think so," Cassie said. She looked at Izzy. "Remember that first night at the Library Hotel? We were talking about a burglar opening a safe?"

"Yeah," Izzy said, smiling faintly.

Drummond returned with a bottle of whisky in one hand and five glasses held against his chest with his other arm. He poured drinks for them all and they toasted each other silently and drank, even Cassie.

"Let's do it," Cassie said to Drummond. "Let's get the books."

Then she looked at Azaki.

"Are you ready?"

Azaki nodded, even though he was nervous.

"How does it work?" Lund asked. He pointed at the door Cassie and Drummond had come through. "This door is bigger than a safe door."

"No idea," Cassie said. "But we're going to find out."

Cassie got up, wiped her mouth with her sleeve, and walked over to the door again. She held the Book of Doors by her side as it fizzed and glowed, and then reached forward with her other hand to open the door. Instead of a corridor they saw a black solid wall, with what looked like the interior of a safe in a two-foot-square recess hanging about a foot off the ground.

"Is that it?" Izzy asked.

"Yeah," Drummond said. "That's her safe."

Azaki watched as Cassie reached in and removed the books. She showed them to him each in turn, and Azaki studied them carefully.

"Can you make versions of these?"

Azaki nodded. He knew that he could, but he also knew the limitations of what the Book of Illusion could do. "But the illusion won't last forever. Hours maybe. A day or so if we are lucky. And I'll have to concentrate the whole time."

He wished he hadn't had quite so much to drink over the last few hours.

"So we need to call the auction," Cassie concluded, "in twelve hours' time."

"It took her that long to drive back," Drummond commented. "When we were with the woman. She's about a thirteen-hour drive away. If the Bookseller calls the auction, she'll have to leave almost immediately."

"So the illusion only needs to last as long as it takes her to get the books and go," Lund said to Azaki. "Easy, right?"

Azaki smiled grimly, even though he thought Lund was trying to be supportive. "Yeah, easy."

"Are we ready to do it?" Cassie asked, looking at each of them in turn. "Because when I call the auction, there's no turning back."

"Why not just take the books?" Izzy asked. "Just take the books and forget about her."

Cassie shook her head. "We talked about this."

"There are more books out there," Drummond affirmed, pouring himself another whisky. "Better she's gone for good."

Azaki felt the tension in the room, a tightly tuned guitar string ready to snap.

"Okay," Cassie said. "Azaki, create the illusions. And then I'll call the Bookseller."

"Leave her the Book of Mists," Drummond said.

"Why?" Cassie asked.

"She likes to make an entrance, doesn't she?" Drummond said. "If she tries to create mist and it doesn't work, she'll know the books are gone before we have a chance to deal with her. Leave her that. We'll just have to take it off her when she gets here."

Azaki nodded, and Cassie returned the Book of Mists to the safe.

Then Azaki went to work, the Book of Illusion in his hand sparking with soft light. He created simulacrums of each of the books they had taken and placed them in the safe. He gave them weight and texture, an illusion of substance, magic for the hands as much as for the eyes.

"It's done," he murmured, keeping his mind focused on the imaginary books in the safe. He stepped away and took himself to the couch, closing his eyes to maintain his focus. He could *feel* the simulacrums in the woman's safe. He kept the Book of Illusion gripped in his hands, and soft colors continued to seep out from the edges of the pages.

He heard Cassie close the door again, the woman's safe with it.

"Are we good?" Cassie asked. Then, presumably after a series of nods, she said, "I'll call the Bookseller."

Soon be over, Azaki thought. One way or another.

The Plan, Part Five (2)

G o ahead," Cassie said. "Take your best shot."

The woman watched her for a moment, and then she smiled at Cassie.

"Is this where you want me to use my books?" the woman asked, tilting her head slightly. "Is this where you want me to realize my books are gone?"

Cassie's brain froze as her plan was knocked suddenly off its tracks; her plan was a train careering down a hillside as the woman looked on calmly.

As Cassie licked her lips, as her insides boiled with fear, the woman peered into the purse hanging from her elbow. She withdrew a book and gazed at it without expression. Almost immediately the book became insubstantial, only a suggestion of a book in the air. And then nothing, just the woman's empty hand.

Her eyes flicked to Cassie.

"Did you think I wouldn't know?" the woman asked, as she pulled out the other books, one after the other, each of them dissipating into nothing at her touch. "I know the books," the woman said. "I know how they feel."

Cassie was frozen to the spot, the woman between her and the ballroom entrance.

She's only got the Book of Mists! Cassie's brain shouted. But Cassie remembered what the woman had done to Yasmin, Drummond's friend, with the Book of Mists.

"I don't know you, though," the woman said, her eyes drilling into Cassie. "I don't know who you are. I don't know how you got to my books. But I saw you with the Librarian. I saw you here, at the last auction."

The woman took a few steps forward.

"Tell me who you are."

"It doesn't matter who I am," Cassie said, her voice croaking, her mind racing and trying to come up with a plan.

"Oh, it matters," the woman answered. She ran her eyes slowly up and down Cassie. "I am going to keep you alive," she said. "But you will wish you were dead. I am going to make you sing to me of your pain. I am going to delight in your agonies for weeks and months."

The woman took another step forward.

"The Librarian is behind this," she said. "Tell me, blond woman, where is the Librarian? What was his plan? Did he think he could stop me just by taking away my books?"

Cassie swallowed, fear a large dry rock in her throat. She couldn't move. She couldn't think.

Then the woman reached into her purse again, but this time she pulled out a handgun, a revolver, the end of the barrel a massive black hole in Cassie's vision.

"Do you think I need books?" the woman asked. "This is the gun I killed my father with. It took him many days to die. I shot off pieces of his body and then dressed the wounds to keep him alive. I didn't have books back then, you see, but I could still make him sing to me."

Cassie found herself hypnotized by the barrel, the dark eye watching her.

"Stop."

Cassie glanced over the woman's shoulder. Drummond was there suddenly, coming out of nowhere, from behind Azaki's veil of invisibility. Azaki was there too, and Lund, and Izzy farther back. Cassie felt relief wash over her.

"Enough of this," Drummond said. His eyes flicked to Cassie, checking she was okay, and then back to the woman.

"The Librarian," the woman said. "And . . . others."

She smiled as if delighted.

And then Lund ran at the woman, his sudden movement surprising everyone. Cassie flinched in shock, but the woman was too quick. She pivoted and fired and Lund was knocked backward as if punched, landing hard on the floor.

Immediately Cassie saw three things.

She saw Izzy shout Lund's name and dash toward him.

She saw Azaki flicker and disappear again.

And she saw Drummond run toward the woman, just as Lund had, his face set in a grimace of determination.

The woman pointed and fired at Drummond, just as she had fired on Lund moments earlier.

Cassie hesitated, unsure of what to do, and when she decided to move, to run at the woman from the opposite side of Drummond, it was too late. The mist was already gathering around her.

DRUMMOND DIDN'T STOP, AND NO bullet seemed to hit him, and Cassie saw the woman's eyes narrow in surprise, even as the mists thickened.

She tried to move, but it was like pushing against sheets, and then pillows, as the mist grew denser.

"Drummond!" she called.

Then the mist was gone, the air suddenly clear and clean, and in front of her Azaki was gripping the woman's wrist, appearing from nowhere to steal the book from her grasp. And while she looked that way Drummond had reached her and grasped her gun with both hands.

"Hard to shoot someone carrying the Book of Luck," he said to her. "Much to my delight."

The woman screamed in fury, spittle flying from her mouth, as Azaki and Drummond wrestled her weapons from her hands, two men easily overpowering one slight woman.

"What are you without your books?" Drummond asked, as he and Azaki took a few steps away from her.

"What are you like without all of your powers?"

The woman didn't answer.

From the back of the room, Izzy called, "Cassie, he's hurt. He's been shot!"

"I'm fine," Lund grunted, his voice weak.

"You're nothing special after all," Drummond said, continuing to stare at the woman.

"You're smaller than I thought," Azaki observed. "Can't believe I've been scared of you all these years." He looked down at the Book of Mists in his hand.

"You killed my friends," Drummond continued, his expression serious. "I've been running from you for a decade. My library . . ."

The woman tilted her head, interested.

"I've been away from my library for so long, just to protect it from you."

Drummond lifted the gun and pointed it at the woman's forehead.

"Why don't I just shoot you now and make the world a better place."

"No," Cassie said softly.

She walked over and put a hand on Drummond's arm, forcing him to lower the weapon, forcing him to look at her.

"She was the one who brought the gun," Drummond protested.

"I know," Cassie said. "But you're not a killer. That's not the way to do this."

The three of them looked at the woman in silence, and the woman stared back defiantly. Cassie could hear Izzy speaking to Lund, reassuring him. They didn't have long, she knew. She didn't know how badly Lund was injured but they had to get him help.

"Time for you to take a trip," Cassie said to the woman. "I want to show you the Book of Doors." She pulled the book from her pocket, and the woman looked at it like she was a hungry man and the book was a meal. "I want to show you the nothing and nowhere. I want to show you where the books came from."

The woman raised her eyebrows at that.

"I've been there," Cassie said. She shook her head slowly. "You won't survive there. It's a place where humans can't exist. It will tear you apart."

Drummond shoved the gun into his pocket, and Azaki tossed the Book of Mists onto the floor, and the two of them approached the woman, one for each arm, planning to carry her to the door at the side of the room, where Cassie would reveal the nothing and nowhere. But before they grabbed her the woman placed her hands on her skirt, palms down on the black feathers.

Azaki reached her first, and he took hold of her arm, and she dropped her head and smiled at him from beneath her brows.

Azaki grunted. His mouth dropped open and he released an awful scream into the ballroom. He fell backward onto the carpeted floor as he threw his hands up to his face, and Cassie saw that the skirt the woman was wearing was glowing now, pulsing dark light.

The woman shot out an arm and grabbed Drummond before he could move away, and then Drummond shrieked, a high-pitched agonized yell, and his eyes rolled back in his head, and he too fell to the floor, both hands on his face.

Cassie backed away.

She had seen this before, in Drummond's memories.

"The Book of Despair," she said.

The woman turned on the spot, pirouetting elegantly like a dancer, her head back and her eyes to the ceiling, as if Cassie weren't there.

Cassie looked again at the skirt of crow's feathers and saw that it wasn't fabric. The feathers were the pages of a book stitched together into a garment.

Before Cassie could react to that, the woman darted forward, not with inhuman speed but quicker than Cassie had expected, and gripped her with both hands, her face a contorted scream of fury, and Cassie was filled up with despair.

Despair

In Cassie's mind, all was lost. It was over.

There was no hope. They were beaten, and she was barely aware of her own body as she collapsed to the floor, as all strength and intention left her.

There was no color in the world. Life was monochrome and austere. There was consciousness and then death, and consciousness was destroyed by the inevitability of death.

Death.

Her own grandfather, a skeleton in loose skin with blood on his lips from his coughing. The air was thick with sweat and pain. Cassie was stuck there, a room with no door, just pain and death forever, and she wailed, and this world of despair enjoyed the sound of her pain.

Then she saw the future, her despair pulling back a curtain and revealing to her what her failure meant. The whole world was empty, silent cities and barren fields. Animal carcasses lay strewn about in muddy fields where no crops grew. The trees on the horizon were hands thrown up in horror at what had become of the world.

This was the world the woman had created, and here she was, a shadow on the horizon, strolling in delight through the misery. She was a smudge of black on the landscape drawing near, her arms spread wide as she promenaded along the road. But the road was not a road,

Cassie saw. The woman was walking on a path made of people, all of them crushed under her feet, all of them screaming wide-mouthed into the gray world. And the world wasn't silent anymore, it was full of the noises of pain and agony.

This was the future for humanity, for mankind. Because of the woman.

Because of Cassie.

Because of the books Cassie had created in the nowhere and everywhere.

Cassie wailed, in the ballroom, and in the dead world where she was in her mind.

And the woman was drawn to the sound. Hungry eyes swept around like searchlights and found Cassie where she cowered. The woman's smile of delight turned into a sneer.

Cassie lowered her eyes, knowing that the woman was advancing upon her. She knew that the woman wanted to add her to the road of bodies and bones, to the screaming path that carried her through the world. Cassie would be stuck there, for eternity, just one of millions of others.

Overhead the sky was gray and flat, and as the woman advanced birds fell heavily to the ground on all sides, squawking and flapping as pain gripped them. And below her, in the mud, insects and worms writhed and erupted to the surface, stricken by the agony inflicted by the woman passing above them.

And the woman reached out toward Cassie, her mouth agape in a scream of pure hatred.

There could be no life without pain and suffering.

Cassie was screaming, the woman's skeletal hand coming near, her mouth wide as she sought to tear Cassie apart with her blackened teeth.

There was nothing but despair.

And then there was fire, sudden and furious and angry and beautiful, because it was *something*, something instead of nothing.

Fire

Izzy was on the floor next to Lund, holding his arm as the man groaned and writhed. The bullet had hit him in the abdomen, in the guts, and Izzy was terrified that some organ had been punctured, that he was bleeding internally.

"Lund!" she said. "Talk to me."

The man was a rock of tense muscle, his eyes clenched.

"I'm . . . okay," he muttered, through gritted teeth.

Izzy knew he needed help, she needed to move him. She glanced up to see what was going on with the woman, and she saw instead Cassie and Drummond and Azaki all on the floor, all of them moaning. The woman was still standing a few feet away, turning on the spot, her face tilted to the ceiling. She looked almost joyous at the agonies that surrounded her.

"What?" Izzy gasped. She had no idea what was happening, what the woman was doing, but she saw the woman's skirt was glowing.

She looked at Lund again, his jaw muscles clenched so hard she thought he would shatter his own teeth. Cassie screamed farther down the room, and she could hear Drummond grunting. Azaki was simply saying, "No, no, no," repeatedly. As Izzy watched he rolled onto all fours and banged his head on the carpeted floor, like he was trying to knock himself out.

The woman turned around and her eyes widened at the sight of Izzy. She advanced, and Izzy was frozen, unable to move, watching as the monster drew near. And then the woman brushed a hand gently across Izzy's cheek, and Izzy flinched back reactively. But she felt nothing, even as the woman turned, pirouetting as if dancing to music only she could hear.

Izzy realized she was safe. The book that Cassie had given her was protecting her. She could feel it, warm and heavy in her pocket, a shield against whatever was affecting her friends.

Izzy looked at the glowing skirt again, as the woman danced. She looked closer at the feathers and realized they weren't feathers. That was why the skirt was glowing—it was one of the books. Her whole skirt was made from the pages of a book somehow stitched together.

The woman continued to dance in the flickering candlelight, her eyes cast upward.

She's not given you a second thought, Izzy said to herself. You are nothing to her.

Izzy hated the woman. She was nothing but a selfish bully. No better or worse than the kids in the schoolyard that used to pick on her when she was younger.

She looked at Lund, at Cassie and Drummond and Azaki. She was the only one unaffected. She was the only one who could do anything.

She looked at the skirt again, seeing coarse, dry paper instead of feathers, the flicker of candles beyond the woman. And then she remembered something Drummond had said to her the morning in Lyon, months before. And she remembered sitting on the beach with Lund in Oregon.

She jumped up and reached into her pocket for the cigarette lighter Lund had used to start the fires on the beach. She sparked the lighter and dashed forward a few steps and put it to the hem of the skirt as the woman was facing away, staring at Drummond and Cassie farther down the room.

The flames were immediate, catching on the thick, dry pages of the Book of Despair, and in a few seconds the whole garment was aflame, the woman now wearing a skirt of fire.

As Izzy backed away, returning to Lund as the woman jerked in surprise and screamed, she saw Cassie shaking herself sensible, and Drummond sitting up again. Azaki stopped throwing his head at the floor and even Lund opened his eyes to see what was happening.

The woman screamed in fury, beating the skirt with her hands.

"Drummond!" Cassie called, and Izzy saw Cassie running to the mirror at the back of the room, the mirror with the secret passageway behind it. The mirror that was also a door.

Across the room Drummond had a book in one hand and it was glowing. He flexed his other arm, and the woman was lifted off the ground, a fireball and fury in the air. Cassie opened the mirror and pulled it back, revealing a dark hole in the wall, a rectangle of nothingness, and Drummond threw his arm toward it. The woman shot across the room, three feet off the floor, a streak of fire moving with the howl of an animal caught in a trap.

The woman disappeared through the rectangle of darkness, rotating to face them, her head back and staring at them as if she were falling off a building and they were on the roof watching her plummet to her doom. She threw a hand toward them as she went, as if reaching out for a handhold, and then she seemed to disintegrate into the darkness, her howl fracturing into a thousand howls, and then nothingness.

Cassie slammed the mirror shut, and the fire and the noise were gone.

Next to Izzy, Lund groaned and closed his eyes once more.

Izzy pulled the Book of Safety from her pocket and pressed it into his hands.

"Come on," she said, tears in her eyes. "Work."

Her friends ran toward them from the other end of the room, and Izzy hoped it wasn't too late. She hoped Lund would be okay.

The Last Act of Hugo Barbary (2002)

In the past, the man who had for many years been known as Dr. Hugo Barbary was sitting on the edge of the reflecting pool opposite Radio City Music Hall on Sixth Avenue. It was nighttime in the city, warm and humid and angry, and Hugo Barbary was an argument of a man.

He had been thrown back to the past again by Cassie, through a door from the ballroom. As best he could work out, when he wasn't distracted by the storm in his mind, it was many years ago. Maybe twenty years. Not as far as the last time, but the past for sure.

He shuddered and grunted, feeling the writhing pain in his skull.

That Bookseller woman had done something to him, he knew. She had used the Book of Pain and she had dislodged something. He hadn't felt right since. He had walked aimlessly when he had first arrived in the past and he knew that he would have looked like just another mad old man on the streets of Manhattan. He had found himself on Sixth Avenue and had stopped at the pool, trying to calm himself.

He felt alternately furious and elated, in agony and delight. He was two people fighting. The Book of Pain had released all of his turmoil, the memories and experiences of his childhood that had made him into the monstrous man he had become. The Book of Pain had *created* his pain anew, giving it a life and an intent of its own, and now it was wrestling with him.

The rest of Hugo, the other parts of him that were no longer in pain, felt as if they had been asleep for decades. He had all of his memories, all of his experiences, but he was a different person, a man horrified and terrified by the things he had done before that woman had changed him with the Book of Pain.

In the noisy night of New York City, his eyes dazzled by the bright lights and headlights, Barbary threw back his head and grunted, and a couple of tourists sitting near him on the edge of the pool threw him a nervous look and shuffled surreptitiously away.

The pain was alive and trying to recapture Hugo, but he did not want that. The part of him that had once been a boy, that had been innocent before injury, resisted.

He screamed through gritted teeth, gripping the concrete edge of the pool with both hands, his neck straining. His scream died in the sky above him, swallowed by the honking of traffic and the rumble of the subway trains beneath Sixth Avenue.

He thought it was over, he thought he felt better for a moment, and he started to relax, but then the pain came back. This pain was a physical thing, and Hugo Barbary was carrying the Book of Health, which was working to remove it from him like poison from a wound, or a long-buried splinter, and suddenly the pain punched its way out of Hugo, a tenebrous, intangible thing that erupted from Hugo's mouth and swam in the air, hiding in the pollution and darkness of the night.

Hugo was suddenly, immediately released. His mind was clear, his agonies gone, and he looked around with wide and wondrous eyes. For the first time in his life he really saw the world around him, the colors, the life, the activity, and it was marvelous to him.

He stood up abruptly, suddenly seized with opportunity and possibility. He was an old man, but he was carrying with him the Book of Health and the Book of Faces. He had many years before him, and many ways to spend his time. As he walked south along Sixth Avenue, his eyes glinting and a smile on his face, he decided that he was no longer Dr. Hugo Barbary. That was a name that another man had chosen for himself to convey certain ideas. It had never been his real name. The man that had been Hugo Barbary for most of his life decided that he would take another name for himself now. He didn't know what, but he had plenty of time to decide.

HUGO BARBARY'S PAIN HUNG IN the air in the hot New York night. It floated above the traffic and the people, unnoticed. But this pain had been created by a special book, pain that if not quite alive nonetheless had intent and a will.

The pain waited, but not aware of what it was waiting for.

Waited until a young family wandered past, the Belrose family on holiday in New York for the first time, enjoying the sights and the bright lights. They sat by the side of the pool and shared some M&Ms and a Coke they had just bought, and then the young daughter, Rachel, left her mom and dad as they spoke about boring adult things and wandered along the edge of the pool, trying to balance herself, teasing herself that she might fall in and get wet.

She stood there on the corner of Sixth Avenue and Forty-Ninth Street, gazing up at Rockefeller Center, the other towering buildings all around. Rachel was so excited to be away from the countryside, the cabin where they lived. She didn't think she was going to sleep when they got back to the hotel; she was going to stay awake at the window all night watching the people and the traffic. At home she couldn't see anything from her bedroom, just darkness and trees. It was so boring.

She looked at her parents now, as they stood up and checked they hadn't left anything behind.

"Come on, Rachel!" her dad called, smiling.

She took one last look around and then jumped off the edge of the pool, and when she jumped, she was taken by the pain of Hugo Barbary. It swallowed her, or she swallowed it, and she landed on her hands and knees on the sidewalk.

For a few moments she was still, just staring at the concrete between her fingers.

She suddenly felt full, *unpleasantly* full, and her head felt funny.

And she felt . . . different.

"Honey! Rachel?"

It was her dad, she knew, and the sound of his voice annoyed her immediately in a way it never had before.

She stood up and saw them looking for her, like she couldn't do anything by herself.

She went to them and saw the relief on their faces, and she despised them for it.

Then another part of her—the part of her that had been Rachel before she had jumped a few moments earlier—asked herself why she was thinking such things.

The Rachel part of her shrugged off the strange feelings and hurried after her parents.

But over time, after their return home from New York City, the Rachel part of her would become quieter and quieter, more and more dismayed at what was happening. After a while it would recede, and eventually it would be locked away somewhere inside.

The pain took her over. The pain lived in Rachel's body.

And it remembered about the books, the books that had created it. And it coveted them.

BEGINNINGS
AND ENDINGS

The Fox Library

In the Fox Library, everything was dark and insubstantial, colorless in a way that made Cassie recall what she had seen in her despair. They stood in silence, a group of shadows in a dark space, as the shape that was Drummond once again threw a page of the Book of Shadows out into the day. And then color flooded in on them, just as it had the last time Cassie had visited the library. The Fox Library was no longer the Shadow House, but a real, solid building sitting on a hillside in the northwest Scottish Highlands.

"Wow!" Izzy gasped.

They followed Drummond out into the courtyard in front of the house, crunching on the gravel. Unlike Cassie's previous visit to the Fox Library, the sky overhead was blue and clear, the sunlight golden and warm despite the chill in the wind.

"It's so nice to breathe fresh air," Azaki murmured, squinting into the day. "Air that doesn't smell like old furniture."

"Where are we?" Izzy asked, so Drummond told her.

They stood in front of the house for a few moments, just enjoying the air and the silence. Lund stood off to one side, the Book of Safety in his hand. Cassie nudged Izzy and nodded toward the large man. Izzy walked over to him and held his arm.

"How are you?" she asked.

"Still okay," he said. "I think."

The Book of Safety appeared to have halted the progress of whatever injury the bullet had caused Lund, but they didn't know if it was a permanent fix or not. Back in the ballroom Drummond had said, "I have something that might be able to help properly. In the library."

So Cassie had opened a door and all of them had stepped through into the shadows.

Now in the daylight, in front of the house, Cassie looked down to the far end of the lawn and she saw another deer there, watching her just like the last time. Or maybe it was the same deer. Then a second deer appeared beside it, chewing lazily as it observed them.

"Look," Cassie said to Izzy, pointing to the deer.

Izzy's face lit up when she saw them. "Bambi!"

"How about a drink?" Drummond asked. "Somewhere comfortable?"

"Oh yes, please," Azaki said. "Something with a bit of kick."

THEY WALKED BACK INTO THE house and through the hallway, Azaki murmuring in delight when he saw the bookshelves that lined the walls. They trooped up the stairs, past the tall stained-glass window, and then Drummond led them into the main library.

To Cassie the room felt even grander than it had during her previous visit. Perhaps it was the soft golden sunlight stretching in from the bay window, but the room seemed larger, the comfortable chairs more inviting.

"Home again," Drummond said, his words a sigh of satisfaction.

He stood awkwardly for a moment, watching as everyone found a seat to sit in or a windowsill to lean on.

"This is an amazing house!" Izzy said, sitting on the arm of the chair that Lund had dropped into. "You own all of this?" she asked.

"He owns the mountains," Cassie said, leaning against the window and gazing out toward the loch to the west of the house.

"And all these books," Azaki said. He was sitting in the chair opposite Lund, picking through the pile of books on the low coffee table. "I assume."

"This is like your dream home, Cassie," Izzy said. "All these books.

No roommate to bug you." She smiled at her tease and Cassie pulled a face back at her. Cassie's and Drummond's eyes met, and then they both looked away at the same time.

"It is beautiful here," Azaki said, craning his neck to take in the view from the window. He jumped up and walked over to stand next to Cassie, gazing out at the day. There was something about the light that reminded Cassie of liquid gold. The whole glen was washed in it, the mountains and the loch.

Drummond smiled and slipped his hands in his pockets "That's because it's sunny, which almost never happens. Wait until it's gray and misty and wet, then you'll see it's even more beautiful. Let me get some drinks. Tea and coffee for everyone?"

Drummond took their orders and disappeared out of the room. Cassie and Azaki poked about among the books on the shelves, and Izzy took herself to the window to inspect the view, telling everyone when she saw deer again. Lund remained in his seat, his head back and eyes closed like he was hungover, the Book of Safety clutched in his hand against his stomach. When Drummond returned, he was carrying a tray laden with mugs. They gathered around the coffee table, taking places in chairs or cross-legged on the floor, and Drummond passed out the mugs.

"I brought shortbread as well," he said, placing a plate of biscuits on the table. "Everyone should eat. Even you, Lund. We all need the energy. It will help you feel better."

They each took biscuits and munched them in silence for a few minutes.

"What now?" Izzy asked Cassie, cupping her mug of coffee between her hands.

"I don't know," Cassie admitted. "Back to normal, I guess?"

Everyone was quiet, contemplating that. Cassie heard a ticking from somewhere else in the house, the rhythm of a grandfather clock filling the silence.

"It doesn't have to be that way," Drummond said, looking at the floor as he spoke. "There are still special books out there. There will still be people using and abusing them."

"That Bookseller woman still has the Book of Pain," Izzy noted.

"What are you saying?" Azaki asked Drummond.

"Well," Drummond said, and then he cleared his throat. Cassie thought he was nervous. "The Fox Library used to be a place where friends would come and talk about books. I'd like it to be alive again. But maybe we need to do more than just talk about the books." He looked at Azaki. "You were a book hunter. And Lund helped you for a while."

"So, what, you want us to keep hunting books?" Azaki asked.

"Why not?" Drummond answered. "But don't do it for the money. Do it for the library. Do it to protect and preserve the books."

Azaki mulled that over, sipping his drink.

"You should do it," Izzy said to him. "I hate these books, and I'd much rather they were locked away here than out in the world."

"You could help too," Drummond said, looking at Izzy, and then at Lund. "Both of you."

"What?" Izzy asked. "I can't help. I have a job back in New York. Or I did. Who knows if I still have it? But I have an apartment. I need to work to survive."

"I'll pay you," Drummond said. "I'll hire you. The Fox Library has considerable resources at its disposal. And we can't let someone else like that woman or Hugo Barbary get hold of the books. We have a duty. The Fox Library has employed people before. No reason it can't employ them again. I'll hire the three of you as researchers. Book hunters. Library assistants. Whatever you want to call it. I need people with the right intentions. People I can trust."

"And that's us?" Izzy asked skeptically.

"Yes," Drummond said, meeting her gaze. "I think so. I would trust all of you."

Izzy looked surprised at Drummond's words, flattered even.

"You should do it," Cassie said to Izzy.

"What about you?" Izzy asked.

"Cassie as well," Drummond said, holding Cassie's gaze, not looking away this time. "All of you."

"Okay, sign me up," Azaki said, taking a second piece of shortbread from the plate. "It would be nice to be doing something positive for a change. What else am I gonna do with my life?"

"What does it pay?" Izzy asked.

Drummond laughed. "I'll match whatever you are being paid now."

"Is that all?" she asked.

"She'll do it," Cassie said. "We both will."

"Lund?" Izzy asked.

The big man nodded and gave a thumbs-up. "But I would really like to not have a bullet in my stomach for much longer."

"Ah . . ." Drummond said. "Yes. Of course. I have something for that." He stood up and nodded at Azaki and Izzy. "You two get the fire going, and we can talk about the new Fox Library."

"I've never lit a fire," Izzy said.

"Lund," Drummond said. "Stay right there, I'll be back in a minute." He looked at Cassie. "Can you help me?" he asked, nodding off to the side of the room.

Drummond opened the bookcase on the other side of the room, revealing the hidden staircase, and then he and Cassie climbed back into the room at the top of the tower, with its cupboards and papers and sunlight flooding in from the windows. Drummond pulled the same key ring from his pocket and walked around the wall to the cupboard numbered "eight."

"Book of Healing," he said to Cassie, as he removed the book there. "This should fix Lund right up."

"Fantastic," Cassie said.

"But there's something else I wanted to show you," Drummond continued. He walked around to cupboard six and unlocked it.

He removed a book from the cupboard and walked over to place it on the table. Cassie gasped in surprise when she saw it.

"That's the Book of Doors," she said, looking at the same book that she carried in her own pocket.

"Yes," Drummond said. "We've had it in the library for over a century, but we didn't know what it was. Nobody could use it. Look."

He opened the book to the first page and Cassie saw that there was no text describing the Book of Doors, like there was in the version of the book she had.

"But it's the same book," Drummond said. "That was why I was so surprised when you showed it to me that day in Lyon. I realized we already had it, we just didn't know. That's why I've been so interested in who gave you the book."

"Where did it come from?" Cassie asked.

"Egypt," Drummond said.

Cassie shook her head slowly and took the book from him. As she held it in her hands it felt warm, and it glowed in that familiar way, and then she saw the first page of the book change, text swimming into focus, the familiar words she knew from her own book.

"'Any door is every door,'" she read.

Drummond smiled and then laughed. "It's still incredible, even after all these years," he murmured to himself, gazing down at the page.

"But two versions of the same book," Cassie said, flicking through the pages. The book Drummond had given her was identical to her own. It was the same book. "How can that be?"

"Time travel," Drummond said. "It's the same book, just at two different points in its own timeline. Just like there were two versions of you in the past; there was only one Cassie, but the younger you and the older you were existing in the same point in time for a while."

Cassie's frown deepened as she thought about that.

"When I asked you to bring me back here the first time," Drummond said, "I wanted to see this book again. I wanted to confirm to myself that it was in fact the Book of Doors. I waited till you were asleep and then I came up here and checked."

Cassie nodded distractedly.

"I thought about destroying it," Drummond murmured, and Cassie looked at him. His eyes were fixed on the book. "But I couldn't. I just couldn't do it. And I knew that if you had a later version of the same book, I could still destroy that if needed, and this version of the book would be safe here in the library, out of reach of the woman."

"You don't need to destroy anything now," Cassie said. "And certainly not this."

"No," Drummond agreed. "I want you to have it. It feels like the Book of Doors has always been yours."

She smiled, touched by the gesture. In that moment she wanted to tell him everything—she wanted to reveal that all of the books were hers, but it still felt too big, and maybe now too unbelievable. Did she still believe it herself? Her memory of the nothing and nowhere was growing increasingly vague.

"Take it, please," Drummond said, as if he thought she was hesitating to accept.

Cassie nodded and ran her thumb over the cover of Drummond's copy of the Book of Doors. "This is the version of the book I got back in New York all those months ago," she said, working out the chronology in her mind. "You give it to me now and then . . ." She smiled because she realized what she had to do. "I have to give this to Mr. Webber," she said. "So he can give it to me."

"If you say so," Drummond said.

She nodded to herself.

"Let's get back downstairs and fix up Lund. And then maybe we can talk about the future, all of us."

Cassie smiled. "I'd like that. And I'd love to stay here. This place feels like home to me. But I need to go do a couple of things first."

She looked around the room, at the numbered cupboards. "Can I borrow another one of your books?"

The Joy at the End

The room was in darkness, and heavy with the smell of sweat and blood and death.

This was Cassie's home, a place that had become alien to her. She had come back to this place using Drummond's copy of the Book of Doors—having to prove to herself that it worked, that it was the same book as her own.

Her grandfather was in the bed, a skeletal shape, moaning quietly. Another Cassie, a younger Cassie, sat slumped in the easy chair in the corner, exhausted. Through the drapes dawn was coming, light creeping into the day.

Cassie walked to the window and pulled one of the drapes aside. She saw the workshop out there, the spring wildflowers growing in the long grass along the side of the building, vibrant colors in the morning light.

"Cassie."

The word was a croak of agony. Cassie turned at the window and saw her grandfather looking at her. He smiled, hollow cheeks and the rictus of a corpse.

She sat on the bed and held his hand.

"I hoped I'd see you again," he said.

She nodded and smiled. "I wanted to be here," she said. "I was asleep the first time."

She looked over her shoulder to her younger self. Her grandfather looked there as well. "You're exhausted. I don't mind."

"No, but I do."

Her grandfather winced then, his eyes rolling in his skull. She remembered how even the morphine wasn't helping at the end.

"I wanted to be here, and I wanted to give you something," she said, not even sure if her grandfather could hear anymore. She pulled out the Book of Joy. The cover was a bright collage of many happy colors, like flowers in full bloom. She placed it in her grandfather's hands, feeling the clamminess, the ferocity of his grip. "I want to give you joy."

As soon as he held the book, his demeanor changed, his face relaxing as the agonies left him, and he looked at her with clear eyes. The Book of Joy sparked brilliantly like a firework in a dark sky.

"Cassie," he said.

He smiled and rolled his head to the side on his pillow. For a moment he just gazed out the window.

"My workshop," he said. "So many memories. I loved you sitting there reading while I worked."

Cassie felt tears in her eyes as she watched him reminisce, as joy dawned on his face like the most beautiful sunrise.

"Look at the flowers," he said, the words almost a gasp of delight. "Look at the colors. So . . . bright and colorful. Isn't it beautiful! Look at how they're blowing in the breeze."

She sat with him for a few minutes more, as morning dawned on an amazing world, as he slipped away, leaving the world in joy rather than in pain.

And then he was gone, and the colors of the Book of Joy died with him.

Cassie stood up, taking the Book of Joy with her, and she walked around the bed back to the doorway. The other version of her was still asleep in the chair, but she would shortly awaken and find her grandfather gone, and that moment would haunt her for years to come.

But no more, Cassie thought.

This was an ending, but it was also a new beginning for her, for Cassie.

She opened the door and left her house for the last time. She had one more place to go, before returning to the Fox Library and her friends and her future.

The Quiet Death of Mr. Webber (3)

In Kellner Books on the Upper East Side of New York City, Mr. Webber was sitting by himself, reflecting on the conversation he'd just had with the younger Cassie. It was about the time that he was supposed to give her the Book of Doors, he knew, and he wondered how it would come into his life.

He looked up from the table and saw Cassie emerging from the door to the staff room at the back of the store. This was a different Cassie, older, *his* Cassie. She smiled at him and put a finger to her lips, and then pointed over his shoulder to the front of the store where the younger Cassie sat in the window.

He nodded and smiled back at her, delighted to see her again. She seemed lighter in herself, he thought.

She reached out and passed him a book, a small leather-bound notebook. He questioned her with a tilt of his head, and she nodded.

He took the book and examined it, ignoring the way his heart seemed to be pumping unusually hard.

He looked at Cassie again and she nodded once more, flicking her eyes to the younger version of herself, as if saying: *You give this to me.*

He nodded himself, acknowledging the message. Then he reached into his pocket and pulled out his pen. He was aware of Cassie watching him as he wrote a careful note to her on the first page, beneath the other lines of text. Then he closed the book and slipped the pen back into his pocket.

When he turned his eyes to Cassie again, she was watching her younger self over his shoulder. She looked at him and seemed sad, he thought.

Then he felt the pain, a sudden, blinding pain, that made him gasp silently.

He grasped at his chest, dimly aware of Cassie standing close to him. He looked at her, in agony but understanding now why her expression was so sad. She held him close, and as he felt consciousness slipping away from him, as he felt the coming embrace of darkness, she placed a single kiss on his forehead, like a blessing and a thanks.

Acknowledgments

Acknowledgments, eh? Who would have thought I'd ever get to do this.

I am writing this almost a year before *The Book of Doors* is even published. Whoever you are, reading this, I'm talking to you from the past. Hello! What's 2024 like? Thank you for buying the book and bothering to read these acknowledgments.

So, who to thank?

Well, firstly, my agent, Harry Illingworth, who signed me on the basis of a mad, complex novel about the invention of time travel. That book died on submission, and when I pitched a bunch of different ideas for what to do next, Harry told me that this book—*The Book of Doors*—was the one to write. Boy was he right. His editorial insights on the first draft ("more wonder!," "put more wonder in it!," "where's the sense of wonder?") were also perfect. Thank you, Harry, and sorry for ruining your holiday with all the submission shenanigans.

Thanks to Helen Edwards for her work selling the book to other territories and for introducing me to the ways of certificates of residence and tax paperwork. What fun we've had.

To my editors—Simon Taylor at Transworld in the UK (possibly the most charming man I have ever met) and David Pomerico at William Morrow in the US—thank you both so much for your enthusiasm for *The Book of Doors*, and the kindness and patience you have shown with my newbie's questions. You've made my first publishing experience an absolute delight. The full teams at both publishers have been amazing, turning this little story into something quite wonderful—thanks to all for the care and constructive feedback.

Over the years a number of people have read things I've written. Thanks to all of you, but particular mentions to Chris Clews, Pamela Niven, and Alison Kerr, who at one point or another have all gone above and beyond in providing detailed and helpful comments.

Thanks to my friend Graeme O'Hara, of Bob's Trainset Productions. Many years ago I wrote a short film script for him—about the invention of time travel—and he told me, "There's enough material in here for a novel." He was right. I wrote that novel and some years later it got me an agent. Without that push, I wouldn't be here today writing these acknowledgments. Graeme, I owe you a few burgers and beers, to say the least, but you do need to accept that *The Mummy* is an objectively excellent film. Also, you will no doubt be delighted by the return of Merlin Gillette in these pages.

Special mention to Clem Flanagan, the Red Pen Vigilante, who gave me brilliant editorial input on my time travel novel and made me believe it was actually good and worth submitting to agents. Again, without you, Clem, I wouldn't be here. I hope you like *The Book of Doors* as much as you liked *TDWITT*.

Almost twenty-five years ago I took a job in the UK Civil Service to pay the bills while I worked on my writing. Since then I have had the pleasure of working with lots of fabulous and interesting people, all of them (including most of the politicians I've met) committed to trying to make the world a better place. There are too many people to mention individually but thank you to everyone I have worked with over the years—you've made my working life far more enjoyable than it might have been. In particular, thanks to The Lard and Leek Club from VQ days, BODS (still the best team ever), and the Exclusive Pizza Club (Erin, Cheryl, Felicity, Alex, and Fern) for the mutual support through Covid and since. Thank you too to Tasmin Sommerfield for your enthusiasm about *The Book of Doors* and your support for this book publishing nonsense.

Thanks to my parents for giving me the best possible start in life and, essentially, creating the conditions that have enabled me to become a writer. Thanks to my brother for introducing me to Tolkien when I thought it was all old-fashioned rubbish. Shout-out to my in-laws and the extended family and friends in Malaysia, all of whom have been interested and supportive along the way.

Finally, thanks to my wife, May, for her continued love and support. She insists that she does little, but aside from proofreading and improving my prose, and the many discussions about what the different special books might look like, or how a woman might disguise the pages of a special book upon her person, May does so much more than she could ever know. She is the inspiration for characters and pieces of dialogue, and has been my enthusiastic travel companion on research trips. She has added experiences and memories to my life that inform everything I write and without her I doubt this book would even have been written. For all these reasons this book is dedicated to her, but perhaps mostly because she has to put up with me living in my own head almost constantly as I try to work out plots. (The soap room is coming soon!)

Thanks also to Dougal and Flora for making me laugh every day. They won't read this, because they're dogs, but they'll know. Dogs always know.

About the Author

Gareth Brown wanted to be a writer from a very young age, and he completed his first novel as a teenager. That novel wasn't very good and he's been working on his writing ever since. For almost twenty-five years he has worked in the UK Civil Service and the National Health Service while writing in his spare time.

When not working or writing, Gareth loves traveling, especially the whirlwind first few hours in a new city and long road trips through beautiful landscapes. He enjoys barbecues, patisseries, playing pool, and falling asleep in front of the television like an old man.

Gareth lives with his wife and two excitable Skye terriers near Edinburgh, Scotland.